SOMMERSGATE HOUSE

GHOSTS AND REINCARNATION SERIES
BOOK I

KRISTEN ASHLEY

ROCK CHICK
PRESS

Sommersgate HOUSE

❧ GHOSTS AND REINCARNATIONS SERIES ❧

NEW YORK TIMES BESTSELLING AUTHOR

KRISTEN ASHLEY

PROLOGUE
SOMMERSGATE HOUSE

Everyone knew that Sommersgate House was built for love.

Its creator, Lord Archibald Ashton, Baron Blackbourne, spared no expense. Every piece of stone, every stick of timber, every pane of glass (and so on) were the best of the very best. He located the finest carpets; commissioned the most extraordinary fireplaces; purchased the most exceptional pieces of furniture; demanded the most magnificent chandeliers.

Every inch had to be resplendent. It was to be a testimony to devotion.

Sommersgate House was built for his wife, the love of his life, the beautiful Lady Ruby.

It was tragic, then, that they both died within months of its completion.

Everyone thought that was enough reason for the curse to settle on the house. After all that trouble, all that expense, all that dedication to an act of love, to have it all, so quickly, turn catastrophic in only a few months time was enough for any house to be cursed.

And cursed it was, Sommersgate, once beautiful (if a bit ostentatiously so), during one dark day and one frantic, devastating evening, turned wicked, frightful and monstrous.

As the decades went by, the curse became local lore. People could feel it, just walking, riding or eventually driving by the Gate House of the great property. Its malevolence permeated the very air. For those who went to the house, they *felt* it, even though they didn't see it.

Sommersgate House was a most unhappy place indeed.

And that didn't even take into account the hauntings.

I

HOPE

That morning Mrs. Kilpatrick had a case of nerves. Mrs. K knew that there was still the possibility that this morning's imminent arrival would get cold feet. That Julia Fairfax would decide, at the last minute, not to leave her family, her friends, her home, everything she knew, to spend the next thirteen years of her life at Sommersgate House.

Yes, that morning Mrs. Kilpatrick was tense. Her daily girl Veronika was tense. And before he left, Carter, the chauffer, was tense.

Worst of all, the house was tense and make no mistake about it, even though it was simply mortar and stone (albeit grand mortar and stone), Sommersgate could most definitely be *tense*.

Mrs. Kilpatrick had been working at Sommersgate for the last thirty-seven years, since she was seventeen years old, and she was proud of it. She'd worked her way up from a daily girl to the lofty position of Housekeeper. She knew every nook and cranny of the house, every noise, every creaky floorboard. She knew that house like she knew her own husband, through and through.

She turned and watched as Ruby sat at the massive kitchen table, her blonde curls bobbing while she coloured in her book. Per usual, the child made no attempt to colour in the lines or utilise a flesh-like tone for skin (in this instance, Mrs. Kilpatrick saw, skin was kelly green) or any other colour that would be appropriate (the sky was silver and the grass was purple).

From the moment four years ago when Ruby was placed in Mrs. Kilpatrick's arms as a babe of no more than a few days, Mrs. Kilpatrick knew there was something unusual about the child. Ruby had spent the next four years proving her right.

As she watched Ruby, Mrs. K heard a car on the drive.

Ruby didn't hesitate in colouring because she hadn't lived in Sommersgate long enough to know how to distinguish the various sounds but Mrs. Kilpatrick knew that Carter was home.

She took a deep breath and sighed in relief. If something had gone wrong during the journey from Heathrow, Carter would have called. They were now home and Mrs. K hoped that, with the treasured cargo Carter was delivering today, months of sadness and despair would begin healing.

Maybe even a century of it.

She put a hand to her hair, testing the bounce of her fashionable bob, the old blonde now having streaks of white. She smoothed the front of her skirt down, trying, as ever, to ignore her somewhat protruding belly, flipped on the electric kettle and shot a prayer to heaven that Ms. Julia Fairfax was indeed the answer to all Mrs. Kilpatrick's prayers. Or, more to the point, Mrs. Kilpatrick's prayers for little Ruby, Ruby's older brother William and sister Elizabeth and perhaps, just perhaps, their Uncle Douglas but most especially, Sommersgate House.

"Come along, luv, your Aunt Julia is here."

At this announcement, Ruby's head shot up and she ceased colouring immediately. Squealing with delight (a sound so foreign in Sommersgate that it startled Mrs. K), she jumped off the bench and ran out of the kitchen at top speed. She was at the front door, struggling to shift its massive weight when Mrs. Kilpatrick arrived.

"Patience, child. She's right outside the door. You'll see her soon enough."

"Auntie Jewel, I'm in here!" Ruby shouted through the door unnecessarily but Mrs. Kilpatrick doubted the ancient, studded wood with its heavy, black-scrolled, iron hinges would do anything but mute the child's call.

She unlatched the door and using all her might, pulled it open. Ruby shot out like lightning, ran across the distance and threw herself at the tall woman standing on the gravel drive next to a shining burgundy Bentley.

"My gorgeous baby!" Julia Fairfax cried. Wrapping her arms around the child, she lifted her up and swung her around in a full circle.

Mrs. Kilpatrick took in the scene. Carter had moved to the boot of the Bentley and was watching it too. It was hard not to smile with relief and Mrs. K felt the easing sigh tremble through the very air around Sommersgate.

❦ ❦ ❦

Mrs. Margaret Kilpatrick had known Julia Elizabeth Fairfax for fifteen years. She'd watched her grow from a young, naive, headstrong girl of twenty-one to a beautiful, sophisticated, even more headstrong woman (so headstrong as to be described as stubborn).

Julia stood in the drive by the gleaming Bentley, which sat next to a glamorous circular fountain. She was swinging her niece, smiling and laughing, looking like she'd been born to stand in the drive of a palatial estate, even though she most definitely had not.

She was very tall, slim but rounded in all the right places. Julia wore an elegant suit of chocolate brown with a fitted pencil skirt and a feminine jacket nipped in at the waist. Her blonde hair was swept up in a chic twist. She was wearing a pair of leopard print, spike heeled pumps and a tawny pashmina dripped casually from her elbows. She didn't look like she'd spent the last fourteen hours travelling through crowded airports, stuffy airplanes and close cars. She looked fresh and rested, as if she was just headed out to lunch.

"I'm not a baby," Ruby exclaimed through her giggling struggles.

"You're *my* baby, always were, always will be," Julia stated and kissed the child loudly on her cheek.

Julia bent to let Ruby down and noticed Mrs. Kilpatrick.

Walking forward hand extended, she murmured, "Mrs. K."

5

The muscles worked in Mrs. Kilpatrick's throat as she tried not to cry and she steeled herself for what was to come. Julia Fairfax, and her mother Patricia, were American and didn't stand on ceremony and had no sense of, or more likely didn't care much for, the firmly hierarchical way things were at Sommersgate. The lady of the house, Baroness Monique Ashton, hated it when her daughter's American in-laws would come to visit. They were far too familiar with the servants, amongst other things, *many* other things.

Julia put her hand on Mrs. Kilpatrick's arm, squeezed gently and kissed the older woman's cheek with familiarity and kindness.

"How's it going, Mrs. K?" she asked, trying to read Mrs. Kilpatrick's face. At that distance, Mrs. Kilpatrick saw that Julia was not nearly as fresh and relaxed as she'd looked from afar. Her skin was pale and drawn and her green eyes, normally alight with mischief, good humour, or stubborn resolve, looked immensely tired, as if she'd not only been travelling for fourteen hours but as if she hadn't slept in weeks.

"I'm well, Miss Julia, how was your flight?"

Mrs. K referred to both Julia and Patricia in a less formal way at each woman's demand. Lady Ashton would never allow Mrs. K any kind of familiarity which would include using their Christian name. Mrs. K firmly refused to call them Jewel and Patty, as she'd been asked to do many a time. In return, Julia and Patricia had firmly refused to answer to Miss Fairfax or Mrs. Fairfax. In the end, they had an unspoken compromise and "Miss Julia" and "Miss Patricia" were born.

Mrs. K disengaged her arm with her own friendly but fleeting squeeze of Julia's hand and walked the woman into the house as Ruby danced ahead of them. Julia hesitated and looked back at the Bentley. Neither Julia nor Patricia had ever been comfortable with being waited upon, having their bags carried for them, unpacked for them, their laundry done or doors opened for them.

"Don't worry, Carter will see to your bags," Mrs. K assured her. "Your flight?"

Julia smiled wearily, giving in gracefully to the gentle reminder of how things were at Sommersgate.

Even though Mrs. Kilpatrick had pulled away from Julia's grasp, the younger woman linked her arm through Mrs. K's elbow and walked forward. "I'm glad it's over, I hate flying." She looked around her and trembled dramatically. "How's this dusty old pile of rocks keeping? I see it hasn't fallen down around your heads... unfortunately."

Mrs. Kilpatrick shuddered a bit at Sommersgate being talked of like that. On a day as tense as today, a body needed to be careful.

Julia had been a guest on dozens of occasions, dating from before Julia's brother Gavin had married young Lady Tamsin Ashton and through to last Christmas. Julia had brought her (rather despicable, Mrs. K always thought) husband there before they were married and came back after they were divorced. Mrs. K believed fully in the sanctity of marriage but she'd said a little prayer on the day she found out Julia had become legally *un*tied to that horrible man.

Julia, like many, both loved and hated Sommersgate, but, like few, didn't have any problem sharing how she felt.

"It's taken good care of those children," Mrs. K responded, nodding her head toward Ruby as they exited the long hallway and entered the enormous stairwell with its cavernous gallery, curving staircase ornately carved from granite that four people standing abreast could ascend and its enormous ceiling made entirely of domed glass and embellished wrought iron. Its walls were decorated with dozens of portraits of serious faced ancestors wearing the fashions of the day replete with dripping medals or jewels, depending on the gender.

Julia stopped and looked around, staring at the huge marble fireplace that once heated this space.

"I expect it's you who have taken good care of those children," Julia remarked and Mrs. K knew this had more than one meaning. "I just can't imagine what was in Tammy and Gav's heads when they demanded the children be brought up here."

"Miss Tamsin loved this house, as does Ruby," Mrs. K replied.

Ruby was standing next to Julia looking up at her with sparkling blue eyes and Mrs. K took that opportunity to study the child.

Ruby had taken the last five months surprisingly well, but then, at four years old, how much could she understand about the horrible events that rainy night? It was William, and especially Elizabeth, who had suffered the most.

Julia seemed to realise where she was and what she was saying. She bent low and kissed the top of Ruby's curls before her eyes returned to the housekeeper.

"I'm sorry, Mrs. K, I'm exhausted. The trip, selling my house, car... the last week has been day after day of going away parties, meals out with friends, finding a place for every last hair pin. It's been insane."

Mrs. K understood; the last few months had to be upheaval for Julia. She'd had to give up everything.

She gave Julia a reassuring smile. "I've got the kettle on. Let me get you a cuppa. A warm drink always helps. Coffee?"

Julia nodded gratefully and Mrs. K shuffled her into what she knew was Julia's favourite place at Sommersgate, a smallish room off the grand stairwell that had a tile and flagstone floor and butter-coloured, stone walls. It had wide entryways to both the stairwell and the drawing room and grand, double French windows that lead to the front gardens.

This space was once the entry to the house in the days when horses clattered to the front. Motor cars, and an ancestral baroness who detested them and refused to see them out her front door, had changed the traffic of Sommersgate. She modified the drive to complete at the studded doors at the side, added the fountain and laid the old front drive to gardens. She then altered the huge space within the house to what was now one of the warmest places you could find, literally and figuratively. It held comfortable, button-backed leather couches, chairs and ottomans surrounding another ornate, grand fireplace with sturdy but fine tables here and there on which to lay drinks, trays, books or puzzles, as the case may be.

Of course, no one used the space much, the lord of the manor and his lady mother weren't the kind who casually wiled away time with games and puzzles.

Mrs. K's mind moved from the space, back to Julia.

"You wait here. I'll be back in a snap," Mrs. K assured her.

She bustled away, hearing Julia's chic pumps hit the floor one-by-one as she took them off and, in a teasing voice, she addressed Ruby. Listening to Julia, Mrs. K. nearly ran into Veronika who was hiding in the shadows by the dining room

"She arrive safe?" Veronika asked in broken English.

The Russian girl had been at Sommersgate for six months, the longest Mrs. Kirkpatrick had been able to keep a daily for several years, and, for that alone, she cherished the girl. It took an extraordinary amount of time hiring staff, training them in the very specific tasks they had to perform, then losing them and having to hire more.

Veronika not only stayed, but she did a job at which many people would turn up their noses and she did it with pride and unending amounts of energy. Especially these last months when so much more was required of them with the arrival of the children.

"She's safe, you'll need to unpack her cases," Mrs. K informed the girl. "But first, I want you to meet her." Her orders were voiced kindly but Veronika shrunk into herself and Mrs. K's heart went out to the girl.

Veronika had not shared much but Mrs. K knew something was not right. She was timid and scared of her own shadow. Monique Ashton unnerved her and Sommersgate House petrified her, both of which weren't unusual and often why the other girls never stayed very long. But Veronika needed the job, or she would likely be shipped back to wherever she came from, something, Mrs. K thought, terrified her most of all.

Where Douglas Ashton had found the petite, young, pretty, dark-haired girl was something that Mrs. Kilpatrick did not want to know. He'd simply told Mrs. K one day that a girl was coming to fill the daily job that had gone vacant for several weeks.

"If she's suitable, keep her. She'll have no references but that's not your concern, just put her to work," he'd said.

The comings and goings of Douglas Ashton, titled Baron Blackbourne and sixth master of Sommersgate House, were none of Margaret Kilpatrick's business and, even if she could know, Mrs. Kilpatrick didn't want to know. Further, she'd never question Lord Ashton, not in a million years. She'd be sacked, without references, even if she had been in his life since he could remember. He'd do it, she had no doubt, and he'd not entertain another thought in his handsome head about it.

Mrs. Kilpatrick had come to Sommersgate when Douglas Ashton was an infant. Even knowing him since he was a wee lad, as a man, she admired him greatly, she feared him and she worried about him, in that order.

Given his privileged birth, he could have chosen an entirely different path. However Douglas Ashton was driven to something else and this drive, to attain whatever it was he desired, was what Mrs. K admired. Although a cold man, Mrs. Kilpatrick felt (with some pride, even though it had naught to do with her) that Douglas Ashton was not a bad man (not like his father). One couldn't say exactly that he was a *good* man but he certainly wasn't cruel and, considering his upbringing, to avoid that end was a feat in itself.

His determination was what she feared, along with his rumoured ruthless tactics. No man should work that hard, that long, sacrificing whatever morals and ethics (and, if gossip could be believed, were all of them) to get what he wanted. Lord Ashton was not a man to be denied, if he wanted something, it was his. If he wanted Mrs. K to employ a pretty, young Russian girl with no references, no experience and nothing but a passport, then he'd have it. And he did. And Mrs. K was just one in a small army of people who did his bidding, or faced the consequences.

She worried about him because he seemed so unapproachable, so cold and so very alone. He had no one and needed no one and Mrs. K couldn't believe anyone, truly, lived like that, at least not happily. Even though Douglas Ashton never gave any indication he cared one whit about Mrs. Kilpatrick, she was the kind of woman who cared about just about everyone. She had a special place in her heart for the two children she watched grow up at Sommersgate, *both* of them, even Lord Douglas Ashton. It wasn't his fault he was the way he was, indeed, he could have turned out very, *very* different. *That* was why Mrs. K loved him, was devoted to him and his house, even though he would never know how she felt.

Margaret Kilpatrick's attention returned to Veronika. "Help me with the coffee, then you can meet Miss Julia and then you can see to the unpacking."

As ever, Veronika did as she was told and they brought a tray to Julia with an exquisite silver coffeepot, a delicate china serving set and a plate of biscuits all sitting on a crisp, lily-white linen serviette.

Julia stood, a smile on her lips, when she saw Veronika.

"Veronika," she started, again putting out her hand to shake the girl's. The girl hesitantly allowed this but gave a small cry of surprise when Julia pulled her in for a swift kiss on the cheek. Julia thoughtfully ignored Veronika's startled cry when she continued. "I hear you've been taking care of my nieces and nephew. Thank you."

Veronika nodded and stepped back, this warm reception was not something she'd encountered before from anyone, not even Mrs. Kilpatrick. Veronika Raykin and Julia Fairfax had met only once and the circumstances at the time were most dire.

Julia smiled at her and Veronika looked at a loss of what to do next. "I unpack your case," she announced finally and then fled the room.

"She's a little shy," Mrs. Kilpatrick explained.

Julia nodded, her face thoughtful as she watched Veronika go.

"Her timing wasn't great, just coming to this gothic monstrosity when..." Julia stopped and looked at Ruby then she started again. "Tell me, how are things?"

Mrs. Kilpatrick knew exactly what Julia was asking.

For the past five months, Julia was at home in Indiana preparing to move to England and care for her brother's children under the strict terms of he and his wife's will. These terms were rigid and, to everyone's surprise, included that the children be brought up in England, live at Sommersgate and be reared under the guardianship of Lord Douglas Ashton and Ms. Julia Fairfax. Unless Julia was willing to give up custody, which she obviously was not, this meant she had to quit her high-paid job, sell her home, disburse her belongings, say good-bye to her friends and family and move to a foreign country to live at Sommersgate for at least the next thirteen years.

Julia had done all of this without murmur, leaving the country four and a half months ago after the funerals and after the will was read, shattered from grief and jetlag, and spent the ensuing time readying herself for this change in life.

In that time, Douglas Ashton and his mother Monique had not changed their habits one iota. They'd left the care of three bereaved children, who also had left their home to move to Sommersgate, in the hands of Mrs. K, her husband, Roddy, Veronika, and Sommersgate's chauffer and handyman, Carter.

Mrs. Kilpatrick didn't mind. She openly adored Tamsin Ashton

Fairfax, who shared not a single trait with her mother, father or brother, all proud and haughty. Fifteen years ago, Mrs. Kilpatrick had immediately fallen in love with the tall, athletic, fair, blue-eyed American boy from the Midwest, Gavin Fairfax, who was friendly and outgoing and who thought Tamsin resided on a pedestal (Mrs. K agreed). And in loving them both, Mrs. K loved their children and would do anything for them.

But she was not their family. Monique Ashton had not showed an interest in mothering her own two children and she showed even less of an interest in her grandchildren.

Douglas Ashton was worse. He worked long, inhuman hours, day and night, travelling from city to city, country to country, continent to continent. On those very rare occasions when he wasn't working, he was playing and he played with the same intensity as he worked. An expert skier, an avid horseman and a collector of tall, young, frighteningly skinny blondes, brunettes and redheads, he was a man who was responsible to no one but himself. And even though, on a dark, wet road five months ago, that had changed, Douglas Ashton had not.

Mrs. Kilpatrick didn't know why Douglas worked so hard. He was born to money, property and a title. He was immensely good-looking and was one of Europe's top bachelors.

Roderick Kilpatrick, Mrs. K's husband, reckoned it was power. Mr. Kilpatrick worked as groundskeeper for both Douglas and his father and he felt in the position to have a pretty reliable opinion on the subject (indeed, Roddy felt he was in the position to have a pretty reliable opinion on a lot of subjects).

Mrs. K would always cringe and more often than not quickly cross herself when thinking of the older Ashton because he surely existed in purgatory, or worse, for what he put his son through. She tried not to think about it, the scenes, the shouting, the ugly, hideous words. As a mere servant, she didn't exist to the Baron, therefore, it didn't matter what she'd heard and she'd heard a great deal.

How young Douglas had borne it, she couldn't imagine but it was a testament to his strength of will. It wrecked Tamsin, who idolised her older brother. Those two were inseparable when they were young, clinging to each other in a home where controlled violence or absent neglect were the only constants.

Mrs. K never saw evidence of beatings, and there were times when she wished for it, for no matter what lofty a position Maxwell Ashton held, Social Services would frown upon physical violence and Mrs. K would have reported it, make no mistake. But there was never any physical evidence of the type of lashings Douglas would endure.

When he wasn't verbally abusing his son, Maxwell spent his time in the pursuit of power and pleasure which were the sum total of his interests for his short sixty years. Years that ended in a massive heart attack on a ski slope in Gstaad.

Monique seemed quite happy to be left to the pursuit of her own pleasures. And this was exactly what she did, leaving her children to fend for themselves most of the time.

Roddy Kilpatrick felt that perhaps Douglas wanted to prove he was worthy of some attention from the both of them, the kind a proud father and mother would show.

Mrs. Kilpatrick didn't believe that. Maxwell Ashton had been dead for years and there was no sign Douglas intended to slow down or settle down. Further, he seemed to regard his mother, as with everyone and everything else, with a cold disregard. She existed and he acknowledged that fact, and that was the end of it.

Rumour had it he'd more than quadrupled the family fortune and the way he did it was, no other way to say it, *suspect*. He had an office in Bristol and held a full staff at his offices in London. What he did to make his money, Mrs. K had no idea. He had a reputation as a dangerous man and it was a fact that he'd mysteriously disappeared for two years, without word or sighting. He had returned with no excuses for his absence looking no longer boyishly handsome but with a thin scar marring his hard mouth and lines etched into the sides of his eyes that were caused by wind and sun, and obviously not from playing polo.

His disappearance was never explained and, as for the rest, it was simply none of her business.

Mrs. Kilpatrick knew Samantha Thornton, Lord Ashton's personal assistant, had been keeping in close contact with Julia and Julia and her mother called the children once or twice a week since the accident. Julia was no fool; she knew that the children had been left in the servants' care.

"We're all well, we're just happy you're here," Mrs. Kilpatrick answered, loyal to the last to her employers who kept her and her husband fed and housed in the Groundskeeper's Cottage up the lane.

Julia looked like she didn't share Mrs. K's sentiments but she was discreet enough not to say so.

She looked down at Ruby. "Well, we'll get things sorted soon enough," she said with considerable feeling, leaving Mrs. K to wonder what she meant.

"Er... well, as you know, Lady Ashton has been called away..." *On a cruise*, Mrs. K thought but did not say. She was as shocked as she was certain Julia and Patricia had been when they heard that Lady Monique would accept an invitation to cruise the Mediterranean rather than welcome a member of the family who was to move into their home. "And Lord Ashton wanted me to tell you he had unexpected business in London and won't be home until late tonight, but I have a nice welcome dinner planned for you and the children..."

"You're a gem, Mrs. K." Julia smiled a smile that did not reach her eyes and then turned to her niece.

Mrs. K inclined her head in an acknowledgement. "Once Veronika has unpacked your bags, I'll show you to your rooms."

On that, she left, hearing Ruby chatter away to Julia while she walked away.

The children adored their Auntie Jewel, who came to visit often and would meet Tamsin, Gavin and the children for holidays. Mrs. K had to believe that Julia would find a way to heal the raw wounds of a family torn asunder.

As for Sommersgate and its master, Mrs. K could only hope.

Fervently hope.

Mr. Kilpatrick thought his wife was slightly mad but Mrs. K had been at Sommersgate long enough to love it. The house, too, had wounds to heal and those were a great deal older and more imbedded than the three Fairfax children's.

What Sommersgate needed was love, laughter and happiness and, for over one hundred years, the house had lacked all three. It was a tall order, to think this headstrong American woman could soothe the overwhelming grief of three young children and cure a century of sorrow that clung to a pile of stone, glass and iron.

Her biggest challenge was to melt the heart of the dangerously cold Douglas Ashton who was the key to it all.

Mrs. Margaret Kilpatrick had been neither seen nor heard in that house for thirty-seven years. That did not mean she neither saw nor heard. And she knew that there was something between Ms. Julia Elizabeth Fairfax and Lord Douglas Ashton, Baron Blackbourne. Something even they didn't know was there and now there were no husbands or siblings to get in the way.

Mrs. Kilpatrick had to admit she was tense, but, still, she had hope.

※ 2 ※

THE CHILL AND THE SCREAM

"I'm on the archery team and next year, I might get to play polo."

Willie was chatting on the phone with Patricia, who had taken the day off work to wait for Julia's call to say she was at Sommersgate, safely ensconced in the freakishly strange Gothic Victorian mansion with the children firmly tucked under her wing. Being thus in the evil clutches of the evil Ashtons who never really welcomed Patricia's beloved son (or at least Monique hadn't) and to whom, Patty maintained, Tamsin had been the result of an unfortunate mix up in the nursery at the hospital.

That afternoon, Willie and Lizzie had come home from Tancote Boarding School, a posh "public school" located forty-five minutes away where they were day students rather than being boarded there. They used to be at the local community school but Monique had quickly taken care of that. She'd not liked the idea that they would be partaking of government funded schooling and had not had a problem telling anyone who would listen to her displeasure.

Julia was annoyed when she'd heard from Sam, Douglas's PA, that the kids had been enrolled in a new school so soon after their parents had died. However, thousands of miles away and powerless to do anything, she'd simply gritted her teeth and waited.

Polo and archery, oh my, Julia thought sardonically as she listened to Willie chattering away to his grandmother while she watched Lizzie studiously doing her homework and Julia tried to pretend that everything was all right.

But everything was most definitely *not* all right.

They'd come home from school in the Bentley chauffeured by Carter, wearing posh school uniforms and had been sat down immediately to "tea" of cucumber sandwiches and a pot of fat free yogurt each.

"What on earth are you feeding them?" she'd whispered to Mrs. K.

Mrs. K shrugged and answered, "Lady Ashton doesn't want them falling into unhealthy eating habits. We've never stocked sweets, crisps or puddings in this house, unless we're entertaining, of course."

"What about those biscuits you gave me earlier?" Julia asked.

"I was entertaining," Mrs. K explained.

Of course.

Even though Julia was sentenced to live in spooky Sommersgate for the next twelve to thirteen years, she was still considered *a guest*.

Monique Ashton wasn't worried about health; she was worried about the kids gaining weight. Monique herself was ten pounds underweight and was of the mind that fashionable, well-bred people emaciated themselves as proof of their fine upbringing. This, too, had been something Julia had heard Monique wax on about on more than one occasion, often pointedly looking at Patricia, who very much liked chocolate, potato chips and puddings of all kinds and looked the sort who did. Tamsin had always had a kitchen full to the brim with food, from grapes, apples and carrot sticks to chocolate covered malt balls and bags of microwave popcorn.

"Okay, she's right here, Lizzie, Grammy wants to speak to you," Willie called, breaking into Julia's thoughts.

Lizzie threw her pencil down and slinked to the phone. She cast a brief glance in Julia's direction as she took the phone from her brother and said, "Hello, Grandmother."

Julia tried not to grimace.

Grandmother.

Patricia wouldn't like that one bit. Monique was called "grandmother". Patricia was Grammy, Gramma or just plain old Gram.

Julia watched Lizzie talking on the phone. The girl's dark, normally lustrous, thick hair was lank and needed a wash. Her face was pale and lifeless.

Her dark blue eyes were dead.

Julia knew from her own conversations with the children over the last few months, not to mention the last several hours, that Ruby was taking the loss of her parents in stride. The child had always been a little strange. However, as Julia never had any children or been around any who had suffered such a tragedy, she couldn't really imagine how a four year old would react.

Willie, on the other hand, was bearing up as any good Midwestern boy would, even though he'd been born and raised in England. He looked and acted exactly like Gavin at ten years old. Tall, straight, blond and blue-eyed, he was a handsome young man and it broke Julia's heart to look at him, he so reminded her of her brother. Perhaps he had his dark moments but he never let either sister see, just like Gav would do. It was all teasing and light and any intense moments were saved for his own company.

Lizzie was remarkably different from both her brother and sister, not only in colouring, she being so dark (like Tamsin and Douglas) to their fair, but also in temperament.

The girl was not bearing up nearly as well. She was not like Gavin, Tamsin or Ruby. She was sensitive, stubborn and dramatic, quite like Julia herself. Normally quick-witted (and equally quick-tempered), smart and brimming with affection, the loss of her mother, who she adored, but perhaps most especially her father, who she was beloved by and loved herself (to distraction) had been a terrible blow. The twelve year old was having troubles and she had nothing familiar around her, her school and old school friends were gone and so was her home... and her parents.

She chatted to her grandmother for a bit, her heart obviously not in it, and then said, "She wants to talk to you again, Auntie Jewel."

While taking the receiver Julia made certain to give her a loud, lip-smacking kiss on the top of her head in the hopes of gaining a familiar giggle but Lizzie just scuttled out from under the embrace and went back to her studies.

"Hi Mom," Julia greeted.

Patty immediately went on the offensive. "All right, that's it. His Lord and Master doesn't even show up to dinner on your first night and *she's* off on a yacht somewhere –"

Julia cut in. "Mom –"

Patty was having none of it and interrupted in return, "That's simply not good manners. Forget it. Find out how to get those kids back home." By "home" Patty meant their little farm town, fifteen miles west of Indianapolis, this topic being a recurring theme of their conversations these last months. "We'll take care of them, you and me. We'll give them a loving, happy home with big Christmases and pink frosting on their birthday cakes. Those two obviously have no interest."

Julia had inherited the drama gene from her mother but never had quite eclipsed Patricia's flair for it. Her mother was right, of course, but the kids had been through enough without throwing an ugly custody battle at them. Julia had to find some way to make this impossible situation work.

And impossible it was. With over a decade of the not-very-nice (to say the least) Monique Ashton yawning in front of her, without any family or friends of her own nearby and with everything familiar to her so far away, it was not only impossible, it was inconceivable.

And that was without taking Douglas into consideration.

Julia walked out to the doorway of the room and whispered, "I've been here a few hours, please give me time, let me see how it goes."

"I'm coming for Thanksgiving. I can't wait until spring term or whatever they call it. I want to see my babies," Patty returned.

Julia's mother wanted to be close to her baby's babies. Gavin had been her pride and joy. She was using her drama to cover her grief and Julia was glad of it. This kind of Patricia she could handle, grand statements, dire threats she never intended to carry out, Julia was used to that. If her mother gave way to the mourning she was covering, Julia would lose it herself and she couldn't, not now. She had to be strong.

"We stick with the plan, Mom. I need a chance to settle in here and the kids need it too. No more upheavals. No more drama. Please, please, let me handle it."

Patricia hesitated for a moment and then sighed extravagantly.

"Thank God you have Mrs. K, she at least, even through that English reserve, has got a heart in her chest. Okay, call me tomorrow. Love you, miss you already my Doll Baby." And she hung up, not letting Julia say her own good-byes.

Julia walked back into the room and replaced the phone. She took a moment to study the kids; Willie and Lizzie doing their homework and Ruby playing some game by herself.

Julia was tired. No, not tired, exhausted. And she knew it wasn't jetlag. Since the phone rang in the deep of the night five months ago, she hadn't had a full night's sleep. That same, awful night, she and her mother had rushed to the airport and then spent the next two weeks dealing with their own grief and the grief of the three children.

A car accident.

Gavin, Julia knew, drove too fast. It was raining. They were coming home from having dinner together at some country pub on one of England's dangerously winding roads. It was dark. Gavin might have driven fast but the driver of the other car was driving faster, he'd lost control and gone over the centre line on a curve. Gavin had died at the scene, so had the other driver. Tamsin had lived for three days and thirteen hours but never woke from her coma.

She just quietly slipped away.

One summer, many years ago, while Julia was in England for a visit, they were in the garden, drinking Pimm's and lemonade and watching Lizzie and Willie run through the hose that Gavin was pointing at them. It was then that they had asked her to be guardian to the kids if anything ever happened to them.

She'd said, "Of course!" In the way someone says when they're honoured but they know they're answering a question that pertains to an event that will never, in any darkest imaginings, ever happen. Ruby hadn't even been born yet and Julia was still married to Sean.

Of course, she thought now as she watched the kids.

She hadn't known that she'd be sharing custody with Douglas but they had told her they wanted her to move to England and she'd agreed to that as well. It wouldn't happen anyway, so why should she worry?

Sean, as usual, had been angry. "It's fucking cold there. I'm not moving there," he'd ranted (even though it was colder in Indiana than it was in Somerset).

"It's not going to happen so there's no need to get angry about it," Julia responded, as always, trying to soothe his foul temper (and, as always, failing miserably).

Now, Sean was gone, which was one less worry but perhaps the reason for another.

Why on earth had Tamsin and Gavin given joint custody to Douglas? Why had they asked Julia to move into this enormous, ghastly house with their kids and share that responsibility with a brother who was responsible to no one?

Julia knew Tamsin loved her brother and saw the best in him.

But Julia didn't see it.

And how on earth did Tammy convince Gav?

A tremor went up Julia's spine just thinking about Douglas Ashton.

It wasn't an unpleasant kind of tremor, not in the slightest. It was a pleasant kind of tremor, exciting and slightly wicked.

Any time over the many years she'd known him, when her mind wandered to Douglas, that same thrilling, illicit tremor would chase its way up her spine.

Julia had had a screaming crush on him the moment she'd first met him. Perhaps, if she was completely honest with herself, she always had one. He was just that type of man.

To a girl of twenty-one, this tall man with his powerful body, thick, dark hair, strong jaw and eyes so intensely blue they were nearly black... well, he was exactly what one would think of as a titled English aristocrat. He had a posh accent and was so arrogant and sexy, she squirmed just being in the same room with him.

But then had come Sean, then Douglas's mysterious disappearance.

Julia had learned a great deal from the mistakes she'd made with Sean, mistakes she vowed to herself (on a daily basis) she would never repeat.

Sean was a great deal like Douglas, reserved, handsome, edgy. Julia knew now that it matters not how dangerous they seem, how attractive, exciting and wealthy they are, or the challenge they represent with their ice-cold aloofness that you were certain you could penetrate.

What a woman needed in a mate was a companion. Someone who would clean the cat litter, pop to the store for milk or fix the sink.

All the passion and intensity was overrated, and in Julia's experience hid biting cruelty and extraordinary selfishness.

The very idea of her and Douglas was ridiculous, Julia knew. Not to mention Douglas Ashton would never in a million years want her. An Indiana girl who'd lived her entire life in a small town where you could drive the length of Main Street waving continuously because you knew every driver in every passing car (and if you didn't wave, once they got home, they'd call your mother and ask, "What on earth's wrong with Jewel? I just saw her driving along Main Street with her head in the clouds. She didn't even wave! She drives like that, she could have an accident!").

Douglas was not like Tammy at all. He wouldn't consider lowering himself to a girl born to and raised by a divorcee. Douglas vacationed on the Riviera. Douglas flew to Paris in a private jet for a one hour meeting. Douglas's gorgeous but stoic face was printed in magazines (normally while escorting catwalk models or Hollywood starlets or debutantes sporting hairstyles that cost more than Julia used to earn in a week).

Julia walked to the enormous windows and stared at the dormant garden, still thinking of Douglas, the man with whom she was now forced to live for at least the next twelve years.

Unlike his mother, he was always courteous to her, often gallant and sometimes fleetingly friendly, but never warm. She learned not to be concerned by his demeanour, that, she soon discovered, was how he treated everyone and was quite like his father's behaviour (for the short time she knew Maxwell Ashton before his untimely death). Douglas's cold indifference was legendary, he rarely smiled and even more rarely laughed.

After he came back from whatever he was doing those two years, something had changed in him. He had a strange, yet magnetic, sinister quality. She couldn't put her finger on it but whatever it was made him no less attractive, in fact, this mysterious allure, including his remoteness, added to his appeal. He used to be quiet, watchful, you could almost, but not quite, forget he was in a room and then be startled when you caught him watching you.

And Julia had caught him watching her a great deal, probably wondering (undoubtedly somewhat clinically) how she had managed to insinuate herself into the Ashton Family Fortress.

Once he'd come back from his Disappearance (made notable in her mind with a capital "D"), even if you hadn't seen him enter a room, you knew he was there. His very presence was forceful and the moment he cut his dark eyes to you, Julia could think of no other way to describe it, except, *oh my*.

Julia knew, though, that her ex-husband had been the beginning and the end of dealing with those kinds of men, handsome, arrogant and entirely self-centred. She'd rather be alone for the rest of her life than endure even a smidgen of the heartache Sean had bestowed on her or the relentless days of piecing together your life and self-confidence when they were gone.

"Dinnertime! Come on children, it's all served up. Get it while it's hot."

Mrs. K had walked into the drawing room. The room was enormous, could easily and comfortably fit thirty (maybe even forty) people. Decorated in ice blue and white, unflinchingly formal with three gigantic crystal chandeliers running the length of it, it was chilly, even with the fire that now burned in its colossal grate.

The kids had headed to that room straight after tea. Not to the warm leather-couched entry, or the slightly more comfortable, book-lined library or the definitely more suitable billiards room or lounge.

"Grandmother Monique says kids are seen and not heard, the drawing room is the farthest away from Grandmother's morning room *and* Uncle Douglas's study," Lizzie had explained while Julia tried not to show any reaction, least of all her extreme, albeit exhausted, irritation.

They all quietly trooped into the dining room. Quiet, Julia was learning quickly, was very important not only for the children but also the staff. The young Russian girl so excelled in it that Julia had been startled by her twice. Veronika drifted about like a ghost.

The dining room, Julia thought while entering it, was the most extravagantly appointed room in the house. The walls richly covered with embossed paper that was created to look and feel like leather and was hand painted in deep moss green, black and rich bronze with accents of gold. The room not only held a long, shining walnut table that seated eighteen but also had two semi-circular windows along one side that held tables that each sat an additional four apiece and an enormous fireplace in which Ruby could set up house.

Mrs. Kilpatrick had gone all out, as best she could without forbidden fattening sauces and delicious desserts. Halved avocados filled with succulent shrimp to start then fillet steaks, steamed broccoli, Brussel sprouts, boiled potatoes and carrots and to end, a fruit parfait separated with layers of thick, rich, honey-sweetened Greek yogurt.

Julia and Mrs. K both tried to make it into an event and the food, even without butter, salt or sauce to season it, was still delicious.

"You're a wonder," she told Mrs. K with all honesty when the older woman whisked the dishes away.

"One does one's best. Now, it's one hour of television or computer and then you know what to do," she told the children who rushed to have their very short bit of fun.

"An hour?" Julia asked once the children left, her irritation growing.

"Lady Ashton doesn't want their brains turned to mush by telly or computer games," Mrs. K explained.

Julia's lips tightened at the very idea that three grieving children were not given an opportunity to lose themselves in pleasurable pastimes, but she held her tongue and nodded.

If she heard one more word about what Grandmother or Lady Ashton did or did not want, her exhaustion and jetlag would cause her to lose her ever-loving mind and she'd scream the house down. Something which, she understood, would not help her impossible, inconceivable situation one bit.

After the children's short hour of fun, Mrs. K and Julia put them to bed, first Ruby and then Willie and Lizzie.

Sitting on Lizzie's bed, Julia tucked her in tight all the way down her sides just as she knew Gavin used to do because that was what Patricia used to do.

"I'm happy you're here, Auntie Jewel," Lizzie murmured sleepily, but even tired, she didn't sound happy at all.

"I'm happy too," Julia lied, bent forward and gave her niece a kiss on her temple.

Julia rose and crossed the room but stood uncertainly at the door for several moments after she'd turned out the light, completely at a loss of what to do for the girl. She wished Gavin was there to tell her but, of course, she wouldn't have had to do anything if he was.

With a heavy heart, she went to find Mrs. K.

"I'm off to the husband," Mrs. K. announced when Julia arrived in the kitchen and saw that Mrs. K was putting on her coat. "Breakfast for the children is at seven o'clock. They have to leave no later than seven thirty. I expect you'll have a lie in tomorrow, you must be done in."

Julia looked at the clock. It was ten after nine. If Mrs. Kilpatrick was here in time to feed the children by seven, she was working incredibly long hours.

"I'll be at breakfast, Mrs. K," Julia, resolute, told the housekeeper and something in her tone made Mrs. K's head come up.

The other woman regarded Julia closely. "I suspect you will, luv, but it doesn't have to be tomorrow. Give yourself a wee bit of a break. And don't you worry. You'll get settled in, you all will." Julia heard more hope than certainty in Mrs. K's voice but she had no time to worry about it because with that, Mrs. K left.

As Julia headed out of the kitchen, she noticed that Mrs. K had put the house to sleep just as she did the children. Curtains were drawn and small lights were on here and there that did nothing to break the dark and everything to extend the frightening shadows of the big house with its large rooms and high ceilings.

Sommersgate House, her home for the next decade.

She shivered at the thought.

It was beautiful, haughtily and even brashly so, but it was not welcoming. Indeed, it was not welcoming in a tangible way, as if it had its own personality, its own set of eyes with which to look down on her with disapproval.

In fact, the house reminded her a great deal of Douglas.

She shook off that thought as she made her way to her rooms.

Julia had not been surprised to see that she had been put in the guest suite, which was off the dining room and down the back hall that lead to a small Chapel (a lovely little Chapel which was really its own building but attached to the house, it nestled snugly in the sloping hill in which the curving drive was cut over a century ago).

Julia was not placed upstairs with the children or the other members of the family, even though all three children had their own room, as did Douglas and Monique. Douglas's rooms (in plural, Tamsin told her after her and Douglas's father died, and by tradition, Douglas had moved into the master suite when he'd inherited the title, the estates and all they contained) included his own private sitting room although Julia had never seen it. Julia knew that upstairs there were still four bedrooms besides and still, she was isolated, away from the rest.

Julia always loved the guest suite but now she felt as Monique meant her to feel, separate and not a part of the family.

The guest suite was decorated in periwinkle blue and clover green with accents of mushroom, silver and gold. This strange colour combination worked, in fact its interior designer won awards for it (according to Monique).

There was an antique, tall tester bed that was kept in pristine condition by Carter, (chauffer, errand-runner and handyman extraordinaire). The bed was draped in blue and green curtains and covered with an undoubtedly three billion-thread-count, clover green, sateen duvet. It was headed with twin stacks of three fluffy pillows with an enormous European square resting in front and a plethora of toss pillows encased in beaded, embroidered, tasselled or ruched satin or silk. There was an ornate, ivory marble-manteled fireplace with a chaise lounge covered in mushroom velvet with a clover green cashmere throw artfully decorating it which sat invitingly in front of the fire. There was a circular window that was the base of the turret that rose up the side of the house and in it were two comfortable chairs with a shared ottoman, this time in a sateen clover specked with periwinkle, one with another throw, this in blue, and a small, circular, intricately carved table in the middle. There was a writing desk facing the room with an ornate chair that had curved legs that matched the desk. The gleaming parquet floor was covered in a variety of thick, silk rugs.

Opposite the fire was a doorway leading to a dressing room that started with a hall which was lined on both sides in rails, inset drawers and shelves. This led to an opening that contained a dressing table built into one side with a huge mirror surrounded entirely with bright lights and fronted by a swirly-legged stool padded in periwinkle velvet. Behind the dressing table, a floor to ceiling three-way mirror was set into the opposite wall. Walking further down, there were more rails, drawers and shelves ending in a sparkling white bathroom which featured a mosaic-tiled floor, a claw-footed, roll-topped bath with gleaming silver taps and sprays and a separate shower cubical. Sumptuous towels in blue, mushroom and clover were hanging from heated towel rails and wrapped, rolled and tucked in various cubbyholes with thick piled rugs strewn appealingly about the floor.

Julia shed the suit she had not found the time to change out of and took a quick shower. Veronika had made certain her shampoo and soap were exactly where they needed to be.

Even though she was exhausted, Julia knew she would not sleep, it was daytime in Indiana and, anyway, sleep had eluded her for months.

She located and then put on a pair of pale blue yoga pants and a white, ribbed tank top and inspected Veronika's work. The fact that she hadn't unpacked her own case made Julia uncomfortable, not that Veronika would be inappropriate, just that Julia was not used to someone else doing her chores. Nevertheless, Julia had to admit Veronika did very good work. Everything was put in place, properly (even obsessively) hung or folded and Julia noted, a bit stunned, ironed. Rows of shoes matched carefully and lined up perfectly. Her toiletries were nicely displayed at the dressing table and, when Julia went back to the bedroom, the framed photographs and scented candles she'd brought with her were arranged to their best advantage.

A photo of the kids, Gavin and Tamsin with Patricia and Julia sat on the bedside table, everyone with their arms around each other in front of Patricia's Christmas tree from two years past. Julia stared at it, felt the familiar hot tears at the back of her eyes and shook her head. She couldn't give in, she'd shed enough tears and now was the time of healing, of moving forward, of making the best of an impossible (and inconceivable) situation.

She sat down and opened the desk. Someone, most likely Mrs. K, had thought to put some writing tablets, pens and pencils and other office supplies in the shelves and drawers.

Just a few days ago, Julia was the head of a grant-making foundation attached to a small group of three non-profit hospitals. She had been responsible for disbursing the profits of the hospitals. With her small team, they called for and assessed grant projects for everything from equipment for basic research laboratories to doctor and nursing fellowships to scholarships for students studying any kind of medicine, be it nursing, physical therapy, midwifery, or the like.

She'd worked there for twelve years. She loved it there. She would miss her staff, her duties, even her damned desk.

Julia shook her head again to oust the melancholy that always seemed threateningly close to drowning her and started to do what she'd always done when a project loomed.

She wrote a list.

She'd need a mobile phone.

She'd need a computer and e-mail.

She'd need a driver's license and a car.

She'd need a work permit and to have her visa extended.

And she carried on writing everything she needed and then prioritising it.

She took out another piece of paper and she wrote down what she knew to be in her bank account and her investment accounts. She'd made a tidy profit from her house and car. She had some savings. She wasn't destitute.

She started to budget her money, what she'd need, what she could afford. She'd have to have a talk with Douglas about a lot of things, including what she would put into the house. Keeping a house like this had to cost an extraordinary amount, anything she contributed would be a drop in the bucket. But she had not been brought up not to pay her way.

As she looked at the figures she realised that without a job she'd be out of money way too quickly. She had a six month visa but did not have the right to work or to healthcare. She'd need insurance... and it went on and on.

Julia started adding to her list and wondered how much insurance would cost and bent her head to the task of diverting her brain in the hopes of exhausting it so she could fall asleep and not thinking of anything else.

She put her elbow on the desk and touched the middle three fingers of her hand to her forehead, closing her eyes and rubbing away the gentle ache that had begun to throb there.

But no matter how hard she tried, she couldn't keep the thoughts at bay.

She hadn't expected very much out of her life. She never had big dreams or ambitions. She didn't want fancy cars, huge houses, jetting around from exotic place to place. Sean had given her a taste of that and it wasn't worth the price you had to pay to get it.

She was not a risk-taker. She liked things steady, familiar and normal. She liked her family close, her friends next door and to know exactly what aisle the cake mixes were in at the grocery store. All her life she did her utmost to keep everything just that way.

She had been pleased with her lot (after she'd divorced Sean, of course). She had a house she loved. She'd lived there five years and just the summer before had managed to renovate the last room so every inch of carpet, every piece of furniture, every last wineglass was exactly what she wanted.

And she had friends she was going to miss. She was going to miss Josie's Margarita Mayhem Night that was held every year on the longest day. And the Christmas Party where they all trooped out in posh outfits to see the Nutcracker Suite and then came back to Tom and Mary's to eat the vast array of delicious nibbles Mary spent days making. And Kelly's Annual Birthday Extravaganza which was always a blast.

And of course there was Mom. She was really going to miss Patricia.

The three of them, Patricia, Gavin and Julia, had always been close. They had to be once Dad left them high and dry with only a token look back every once in awhile at the family he created and then abandoned.

Patricia was never the "cool" Mom. She was the stern and loving Mom and she was very wise. Life hadn't dealt her a good hand, divorced young with two kids and an ex who forgot to pay the child support far more often than he remembered. He also forgot he had another family, vastly preferring (and not too concerned to show it) his two daughters and son from his beautiful, wealthy and upper class second wife. "The Izod Family" Gavin used to call them as a joke but it was too real to be truly funny and it always made Mom's mouth tighten at the corners to hear him say it.

But, despite all this, Patricia had made a happy home, full of laughter, good times and support (with a great deal of meddling). She tried to fill the void (although sometimes failed) of an absent, careless father.

And as the years went by, Patricia and Julia's relationship had changed from mother and daughter to confidants and friends.

Julia needed that. After she'd left Sean, her heart in tatters and her self-esteem so low she had to dig a ditch to drag it around after her, with the added burden of living a life as the unwanted daughter, Julia had decided she did not ever want another man. The men in her life had torn her heart out and kicked it around. Her father by not wanting her. In Sean's case, four years she suffered his bad moods, cruel words, relentless attacks on her confidence, flirtations and infidelities. She figured she might find someone else eventually (although she didn't really look). But Julia had rules. Whoever that someone would be, he wasn't going to be handsome, wealthy or accomplished. He just had to be *there*. There to listen to her when she had a bad day. There to help her unpack the groceries. There to drive the car every once in awhile.

She was tired of always having to be the one to drive the car. She just wanted to get in and let someone else drive.

But now, any thought of that was far away. Now she had the children and this inconceivable situation and would likely be driving the car forever.

On that thought, she felt it and her head come up as her hand dropped.

What *it* was, she didn't know. A draught against her ankles, but not just any draught, this was intensely cold and felt, somehow, menacing. She had kept the door to her room open just in case one of the children called, maybe it came from there.

She felt it again. It wasn't a chill throughout the room, just a draught at her ankles. It was mid-October, and cold, but even the chill outside was not of the fierce arctic of the draught at her ankles.

She looked around the room and saw nothing. She'd turned on most of the lights but had not drawn the drapes. She stared out into the dark night wondering if Douglas had come home and opened the front door letting in the cold. Surely she'd have seen the lights of his car as the length of her suite ran along the front drive.

She got up to look out the windows and then she saw them, two headlights coming down the hill and around the bend where the Chapel was ensconced. Douglas was just arriving home, Julia watched him park by the fountain.

Then she heard it.

A scream.

A frightening, terrible, blood-curdling, high-pitched woman's scream.

"Dear God, the children..." Julia whispered and she ran out into the hallway as fast as she could in the direction of the scream.

THE PROBLEM

Douglas Ashton drove his Jaguar through the winding country roads outside Bristol Airport.

Normally Carter would have collected him from the airport. However that morning when he left, Carter had to get to Heathrow to pick up Julia.

Douglas thought, at the time, this was likely the first in a long line of inconveniences he'd have to put up with concerning Julia.

Now he was glad for the chance to be alone, behind the wheel of the car, on the dark, deserted roads.

He thought ahead to the call he'd be getting from Japan in a few hours time, to his trip to Munich tomorrow, the meeting there in the afternoon and then on to the business he needed to see to in St. Petersburg. When he was certain that all plans were in place and nothing had been left to chance, he let his mind turn to Sommersgate and what awaited him there.

Julia Fairfax.

She'd changed her name back after she'd divorced her ass of a husband.

Douglas's mother had loved Sean Webster. "How she would even dream of finding someone better than him is beyond me. She doesn't know how lucky she was to trap him in the first place," Monique had declared when she'd heard the divorce was made final.

Douglas had wondered distractedly why Julia had *settled* for the bastard in the first place. He was from money, as Monique mentioned more than once, but Julia very obviously outclassed him from the first.

What Monique didn't know about Sean, and probably, Douglas thought, wouldn't have cared about, was that Sean made a pass at anything in a skirt, including Tamsin.

Tamsin never told Gavin, but she told Douglas.

His sister had always been a smart girl. Gavin, being Gavin, mellow and good-natured most of the time, but fiercely loyal and, in Tamsin and Julia's case, protective, would have immediately lost his mind and done something immensely stupid.

Douglas wasn't so impetuous.

Julia may have been blinded by love (or, more likely, from Douglas's vast experience of women, money) to fall for Sean Webster, but Douglas was counting on the fact that she was smart enough or, at the very least proud enough, not to keep him around.

She didn't.

Everyone was surprised at Sean's accident three months after the divorce was final.

Douglas was not.

He felt no remorse. He had ordered that Webster would not sustain a lasting injury. But there was only one human being that Douglas Ashton had ever loved in his thirty-eight years and that was his sister. He could not allow anyone to make her even the slightest bit uncomfortable.

Sean Webster had made that mistake therefore Douglas had made him uncomfortable.

Smoothly negotiating a deserted roundabout, Douglas allowed his thoughts, as they had for obvious reasons of late, to move to his sister.

Growing up, Tamsin had been the only bit of warmth in their cold home, save the Kilpatricks but they were servants and therefore, it had been drilled into Douglas and Tamsin at an early age, had their place and that place was not a familial one.

But Tamsin, she was like a changeling, not born of their family.

Sweet-tempered, kind-natured and she loved Douglas openly. She thought he could move mountains, she thought he could rule worlds. Until Gavin, the sun rose and set for Tamsin through Douglas.

She saw the best in him even when Mother ignored him or after one of Father's fierce tirades. Douglas rarely permitted his thoughts to turn to his father, mainly because there was no purpose to it. Maxwell Ashton was dead, but he had been dead to Douglas years before his father's heart exploded. This, Douglas thought, was the ultimate irony because he'd always thought his father hadn't had a heart.

His sister's death meant certain unbidden, long-buried memories resurfaced, though Douglas had long since grown too detached for them to affect him. He allowed them to drift through his consciousness now but he was, as always, immune.

If Douglas brought home a poor grade (anything less than a first was an excuse for a screaming, red-faced lecture that lasted at least an hour) or he had not been made captain of the rugby or cricket teams (no matter that he was the best player at both) or any of number of the myriad other ways Douglas disappointed his father, Maxwell would unleash a verbal fury on Douglas that shook the windows.

And Douglas disappointed his father often.

Maxwell had never once used his fists on his son but back then Douglas often wished he would. Douglas had seen, and done, violence in his life and those kinds of wounds healed a great deal more quickly.

"Jesus, I look at you and wonder if you're even my son," Maxwell spat at him once, his eyes narrowed with contempt.

It was a ridiculous pronouncement. Douglas looked almost exactly like his father, except he was three inches taller and ten pounds leaner.

At first Douglas worked to prove his worth to his father, to make him proud, exhausting himself in the effort.

He'd stopped doing that somewhere in his teens, learning the lesson that no matter what, no matter how much, no matter how well, nothing would make his father proud.

Through all of this, Monique blithely went her way, never once defending her son (but often defending Maxwell), never once dirtying her hands with the sordid little secret their family shared (but often accepting bribes to keep her silence or to encourage her to go on her way).

After he'd given up on his father, the only thing Douglas had to prove was Tamsin's faith in him.

Through all these times, Tamsin had been there. She soothed his brow when they were children and she cheered him on when they were older. After an episode, she'd seek him out and try to make him smile or she'd defend him fiercely in whispers, hidden away from Maxwell or Monique's ears.

"Doug, you're worth *ten* of him! Maybe fifteen! Don't listen to a word he says," she would say.

Douglas never knew what he'd done to deserve such devotion from his sister.

On the other hand, Maxwell had adored his beautiful daughter. She'd never borne the brunt of his anger and scorn. She had her own tortures to endure from a Mother who simply didn't care. But Tamsin held little love for her father, always loyal to Douglas and the two of them grew up like children without parents. The adults who bore and sired them being necessary evils on a path that they both hoped would lead to freedom.

Douglas allowed himself a rare moment to feel pleased that Tamsin enjoyed a taste of that freedom if only for awhile.

For his part, he had found his own escape. If Tamsin had known what he did or how he spent a great deal of his time, Douglas had no idea how she would react. Perhaps proud, he thought, and frightened, to be certain. She, and everyone else, thought he was bent on money and power, and this was true, he enjoyed the tactics of business. But it was not a challenge and Douglas was very like his father in many ways, he enjoyed a challenge.

Now Tamsin would never know (not that he would have ever told her, he wasn't free to tell anyone).

His sister was dead and she left him responsible for a mess. What possessed her, he'd never know. Tamsin's mind worked in mysterious ways and her wishes for her children, Julia and Sommersgate was just another one of those mysteries.

Or perhaps, Douglas thought absently, not so much of a mystery.

Tamsin had always been a hopeless romantic and since she was a little girl she believed in the legendary Myth of Sommersgate, its awful history and its alleged curse. She'd told him more than once she'd hoped he'd free the house she loved from the curse and free the long line of barons who presided over it from the tragedy and unhappiness that plagued them.

In other words, his sister desperately wanted Douglas to fall in love.

This desire increased substantially after she'd found Gavin, wanting some of the bounty she had for her beloved brother. Douglas thought this had to be her reasoning, throwing Julia into his life. Douglas had little doubt that in Tamsin's romantic imaginings he would fall for Julia and end the curse she foolishly believed rested on Sommersgate and, in so doing, afflicted Douglas himself.

Driving by a still-lit country pub going about its business of closing down for the night, he turned his thoughts to his current challenge.

Julia Fairfax.

He was surprised Julia hadn't remarried. It couldn't be for lack of offers.

He wished she had. If she'd had a loving home with two parental substitutes to offer the children, no doubt Tamsin and Gavin would have left them to Julia alone.

Douglas would have accepted that, unless she'd made another fool-hardy choice in husbands, which seemed to run in her family. Patricia Fairfax had married a philanderer who had run off with an heiress but he continued to work as a surgeon at the same hospital where Patricia was a nurse. Trevor Fairfax set up house with his new woman, having three more children and daily rubbing his former wife's face in it until Patricia had become fed up and moved to other employment.

Gavin and Julia rarely saw their father when they were growing up; Trevor Fairfax was so consumed with his other family. By the time Gavin had his assignment in England as an electrical engineer with a multi-national construction company, his brother-in-law hadn't seen his father in years.

According to Douglas's research (and he most definitely investigated his future-brother-in-law), Gavin and Julia hadn't missed much with their father. Trevor wasn't invited to the wedding and had never seen his grandchildren. And, as far as Douglas was concerned, that was the end of that.

Which meant, of course, that, indeed, was the end of that.

But now, the Fairfax family was causing another problem and Douglas may have had a great deal of patience with a lot of things but he had no patience with problems.

Julia Fairfax would be living in his house, with his mother, and that was not going to work.

He had no affection for his mother but she *was* his mother. He owed his existence to her if nothing else. But she was a difficult woman and even though she tolerated Gavin, barely, she loathed his mother and sister.

Julia was Gavin's sister and Douglas liked Gavin. He was one of the few acquaintances who held both Douglas's regard and respect. Julia was also the chosen guardian of Tamsin's children and that, in addition to his regard for Gavin, meant Douglas had to find some way to make the situation work.

In any other circumstances, he would have been happy to settle a monthly amount of money on Julia and allow her to take the children to whatever backwater town she lived in. Or settle an even larger amount of money on Julia and have her just go away. If she had taken the children, Douglas would have been content with Samantha gathering progress reports and sending appropriate gifts during holidays and birthdays. He quite liked Tamsin's children, even held some affection for them, but he had no desire to raise them.

However, that wasn't what Tamsin wanted. Tamsin wanted her children to be raised at Sommersgate and for himself, and Julia, to do it and Douglas would respect his sister's wishes, regardless of how inconvenient they were.

However, there was another issue with Julia.

He remembered when he first met her, or more to the point, he remembered that he wanted her the first moment he saw her.

She was a great deal different then. When she first visited them in England it was the first time she'd left her home country. She was uncommonly pretty, tall and shapely with thick blonde hair, green eyes and long, long legs. She held herself with a posture that demanded attention, effortlessly wearing clothes that were both timeless and vogue. The Americans called it "cool" and Gavin had been the same way, it was one of the reasons (Tamsin had told Douglas) why the American had caught his sister's discerning eye.

Douglas had overheard a cousin at Tamsin and Gavin's engagement party referring to Julia as "a bit intimidating." At the time, he'd been surprised by the remark but watching Julia, who conducted herself with the grace and confidence of an old-fashioned movie star, he could see how those less confident would think it was true.

When Julia was younger, she lit up a room with her laughter. She was affectionate and cuddled up to Gavin and her mother, and eventually Tamsin, without any embarrassment.

But she'd grown out of that or more than likely Webster had worn it out of her.

Now she was still affectionate with the children. She also had the American, or perhaps Midwestern trait of touching your hand or arm when she was talking to you or hugging when you saw each other after a long period of time.

Monique detested it.

Now, he knew, Julia was no longer naive or unsophisticated. And the natural grace had been refined to unaffected elegance, an elegance that had just the slightest bit of an edge. His cousin would no longer find her "a bit intimidating" but undoubtedly very much so.

This appealed to Douglas.

Julia appealed to Douglas, through the years, she always had.

She'd gained her degree from the same university as Gavin, she'd acquitted herself well even after she'd chosen an ass like Sean Webster and she'd shown unconditional love to Tamsin as a member of her family and the same, in wild supply, to Tamsin's children. Unquestioning, she'd left every scrap of her life and any future she might have had behind her to do as her brother and Tamsin asked and moved to Sommersgate. That showed loyalty and Douglas valued loyalty above all. It was in short supply, he himself had only had four people in his life show it to him, his sister, his friends the Forsythes, and Nick.

In all the time he knew her, Douglas could have easily, and pleasurably, become entangled with Julia and he had thought of this option often.

Always, he controlled these thoughts, not wishing the nastiness which would no doubt ensue when he ended it (he didn't relish the idea of angering Gavin who was a very genial man but who was also immensely protective of not only his wife, but his mother and sister, and Douglas wouldn't even consider eliciting the response Tamsin, who adopted Julia as her sister, would have).

Now, he would be living with her, and his mother who detested her, and his sister's grieving children and he had to find a way to make it all work, not only for them but also for his own peace of mind.

And this was a problem. A problem with no solution. And that made Douglas impatient. He had not encountered a problem he couldn't solve and he didn't like that feeling.

He had a half-formed plan. Of course, he always had a plan.

He would have to do something publically to demonstrate clearly to his mother exactly what place Julia held at Sommersgate. If left to her own devices, Monique would relegate Julia to nannydom in the expanse of a week. But Julia was about as much of a nanny as Grace Kelly was a wallflower. Unfortunately, part of being an Ashton meant they lived their lives relatively publically and Douglas had every intention of putting Julia in her rightful place as Tamsin's children's aunt, and thus a member of the Ashton family. And he intended to do it immediately.

As for the rest, he'd managed to control his impulses when it came to Julia for fifteen years, another fifteen would not be difficult. Douglas managed to control a great many of his impulses with very little effort. He was rarely home anyway and Julia would just be a woman, albeit a very alluring one, who happened to live in his house.

Nothing else, except Monique's attitude, need change.

And that, he could, and would, also control, of this he had no doubt.

He drove down the lane and around the chapel, skirting the fountain. He left the Jaguar in the front drive, knowing that Carter would have heard him arrive and would take the car to the garages and put it away.

Douglas grabbed his briefcase and walked to the door. He noted the lights were blazing in Julia's suite and the curtains were opened. He wondered vaguely why she was awake at this hour, it was well after eleven and she had to be exhausted.

He shoved open the heavy door, not bothering to lock it behind him. Carter would see to that as well.

He intended to go straight to his study. Even if Julia was awake, she would most likely not wish his company this late at night and, with the call from Japan coming soon, he did not wish hers. The last time he had seen her, he remembered her eyes were sunk in their sockets with heartache but she had been resolute in telling him she'd be moving to Sommersgate directly after she arranged things in Indiana. And she had been true to her promise.

He moved down the hall, his study was opposite the dining room and he was about to turn into it when a flash of white caught his peripheral vision.

Immediately on alert, he turned toward the dining room and saw Julia running directly at him.

Taken off guard at the sight of a woman running through his house in the dead of night, he wasn't prepared and she crashed right into him, rocking him back on his heels. Then she pushed away, disengaging herself from the arm he'd automatically thrown around her waist.

"The children..." Julia muttered urgently before he could say a word and then she pulled away and ran up the stairs, taking them two at a time.

He stood there, staring up the stairs, wondering if this was some strange manifestation of jetlag or if he should follow her. The house was silent, save for her footsteps pounding down the hall. His keen sense of danger, bred in him through a lifetime of assessing his mother and father's moods and honed through the secret life he had chosen, registered nothing.

He made his decision and walked calmly into the study, turned on the lights, deposited his briefcase on the desk, pulled his tie free, shrugged off his suit jacket and tossed them on the couch before he walked out to see what was happening.

By the time he exited the study, she was racing back down the stairs.

Regardless of the madness she seemed to be exuding, she managed, as ever, to do it in style. She wore a thin, fitted top and a pair of light blue pants that hung low on her hips and clung to the right places. She was barefoot, her toes painted a deep, rich red, and her thick, blonde hair was waving softly around her face and down past her shoulders. However flimsy her clothing, she looked like she could walk down the street in them and have every woman wanting the same outfit and every man staring at her just as Douglas was staring at her now.

She skidded to a halt in front of him.

"I heard a scream," she told him, breathless.

That was not what he had expected to hear.

Before he could respond, she put her hand on his chest in that familiar way of hers, bent slightly at the waist and took in two shuddering breaths.

She pulled herself straight again and said, "The kids are okay, sleeping. But I heard this awful scream."

He looked down at her hand on his chest and then at her, regarding her silently.

He could turn on his heel, walk into his study and close the door, leaving her to her bizarre moment of insanity. Or, a far more pleasant idea was to pick her up, carry her to her rooms and make her so exhausted she'd cease these ridiculous actions, go to sleep and let him get back to work.

He nearly had to shake his head to clear that unbidden and unwelcome but very interesting thought from his mind. Dragging her to bed on her first night and seducing her while she was displaying symptoms of temporary insanity was most likely not the best way to welcome her to Sommersgate House.

He couldn't let this woman, who was letting jetlag, unfamiliar surroundings and a highly emotional situation the like of leaving everything near and dear to her behind and starting a new life in a foreign country, lead her to strange delusions, stand in a cold hallway.

"Come to the study, let me get you a drink," he offered.

She didn't move even as he did. "Did you hear me? Douglas, I heard a woman scream. A... woman... scream."

He continued walking and, as he expected, after a moment's hesitation, she followed him. He poured a whisky for himself, a sherry for her.

He handed it to her.

"Drink," was all he said.

She took the glass but did not drink. He lifted his whisky to his lips and sipped from it, watching her over the rim of his glass.

She was staring at him as if it was he that had lost his mind, her lovely green eyes managing to look both rounded and narrowed at the same time.

"Douglas –"

"Julia, calm yourself. Sit down, drink," he commanded and expected her, as he would anyone, to obey.

"Douglas! I heard… a woman… scream!"

He sighed. He'd lived at Sommersgate his whole life, he had, of course, heard this story before.

"You heard nothing. You have jetlag. You were probably asleep and dreaming."

"Jetlag doesn't make you start hearing things. I know what I heard. And I wasn't asleep," she retorted sharply.

Douglas watched her. Her breathing had slowed but she still kept looking out the door as if she was going to see something there.

She hadn't sat, she hadn't drunk, she hadn't done anything he told her to do.

He couldn't remember the last time anyone had spoken to him in that tone. In fact, outside of his father, there might never have been a time when anyone had spoken to him in that tone.

He also couldn't remember a time when he'd issued an order that hadn't been carried out immediately.

This was a new sensation for him and it was intriguing.

"Do you hear anything now?" he asked, feigning concern.

"No."

"What were you doing when you heard this… scream?"

"I was making lists. I was doing a budget. I was wide awake and…" She stopped herself and looked back out the door. She tipped her head to the side and seemed to be listening for something or thinking about something.

Then she took a deep breath and her teeth bit into her generous bottom lip. When her eyes came back to his, she seemed to have come to some conclusion.

"Yes, yes, you're right. It was just... I'm exhausted. I'm sorry. I can't sleep. Haven't slept well in a long time. I'm sorry."

When she stopped speaking, he raised an eyebrow then motioned to the couch with a nod of his head. This time she obeyed his unspoken command and sat down. She took a drink and then opened her mouth wide and breathed out like something burned her tongue. Her expression was so preposterous, it almost made Douglas smile.

"What *is* that?" she asked, lifting the glass to indicate the source of her question.

"Sherry," he replied, walking to the desk and leaning a thigh against it. Then he took another sip of the whisky while he watched her.

"I'm sorry but it's awful," she told him, setting the glass down on the table in front of her.

"That's a sweet sherry, would you like something dry?"

She raised comically horrified eyes to him at the thought of anything sherry and said, "No. No, thank you, no. No sherry, sweet or dry. Sherry, blech. Are you drinking sherry?"

As he regarded her sitting on his couch in her tight, fetching outfit, Douglas thought that this was a very bizarre conversation and would have preferred not to be having it. He also didn't have time (nor would he allow himself) to consider the many things he would have preferred to be doing, most specifically with her or, to be precise, *to* her, as his call would be coming through shortly.

"Whisky," he replied, seeking patience.

"May I have some whisky?"

Obliging her, he walked to the drinks cabinet, thinking to give her some spirit to soothe her mental state and get her to go to bed. There were a number of things to do and she was distracting.

"Do you like whisky?" he asked.

"I hate it," she answered and when he turned on that strange comment, he saw she was again looking out the door. She had lifted her hand to pull her hair off her face and then she looked back at him, dropping her arm. He couldn't help but notice how even these superfluous movements were innately graceful. Her face was free of makeup and her hair was slowly falling back into place around her face. He knew that she was thirty-six years old but she looked a decade younger.

Her voice was low and deep but entirely feminine and very sensuous. He'd always liked the way she'd said his name in that voice.

He'd forgotten that.

She lifted her legs to sit crossed-legged on the couch as he brought her the whisky. His mother would have had a coronary, to see a woman at Sommersgate sitting cross-legged, wearing whatever it was Julia was wearing, no matter how fetching (and whatever it was, it was not couture), with her feet tucked underneath her. That thought, as well, almost made Douglas smile.

"It feels warm going down," Julia said.

"I'm sorry?" he asked.

"The whisky. It tastes terrible but feels warm going down. I'm chilled the bone." And as if to demonstrate, she shivered dramatically.

He wasn't surprised she was cold. She was barely wearing any clothes.

With effort, he pulled his eyes from her body and his thoughts away from the better ways there were to warm her and said sardonically, "Welcome to Sommersgate." And to that, he lifted his glass to her in salute.

Her green eyes, which had been staring into her whisky glass, moved to him and in the briefest second, they lit right before she laughed.

He could not recall ever making her laugh before although he'd seen others do it. She'd always had an uninhibited laugh, throaty and rich, which engaged her whole body, rather than just her mouth. He'd always enjoyed hearing and watching her laugh.

He'd forgotten that too.

There was something quite unusually... *pleasant* about being responsible for that kind of laughter.

What was unpleasant was noticing that she did look exhausted. As her face lit up, the exhaustion was replaced by a light that he was far more familiar with when it came to Julia. And, as soon as the laughter died, the exhaustion settled back on her features. This was not evidenced in haggard lines, in fact, she hid it well. He hadn't noticed it until she laughed. But she was pale and, once the laughter died away, there was none of the usual brightness to her eyes.

She lifted her glass to return the salute and downed the contents after which she grimaced.

"I'm sorry," she said when she'd wiped the grimace from her face. "You get home late and have some crazy female running around your house like an idiot. You're probably wondering what you've gotten yourself into. I promise, this is not an indication of the years to come." And with that, she gave him a small smile that did nothing to transform her face and most certainly did not reach her eyes.

He had no reply and she didn't seem to expect one. She stood and gathered the glasses.

"I'll just take these to the kitchen and leave you in peace." She turned toward the door finishing with, "Goodnight, I'll see you tomorrow?"

"Julia," he stopped her and she turned back. "Just leave the glasses. Veronika will see to them."

She hesitated, looked at the glasses, at him then put the glasses on the table seeming somewhat confused.

"I'll see you in the morning," he finished, done with the episode, done with her.

She hesitated again and he wondered, in a detached way as his mind was already moving forward to when she would be gone, what she planned to do next.

Then she walked up to him, put her hand on his arm, leaned into him and kissed his cheek.

She smelled of tangerines and jasmine.

"Goodnight," she said softly. "See you tomorrow."

He stood leaning against his desk, his arms crossed on his chest and he watched her walk out of the study and into the dark hallway until she disappeared out of sight.

Yes, he had a problem and that problem was Julia Fairfax.

Then the phone rang and she went completely out of his mind.

❦ 4 ❦

RUBY'S FRIEND

The next morning, Julia sat down to her sugarless porridge and stared at it with distaste.

After leaving Douglas last night, she'd tossed and turned in the big, soft bed with its even softer sheets. She couldn't get her strange behaviour out of her head. Behaviour which, if it ever came down to a nasty custody battle, could and would no doubt be brought up to prove she was a raving lunatic incapable of raising three children.

What had come over her last night?

It was the house, the damned house. It was creepy.

She hadn't heard any scream or felt any spooky arctic draught.

She was disoriented and over-emotional, exhausted, jetlagged and homesick.

At least that's what she told herself but the entire night she couldn't get it out of her head that something, not someone but some*thing,* was in the room with her.

She'd managed to drag herself out of bed at an ungodly hour feeling as if she'd only had moments of sleep, which, in reality, was all she had. She was determined to help Mrs. K get the kids ready for school. Mrs. Kilpatrick had taken enough on and it was now time to alleviate her burden.

It was chaos, but quiet and controlled as Douglas was in the house and it was clear the children had long since learned that Douglas was not to be disturbed (although, she soon learned from Mrs. K that Douglas was *not* in the house but out taking his morning run).

Lizzie and Willie were now bolting down their food, no matter that it tasted like cardboard, or maybe because of it.

Julia had made sure they were up, washed, dressed and their rucksacks were filled. After all this, Julia appeared in the kitchen to help with breakfast but Mrs. K had shooed her out and ordered her to sit in the dining room to await the meal. Julia was surprised they sat in the huge, formal dining room for breakfast. Dinner her first night there as a celebration but breakfast?

She'd made an effort when dressing for the sake of the kids and Mrs. K. She didn't need anyone worrying about her and she knew she looked terrible. She tried to hide the dark circles under her eyes behind a mask of light makeup. She'd put on a pair of charcoal grey, boot-leg, corduroy trousers, the belt loops threaded with a heavily embossed, wide leather belt that ended in a huge, silver, Western-style buckle. She wore high-heeled black boots and a fitted black t-shirt that had a scooped neck and long sleeves that fit snugly down the arms but flared out slightly from the elbows to hang gracefully passed her wrists. She'd thrown on a necklace made of a strip of black leather from which dangled a hammered disc of matte silver and she'd completed the outfit with big, wide, silver-hooped earrings.

"You dress like a rock star's wife," Gavin used to tease her.

"She does not!" Tamsin would defend.

"Okay, you dress like a rock star's somewhat-classy wife," Gavin allowed.

Pushing the once happy, now devastating memory and the porridge, aside, she reached for her coffee and took a sip just as Douglas strolled into the dining room.

At his arrival, Julia nearly choked. He was supposed to be out running, she never imagined he'd join them for breakfast. In fact, she had hoped to avoid him completely this morning after her behaviour last night.

Her eyes surreptitiously slid over him and she noted he wore a superbly-cut navy suit with wide-set pinstripes, a crisp, wrinkle-free white shirt and a subtly-patterned, obviously-expensive, navy tie. His thick, dark brown hair was still slightly wet from a shower and curling, overlong, at his collar. His jaw was smoothly shaven and the scar on his upper lip stood out making him look both menacing and sexy.

He sauntered into the room the way only a man who owned such a room could saunter into it, with sheer arrogance.

"Morning Unka Douglas!" Ruby called loudly, her mouth full.

"Good morning, Ruby," Douglas replied evenly, walking behind Lizzie's chair as she sat beside Julia, touching the girl lightly on the shoulder as he did so. Julia watched as Lizzie lifted her shoulder, as if seeking to deepen the gesture, but it was soon gone and, just as quickly, both the girl's shoulders drooped.

"Will... Elizabeth," Douglas said as he sat down at the head of the table to Julia's right and put his napkin in his lap.

"Mornin'," Willie said, also with mouth full.

Lizzie just made an indistinct noise.

Douglas turned his indigo eyes to Julia, she noticed (again, as she had many times over the years) that they were thickly lashed, somehow making the vivid blue seem darker.

"Are you recovered this morning?" he asked.

Of course he wouldn't just let it go. He had to bring it up.

"Absolutely," Julia lied with a bright, false smile making a show of pulling her porridge back towards her as if it was a delicious bowl of ice cream which she couldn't wait a moment longer to devour. "Fit as a fiddle," she added for good measure.

There was the briefest hesitation and then he drawled (actually *drawled*), eyes still on her, "I can see that."

There was something in that drawl and in his eyes that made Julia's stomach lurch in a not altogether unpleasant way.

"Recovered from what?" Willie butted in, thankfully interrupting the moment and reaching for a piece of toast that carried the barest hint of butter.

"Nothing, I didn't get settled in last night, but I'm okay now," Julia fibbed again, eating a mouthful and then making the Herculean effort to stop herself from gagging. Douglas was still regarding her rather closely and she really wished he wouldn't.

"It's the house," Willie stated. "It doesn't like strangers. It'll get used to you though."

Julia lost all composure and gaped at her nephew open-mouthed as Ruby giggled.

Lizzie had no response.

"What?" Julia asked.

Willie cut his eyes to Douglas and took a big bite of toast.

"Nothin'," he muttered and Julia decided after her behaviour last night it was prudent to drop the subject.

Mrs. Kilpatrick swept in, deposited poached eggs, two crisp rashers of bacon and fresh toast in front of Douglas and swept out, not making a sound throughout the entire exercise.

Julia stared hungrily at his plate and wondered what she had to do to get eggs and bacon for breakfast (especially when she couldn't even get in the kitchen to make it for herself) as she took another mouthful of oatmeal. At that point, she'd sell her soul for just one rasher of bacon.

"This weekend," Douglas started as he poured himself some coffee out of the silver service, "we'll all go to London. You four can go sight-seeing during the day and Saturday night, Julia, I'd like you to attend an art opening with me."

Julia had barely stopped gaping at Willie only to turn and gape at Douglas.

"I'm sorry?" she asked after she forced herself to stop gaping.

Her question was lost in loud whoops from Willie, the volume of which surprised even Julia considering the careful quiet the children and servants observed constantly.

"London! Wicked!" Willie declared, pumping his arm like he was a trucker repeatedly blowing his horn.

Ruby decided this was a good indication that she, too, could get excited and she let out childish screech of delight.

"Elizabeth, would you like to go to London?" Douglas quietly asked his niece.

Surprisingly, Lizzie answered.

"Kensington Palace, where Diana's dresses are?" she inquired of her bowl of porridge, not lifting her head to look at her uncle.

"If that's what you'd like," Douglas told Lizzie and turned back to Julia. "Take Veronika as well, so you won't be overburdened."

And with that, the weekend plans were made with Julia only being able to utter two, unacknowledged words in the process. Julia wondered if Veronika might have plans of her own but she decided not to ask as clearly, to Douglas, it didn't matter.

She wanted to say something about not wanting to go to London, but rather wanting to sleep in and get used to her new home and not traipse around an unfamiliar, bustling city. Or, she wanted to say something about wanting a pot of jam or a sugar bowl on the table, because at the very least she took sugar in her coffee, not to mention her oatmeal. Or she wanted to say something about how it might be a good idea for Douglas to speak to her about these ideas before he presented them to the children.

But then she noticed Ruby.

The little girl was staring over Julia's shoulder and out the window.

Julia turned to see if it was Carter who had caught the child's attention but when she looked, she saw nothing.

When she turned back to the child, Ruby was waving.

Julia, again, looked out the window and saw nothing.

"Ruby," she called, "who are you waving at?"

"Ruby has an imaginary friend," Willie replied, clearly the speaker for the group.

"He is not imaginary," Ruby fired back. "He's standing right there at the window, looking at Auntie Jewel."

A chill slid down Julia's spine as she turned again to peer out the window.

"I don't see nothin'," Willie declared.

"Anything," Julia corrected distractedly, still seeing nothing.

"I don't see anything," Willie amended, overly sweet and teasing Ruby by bugging his eyes out to her.

"He's right there and he's my friend. He likes me. And he likes Auntie Jewel," Ruby shot back.

"That's enough, Ruby. Eat," Douglas ordered and without a word, little Ruby obeyed, but then, at that tone of voice, a Marine Sergeant would have obeyed.

Mrs. K came back in and announced that Carter was ready to take the children to school.

They all, even Ruby, rushed from their seats, leaving their dirty dishes on the table and heading out the door.

"Hang on a second…" Julia called and they stopped. "The dishes…" she started to say but was interrupted.

"The staff see to the dishes, Julia," Douglas reminded her.

Julia made another Herculean effort at control. She had not been raised to leave her dirty dishes on the table and she knew neither Tamsin nor Gavin had raised their children to leave their dishes. They'd had a nanny, to be certain, Gavin travelled a great deal. They also had a maid, who came in three days a week, and why not, Tamsin was rich. But the children were only half-aristocrat. The other half, both Gavin and Tamsin had assured, were polite, courteous, well-behaved Midwesterners.

Momentarily defeated, Julia changed tactics. "Well then, I want kisses. You aren't walking out of here without giving me kisses."

Willie rolled his eyes and slouched forward, making a show of hating every second and pecked her cheek so quickly he appeared to be going for a world record. Lizzie didn't rush forward either but did as she was told. They both ran out of the room as Julia caught Ruby in a hug and lavished the child's face with kisses as she squirmed and giggled.

"Off with you, Ruby-girl, say good-bye to your brother and sister for me," Julia said.

With that, Ruby dashed out of the room.

Left alone with Douglas, Julia was at a loss, so she stared longingly at his breakfast.

"I thought…" he began and then stopped, regarded her for a moment then he continued politely. "Would you like for me to ask Mrs. Kilpatrick to make you some eggs?"

Flustered, she stopped staring and took another spoonful of porridge.

"No, no, I love oatmeal! Yum, yum," she lied and was about to put the spoon in her mouth when a masculine hand came into her sight, its fingers clamped on her spoon and it was firmly pulled out of her grasp by Douglas.

Stunned, she watched as he dropped the spoon into her bowl and removed the bowl from her place setting. He then set his plate of food in front of her.

Julia could not believe what he'd just done and couldn't think of a thing to say to him. It was his house and she was a guest there, but still, the arrogance! She tried to think of some way of responding to his outrageous behaviour and decided diplomacy was best.

"I can't..." she started only to be interrupted again.

"You can and you will," he commanded, dipping his head to her plate, his gaze firm on her face and she found herself too tired, too stunned and too hungry (and maybe a bit too chicken), to argue.

Therefore, she tucked into the food.

"Sunday evening, when we get back from the city, I'd like to have a talk about our arrangement," Douglas announced.

She took a bite of bacon and watched him. He showed no signs of anything, no emotion, no sadness at his sister's passing. Last night he got home late after a day of whatever it was that he did, and was up again, early, dressed and ready to go back to whatever it was and he looked like he just left a spa.

"Julia?" Now he no longer looked emotionless, he looked impatient.

"Yes, that's fine. That's a good idea. I look forward to that." She was babbling.

"Good." He took a last sip of his coffee and threw down his napkin. "I'll see you Saturday evening."

She nearly choked again.

Saturday evening!

"Saturday evening... but it's Wednesday!" she cried.

She said it to an empty room.

He was gone.

And Julia still felt like she was being watched.

Veronika was surprised to find Miss Julia's bed made when she walked into her room.

She'd heard the American woman on the phone in the kitchen and she'd hurried to do the cleaning while Julia was otherwise engaged. She bustled around the room, intent to perform her duties to the exacting standards that Lady Monique Ashton expected them to be done.

Bathrooms cleaned thoroughly, daily. Used towels were taken away and washed, daily. Also, dusting and hoovering done, daily. Sheets were changed on Wednesdays and Fridays. Clothes were picked up off the floor and all of the outerwear was put in cleaned and pressed linen sacks and taken by Carter to the dry cleaners. Unmentionables carefully hand washed and air dried. Towels, sheets, serviettes, tablecloths were all washed, starched and ironed, by Veronika. The heavy cleaning was done on a strict rota that Mrs. Kilpatrick oversaw with a devotion akin to religion.

The American was like no one Veronika had yet met in England. She made her bed. She folded her towel and put it back on the rail. She spoke to Veronika in a normal voice and smiled at her, even when Veronika was just passing.

Veronika didn't know what to make of her.

The Lady Tamsin had been quite like that but careful not to be overly familiar when Lady Ashton was around. Veronika had only seen Mister Gavin once, for the briefest of moments, and he'd been kissing Lady Tamsin at the time so Veronika had left them to it.

Veronika felt a great deal of guilt as she was the only one in the household who had gained from the lovely couple's deaths. Mrs. Kilpatrick's hours went from abnormally long to ungodly long. Veronika, who worked Wednesday through Sunday and had Monday and Tuesday off had gained a lot of extra hours and overtime pay the last five months. This had eased her burden tremendously.

She was able to move out of the cold and cramped old servants' quarters and she got herself a small, shabbily furnished bedsit in the local town. She was also able to buy a beat-up old car. She put in a telephone (even though she had no one to call). She even bought plates, cutlery and pretty plastic glasses at the local Tesco that had bright circles printed on them.

Even with all the good luck Veronika had since meeting Lord Douglas Ashton that dark night nearly seven months ago, she still didn't trust it.

Veronika was not a lucky girl, never had been.

And in that dark alley, so many months ago, she was certain her luck had run out. She was vulnerable, alone and the men who had been tracking her finally had made their move. They'd trapped her in that alley, beat her about the face until she tasted the blood in her mouth, and her belly until she found it hard to breathe, pushed her up against the wall and put the knife to her throat making such demands, such *hideous* demands. She knew she'd die, or go missing, perhaps sold into a life even worse than the lonely one she was living.

Then, out of nowhere, Lord Ashton appeared.

Veronika never knew what he was doing there but she prayed to God nearly every night a prayer of gratitude that he was.

There had been three large men but Lord Ashton dispatched them without breaking a sweat. When he turned his dark eyes to her she noticed he wasn't even breathing heavily and his expression was not angry but strangely remote. The controlled and practised violence he showed when dealing with her attackers was almost more frightening then the knife pressed to her throat.

"Come with me, you'll be safe," he'd commanded, speaking fluent Russian.

She went, too afraid not to go at the same time knowing somewhere deep in her heart she was safe.

He took her to a hotel and signed her in, paying a week in advance.

She expected he would want something, something she'd never given anyone, and, although she was frightened, she knew she would have given it to him. He had saved her life for one thing and for another, he was very handsome, except for the scar on his mouth which made him look slightly menacing.

He was tall, lean and utterly perfect.

And he was her hero.

But instead, the moment he saw her safely into her room and handed her a wetted towel to wipe the blood from her mouth, he turned to go. She became so scared at the thought of being left alone, she blurted out her whole life story in quick, frightened sentences.

He listened, his impersonal expression never changing throughout her sad saga. When she was done, he nodded and left without a word. She thought that was it and she didn't know what to do. She couldn't stay and she was too frightened to leave.

In fifteen minutes, the phone rang in the room and an efficient woman was on the line, telling Veronika in somewhat broken Russian what would happen to her. In a week, she had a passport and a ticket to England.

That was it and here she was.

She'd started her job immediately in this big, frightening house with its many chimneys and gables, wrought-ironed scroll work, twisted, strange fancies shooting toward the sky, its curved turrets and graceful chapel.

Mrs. K was nice to her from the first but it still took Veronika months to trust her. Carter was gruff and quiet but she noticed he, and Mr. Kilpatrick when he was around, both looked after Veronika either under Mrs. K's request or Lord Ashton's edict. Even with their easy acceptance and their kind, efficient training of her in her new duties, she was still frightened. The men Lord Ashton had bested were not of the kind to lose gracefully.

She lived in fear that they would find her, one day.

In her new life, though, somehow, with all of this hanging over her head, the house scared her most of all. Especially at night, when she watched over the children and heard the noises, felt the draughts and saw the shadow of a man walking around outside.

No, the house didn't scare her most of all. Losing her job did. She couldn't go back to St. Petersburg.

And she feared losing her job every second of every day because Lady Ashton was not an easy mistress.

Everything had to be perfect, no feather left on the floor by the vacuum, no wet washcloth forgotten in the shower, no familiarity with family or guests. If it happened, the results were terrible. Veronika had felt Lady Ashton's displeasure, the razor sharpness of her tongue and her angry eyes. There were rules and responsibilities that had to be seen to with the utmost care, Veronika had twice been careless, one more time and Veronika knew she would be gone.

"Oh! There you are," Julia greeted her as if she was actually looking for her and wanted to speak to her. Veronika was finishing in her bathroom and watched as the American approached.

"Look at these... can you believe? I told Sam I needed a mobile phone and a computer, what... two hours ago? And look."

Veronika shrank back as Miss Julia showed her a sheaf of papers, all of which had tiny writing and pictures of phones or computers on them.

"'Pick one,' Sam said, 'and I'll have it delivered to you this afternoon.' This afternoon!" Miss Julia shook her head and Veronika watched the shining, fair hair move around the woman's tired face. Unlike Lord Ashton and his mother, this one, Veronika could tell from her own awful experiences, was in mourning.

In Russia, when you lost a loved one, you wore black and you beat your chest and you cried and screamed and followed the coffins throwing yourself on the ground while you cursed God. Veronika knew this, she'd done it three times in her short life.

Not here, not in England.

Here, one day Lady Tamsin and Mister Gavin were alive, the next day, they were not and it was business as usual.

Veronika had walked in on Mrs. K snuffling into her handkerchief and Carter hadn't spoken for a week, walking around tight-lipped and pale.

But, the family had showed no signs that the slightest thing was amiss.

But Miss Julia looked like she could use a black shawl around her head and good scream and beating of the chest. Her grief was etched in every line of her body.

In her short, sad life, Veronika had lost her mother, father and sister. She knew grief and the look behind Miss Julia's eyes was a look Veronika had seen in the mirror many a morning (and sometimes she *still* saw it in the mirror). She could try to hide it but it showed.

"Which one should I pick?" Miss Julia asked, sounding genuinely like she wanted an answer.

Veronika stared at the papers, not understanding the words written on them.

"I do not know," she answered in her heavily-accented English.

"I don't know either," Miss Julia sighed and walked down the hallway. Little Ruby was laying on her back on the bed, arms and legs splayed out like she was arrested in the act of making a snow angel. Julia jumped on the bed and pulled the child's t-shirt up and blew a raspberry so loud on her belly that the child shrieked with laughter. It made Veronika want to smile. She hadn't heard laughter in this house in... well, she'd *never* heard it.

Though, of the three children, Veronika knew Ruby would one day find it the hardest. She didn't know what she felt now, just loss and bewilderment. To her, Mummy and Daddy could come back any day.

But one day, without the precious memories the others enjoyed, Ruby would have the hardest time of all.

"So, you're coming with us to London?" It took a moment to register that Julia was speaking to her she was so used to being ignored. Veronika stood there, carrying the towels Julia had used the night before.

"I... yes. To look after children," Veronika answered.

"Have you ever been to London?"

Veronika shook her head.

"Then you'll go with us on Saturday," she decided and Veronika just stared. "We're going to Kensington Palace to see Diana's gowns and to Madame Tussaud's to see all the waxworks."

"And the Tower of London where they chopped off people's heads!" Ruby shouted, even though both women were close enough to hear.

Julia turned and looked at Veronika, her tired, sad eyes kind.

"Would you like that, Veronika? To see Diana's dresses?" she asked.

"And the place they chop off heads!" Ruby shouted again and Julia smiled indulgently at the child.

Veronika didn't know what to say. She was paid to do what she did. Would she get sacked if she went sightseeing in London? Mrs. K said the American was now a member of the Ashton family and should be treated thus. If Miss Julia told her she must go then she couldn't refuse.

She'd always wanted to go to London, she'd always wanted to go anywhere and everywhere, to travel and have adventures, see things, meet people, eat different food and hear different music. But those were dreams and even though she was only seventeen she knew that her life was this. Work and loneliness, not sightseeing in London. Any dreams Veronika had were long since dead.

"Don't worry, Veronika, we'll take care of you," Miss Julia assured her in her soft, throaty voice, watching Veronika closely.

"Yes! Auntie Jewel takes care of everyone. That's what Daddy always says."

Both women looked at the child who was now on her knees, her hands clasped in front of her, her eyes bright with excitement at the prospect of London.

Veronika turned to the American and saw the tears shimmering in the other woman's eyes. Knowing instinctively what to do, before little Ruby could see her aunt's despair, Veronika rushed forward.

"Come, girl. We take a walk to see what Missus Kilpatrick is doing, maybe she makes bread. You help her."

Ruby, always up for an adventure, shot out of the room.

Veronika quickly followed her but when she turned to close the door behind her to give the American some privacy, Julia was there, one hand on the door to stop Veronika.

"Thank you," Julia whispered, her voice such an absolute ache Veronika felt it lodge in her own throat just hearing it.

Veronika nodded and gently closed the door.

No, Veronika didn't know what to make of the American. But somehow, she felt maybe she could believe her luck *had* changed.

DOUGLAS'S PROTECTION

The doorbell rang at Douglas's house in the posh Kensington area of London just as Julia was walking down the stairs. She saw Veronika come out of the room where she and the kids were watching a DVD and she waved her back.

"I've got it," she told the girl, Veronika nodded and walked back from where she came.

Julia opened the door and a short woman with dark hair highlighted expertly with blonde streaks charged in.

"Okay... I hope I'm not too late but I had a million things to do," the woman announced without saying hello.

But she didn't have to say hello.

Julia had never met Sam Thornton but she would know her voice anywhere.

Sam whirled around once she'd gained entry and stopped. Julia saw Sam was wearing a well-cut, black suit with impossibly high-heeled black pumps and still she was at least four inches shorter than Julia.

"Well, I can see I didn't need to rush. Wow, that's quite a dress," Sam pronounced, her eyes giving Julia a head-to-toe.

"Sam," Julia said and walked forward, bent down and tightly hugged the woman she'd known for months but had never met.

The last three days, as with the last five months, Sam had been her lifeline. She'd arranged for Julia to have a mobile phone, a laptop and had the technician come to Sommersgate to connect Julia's new computer not only to the high-speed broadband that was already laid to the house but also to connect it to Douglas's complicated, wireless network in the house. Sam acquired an e-mail address for her as well and this meant Julia was in touch with family and friends back home and for that she'd be forever grateful.

Sam had sent Julia all the forms she needed for her driving license and from the Home Office. She'd researched health insurance and sent her job openings and volunteer opportunities in Julia's field. She'd even looked into getting Julia a bank account, which right now seemed impossible due to laws put in place to prevent terrorist activities and thus Julia had to be a resident of the country. It appeared Douglas had to open an account for her which was an aggravation Julia did not need and something she had to discuss with him on Sunday.

As the days went by, Julia was getting more and more uncomfortable with the "arrangement", as Douglas had called it, and needing to rely so heavily on him, even when he wasn't there. Her debts to him were mounting up and Julia was making carefully updated lists to tally these debts so she could (if she ever saw him for long enough to have a conversation with him) settle them.

Once Julia stepped back from Sam, the other woman started talking in her usual rapid fire way.

"Good to meet you too," she said, obviously flustered at Julia's show of affection. "I brought half a dozen frocks just in case you didn't have anything suitable to wear tonight but it seems I didn't need to worry." She gestured at Julia's outfit and then quickly on to another thought, she glanced around her. "Where are the kids?"

Without a response from Julia, Sam headed directly towards the lounge and the other woman's command of the situation and everything around her made Julia smile.

She looked down at her dress thinking with amusement about Sam taking charge of even her wardrobe. Julia's dress was jade green satin, with a high, mandarin neckline with intricate aquamarine frogs and scrolled cording. The hem was embroidered extravagantly in pale yellows, deep pinks, aquamarine with accents of black and gold with high slits up her thighs on either side. She wore a pair of delicate but dangerous-looking high, spike-heeled, slingback pumps. She'd twisted her hair up at the back, clipping it at the crown with a gold barrette inset with jade allowing the thick, waving blonde mass to fall over the clip.

She followed Sam into the lounge and it was clear the children knew her as they crowded around and Sam gave them affectionate hugs. Either they knew her or they were overwhelmed by the big chocolate bars she was freely distributing from her handbag.

Julia's week had been hectic, settling in, getting sorted, understanding the children's schedules which included daytime trips for Ruby to gymnastics and ballet classes and evening piano and violin lessons for Willie and Lizzie with Lizzie also taking ballet. There was also homework and instrument practice and the rigid schedule of the house mealtimes and bedtimes to keep.

That day they'd left early and Julia was thrilled to be free of the forbidding house that, even as enormous as it was, still felt claustrophobic. She sensed a strangeness there she couldn't put her finger on and Ruby's imaginary friend (whom the girl talked about all the time) was giving her the creeps.

Carter drove them to London where they spent an excruciatingly busy day visiting Kensington Palace, the mad, tourist-filled crush of Madame Tussaud's and the equally crowded Tower of London.

Still not sleeping well, with a day on her feet fighting crowds, watching over the children and hustling from one place to the next, Julia was shattered.

All week, when she did eventually sleep, it was fitful, filled with strange dreams she couldn't quite remember or disturbed by an odd tapping at the window that was most likely the branch of a tree or shrub but in the dark of night seemed something else, something sinister.

Tonight, Sam had told her, she would be having dinner with Douglas and two of his friends, Charlotte and Oliver Forsythe. Julia had met Charlotte and Oliver on several occasions when she'd visited Tammy and Gav. Charlotte was the editor-in-chief of a glossy fashion magazine and Oliver's family was in banking. "In banking" was Tammy's way of saying his family owned the controlling share of a bank with hundreds of branches nationwide. Julia liked them both. Even though she didn't know either of them very well she knew they'd been good friends to Tammy and Gav.

They would all then be off to an art gallery opening. There, Sam warned her, she would face the "paps". Thus the need for Sam's "frocks" as Sam had informed her she wanted Julia to be confident in the face of the onslaught.

"And every girl knows, confidence often comes in the form a fantastic outfit!" Sam had proclaimed (quite rightly).

This was something Julia had not anticipated. She did not look forward to this evening, dressing up and having dinner with people she didn't know very well was enough of a drain on her flagging resources. But facing "paps" made it all the worse.

"Paps" was English slang for "paparazzi". Tamsin and Gavin, she knew, were both photographed frequently at balls and other events that Tamsin supported in her role as Lady Tamsin Ashton Fairfax. But Douglas was positively hunted by the photographers. Julia had seen his face dozens of times in various magazines in The States. Until Sam reminded her, it hadn't occurred to Julia that, in being with him, she would also face the paparazzi. This would be a unique experience but she couldn't imagine they'd have an interest in her when Douglas was there as a target. Perhaps, she thought (or more to the point hoped), it wouldn't be that bad.

"I thought I'd take the kids to a movie tonight, if you don't mind," Sam said, interrupting Julia's thoughts.

"Wicked!" Willie shouted what Julia was coming to learn was his favourite word.

"In Leicester Square, Lizzie, where they have all the big premieres, like *Harry Potter*." Sam went on when Lizzie didn't act as thrilled as Willie.

"Okay," Lizzie muttered, too well-mannered to ignore someone speaking directly to her but also not willing to show any excitement.

"Is that okay?" Sam asked Julia and Julia nodded and smiled. The kids would love it and they certainly had enough of being holed up in austere, posh houses.

She saw Veronika standing away from the group, her face carefully blank and Julia had an idea.

"Could you take Veronika as well? I'm sure she'd like to see Leicester Square and she'd help you out with the kids," Julia asked Sam quietly, looking at the young girl across the room and giving her a wink.

"Sure thing. Ronnie you're coming with us!" Sam announced and Julia watched with satisfaction as Veronika's studiously controlled face positively lit up.

The Russian girl had been a godsend that day. She carefully looked after the children, was immensely gentle with them, occasionally cautiously affectionate and she obviously took her job very seriously. She'd also noticed that, several times, Veronika lost herself in wonder at the sights they'd seen and Julia was pleased that she'd brought her along instead of leaving her with Carter while just she and the kids enjoyed their activities.

"But we must go, on the double, or we'll miss our showing. Come on! Chop chop!" And Sam clapped her hands as the kids and Veronika trooped into the hall to get their coats.

Julia was carrying her evening bag and walking beside Sam and she pulled it open to take out some money for the kids and Veronika.

"You have a car big enough for all of them?" she asked, sorting out two fifty pound notes because she had no idea how much an evening out to the movies in London would cost. Considering the exorbitant cost of everything else that day, a hundred pounds might not even cover it.

"No worries. We'll take a taxi. Haven't experienced London unless you've had a ride in a London taxi. I have one waiting outside with your frocks. We'll swing by my house, drop off the dresses and off we go," Sam assured her as they stopped several feet from the front door.

"Can you come directly back after? Ruby shouldn't be out late," Julia requested.

Sam laughed. "I've got five nieces and two nephews. Don't worry about us, I know the drill. We'll be fine."

Julia started to hand her the money when a deep voice came from behind them.

"What's happening here?" Douglas asked.

Julia whirled around and saw Douglas was standing in the open doorway looking sophisticated wearing another superbly-tailored navy suit, this one without pinstripes. It was accompanied by a deep burgundy shirt and monochromatic tie.

She hadn't seen him since Wednesday, hadn't even spoken to him on the phone. She'd just managed to force him, and the disturbing and confusing rush of feelings she was having, out of her mind. At the sight of him standing there managing to look both dashing and unapproachable, those feelings crowded in on her uninvited and she felt her breath momentarily quicken.

Ruby dashed to him and threw her arms around his legs. He touched her head lightly, this she accurately took as a signal to disengage and Douglas nodded to Willie's, "'Lo, Uncle Douglas," and briefly and distractedly touched Lizzie cheek as he walked by the girl.

"Sam is taking the kids to the movies. I was just giving her some money," Julia explained.

Ignoring the proffered notes, Sam ordered, "I'll put it on my expense account. Right boss?" she said with a cheeky grin at Douglas and, not waiting for an answer, she addressed the crowd. "We'll be late if we don't go and you two will be late if you don't go... children! Onward!" she ordered and trooped the kids to the door leaving Julia standing there, still holding the notes in her hand.

"Hang on!" Julia called. "Kids... kisses!" And they all came back, briefly pressing kisses to her cheek and rushed, followed by a quiet Veronika who appeared to be trying to make herself invisible, out the door.

When Julia turned around, Douglas was gone. A light was now on in what she knew was his study and she stuffed the notes in her purse as she walked to the doorway. He'd laid his briefcase on his desk and had the phone in his hand.

"Carter," he said into the receiver, "we'll meet you at the front door." He turned his head to look at her as he replaced the receiver. "Are you ready?"

In response, Julia put her arms out slightly at the sides, looking down at herself.

"I see you are," he said, his tone no longer businesslike but vastly different. He was looking at her, his eyes moving down her body in a lazy way.

From the look in his eyes, she felt that familiar tremor slide up her spine and her stomach lurched, then clenched and she felt pleasantly warm, unwelcomely so.

What was he playing at? He hadn't even said, *Hello, how were the last three days of your new life?* Now he was eyeing her like she was dinner.

She didn't have the time, or the energy, to think about it.

Instead, she said, "I'll just run upstairs for my wrap."

Then she turned and escaped, ascending the stairs to her room. She grabbed her pink pashmina from the bed and wrapped it around her, throwing a free end over her left shoulder. She took a deep breath and thought, *I can do this, just a few hours, I can manage not to fall face forward in my soup and then it will be over and I can come back and sleep.* Once she told herself this (and almost believed it), she headed back down the stairs.

At the curb, Carter opened the door to the Bentley for them, closed it behind them and they were whisked into the London night.

Julia stared out the window feeling strangely shy and decided to put it down to tiredness and Douglas's earlier look. She had always been outgoing and found talking to anyone from any background easy. You just found out what their interests were and then asked questions. Nearly everyone loved to talk about themselves. Simple.

But she was so exhausted, she couldn't think how to make small talk with Douglas and then she realised belatedly that Douglas wasn't speaking either. She turned to look at him and saw he was staring at her legs which were crossed. It was too dark to see his expression but she sensed something in the car and that something made her cheeks warm.

"How was your week?" she asked in an attempt to dispel her bizarre feeling.

"Long," he answered shortly, not offering any more information as he shifted his gaze from her legs to her face. "Yours?" he asked.

"The same."

And that was it, the extent of their conversation. Not long after, they slid to a halt at the front of a fashionable restaurant, so fashionable that Julia had heard of it, even in Indiana, *and* all the celebrities that haunted it.

The place was a crush at the front but the moment the doors closed behind them it was serene, decorated with an overdose of trendy bamboo and lots of glass. The hostess immediately stiffened and came forward, oozing courtesy as she guided them to the table Charlotte and Oliver were already occupying.

Julia was pleasantly surprised when both the petite, slim, stylish, black-haired Charlotte and the tall, straight, sandy-haired Oliver greeted her with friendly familiarity.

They'd barely taken their seats when a waiter appeared at the table.

"Would you like drinks, Lord Ashton?" he asked reverentially.

Douglas didn't even look at Julia before saying, "Miss Fairfax will have a dry vodka martini, up, with an olive. I'll have the same, with gin, no olive."

Julia was stunned speechless.

It was true, she had a strict regimen of drinking. Margaritas while eating Mexican or on hot summer evenings. Micro-brewed beer while watching sports. Spiced rum and diet cola while lounging at home with friends or on the rare occasions when she was at a beach. Dry red wine with dinner. Amaretto with coffee after dessert. Mojitos when she was feeling saucy or eating Texas chilli. And, on posh nights out, a dry vodka martini, up, with an olive.

She didn't know what was more shocking, that Douglas knew her preferred drink or that he hadn't bothered consulting her when ordering it. No man, not even Sean, had ordered for her without taking her request. The sensation was alarming because even though it was irritating, it was also somehow delicious.

She tried to hide her contradictorily pleased annoyance but when she glanced at Charlotte, the other woman was watching her closely.

"So!" Charlotte cried suddenly and Julia jumped. "How are you settling into the spooky manse? I see Monique hasn't driven you to tearing your hair out yet, which, I must add, is a shining testament to you, my dear." Then she lifted her drink in an amusing salute to Julia.

"Monique is on the Mediterranean," Douglas announced, the

waiter long gone, rushing to do the bidding of a very famous and powerful client.

"Oo, what luck. So, you've been spending this time counting your lucky stars," Charlotte asked Julia, a twinkle in her eye.

Julia didn't know what to make of Charlotte, nor how to respond, but was spared by Oliver who said warningly, "Charlie."

"She's been around long enough, I think she knows what she's in for," Charlotte told her husband with blithe unconcern at his warning and turned back to Julia. "I'm putting my money on you." Her eyes still sparkled but there was something kindly speculative in them that told Julia that Charlotte Forsythe understood very well and not just about Monique.

With that firm announcement of support, Julia began to relax and enjoy the evening.

Dinner was delicious, even if the servings were sparse, and Charlotte and Oliver were good company. She learned that Oliver and Douglas had gone to school together, played rugby and cricket together and raced cars, horses and anything else that was fast or dangerous while Charlotte, at a sister school for girls "across the lake", tagged along after them, naughtily egging them on whenever she could.

Julia realised almost immediately that she liked Charlotte immensely. She was witty, obviously in love with her husband and not at all reverential of Douglas.

Julia's enjoyment of the meal and the company was only marred when, after they were finished and enjoying coffee, Douglas leaned back and rested his arm across the back of her chair.

It was an entirely male gesture and incongruously familiar. And the way Douglas did it was somehow... *predatory*.

What was more, their table was the focus of a great deal of attention from the other diners and even the staff and Douglas's behaviour was odd in the extreme.

True, she and Douglas had known each other for years, spent holidays together, ate many a meal in each other's company and had even engaged in a variety of conversations both with others and alone.

And there had been three times, three very memorable times, when Douglas had shown her fleeting moments of tenderness.

The first was during one of her early visits, a summer holiday. They'd been outside Tamsin and Gavin's house, Gavin at the barbeque with everyone else eating and drinking. Julia had turned her ankle walking back into the house. Douglas had just arrived and had been close enough to catch her before she fell. Unfortunately, she'd turned it quite badly and he assisted her to a chair, his strong arm supporting her. Once he had her seated, he bent to her foot, carefully, even fondly, lifting her ankle and inspecting it. Gavin had come forward to take over but Julia had never forgotten Douglas's (strange, for him) thoughtful attention.

The second was during her first visit to Gavin and Tammy's after her divorce was final. When they'd had a moment alone, Douglas had asked quietly if she was all right and she had the distinct impression that he genuinely cared about her answer. Douglas had been quite obvious about the fact that he never cared for Sean, unlike Monique who doted on her ex-husband. However, with no small surprise, Julia felt that it wasn't the fact that Douglas disliked Sean and was making some point in asking, it was that he wanted to be certain she was, indeed, all right.

And last, after Tammy and Gavin's funeral, Julia had found a quiet corner in the library at Sommersgate where she thought no one would find her. Douglas, to her stunned amazement, not only found her, she had the impression he'd come looking for her and, without a word, pulled her stiff body loosely into his arms. At this act of compassion, she'd clutched his shirt, buried her face in his chest and burst into tears, the grief shuddering through her body as the gravity of her loss settled on her soul. Through this, he silently absorbed it, the whole time stroking her back in a way that was both absent (for him) and comforting (for her). Then Patricia walked in and Douglas turned her into her mother's arms, again without a word, and walked away.

Putting these things out of her mind, Julia also tried to shrug off her feelings at Douglas's arm on her chair. Gavin would and did put his arm on the back of her chair and it was obviously never predatory or possessive (but maybe protective). Perhaps, Julia told herself, it was a brotherly gesture.

Once she had that comforting thought settled in her mind, she relaxed. Until she saw Charlotte, who Julia was realising didn't miss a trick, had noted the action with raised brows and a feminine glance at Julia that spoke volumes. This was something else Julia decided to put out of her mind.

After their coffees, Charlotte and Oliver took their own car to the gallery while Carter drove Douglas and Julia

"I'm not good company this evening," she told him and she watched as his head turned to her. "I still think I'm a little jetlagged and it's been a long day. I'm sorry."

He nodded but didn't respond.

"Dinner was lovely and I like Charlotte very much," she tried again, desperately wanting to dispel her awkward feelings.

No response for a moment, then he asked, his deep voice sounding strangely lower, more throaty, "Your perfume, what is it?"

She blinked in the darkness. "Wah... why?" she asked, thrown by his odd question.

"It's extraordinary," he said it in such a tone that she didn't know if it was good-extraordinary or bad-extraordinary. "What is it?" he repeated.

"It isn't from a shop. A friend of mine makes it for me. She's a bit, er... unusual, my friend. She says it's an aromatic manifestation of my 'essence'." He made no response to this so Julia inquired hesitantly, "Is it too strong?"

"No," Douglas answered and said nothing more.

She sat there, bewildered, and thought it best to let it go. Then curiosity (as often was the case with Julia) overrode common sense.

"Why do you ask about my perfume?"

"It suits you," was all he said in reply.

At that moment they slid to a halt in front of the gallery and Douglas threw open the door before Julia could form a thought. She was still reeling at the strange conversation. Julia thought he had just called her extraordinary, though she still didn't know if that was good or bad but she had the feeling it was good.

Then she could think about it no more. The flashbulbs started popping and the shouts were frenzied while he alighted and she saw his hand offered through the door to help her. She put her own in his and exited the car to the blinding lights. She instantly became discombobulated and dropped his hand as the shouts became louder, more frenzied. She heard his name repeated again and again while the blinding flashes came with such swiftness there seemed no pause between.

She felt her hand taken again in a firm grasp as she was pulled forward, Douglas guiding her, or more to the point, dragging her towards the door.

They made it through the door and crush outside was nothing to the crush inside. It was wall-to-wall people.

Someone rushed forward to Douglas the minute they entered the gallery.

"Lord Ashton! You're here!" It was a young, eager, overly-made-up woman who turned curious eyes to Julia, looked her from head-to-toe, made a judgement and, Julia thought, dismissed her. "Can I get you some drinks?"

"Champagne," Douglas commanded shortly and then completely ignored her.

He'd dropped Julia's hand upon entering but now he slid his fingers, starting at the side of her waist, to the small of her back and guided her forward, stopping her by wrapping his arm fully about her waist and pressing his fingers gently and firmly against her side as they arrived at the first wall filled with art.

She barely had a moment to get her breath or process the pleasant warmth of his hand at her waist and his body at her side when she heard a call.

"Douglas!" a man shouted, far louder than needed even in the din of the crowded gallery. Douglas dropped his arm but kept himself positioned close to Julia's side. The older man was paunchy with a shock of bright white hair and very red cheeks. "You've done it again. It's the next Picasso. I've already bought two. How do you find them?" he asked, apropos of nothing.

He too looked over Julia and didn't bother to hide his curious interest before he again turned his eyes to Douglas.

Douglas didn't answer as the man babbled on, "Masterpieces, all, the like I've never seen before."

As Julia finally realised what the older man was referring to, she turned her attention to the artwork on the walls.

Each piece was suspended between two sheets of plexiglass with no other adornment. They were drawn on bits of wrinkled scratch paper and each one, she saw, looked like a doodle done in pencil while the artist was taking a telephone call.

Julia couldn't claim to be an art aficionado but even she could doodle better than this. And without the theme of blood, guts and violence that ran throughout the works she could take in from her vantage point.

"These are hideous!" Charlotte shrieked gaily as she and Oliver joined them, the white-haired man obviously taking the hint of utter silence from Douglas and moving off. "What on earth made you become patron to this person? Dear God."

Julia was surprised. She didn't know Douglas was the opening's patron and she peered more closely at the disturbing doodles. She also looked at the prices discreetly affixed on the walls to the side of each piece and gasped in shock, each piece cost a small fortune.

The girl arrived with their champagne, Douglas handed Julia a glass and his to Charlotte. "Two more," he told the girl without a thank you and, apparently not expecting one, she immediately melted into the crowd to do his bidding.

"I've never seen these," Douglas belatedly answered Charlotte. "Samantha finds it amusing to use my influence and money to do shocking things that will make people wonder about me."

"Well, she's succeeded," Oliver replied, laughter in his voice. "From the looks of these, you're a very disturbed individual."

"Hideous or not, most of them have sold," Charlotte noted and then she came forward and wrapped her arm around Julia's waist. "We're off to the ladies," she announced and pulled Julia along with her and through the throng of the crowd before Julia could say a word. "We're not off to the ladies, I've *got* to have a cigarette and Ollie doesn't know I've started up again," she confided to Julia conspiratorially, still giving Julia no time to respond.

She guided Julia through the gallery, down a hall at the back and outside into an alleyway. Other guests mingled with staff to enjoy their cigarettes in the surprisingly tidy but smoky alley.

Charlotte pulled Julia away from the smoking crowd and down, stopping them within sight but out of hearing distance and surreptitiously lighting a cigarette with a slim, gold lighter.

"Thank you for coming with me," Charlotte said, even though she hadn't given Julia much choice. "Now, we can really talk. Tell me, how are you getting on?"

Her words were not gossipy but kind. Nevertheless, Julia was aware this was a family friend and she forced herself to be discreet even though she desperately wanted to talk to someone, *anyone*.

"I'm settling in..." she started.

"Codswallop," Charlotte announced, the strange word forcing a giggle out of Julia and making her relax.

"Okay, it's been tough," Julia allowed.

"Tough is when you break the heel of your favourite pair of Jimmy Choos. There's another word for it when your whole life turns on its head." She took a drag from her cigarette and blew the smoke away from Julia. "Come on, you can tell Auntie Charlie," she coaxed with an encouraging smile.

Julia smiled back. She needed someone to talk to and Charlotte seemed genuinely concerned so she gave in. "I'm tired, exhausted... the kids are, well... things are not good."

"Monique," Charlotte guessed, making the name sound like a curse and correctly judging the state of affairs at Sommersgate. "That woman is a nightmare. She wasn't a good mother and she certainly isn't a good grandmother."

Julia was stunned by her frankness and curious at her words. Tamsin (and certainly not Douglas) had never spoken about her relationship with her mother even though Julia knew it was obviously nothing like what she and Gav had with Patricia. She knew, though, that it was none of her business.

"It'll get better," Julia assured her, trying to believe it herself. "I haven't even been here for a week. I haven't had the chance to really talk to Douglas."

"Who ever *really* talks to Douglas?" Charlotte asked with further brazen honesty as she waved her cigarette around in the air. "I love him but he's about as approachable as The Guards." She took another deep drag and then glanced at the crowd, obviously worried that Oliver would discover her habit then her eyes moved back to Julia. "Listen to me, I was Tammy's friend, I miss her. She was wonderful and an important part of my life. But I cannot imagine what possessed her to do this to you and Douglas. She loved that house, God knows why, it's the creepiest place on earth. But she connected with it. I figure she talked Gavin into having the kids brought up there and to protect you, they made Douglas guardian too."

Julia couldn't hide her surprise at this announcement. She, too, had spent hours trying to figure out what intentions Gavin and Tamsin had when they put her and Douglas in what was seeming, more and more, not only an impossible, not even an inconceivable but maybe a catastrophic situation. Especially if Julia couldn't control the avid clenching of her stomach any time Douglas was near.

"Do you think?" Julia asked.

"I can't imagine why else. Tammy adored Douglas but she didn't fool herself about him. He's a good man but, let's face it, he's no father figure." Julia couldn't help but laugh out loud at that, Charlotte threw her a grin and carried on. "So, Tammy wanted the kids at Sommersgate and you to raise them because they both thought you were fabulous and everyone knows you love those kids. But they had to know Monique would be a problem. Ergo, Douglas is thrown into the fray, poor man. He worshipped his sister, you know."

No, she didn't know. Worship was the kind of thing people did *to* Douglas, not the other way around.

Charlotte continued. "It's clear he's already decided on protecting you, if you know what I mean. So, my advice to you is to take him up on it."

Julia frowned. "I don't know what you mean."

"The possessive arm thing, wasting no time in dragging you in front of the paparazzi as a declaration of your position and his favour. Trust me, everyone in there..." she gestured with her cigarette to the gallery, "knows who you are and why you're here and that you are not, upon arrival in this country, being hidden away like a poor relation whose role is now nanny of her Lady Sister-in-Law's children. No, instead, you're out here, looking fabulous... and you *do* look fabulous by the way, that dress is *amazing*... and drinking champagne. And Douglas's favour is a sought after commodity. He shines his light on you, not even Monique could dim it. Believe me, there is nothing, not one thing that Douglas does that doesn't have a purpose. This…" she gestured lavishly to the alley, "is his subtle way of telling his mother, when she returns, and anyone else for that matter, to back, the hell, off. Well done him!" She finished, clapping her hands, rather dangerously in Julia's opinion, considering the lit cigarette.

This news, coming from a woman who had known Douglas for years, was so welcome that Julia felt the tears sting her eyes.

"Oh no, don't do that!" Charlotte cried, coming close to Julia and squeezing her arm reassuringly. "Your makeup is gorgeous and everyone's going to be looking at you. You can't ruin it. Here, have a cigarette, it'll calm you down."

"I quit ages ago," Julia admitted, taking a deep breath to fight back the tears.

"Well, I suppose since you're currently the moral compass for three children, now isn't the time to start up again. I *must* quit too or Ollie will divorce me." She gave Julia's arm another squeeze before she took her hand away. She dropped her cigarette and crushed it under the toe of her beautifully-shod foot. She straightened her shoulders, tucked Julia's arm in her elbow and started forward but Julia pulled firmly back and looked at the woman. For the first time in months she felt less tense and less worried and those feelings lit her green eyes to sparkles, even in the dark alley.

"I…" Julia hesitated, not knowing how to put her feelings into words, then she continued, "thank you. I appreciate you telling me this."

Charlotte shook her head and patted Julia's arm, her eyes kind. "Enough of this, let's go show them how fabulous you are."

And that was what Charlotte did.

For the rest of the night, Julia had a wonderful time. She was wrong, Charlotte wasn't just witty, she was hilarious. They drank glass after glass of champagne and Charlotte introduced her to everyone, making outrageous comments that made Julia laugh so hard she nearly cried.

Douglas hadn't been lost in Charlotte's determined efforts for the evening, even as she whisked Julia from person to person, and drink to drink, they always came back to Douglas. Charlotte would deposit Julia firmly at his side for just enough time for him to smile down on her or lean over and comment in her ear, showing everyone clearly, and they were most definitely watching, that Julia did indeed have his "favour". Then Charlotte would whisk Julia away to show her off again.

By the time Julia stood on the pavement beside the Bentley with the paparazzi flashing away and Carter calmly holding the door, Julia was still exhausted but more relaxed than she'd been in months.

After giving her a brief hug and kiss on each cheek, Charlotte pressed a card in her hand.

"My info, phone, mobile, home, my assistant, my e-mail... you need anything, you call me, anytime!"

Julia nodded. "You're lovely, Charlotte."

"Charlie, all my friends call me Charlie." And with those words, and the meaningful look she gave Julia to accompany them, she and Oliver were off.

Once they were in the Bentley and moving safely through the streets, she heard Douglas say, "It appears you had a good time."

"Charlotte is a love," Julia declared happily, thrilled to have her first new friend and perhaps an explanation about Douglas's behaviour, and Tammy and Gav's wishes, that would make her life a lot easier.

They drove home in silence and alighted from the car in front of the house. As they walked to the front door, Julia tripped, her heel getting caught in a crack in the pavement, and lurched forward. Douglas caught her against his body, an arm going around her.

"Steady," he warned on a murmur, looking down at her just as she looked up, a small relieved smile still on her face, when the bulb flashed beside them.

"Off with you!" Carter shouted, moving threateningly, yet surprisingly nimbly, toward the photographer as Douglas hustled her inside.

But even with that end to the evening, nothing could stop Julia's feeling of calm.

Douglas said a curt goodnight, already preoccupied with something else, and went straight to his study.

As for Julia, she checked on the children then prepared quickly for bed and slept soundly for the first time in months.

6

THE ARRANGEMENT

By the time she'd put the children to bed Sunday evening, Julia's sense of calm had gone.

She'd woken up that morning in the Kensington house feeling refreshed. She'd put on a long, A-line skirt of dove grey wool, a matching turtleneck that was ribbed from the waist to just under her breasts and from wrist to elbow, the effect making her waist look tiny. She added a pair of soft, soot-grey, suede boots and the diamond studs her brother and Tammy had bought her for her birthday years ago. She pulled her hair back in a ponytail at the nape of her neck and went forward to face the day for the first time in a long time in a light-hearted, maybe even good mood.

She found Douglas, not in his study but in the lounge reading the paper. He wore dark brown corduroys and a matching turtleneck and he looked casual and relaxed and, for once, was not working.

"Good morning," she said as she walked into the room.

He looked at her over the paper.

"Julia." His face betrayed nothing but his eyes again slowly trailed the length of her body.

She ignored his gaze and smiled at him. Charlotte's words about him protecting her through Tamsin's bizarre last wishes and his quiet assumption of the duty of protector were still at the front of her mind.

At her smile he dropped the newspaper and lifted an eyebrow asking without words what was on her mind.

"So... today?" she inquired.

"Today," he said shortly, folding the newspaper and throwing it on the table in front of him, "Carter is taking you and the children to Patisserie Valerie for breakfast. I've a couple of calls coming through, so I'll need to stay behind. You'll make a few more stops with the kids to see the sights. You should find something to bring home for lunch. Then we'll go back to Sommersgate."

She wasn't listening; instead, she was looking at the paper he'd thrown on the table. In it, a large, colour photograph of her and Douglas was displayed.

They were walking into the gallery, their hands clasped firmly, their arms stretched out between them as Douglas pulled her forward. He was in profile, his expression hard and showing nothing. She was staring at the ground, her pashmina had dropped off one shoulder and was hanging in the crook of her elbow. To keep up with Douglas, her stride was long and the slit at the side of her skirt had opened to accommodate it, showing a shocking expanse of leg.

Regardless of the distance between them and their expressionless faces, the clasped hands conveyed a closeness that could easily be misunderstood. In fact, if she had been looking at two other people in the same positions, she would have assumed they were lovers. Friends or siblings didn't walk together like that, hands clasped tightly, the man forging through the crowd leading, and protecting, the woman.

"Oh my God," she breathed, losing her composure as she stared at the photo.

Douglas's eyes dropped to the paper.

"Forget it," he said in a tone that Julia was beginning to wonder if he expected would be readily obeyed regardless of the ridiculousness of his demand. She just couldn't "forget it" simply because he told her to.

It was the first time in her life she'd ever had her picture in the paper, for one thing. They looked like a couple of lovebirds on a night on the town, annoyed at being trapped by the paparazzi.

What would the children think if they saw it?

"But –" she started.

"It's nothing," he interrupted her, rising from his seat and then he prompted her, "Children. Breakfast."

And that was all he said, leaving her in the room alone with the photo and his final command to see to the kids.

She stared in complete disbelief and diminishing calm at the doorway he'd walked through. Then she grabbed the paper and ran upstairs with it, shoving it in her bag so none of the children would see it.

Leaving Douglas behind, they'd had a beautiful breakfast at a fabulous patisserie. Afterwards, Carter drove them to Buckingham Palace to the now unhidden delight of Veronika. The children had seen it before, save Ruby who walked hand-in-hand with Veronika and gazed in awe upon the palatial estate with its huge black gates with gold crests. Instead of being driven, Julia decided they'd walk the short distance to Westminster Abbey and Big Ben, then across the bridge to stand in line for what seemed like forever eventually to take their spectacular ride on the London Eye.

A fight ensued between Willie and Ruby as to what was for lunch, burgers (Willie) or fried chicken (Ruby) which Julia solved by making Lizzie decide. She'd been trying to draw out her older niece and although she'd managed to force her to take a shower every morning, wash her hair and have more than a few bites to eat, Lizzie was still resolutely withdrawn.

Upon Lizzie's verdict, they took home a big bucket of chicken and Julia helped Veronika get the children settled, then Carter and Veronika disappeared.

Julia went to find Douglas who was in his study on the phone. She knocked and, at his command, opened the door. He was standing rather than sitting behind his desk, his arm outstretched and pointing to a place on a piece of paper when he looked up at her.

Having his gaze levelled on her made her legs feel like jelly. He was so damned attractive, tall and compelling, his dark eyes intense.

She recovered her composure, setting such silly thoughts aside with a silent curse to herself.

She stood politely in the doorway and used the universal sign language to communicate silently that food was available (in other words, she pretended to fork food into her mouth and chew). Realising what she was doing, feeling like all kinds of fool, she quickly left him to his call.

The kids were devouring the fried, fatty, forbidden treats that had been a hallmark of the weekend when Douglas walked into the dining room.

"I saved you a leg!" Ruby announced by shouting at him and Julia tamped down her awkward feelings from before. She was letting strange things get to her and she allowed herself to trot out what were becoming familiar excuses – exhaustion and homesickness – and she felt marginally better.

After they were done, Veronika cleared the table and Julia made certain the children were packed and they all trooped to the cars. Douglas had his Jaguar in London and he decreed in his usual bossy manner that Julia was to ride with him. He then swept her in the car so quickly she had no chance to call good-bye to the children.

She had wanted Lizzie to ride with him. Lizzie who looked at him with a longing that tore at Julia's heart. She was looking to replace Gavin, Julia knew, and the only replacement available was Douglas. However, it was clear Douglas was entirely uninterested.

Julia turned in her seat and looked back at them. Lizzie was climbing in the backseat of the Bentley while Veronika was settling into the front. Willie was impatiently dancing behind Lizzie, waiting his turn, and Ruby was jumping up and down, waving at Julia.

Julia waved back.

Douglas expertly manoeuvred through the streets of London and finally found the motorway, all this was accomplished in complete silence.

Once they made it to the far right lane, flying by the two other lanes of traffic as if they were going a snail's pace, to her chagrin, the smooth ride of the car and constant sleep deprivation caused her to fall asleep, her head on the window.

She was awakened by a hand on her thigh squeezing it gently. Her eyes flew open and she saw that Douglas was leaning over her, his face close to hers, his hand still on her.

"Wake up, we're home," he said, his deep voice strangely, and invitingly, soft.

She glanced around dazedly, shaking her head and cursing herself for falling asleep. She hoped fervently that she hadn't drooled or snored or done anything else utterly humiliating.

They were parked in the drive at Sommersgate. The sun was setting but light still covered the house, gardens and the rolling fields to the west. They'd enjoyed wonderful weather all weekend, chilly but dry and mild.

Once she'd pulled herself together, she realised *both* the jelly-feeling legs and the pleasant warmth in her belly were present at his proximity.

Therefore, Julia announced, "Great!" in order to dispel the intimate mood in the car and turned to let herself out but Douglas's hand on her thigh tightened.

"Julia."

She turned back even though she didn't want to. In fact, she *really* didn't want to.

"Yes?" she asked when her eyes met his.

I am innocence and light, blithely unaware of his hand on my leg, innocence and light, innocence and light, she repeated in her head.

For some reason, he grinned, the effect was a shock to her system and she watched the wrinkles crinkle handsomely at the corners of his eyes and those same eyes warmed lazily as they stared into hers, so very close. She felt her stomach flip nervously as that familiar thrill chased up her spine.

To hide it she repeated, "Yes?" Clipping the word's sibilant end tersely to try and convey an impatience she really didn't feel. In truth, even though she hated to admit it, she could have sat there forever.

His grin widened to a smile as if he knew her thoughts exactly, the brilliant flash of his teeth against his tanned skin and that deathly alluring scar on his lip disarming her completely.

"We'll talk tonight," he said, leaving her to think that he had thought better of what he was about to say... or do. Thankfully, he removed his hand and she exited the car with all haste, practically running into the house (after a brief struggle with the impossibly heavy front doors) and straight to her rooms.

Tonight they would talk about their "arrangement".

This was good, she told herself. They had to get some things settled.

No, *she* had to get some things settled. She had to get herself sorted, get some rest, get her thoughts together and get her body under control and find out where the rest of her life was taking her.

One place she was determined it wasn't going to take her and that was into some ill-advised fling with the man she was forced to live with for the next however-many years.

No matter how damned handsome he was.

Or how beautiful his smile.

She changed from her lovely outfit into a pair of faded jeans and an equally faded, tight-fitting black t-shirt that said, "Harry's Chocolate Shop – Home of the Great Indoorsman" in yellow printing which promoted a popular bar at Purdue University where she and Gavin went to school. They were comfortable clothes and reminded her of home.

She donned them like armour.

To prepare herself, she gathered her notes and wrote more, reading through them carefully.

When the kids arrived a half hour after Julia and Douglas, she and Veronika dealt with them, their bags, their homework, their dinner and then put them to bed. Douglas emerged only during bedtime, looking in on Ruby, who had already been in bed for an hour and was sleeping, and taking care of Willie while Julia tucked Lizzie into bed, all the way down her sides, like she'd been doing since the first night she arrived.

"Are you okay, Auntie Jewel?" Lizzie asked to Julia's surprise.

Julia's first response was to kiss the girl on the cheek and smooth her dark hair back, smiling into her sad, worried eyes. She'd underestimated her niece, no doubt in her sensitive state she was sensing Julia's agitation.

Julia decided to be honest. Honesty, Patricia always told Julia and Gavin, was the best policy.

"No, Lizzie-babe, but I will be. Don't you worry about it though, go to sleep."

Julia kissed her niece again and left the room with the unfortunate timing of joining Douglas at the head of the stairs.

"Is it time for our chat?" she asked with studied politeness as they walked down together.

"I've a call to make," he responded.

"That's okay," she said airily, as if she had all the time in the world, "I'll wait."

She went directly to her rooms, looked in the mirror and ran her fingers through her hair. She found herself wishing she had a stash of liquor for some liquid courage and then shook the thought off.

This was a good thing, she told herself, they had years of this ahead of them and they needed some ground rules.

She sat in the turret, went back over her notes and she waited.

Then she waited some more.

She supposed he would come and get her when he was ready but, after thirty minutes, she heard nothing. And with each passing minute, her anger increased.

This was his house, of course, but did this mean she had to wait for his bidding, like Mrs. K or Veronika? Was this to be her life?

Not bloody likely.

Angrily, she grabbed her notes and headed to his study.

The door was open and she walked straight in without knocking. He was on the phone again, sitting behind his desk and at her arrival he lifted his dark-eyed gaze to her.

She had to steel herself against the gaze and just how perfectly he fit in the richly-appointed, masculine room. It, too, had an enormous fireplace that took up most of one wall, beside it an ornate cabinet sat, topped with intricately cut, crystal decanters filled with liquor surrounded by sturdy, cut-crystal glasses that were built to be held in a man's hand. The opposite wall was lined with bookshelves and filled with books, liberally interspersed with (most likely priceless) objects d'art. An enormous, comfortable couch faced the fireplace, covered in a rich, tan suede and flanked by two matching wide-seated armchairs. In the centre of this was a heavily carved, rectangular table, its wood buffed to a dazzling shine. Two more chairs faced his desk and there was an ancient standing globe in the corner beside the floor-to-ceiling windows that faced the garden. The highly-polished wood floors were covered with deep-pile, patterned carpets that screamed money.

As she stood there, Julia wondered for a moment what to do. She knew she was being rude but she'd had enough of working to Douglas's schedule. She came to England on a Tuesday, Monique gone, he arrived well into the night, offered no help, no direction and then he left on Wednesday not to return for days. No phone calls, e-mails, nothing. He planned her weekend for her without asking her thoughts on the matter. And it was Sunday night, for goodness sake, who worked late on Sunday night?

Her options flitted through her mind. Sit comfortably on the couch and appear like she had all night to wait while he rudely did exactly what he wanted? Make herself a drink? Make him one? Sit in one of the two chairs that faced his enormous, aptly-described baronial desk and stare at him pointedly?

She liked the idea of him not being able to ignore her, which she knew he could and would do. Instead of sitting in a chair, she walked to the front of the desk, positioning herself right across from him and she twisted her hip slightly to rest it against the edge. She bent her head to read the notes in one hand while the long fingernails of the other tapped impatiently on the surface of the desk. She would have whistled if she could carry a tune but she thought that might be overdoing it.

"Something's come up." She heard Douglas say and when she looked down to him, he was leaning back in his chair watching her, his eyes inscrutable, "No. I'll call you."

Without saying good-bye, he replaced the receiver.

"I gather you want something?" he asked.

"Yes... you." His right eyebrow rose arrogantly and her stomach lurched. "That is... to talk to you," she finished.

She could have kicked herself. Not a great start.

He rose and walked around the desk.

"Would you like a drink?" he inquired.

"Yes." She so very much wanted a drink, she wanted to shout it (but she did not).

"Whisky?"

What she really would like was a shot or two of tequila but she doubted any of the unquestionably invaluable crystal decanters held anything as common as tequila.

"That'll do," Julia replied.

He poured the drinks and brought one to her. After he handed her the glass, he took a sip from his and shoved his other hand in his pocket, rocking back on his heels.

"Would you like to start? Or shall I?" he asked politely.

She watched him carefully. As far as she could tell, in the last week he'd spent approximately two hours in the company of the children. What he had to say she could not imagine and curiosity almost made her let him go first.

Instead, she took a sip, winced as the fiery liquid went down and said, "I'd like to start, if you don't mind."

"Be my guest," he said and motioned courteously to the couch.

She sat, thinking he, too, would sit, but he stayed standing. She realised her mistake immediately as she'd have to look up at him. She hid it by pretending she didn't care. She casually pulled her legs up on the couch, tucked them beside her as if this was a cosy little arrangement and she was as comfortable as if she was ensconced in front of the television in Patricia's living room.

He again put his hand in his pocket and surveyed her and she had the distinct feeling she wasn't fooling him, not one bit.

"I have a list," she announced.

"I can see that." His voice was carefully controlled but she had the impression that he wasn't biting back anger but rather hiding amusement. She shot a sharp glance at him but his face was just as blank as his voice was controlled.

With no further ado, she launched into it. The children's food, their schedules, their boarding school, the time they were allowed on the computer or in front of the television, the unnatural quiet they had to observe.

She had a few things to say about Monique as well, but she did so carefully. She made no accusations but instead made it perfectly clear who, exactly, had been chosen to raise the children and how that was going to carry on from this point forward.

She also informed him that she needed to settle in, for herself and for the children. She needed a bank account, a job, a means of making money and continuing her contribution to her pension for the time when she was back home, alone and facing the wrong side of middle age (although she didn't share that last bit). She explained her concerns about health insurance, the urgency of getting a driver's license, a car and an open-ended visa and work permit.

She also told him she'd like to contribute financially to the house and the children's expenses and asked him to assess a monthly figure she could pay and they would discuss it.

When she finished, she was very proud of herself. She had been succinct, logical and controlled. For his part, he listened patiently and without interruption.

He walked back to the drinks cabinet and poured himself another whisky. She took a cautious sip of hers that had heretofore gone forgotten.

He turned back from the drinks cabinet, leaned his thigh against its edge and regarded her.

She regarded him right back.

Moments passed.

Finally, she could stand it no more.

"Well?" she asked, her tone more sharp than she would have liked and she berated herself for allowing him to shake her control. She needed that control, for a variety of reasons.

"Julia, the children go to boarding school because it's far superior to anything the government could offer them. They take lessons because they should have accomplishments outside of school. That won't change."

"Douglas –"

He lifted a hand to stop her interruption and she shut her mouth only because he'd let her speak her piece uninterrupted. She should give him the same opportunity and *then* let him have it if she didn't agree.

"As for their food, what lessons they have and how many, their schedules, television..." he trailed off, obviously beyond these petty details, "I leave that in your capable hands."

She immediately felt relief flooding through her; he wasn't going to argue with her.

"And how will Monique feel about this? Will you talk to her?" she asked.

"I'll control Mother," he answered in a tone so implacable, Julia almost felt sorry for Monique. "As for your job, visa, license, I'll get Sam on it. And I'll ask her to clear my schedule so I can take you to the bank and get you an account."

"Thank you," she said and she meant it. She was so relieved, if she could trust herself and her crazy emotions, she would have given him a hug and a big, sloppy kiss. "Speaking of Sam, she's already helped a great deal, she's been a godsend. She got me a phone, a computer..." Julia sifted through her lists and quoted to him how much she figured she owed him. "I'll need to pay you back right away. Can Sam help me arrange a transfer to your account?"

"Don't be absurd," he replied in a way that would make Einstein feel ridiculous for presenting his theory of relativity.

"You can't buy me computers and –" Julia started.

"Even suggesting you'll pay me is insulting," Douglas cut in. "You gave up your entire life to be here, the least I can do is make it convenient and comfortable for you."

That shut her mouth. She didn't know whether to be pleased or annoyed. It was a lovely sentiment but she most certainly didn't want to feel indebted to him.

He seemed not to notice her warring emotions and carried on. "As for a car, you'll take one from the garage. I use the Jag, Mother the MG, Carter the Bentley. You can have one of the others and, if you don't like them, just tell Sam what you want and she'll arrange for it to be delivered."

Julia's mouth dropped open.

He'd have *a car* delivered?

That was too much, any thoughts of lovely sentiments went out the window and her relief was chased away as quickly as it came.

Before she could say a word, he continued. "And we won't even discuss a monthly..." he hesitated then went on, "*payment* for living here." He said the word "payment" like it tasted vile. "That idea is even more absurd than the other."

"But I can't –" Julia started again.

He threw his whisky back and put the glass down with a thud, effectively interrupting her.

"I can provide for my family, Julia," he announced inflexibly and while she was trying to wrap her mind around the extraordinary fact that he thought she was family, he continued. "I'm uncertain why my sister trusted me with a task for which I have no skills or desire, but the one thing I can do is provide for you and the children. And on that point, there will be no discussion."

He told her there will be no discussion as if that was the end of the discussion just because he said so.

She couldn't, and wouldn't, let it go. It wasn't in her nature or her upbringing. She'd been working since she was sixteen, getting a job at the local Dairy Queen so she could buy herself clothes and go out with her friends and not put a strain on her mother's already seriously strained finances. She wasn't about to let him "provide" for her.

She pushed it. "Douglas, I understand but –"

"The subject is closed," he announced.

She stared at him, not knowing whether to laugh out loud or scream, wishing she could do both at the same time.

"I can't –" she began again.

"How, may I ask, do I get you to do what you're told?" he queried calmly but he didn't look calm. His eyes were glittering and she was so used to Douglas's complete indifference she couldn't tell if he was enjoying himself or if he was immensely annoyed.

"I never do what I'm told," Julia informed him, having decided that, for her part, she did not find this amusing at all.

"*That* does not bode well for the next thirteen years," he declared, his tone showing he had chosen the opposite.

"I'm sorry, I can't just live here and contribute nothing."

"You'll be taking care of the children."

"One day, I'll be working too. What then?" she asked.

"We'll cope, people do these things every day," he replied with a shrug of his shoulders.

"Yes, but I'll need more commitment from you with the children. Especially now, especially Lizzie. I think she's looking to you –"

He stiffened, all amusement gone, and he interrupted her again, his words curt. "I have no idea how to heal her grief and further I have no intention of filling Gavin's shoes."

"But –" Julia began, stunned at his reaction and his words.

"Have we covered everything on your lists?" he asked politely and pointedly, this discussion, according to Douglas, was obviously closed.

"Yes. But, Douglas –" Julia tried again.

Douglas interrupted again. "Good, I have a phone call to finish."

And to her amazement, he walked to his desk.

She was dismissed.

She stood there not knowing what to do. She'd never met the like of him. One minute, he was so good-looking, so damned sexy that he made her legs tremble and her stomach pitch, the next minute he was so impossibly autocratic, she felt like throwing something at him.

He picked up his phone as he rifled through some papers and she realised that he didn't even intend to acknowledge her presence in the room.

She'd been there less than a week, she'd left her entire life behind, the life before her was still uncertain and in the midst of all this she had three children who depended on her and, by the way... *him.*

She wasn't supposed to do it alone. Tammy and Gav wanted her to have help and that meant far more than a free meal ticket, the use of a car and Douglas publically bestowing his "favour" on her at art galleries.

She didn't even wage the battle to control her temper, she just let it lose. She downed the contents of her whisky, gagged momentarily as the fire hit her throat and stormed his desk.

"Excuse me!" she slammed her glass down on its shiny surface making his head come up with a jerk. "I'm sure you're used to strolling into a board room or wherever you work and making everyone do your bidding but I'm afraid that does *not* work with me. May I remind you that *your* sister and *my* brother expect us, no, they trusted us, *no*, they *honoured* us by allowing us to raise those children together and I'm not going to let you throw money at it and then get on with your life like nothing's changed. You'll pull your weight, you'll get involved and you'll damn well quit telling me what to do all the time, because I'm up to here..." she indicated her chin with an angry thrust of her hand, "with it."

He had the receiver in his hand but, after she finished, he slowly returned it to its cradle.

"Are you finished?" he asked, his tone completely civil.

She took a deep breath.

Was she finished? She didn't know. Maybe she went too far.

"No, Julia," he said quietly, "that was too magnificent to question. Simply score your point and go."

She faltered. "Did I?" He raised his brow in question. "Score a point," she explained.

He inclined his head briefly.

She was stunned. She was pleased.

For some reason, she was also scared.

One point meant only one point which meant there was a game afoot here. And she did not want to play games with Douglas Ashton. Douglas Ashton always, *always* won.

Nevertheless, she thought it prudent to take his advice.

"Well then, thank you for the chat. I feel much better," she lied. "Goodnight."

She turned to go but his voice calling her name stopped her.

She turned back.

"Yes?" she asked.

He was looking at her in that pleasant way again, something akin to admiration in his eyes, a look that stole her breath away.

His voice was smooth as silk when he spoke. "Last time you said goodnight to me in this room, it came with a kiss."

The pleasant tremor slid so far up her spine, it went up her neck and made her scalp tingle just as her stomach flipped.

With a supreme effort of will, Julia ignored it.

"I wasn't annoyed with you last time," she informed him haughtily.

There was definitely a game afoot and even after this discussion of their "arrangement", she wasn't sure of the ground rules.

"I'll bear that in mind the next time we have a late evening conversation," he replied, then he picked up the phone and she felt her best bet at that point was to flee the room.

Which was exactly what she did.

7

DOUGLAS'S DECISION

The next morning, Douglas rose early and, instead of his usual run, he went to the stables to take one of his horses out to be exercised. They were getting fat and lazy with inattention. Tamsin and Gavin used to come to Sommersgate once a week to take them out but now that they were gone, he was the only one who could do it.

He saddled his chestnut stallion and for over an hour rode him through the wood surrounding Sommersgate. When he was done, instead of leaving it to Carter, Douglas brushed the horse down himself. When he was finished, he went back to the house where he showered, dressed and picked up the phone to call Samantha.

She answered, her voice sounding as if she'd been awake for hours and in that time had arranged peace in the Middle East while baking a complicated soufflé.

He instructed her to clear his schedule as best she could so he could be at Sommersgate in the evenings and to make an appointment at his bank for himself and Julia.

"I see," she responded meaningfully. "Does this decision have anything to do with a fab... you... *las* green satin dress?"

Sam had been with him for several years and had lasted longer than all of his PAs. She was able to do this because she was incredibly bright, had the energy of a litter of four week old puppies, was completely circumspect and didn't fear him. Therefore, he often cut her a fair amount of slack which he would never do for others.

"Just do it," he told her.

"Righty-ho, boss," she confirmed jovially and rang off.

He headed to the dining room and could hear the children's chatter and Julia's husky-soft voice floating up the stairs.

Yes, in answer to Samantha's question, it was the green dress. The green dress Julia wore on Saturday evening was superb. That green dress could even be described as sublime.

It was also the green eyes, the way they looked when Julia laughed with Charlotte or when they flashed at him last night when she was angry.

It was also something else, something surprising.

He'd been partial to acquiring empty-headed women because they were easy to acquire and just as easy to throw away.

There was something different about being with Julia.

Julia Fairfax was anything but empty-headed.

He watched as she chatted away with Charlotte and Oliver at dinner, drawing both of them out skilfully and allowing Charlotte to animate the dinner with her usual flair without competition. Then, as Charlotte introduced her around at the gallery, he noted how Julia listened intently to what people said and the judgmental faces changed as she melted their reserve with her natural charm, charm she was able to command even though she admitted to jetlag.

He found he felt what could only be pride when she returned to his side to smile up in his eyes and cock her ear to hear some banal thing he forced himself to say simply to keep her attention.

She rarely seemed ill at ease with anyone (although often appeared that way around him). She picked up remote friendships, as she apparently had with Mrs. Kilpatrick, and acquaintances, as with Charlotte, as if thousands of miles and months had not divided them.

Last night, however, there was a different Julia. Impassioned and eloquent, he found himself admiring her not only when she calmly read from her lists, smoothly stating her case, but most especially when she lost her temper with him.

"No man has a prayer in the world with Jewel." Douglas heard Gavin say once, loud enough so Julia could hear him. "She's bossy, stubborn, too damn fiery and she's got attitude. She's more of a headache than she's worth."

Gavin may have said those words to tease but the look on his face said he felt they were valuable qualities.

Douglas was beginning to agree with him. He had known many women who attempted to be a challenge in order to make themselves seem more attractive, less easy, more interesting.

He had never met a woman who was an actual challenge.

Thinking of this, Douglas recalled several times in the past when Julia had caught his attention with her passionate nature and natural eloquence.

He remembered once when Julia and Gavin were having a discussion on politics which escalated into an argument. Tamsin had wisely kept neutral and Douglas had just watched as Julia's magnificent moral fury built up in the face of Gavin's teasing goading. Remarkably articulate, Julia finished her tirade with a crushing set down that shredded even the mellow Gavin and forced him to accede the point.

The problem with Julia, Douglas thought with satisfaction, had turned vaguely interesting.

Before he arrived at the dining room, Carter stopped him.

"You have a... call, sir," Carter said and this practiced speech was not lost on Douglas.

Instead of going into the dining room, Douglas went to his study. He should have closed the door but he could see Julia and the children sitting across the hall and they'd not hear him from this far away. He found he had the unusual desire to have their pleasant chatter in the background.

He saw which line was blinking, blew out a sigh and picked up the phone.

Nick was on the other end. Douglas listened and his mouth thinned into an angry line at what he heard.

"I'll be there by the evening," Douglas said before he hung up. He quickly rang Samantha and explained the change of plans.

"You know, you've got to stop doing this. Those kids –" she started to say, her words and tone highly inappropriate. Douglas might be lenient with Sam but now she was treading on dangerous ground.

He cut her off. "If I wish your opinion, I'll ask for it."

"Okay then, I'll make it so." Efficiency restored in her tone, she rang off again but this time he could tell she did it with disapproval.

He put Sam out of his mind and walked into the dining room amidst the children's welcoming voices. Julia looked up and quickly looked away. He could tell she was tired and she looked drawn and, he regarded her closely, a little angry.

He nearly smiled to himself.

She hadn't wasted any time; there was a sugar bowl, a butter dish and three pots of jam on the table.

"Look, Unka Douglas! Marmalade!" Ruby shouted, apparently in a phase where everything had to be said at the top of her lungs. She was waving a piece of toast so exuberantly that marmalade went flying, landing with a splat on the floor behind her.

"Yes, Ruby," he said while he sat down, "perhaps you should *eat* it rather than making the dining room *wear* it."

Ruby giggled and Douglas saw Julia's lips twitch but she wouldn't allow herself to break out in a full smile.

Douglas spared Lizzie a glance and his amusement faded.

The girl bothered him. She was obviously taking the death of her parents very hard. Julia thought Douglas should take her in hand but he was at a loss of what to do.

He found the girl difficult to be around. She looked almost exactly as her mother did at twelve years old, big, dark blue eyes and a mass of shining brown hair. He was counting on her eventually pulling herself together and in a short time Julia had managed to at least achieve some small success. Lizzie's hygiene had been slipping and she was losing weight. Now, her hair had some of its lustre back and she sat eating a stack of toast slathered with butter and jam.

In fact, looking around him, he noticed all the children were eating their food with relish. The last months, they had been eating quickly but he saw that they were eating quickly to get it over with. Now they were devouring the food with enjoyment and, although Lizzie wasn't bright eyed and giggling, she was eating. Both Will and Ruby were acting as if they'd just won the lottery.

"Children, what did we talk about?" Julia prompted.

Julia, he saw, had no food in front of her and was sipping only at a cup of coffee.

"Thank you Unka Douglas!" Ruby shouted at the top of her lungs.

"Thank you for the weekend in London, we had a good time," Will recited as if he was reading it from a script, the blankness of his tone belied the look on his face which one could only describe as goofy. This effect, Douglas saw, was to draw out Lizzie who didn't bother to respond to her brother.

"Yeah, thanks," Lizzie chimed in half-heartedly.

Douglas looked at Julia, her chair was pushed back and she was twisted in it, her back slightly towards him, her legs crossed in front of her. Her bare foot with its pale pink varnished toes bounced casually, or angrily, he couldn't tell which.

She was cupping her coffee in both hands like it was providing warmth against an arctic freeze and staring into it like it could tell her the meaning of life.

He reached for the coffeepot and poured himself a cup.

"You're welcome," he told the children.

"Can we go back? Can we, can we, can we?" Ruby asked.

"Of course, Ruby, when would you like to go?" he inquired, sipping his coffee and feeling the full weight of Julia's feigned aloofness, just as she intended.

"Tomorrow?" Ruby tried.

He smiled at the child and said in a gentle tone, "No, Ruby, tomorrow would be too much of a good thing. But soon."

"Promise?" she shouted.

He nodded and Mrs. Kilpatrick walked in, setting his breakfast in front of him and announcing that Carter was ready to take the kids to school.

They rushed around like dervishes, all stopping at Julia for hugs and

kisses. Douglas watched in dawning realisation that this unusual practice of affection was now an expected agenda item for the morning
schedule, or indeed any time they left Julia. Ruby even stopped and gave
him a kiss before unnecessarily chasing after the siblings who would
leave her behind.

Unable to keep her back even partially to him and not appear rude,
Julia turned back to the table but didn't say a word.

"Have you had breakfast?" he asked.

"I'm not hungry," she replied, her tone not inviting further conversation and her eyes were now gazing in fixed fascination on the wall-
paper across the room as if she were counting the seconds to when she
could leave and not seem ill-mannered.

"Would you like to explain this new morning ritual?" he asked.

This shook her out of her feigned remoteness and she turned startled green eyes to him.

"You said that I could decide what the children were to eat," she
looked down at the pots of jam.

"I'm not referring to the sugar bowl, Julia," he explained. "I think
it... unusual to demand the children display physical affection every time
they leave you." His tone sounded more judgmental than he intended
and she stiffened in response.

"It's tradition," she told him, her voice terse.

"An odd tradition," he commented, regarding her levelly and she
raised her glittering eyes to his.

"Not really. My mother always made us kiss and hug her before we
went to bed or school or, when we were older, out with our friends. We
used to hate it. Especially if it was in front of someone else or we were
quarrelling with her. Even then, we had to kiss her goodnight. One day,
when I was a senior in high school, she got sick. A really bad case of
pneumonia and she had to be in the hospital for a long time and, for a
day or two, it didn't look good. I couldn't give her a kiss or hug before I
went to bed and I found I missed it, was actually desperate to do it
because I was so scared at how sick she was. It was then I realised her
wisdom, because anything can happen when you least expect it. And, if
the last thing you did was give someone you loved a hug or a kiss, it
would make dealing with whatever happened just that tiny bit better."

She stopped and he realised, with some surprise, she was having trouble breathing. Regardless, she continued, but this time, her voice was shaking.

"I know Gavin and Tammy did the same thing with those kids for the same reason and it makes it all a tiny bit better knowing that the last things those kids did was kiss and hug their parents good-bye."

It was then Douglas realised why her breathing was laboured, why her voice was shaking. She was holding back the tears that were gleaming at the rims of her eyes. He himself felt a strange lump rise in his throat and his hands involuntarily formed into fists in an effort not to touch her, something that was becoming a habit, this consistent effort not to touch her.

And he very much wanted to touch her now. He wanted to touch her last night after she blazed at him in anger and when she was seated demurely on the couch listing her grievances regarding the children. He wanted to touch her in the car when she was sleeping away her exhaustion and jetlag. And he had wanted to touch her in the Bentley when they were driving to the gallery and all he could smell was her perfume and all he could see were her endless legs.

It wasn't often that Douglas didn't simply do what he wanted to do. Now, most especially, as he watched her struggle with her emotions, sitting there looking alone and tremendously sad, he found himself wanting to comfort her. If he was honest, he may have even needed her to comfort him as he felt his chest tighten with something he hadn't felt for years.

"Julia," he murmured softly.

She took a deep shuddering breath.

"So, you see," she finished, a tremor still in her voice but the subject, most definitely, was closed, "it's tradition."

He allowed her a moment to collect herself, reading correctly that she would prefer to be in control rather than let go. He understood that. However, he did so while watching her.

She was immensely watchable. Her face wasn't just lovely, it was also expressive. Her emotions, now raw and right on the surface, made her all the more alluring. He could never countenance female tears but then, he'd never seen any that were genuine.

He felt the familiar pull of what he recognised as a growing attraction to her. He'd always known it was there but the strength of it was surprising.

He didn't just want to touch her. He wanted to kiss her. He'd wanted to kiss her in the car when she had so obviously enjoyed the night out with Charlie, her cheeks flushed, her voice happy and he was surrounded with her captivating scent and knew *exactly* how her legs and ass looked in that unbelievable dress. And again, when he had awakened her after they arrived home and her eyes were heavy-lidded and her voice was husky with sleep. And also, after she had vented her anger at him last night.

No, last night he hadn't *wanted* to kiss her, he *ached* to do it and far more than that. He'd had to put the desk between them to stop himself.

And now, while she was struggling for control, he wanted very much to coax her to lose that control. He wanted to taste her lips, hear her whisper his name with her voice throaty with passion.

He wanted her.

Yes, the problem of Julia was definitely becoming quite intriguing.

As she seemed to get a hold of herself, his mind came to terms with this development and he immediately came to a decision and formed a plan. It was, he realised, an excellent solution to *all* his problems most especially Julia and the children.

"I'd like to ask you a favour," he stated.

She turned her eyes to his, the grief barely masked and its presence made his tone gentle when he continued.

"Tamsin was on a committee for years to organise a ball to raise funds for a local charity that provides research funding for breast cancer. This year, she was chair of the committee until..." he broke off, not needing to continue.

"Yes?" Julia prompted, her voice deeper than normal with the effort to control her emotions.

"I'd like you to attend with me, to represent the family, to represent Gavin. I think Tamsin would have wanted that."

Tamsin would have wanted Julia anywhere and everywhere. They were like sisters, e-mailing and sending care packages full of little gifts they'd purchase for each other the minute they saw something that reminded one of the other.

Douglas watched Julia nod, her sadness melting as she gave him a small, tentative smile.

"I'd be delighted," she agreed and a truce was established, albeit soon to be made very brief.

"Well, well, well, isn't *this* cosy?" A refined, but glacial, female voice sounded from the doorway and Douglas looked up to see his mother standing there, staring down her nose at Julia.

Monique was wearing a white suit with a filmy black blouse and a huge black and white hat. Douglas regarded his mother with remote disdain. She looked like she'd walked right out of a rerun of *Dynasty*.

She was sixty-four years old and through a strict diet and exercise regime, monthly visits to the spa and hairdressers, twice-yearly visits to a plastic surgeon and sheer determination, she looked twenty years younger.

She was carrying a newspaper and walking forward, the expression in her eyes was frosty.

He stood, as a gentleman should, but for no other reason.

"Mother," he greeted her warily for he could see she was in a mood.

She ignored him.

"You!" she pointed, her tone accusatory, her gaze malicious, at Julia who was staring at her brother's mother-in-law, her expression a study in shock, her eyes riveted to the finger pointed in her direction.

Monique then threw the paper she was carrying and it slid down the table, over the children's dirty dishes and spilled onto Julia's lap taking marmalade and butter with it.

Julia caught it reflexively, jumping up from her seat.

Douglas gritted his teeth.

"Mother," he said through them, his voice a warning.

"Didn't take *you* long did it?" Monique hissed. "Went right in for the kill, didn't you?"

Julia was looking down at the paper and Douglas saw in it was a printed the photo taken of them outside his house in Kensington.

He had to admit, it looked damning. He knew he'd just caught her after a stumble but they looked like they were two lovers embracing. He was forced to subdue a pleased smile at this turn of events as this was fortuitous to his new plan.

Julia looked at it horrified.

"This is all a mistake. I –" Julia started.

"You're a parasite, is what you are... which was expected but I cannot believe how quickly you've managed to latch on."

At that piece of rudeness, Douglas cut in curtly.

"Mother, we were in London for an art opening. Julia tripped, I caught her, the photographer got lucky. Did you come all the way back from the Mediterranean for this?"

His words and tone made her actions sound ludicrous.

She tore her angry gaze away from Julia who was visibly shaken. Julia looked from Monique to Douglas then back to Monique.

For her part, Monique looked to be trying to decide the veracity of his words. She also looked at him and then Julia.

He looked annoyed, which he was. Julia looked stricken and offended.

And he noted passingly, rather glorious.

Even standing there, barefoot, wearing snug-fitting jeans and an equally snug-fitting chocolate brown t-shirt that said "Eat at Ed's" in pink on the front, she somehow appeared to match Monique in panache. Even injured and caught off guard, there was something almost regal about her that even Monique, with her wealth of aristocratic background and good breeding, couldn't match.

Douglas tore his gaze away from Julia and watched as his mother made her decision. Perhaps believing Douglas, perhaps realising that her opponent may not be as much of a pushover as she anticipated, perhaps sensing she wouldn't have Douglas's support, she backed off with ill-grace.

"That," Monique answered Douglas belatedly, her tone no longer icy but now airy, "and Beatrice was getting on my nerves. I forgot I can only stand the woman for hours at a time, why I thought I could spend three weeks with her is beyond me."

Deciding to give up her tirade, without another word, she turned and began to walk away, as usual without any kind of greeting, asking after Douglas, who she hadn't seen in weeks, or inquiring about Julia, who had moved an ocean away from her home to take up the care of Monique's grandchildren.

"Mother," Douglas called, his voice so unyielding even Monique stopped and turned.

"Yes, my darling?" she replied.

He stared at his mother and saw her eyes glittering with malice. Her words were uttered in a sugar sweet tone that he knew from years of experience she didn't mean. He'd been enduring her faux motherhood for thirty-eight years and he'd always been able to ignore it. For some reason, today, he found it grated.

"I think there are a few things you should say to Julia," he informed her.

Her eyes narrowed and she tried to stare him down. Instead, he calmly sat, picked up his coffee cup and took a sip, watching his mother the whole time.

Once he replaced the cup in its saucer, he quirked an eyebrow to her.

His mother sighed dramatically, giving in with anything but good grace.

"Welcome to Sommersgate, Julia. My apologies for the misunderstanding."

She looked Julia up and down and her expression showed she found what she saw lacking. Then, without another word, she walked out of the room.

Douglas sighed.

Then he turned his eyes to Julia, who was staring after Monique, her face a mask of pure incredulity.

"Sit down, Julia," he commanded quietly.

For once, she did as she was told.

"What... was... *that?*" she asked, her voice horrified.

"I'm afraid the gloves are off," Douglas explained, watching her.

Her eyes moved to him and he saw they were huge and uncomprehending. She looked at the paper in her hands and then threw it on the table as if it burned. She lifted a shaky hand to pull her hair away from her face and took a deep breath.

"It'll be okay," she murmured as if trying to convince herself. "It'll *all* be okay."

Douglas watched her as she tried to fool herself. This time, with him standing beside her, she emerged virtually unscathed. Given her mental state, she was, he knew, no match for his mother's callous, unrelenting venom. Even if she had exhibited fire and spirit, she was exhausted and still coping with the loss of her brother and Tamsin. She'd be torn apart within a week; he'd give it two at the most.

And somehow understanding this went beyond annoying him.

Ten minutes ago, knowing that Julia and his mother and this arrangement would be difficult was a simple inconvenience, something he understood that he needed to control.

Now, watching his mother square up against the woman he just decided to make his wife was simply unacceptable.

"Oh for God's sake," Douglas muttered as he rose, frustrated with denying himself. He grabbed Julia's hand and pulled her roughly out of her chair and straight into his arms.

She stiffened and pushed against him, her hands at his chest, her eyes alert and surprised.

She tilted her head back to start to ask, "What are you –?"

He ignored her reaction and did what he'd wanted to do since her first night at Sommersgate, indeed, since he first saw her fifteen years ago.

Douglas kissed her.

While one arm held her tightly against him, wrapped around her waist, his other hand slid down her back to splay across the small and press her hips more tightly against his.

She pushed against his chest with more strength and moaned a suffocated denial against his lips, opening her mouth under his. Given this golden opportunity, he took unfair advantage, sliding in his tongue and deepening the kiss.

The moment his tongue touched hers, his body ignited. She tasted of a hint of coffee with an underlying sweetness that was intoxicating. Both his arms closed around her pulling her more deeply into him as his tongue went from invading to coaxing. He used it to tease her and his hands to mould her against his hard body.

This, he was pleased to note, worked.

He felt her hands abruptly stop pushing against his chest and they started to slide up, stopping when her fingers curled at his shoulders to hold on. Her lips relaxed and her head slanted to give him better access.

He didn't hesitate in accepting her invitation.

It was then the kiss went wild.

She clung to his shoulders, her fingernails biting into his flesh as she matched his heat, her tongue duelling with his. He felt his blood heating, his heart pounding, her body remarkably hot through her clothes.

Finally, one of her hands lifted, gliding up his neck, her fingers slid into his hair as she held his head to hers, giving herself fully to the kiss. She pressed her soft body to his, the heat of her searing his skin through his clothes as her passion exploded. She gave him everything he wanted and he took it, gladly, and then took more. He heard her moan again but this time not in denial but with desire, the sound of it sending his blood speeding through his veins and he pulled her body even closer to him, trying to absorb her very essence.

He had expected it to be good but he hadn't expected it to be like this.

She tasted sweet and she smelled of tangerines and jasmine. All he could do was feel her, taste her and smell the exotic scent which defined her – delicious, tangy, soft, wet and gorgeous. She surrounded his senses so completely that everything else but her faded away. The sensations were so extreme, he was sorely tempted to throw her on the ground and have her right there in the dining room.

His body tightened at the thought and before he could lose all control, he tore his mouth from hers and took a ragged breath.

"Jesus," he muttered.

She pulled out of his arms and stood shakily in front of him with the fingers of both hands pressed to her lips. Her green eyes had darkened to jade and she was staring at him in wonder.

"Jesus," he repeated, this time as a curse to stop himself from reaching for her again before her reason returned and the moment was shattered.

He knew, though, that it was way too soon and Douglas was an expert strategist. He would never make a move toward a desired goal before the time was right.

"Why did you do that?" she asked, her voice low and soft, nearly a whisper, but there was accusation in it.

"I'm leaving for a few days, I'm not certain when I'll return," he returned instead of answering her, trying to regain some control.

"No!" was her startling reply. She sounded frightened and her eyes flew to the door where Monique had exited.

"Julia," he said her name but watched as she looked away from him and seemed to be fighting to gain some control.

"Fine," she replied, changing her mind like quicksilver. "Fine, I'll be fine, we'll all be fine. Just go."

She wouldn't be fine and she was beginning to understand it. And, for some reason, this pleased him.

"I'll leave you my mobile number. Call if you need me or you can always get me through Samantha."

She squared her shoulders and tilted her chin. "We'll be fine."

"I'll leave you the number, just in case."

"Why did you kiss me?" she asked again, her voice stronger, her eyes flashing, her tone demanding.

Why *did* he kiss her?

And, more to the point, why had he decided she would be his wife?

Because of her poignant story about the children kissing their parents good-bye?

Because in less than a week, the children were already responding to her when over four months under his mother and his nominal care they were more and more withdrawn and detached, going through the motions of childhood without anchor?

Because his mother was such a bitch and any relationship he had with Julia would drive her insane, an idea which, he had to admit, he found he liked very much?

Because of her charm and grace and the way she looked just as resplendent in blue jeans as she did in satin?

Because of that green dress, her long legs, her shapely ass and her flashing eyes?

Because he'd been waiting fifteen long years to have her underneath him and he decided he was finished waiting?

Or simply because he'd just decided she'd make an excellent baroness, that perhaps Tamsin wasn't so crazy after all and this lovely creature before him would do spectacularly well in a life by his side?

"To say good-bye," was all he said to explain.

She stared at him like he was mad.

"Call me if you need anything," he finished.

And before he grabbed her again, which was exactly what he wanted to do, he turned on his heel and walked away.

❧ 8 ❧

THE GAME

Julia lay on her bed and stared at the dark ceiling. The scratching was at the window but she'd drawn the drapes.

She had to draw the drapes because last night, she'd seen what was scratching.

It was Ruby's imaginary friend. Except, he wasn't imaginary. He was real. Not real, exactly, a ghost. A man, handsome and tall and wearing an old-fashioned suit from some time that Julia didn't know. He had dark hair and dark eyes and the only good thing about him was that he wanted to get in but he couldn't. She knew that because she saw him try... and fail.

"Damn," she whispered, tossing in her bed, "damn, damn, damn!"

The last two weeks had been an absolute nightmare.

A nightmare named Monique.

The woman was awful, she was truly awful.

Julia tried to find something good or nice in everyone and every night she'd been wracking her brain trying to find one teeny, tiny, little characteristic that Monique had that was likable or even acceptable.

There were none.

The staff feared her, Veronika most of all. And Julia could see why. At the best of times, Monique was imperious. The worst of times, she was scathing. Julia had witnessed her coldly tearing apart Veronika for missing some speck of dust or not polishing the banister to a high enough sheen and she'd been astounded by the woman's sheer evil. She acted like Veronika had thrown a wild crack party and accidentally burned the house down.

And the children didn't know what to make of her or the relationship between her and their aunt. She was no less dictatorial with the kids though she cut herself short at any disdainful remarks. Most likely because, if she tried, she knew Julia would scratch her eyes out which made Julia wonder how Monique had been with the children before Julia had arrived.

And Monique didn't waste any time.

In fact, it started the day after Douglas left.

On Monday, Monique had been absent all day, staying in her room or her morning room and completely avoiding Julia and ignoring the children.

On Tuesday, she sent Mrs. K to find Julia and invite her to the morning room for tea.

Ruby was, pointedly, not invited.

Julia appeared as requested, hoping to negotiate a truce. Monique was dressed in a pale pink blouse and cream tailored trousers with a pair of expensive matching pumps. Her dark brown hair was swept up in a neat chignon. Her smooth, high cheekbones shone with artfully applied blusher.

She regally inclined her head toward a chair covered in flowered chintz, which was, Julia guessed, her invitation to take a seat. The morning room, just as the drawing room, was decorated in ice blue and white but in this room it seemed only slightly less formal, no less cold.

Julia sat and Monique asked with feigned sweetness, "Tea?"

"No thank you, I don't drink tea," Julia replied.

Monique ignored her and poured tea into a dainty, china cup, added a wedge of lemon and handed it to her.

Julia held it, stunned into immobility by the woman's rudeness.

"Let's not misunderstand ourselves, you and I," Monique said, sipping from her own cup and gazing dispassionately at Julia like she was something that crawled out from under a rock.

"Monique," Julia started, in hopes of laying the tentative groundwork to heal relations, "I just want to do what's right for those children and get along with you and with Douglas."

"Douglas, my dear, is what I'd like to talk to you about."

Julia tensed and Monique didn't delay in explaining *exactly* what the tête-à-tête was about.

"Your brother, God rest his soul," she touched her hand to her heart in false grief, "convinced my somewhat misguided daughter that he was worthy of her attention. But I shall tell you right now what I should have told him. He was *not* worthy of my family and you, particularly, are not worthy of my son. I know what kind of woman you are. I know what those pictures showed. I know your intentions. And I will not allow you to..."

But Julia was no longer listening to her. Monique had made a fatal mistake in her little interview. She could have attacked Julia, which would mean that Julia would have tried to react kindly or at least diplomatically.

But she should never have said a word against Gavin.

Julia put her cup down with such force that it clattered, stood up and stared down at the woman.

"Don't you *dare* speak about my brother to me ever again, Monique. Do I make myself *perfectly* clear?" she whispered, her voice an enraged hiss.

For a moment Monique looked startled but she recovered quickly. "Should I remind you that it is *my* home you are living in, *my* sheets you are sleeping on, *my* –"

"I beg to differ but on the death of your husband, is it not true that all of that became Douglas's? If you have an issue with me staying here, I'll ask you to skip chats such as this and take it up directly with your son."

And without allowing Monique to say another word, she'd walked out.

She'd been shaking with fury and when she exited the room she nearly ran into both Mrs. K and Veronika who, if she had thought about it at the time, were more than likely listening at the door.

She wanted someone to talk to (or more precisely someone to vent to) but Mrs. K looked at her kindly and Veronika gave her a shaky smile and they both scurried away as quickly as they could.

That meant, obviously, both of them were out as confidants.

She would normally call Patricia but her mother, she knew, would have lost her mind and flown out on the next available plane.

In a moment of temporary insanity, she considered calling Douglas.

Instead she phoned Charlotte.

Charlotte listened and before Julia could relate the whole story, her new friend interrupted with, "That woman is *vile*."

For some reason, this comment made Julia relax.

"It was like a scene out of a bad soap opera," Julia told her and couldn't stop herself from laughing at the memory which, looking back, seemed ridiculous and *exactly* like a scene out of a bad soap opera (unfortunately, it wasn't).

"If Douglas is away and you need a break, you just pack up those kids and come to London. Ollie and I have *plenty* of room."

"Charlie," Julia explained, still laughing and touched by this offer from her new friend, "I can't drive. I don't have a car or a license yet."

"Then I'll come get you!" Charlotte declared.

Julia had to decline. As much as she wanted to escape, it would mean taking the kids out of school, shaking up their lives yet again and she couldn't do that.

No, she was stuck and she had to do the best she could.

However, sadly, Monique wasn't nearly finished yet.

All sign of sugar bowl, butter and jam was away the next morning at the breakfast table. When Julia asked Mrs. K where it was, Mrs. K explained that Lady Ashton had told her not to include it when laying the table.

So Julia put it on the table herself.

The next morning, it was gone again.

So Julia put it back.

And this went on.

Evening meals were the same struggle. Eventually, Julia commandeered Carter, grabbed Ruby and went to the grocery store herself.

Mrs. K continued to make healthy meals. Julia, with Ruby's "help", worked alongside her adding buttery garlic bread and thick gravies and making cakes and pies.

It was the fourth night Monique was home, and the first night she deigned to dine with them, when pecan pie with ice cream concluded the dinner.

When Julia brought in the dessert, Monique stared at it in disgust.

As Julia cut a healthy piece for the still introverted Lizzie, Monique announced, "You do that child no favours, she's already fighting a weight problem as it is."

Lizzie's twelve year old girl ears registered this insult and she stiffened.

Julia stared at her niece, the girl's eyes haunted, her cheeks hollow. Lizzie had most likely lost ten pounds she couldn't afford since her parents died. She had no weight problem.

The courteous thing to do was hold her tongue and have a word with Monique during a private moment but Julia was too incensed for courtesy.

"Monique, you may be under the ludicrous impression that those Hollywood lollipop girls with their stick-thin bodies and enormous heads are attractive but they... are... *not*. They look like aliens from another planet! Lizzie needs to put *on* weight, not take it off."

Monique had stared at her with murder in her eyes and, with no other option, Julia simply stared back. All three children watched in stunned silence but finally Julia broke the staring contest and carried on serving dessert like nothing happened while Monique left the table in icy silence.

After that episode, she wanted to call Douglas again, which she knew was an irrational idea. She was saved from doing that by Charlie calling her.

She told her friend about the lollipop girl comment and Charlie hooted with laughter.

"Forget coming here, I'm coming to visit you. *This* I have to see."

Julia laughed with her but no matter how fun Charlie was making it seem, it was anything but fun and the next day, it became worse.

When she asked Carter to take her to the grocery store, he declined

saying that Lady Ashton told him that he could only take Julia somewhere if *she* approved it, personally.

"I see," Julia replied quietly as Carter wrung the cap in his hands
either nervously or angrily, she couldn't tell as his face was carefully
blank but his lips were thinned. "That's okay, Carter, it's a beautiful day.
I'll walk!"

It was not a beautiful day. It was chilly and grey and threatening
rain. But that wasn't going to stop her. *Nothing* was going to stop her.

There were footpaths crisscrossing all over the United Kingdom,
Gavin had introduced her to them. She found a walking map in the
library, plotted her course, grabbed a couple of umbrellas and she and
Ruby went on an expedition. It was more than two miles there and
back and both of them were exhausted and drenched by the rain that
came in the last half mile but it didn't matter. Ruby loved it and Julia
was determined that woman was not going to beat her. Monique was
not going to use the staff against her and Julia was not going to allow
the servants' already unhappy existence to suffer for anything
Julia did.

Luckily, the next day, her driving license came in the mail.

"Relief!" she shouted as she opened her mail and Veronika, who was
clearing away the breakfast dishes jumped. Julia walked straight to her
and grabbed both her cheeks and kissed the girl on her forehead.
"Freedom!" she crowed to Mrs. K who had just walked in to witness her
exuberance and Julia waved the license at them and strode away to e-
mail her mother and call Charlie and Sam.

That evening, just when she thought things would start swinging
her way, she saw the man behind the window. He was looking at her
imploringly and trying to reach through the glass toward her. The
minute his hands tried to push through the glass, he disappeared, the
vision of him shimmering and melting until he was gone.

Julia had stifled a scream upon seeing him, stood staring at the space
he was in for moments after he was gone and then she slapped the
draperies shut. She spent the rest of the night trying (and failing) to talk
herself out of believing what she saw.

There were no such things as ghosts.
Were there?

The next day, Monique thankfully left for a spa visit in London with no word on when she would return and no good-byes.

With the vision of the man still foremost in her mind (and seeing a ghost was *not* a relief from having Monique or Douglas's bizarrely passionate kiss good-bye (he'd *never* kissed her, passionately or otherwise) being the things foremost in her mind), Julia approached Mrs. K and Veronika in the afternoon while they were in the kitchen.

Without leading into it gently, she simply announced, "I saw a man outside my window last night."

Veronika, who had spent the last week desperately attempting to be neither seen nor heard, especially when Lady Ashton was around, let out a little scream.

Mrs. K turned from the stove where she was making a delicious-smelling stew, taking advantage of Monique's absence to fatten up the children.

"Oh dear," she muttered.

"Oh dear is right," Julia replied even though she felt *oh dear* was an understatement. "And Ruby sees him too. She waves at him and I even saw her talking to him the other day."

Ruby was off with Carter picking up Lizzie and Willie. Mrs. K looked at Veronika who looked back at her, the young girl's face pale and frightened.

"All right, there's nothing for it. You two, yes, Veronika, the both of you, sit down," Mrs. K ordered, dipping her head to the kitchen table.

Without further coaxing, Veronika and Julia sat together at the big, wooden kitchen table with its friendly yellow oil cloth. Mrs. K put the lid on the stew and was about to turn to them when Mr. Kilpatrick walked through the door.

Julia had only met Roderick Kilpatrick a couple of times. According to Mrs. K, her husband took care of the grounds, oversaw the gardeners, allowed or disallowed hunters as the case may be and also maintained and oversaw several other properties and farms that Douglas owned in the vicinity. He had a wealth of coarse grey hair, a big, droopy moustache and ruddy cheeks.

"Miss Julia. Veronika," he touched his cap to them and looked at his wife, "I'll come back later."

"You'll stay, Roddy, she's seen The Master."

That brought Roddy up short and he swung his head toward Julia and then looked like he'd try to make good an escape before he saw the severe look his wife gave him. Upon seeing her look, he reluctantly entered the room.

"Veronika, have you seen him?" Mrs. K asked, her voice losing its wifely authority and turning kind.

Veronika nodded, her eyes wide.

"Nothing for it, Rod," Mrs. K said decisively, her eyes swinging back to him.

Mr. Kilpatrick sighed and both the Kilpatricks sat across from Julia and Veronika.

"There's nothing to fear, lasses. Really there ain't. He's been around, and so has his missus, for as long as this house has been standin'," Roddy Kilpatrick announced.

Julia glanced at Veronika who returned her look, her dark eyes frightened.

"No one knows the real story," Mrs. K began. "Some say he killed her, some say someone else killed them both. The truth is, they found his body outside, dead from exposure and looking like he'd been trying to get in. They found The Mistress in the house and she'd been strangled."

Veronika's English may not have been the greatest but she understood *that* and let out a frightened peep.

"Nothing missing, no forced entry, all the doors were locked from the inside and no one knew of any enemies that would hate either of them enough. No one knew, either, of any troubles they were having," Mr. Kilpatrick went on.

"Who were they?" Julia asked.

"Lord and Lady of this very house," Roddy Kilpatrick explained. "He built it for her, the biggest, grandest house in the county. He was rich, just became the Baron on the death of his father, and everyone says he loved her more than money or titles or anything. She was a merchant's daughter, not of his class but enough so that he could court her. They said she loved him just the same. They lived in this house for weeks, maybe a few months when it happened."

"She left a baby boy," Mrs. K added. "He was raised by her mother and the line was safe but, ever since, he's been trying to get in and she, well no one knows what she's doin'."

"She?" Julia prompted.

"Ever feel a draught around yer ankles? Or hear any whispers? People say sometimes that she screams," Mr. Kilpatrick explained, Julia's mouth dropped open and Mr. Kilpatrick nodded. "Yep, that's her. No one ever sees her but they *feel* her. No one knows if she keeps him out or if she's tryin' to let him in."

Mrs. K took the story from there. "They say, and Lady Tamsin believed this, that this house is cursed. That the curse will only lift when a living Sommersgate baron finds a bride that he loves truly, and she truly loves him in return, then The Old Master will be let in to reunite with his bride and then they'll be at peace and so will Sommersgate."

"But," Julia began, "this house is over a hundred years old. There has to have been some baron that loved his wife in that time."

The husband and wife looked at each other and then looked at Julia, shaking their heads.

"It wasn't often done in that class, my love," Mrs. K explained.

"But now, these days it is… isn't it?" Julia asked, wondering about Monique and Maxwell (not that she could imagine Monique loving *anyone*, including her dead husband).

Julia received more shaking of the heads.

It was then the kids came home, crashing loudly into the kitchen and story time was over.

But Julia found a moment to search out Veronika before the girl left for the day. When she did, Julia touched her arm.

"Are you okay?" Julia asked. "With this, er… ghost business," she went on to explain.

"Sad," Veronika said, her eyes making that one word far more expressive.

Julia nodded and smiled and was about to walk away when Veronika stopped her.

"You?" she asked and then went on hesitantly. "Okay?" Julia nodded again but Veronika forged on, looking scared but determined.

"Not with ghosts, with…" She let that hang and Julia knew exactly what she meant.

Without thinking, Julia pulled the girl into a hug and after a moment Veronika returned it.

"I'm fine," Julia whispered. "Don't worry about me. It'll be okay for all of us," Julia stated with feeling. "I promise."

This time, Veronika nodded, pulled away, gave Julia a pretty but tentative smile and then walked away.

That was yesterday. Tonight was different.

The scratching was back, intent and determined. *He* was out there.

It was late and although Monique was gone, the scratching and everything on Julia's mind wouldn't allow her to sleep. She was averaging less than five hours a night and she was constantly exhausted.

Douglas had disappeared, no word, no sign. Pride was now stopping her from calling both him and Samantha to find out what he was doing and when he would return. He should be home; he'd been gone for over two weeks. He was supposed to be helping her with the kids and he'd not even had the courtesy to phone. She was furious and the minute she saw him again she was going to let him have it.

She had to think that way. If she allowed herself to think of the way he sometimes looked at her and the fact that he kissed her…

Kissed her!

She still couldn't fathom it.

She'd been right, a game was afoot. Perhaps he was trying to get her to slip up, seem like the gold-digging monster his mother thought she was. Perhaps he was going to try to prove her unworthy of taking care of the children by seducing her, making her look the brazen hussy. Why, she did not know, as he had little interest in the children but who knew exactly how Douglas Ashton's mind worked.

If she wasn't careful, he would succeed. It had been a long time for her. She'd not had a lover since Sean. When Douglas had kissed her, she kissed him back, she didn't want to but she couldn't help herself.

He was a good kisser.

No, he wasn't a good kisser, he was an *excellent* kisser.

And he was Douglas.

There was a time when she'd dreamed of him kissing her, when she'd have practically paid him to do it (not that he'd need or take the money). She never imagined that he would even want to kiss her, let alone do it.

And it had been good, oh so very good to have that hard, sexy mouth with its mysterious scar on hers. He tasted like... like... well, he tasted like all man and like *sex*, touching her tongue to his, feeling his tongue in her mouth, the only thought on her mind was having his mouth on her body, *everywhere* on her body. He barely had to try before he broke through her struggle and she was clinging to him and kissing him back like a wanton.

His body was so warm and hard and...

She shook her head to clear it. She would not, *could* not think of Douglas. She had to get a hold of herself. She could not live the next more than a decade panting after the Lord of the Manor. It was humiliating and she wouldn't allow it to happen, not ever again.

The scratching was fraying her nerves and when she could take it no more, she threw the covers back and stalked to Douglas's study to get a whisky to soothe her tension and hopefully put herself to sleep. She'd get drunk if she had to, sleep on the sofa in the study to avoid the infernal, constant scratching. She threw her lilac, cashmere robe on over her pyjamas and headed out of her room.

The draperies were open in the study and moonlight lit the room. The moon was so huge and bright, she didn't bother with the lights, walked directly to the drinks cabinet and picked up the decanter she'd seen Douglas using. She was reaching for a glass when she heard a deep, baritone voice.

"Can't sleep?"

She jumped, whirled and almost dropped the decanter.

"Douglas!" Julia cried in surprise.

He was sitting in the armchair that faced away from the door, towards the window. He was lounging with feet up on the table in front of him like he had no cares in the world. As if he didn't have three children he was supposed to be looking after. As if he didn't have a harridan of a mother who was making everyone's life at Sommersgate a living hell and had been for years. As if none of this touched him.

Something about this made her both angry and on edge.

She could see the glint of a glass in his hand.

"Julia," he replied calmly in greeting.

"You're home," she noted unnecessarily, feeling foolish.

She should be shouting at him because he'd abandoned her to the fate worse than death that was Monique. But something made her stop.

Something made her nervous.

He didn't reply, just looked up at her, his face partially in shadow, partially lit by the moonlight and the effect was decidedly ominous.

"What are you doing, sitting in the dark?" she asked.

"Thinking," he answered shortly.

She stood there mutely, holding the decanter and waiting for him to say more.

He didn't.

She twisted, put the decanter down and turned back. In that time, he had silently risen from his chair and her faint feeling of dread intensified as ominous turned menacing.

What was he up to now?

She wanted to escape but curiosity got the better of her.

And curiosity killed the cat, Patricia always used to say.

"Thinking about what?" she asked.

He walked forward a couple of steps, stopped a foot away and leaned into her.

She inhaled sharply with alarm but he only reached around her, grabbed the decanter she had just set down and refreshed his drink.

He leaned back in to replace it and she said belatedly, "Let me get out of your way."

"Thinking," his deep voice rumbled, rooting her to the spot as he paused to take a sip from his glass, "about a woman who would give up everything to come and look after three children. Children who lived thousands of miles away from her and who, upon reflection, she barely knew. Why would someone do that?"

"Do you mean me?" Julia asked stupidly.

He didn't answer.

She slid away from him in order to put a healthy distance between them. He was frightening her with his tone and his question and with his overall *mood*.

Douglas didn't have moods. Douglas glided through life guarded by Teflon.

"Why do you think I did it?" she inquired, trying to read him.

"You tell me," he responded.

She'd escaped to stand in front of his desk, putting furniture between them. He had to turn and his face was again illuminated by the moonlight. It was blank, not naturally so, carefully so.

"I did it because Tamsin and Gavin asked me," Julia gave the obvious reply. Again, he said nothing and her nervousness made her go on. "It isn't as if I barely knew the children. We spoke on the phone regularly. We spent holidays together, I'd come over for vacations. You know, you saw me every time I came out." That was true, she realised in distracted surprise; he did. Regardless of how busy he was, every visit she made to England, (save for the ones during the time of his Disappearance) she saw Douglas.

He leaned his hip against the drinks cabinet and continued to watch her, his face showing nothing.

"Can we turn on a light?" she requested, her voice pitched a little high, her tone sounding damnably, and obviously, uneasy.

"No." Her anxiety escalated at his answer and he continued. "You've damaged your career, sold your home, left everything behind. It seems a noble sacrifice, extraordinarily so. One might say unbelievably so."

"Gavin would have done it for me," she told him, her anxiety beginning to fade to anger as the intent behind his questions began to dawn on her.

What *exactly* was he inferring? Did he think this was a walk in the park for her? Did he honestly think that she was thrilled to ruin her life, stall her career and live with his Attila the Hun of a mother in this beautifully scary but incredibly ostentatious house that was so far from a home it wasn't funny?

He didn't respond, just kept watching her and she felt compelled to explain.

"In fact, he did do it for me, in his way. We take care of each other, we always did," she said with feeling.

"Gavin gave up his life for you?" he asked, not attempting now to hide his disbelief. "When did this happen?"

"With Sean. And he didn't actually 'give up his life' but if he'd been caught..." Julia stopped, her voice still sounded nervous but it had a slightly belligerent edge.

"Webster? How?" Douglas questioned, his tone still disbelieving.

Julia shook her head. Could she trust him with this information? Obviously he was leading somewhere with this attack and she had the distinct impression she knew where he was leading. He'd obviously taken Monique's accusations to heart and, with so very much time away to think about it, he decided that Julia had come for the same reason that Monique did. The kiss, she had to admit, undoubtedly helped.

As angry as that ridiculous and arrogant assumption made her, she felt it necessary to explain if just to throw it in his face. Gavin was now gone and even if it changed Douglas's opinion of her brother, so be it. She'd never spoken to Gavin about it, never told him she suspected but, with Gavin gone, what would it matter?

"I told Gavin what Sean had... done to me," she started tentatively.

"The cheating," Douglas interrupted and she was surprised he knew.

But then again, everyone knew, even Julia.

She shrugged lightly and said, "Yes, that..." she paused not willing to share more so she finished, "and other things."

His eyes narrowed before he put his drink down and took two steps toward her.

She took two steps back and her bottom hit the edge of his desk. She might be angry but she didn't like talking about this and, furthermore, it was none of his concern. She was beginning to be furious he'd put her in a position of defending herself, just as furious as she was scared of him. He was frightening when he was brooding like this, immensely so.

"What other things?" he asked when he'd stopped advancing.

"Nothing, just... it seems silly now but at the time –"

"Yes?" he prompted, obviously not willing to read into it and demanding she explain.

"Sean could be very cruel," Julia replied simply.

Cruel was not the word for it. It was more than cruel the way Sean spoke to her. It was soul-destroying.

"How so?" Douglas pushed.

She sighed deeply, wondering how to explain it, wondering if a man like Douglas could even understand it.

"He didn't hit me or anything." Her eyes skittered away. She hated to think about it and had learned, over the years, to set it aside. It wasn't her, she told herself over and over again, it was Sean. He was destructive, belittling, domineering and hurtful. She didn't make him that way; he'd been that way always. It still made her heart ache, even after all these years. "He would just... say things," she finished.

Silence.

Then in a tone that was far quieter, dangerously quiet, Douglas pressed, "Say things?"

"Yes, things. Stupid things. Hateful things. Just things meant to hurt me. They were just words and it was silly of me to give them power."

Again, he was silent and she felt it sounded foolish even to her own ears.

"He was mean, a bully," she explained, exasperated with herself at the memory of how she was so weak, and further angry at herself for letting those long ago memories tear at her insides now. "He just wanted me to feel small so he could be the big man. I shouldn't have let it affect me but I loved him and wanted him to love me, so I did. Let it affect me, that is. It was... he meant to... it just..."

She didn't know how to explain it to a powerful, rich, fit, tall, famous man who probably never felt small in his whole life. She couldn't put into words how, day-by-day, Sean would methodically strip her of her sense of humour, sense of fun, sense of self until he shredded her confidence and made her a quivering wreck. He never stopped and she was always scared of him, scared of what he would say and do, scared to do anything to cause his displeasure. She became scared of what others felt about her and wondering if they saw all the same ugly things Sean seemed to see. She had to build a wall of bravado around her simply so she could function.

Then, of course, there was the long and difficult journey to find herself again when Sean was finally gone.

"*Hurt*," she finished and her voice betrayed vividly in that one word just how destructive Sean had been.

Douglas walked forward again and Julia had no place to retreat so she held her ground.

"And what did your brother do about this?" he asked, his tone still quiet, the menace somehow gone but that didn't make her less frightened. If anything, she was more so because now his quiet tone was also, shockingly, gentle.

He looked down on her; he was so close she could feel the heat from his body. She ignored it and pressed on and she did this in an effort to finish this discussion and move on.

"Well," she hesitated, staring in his expressionless face, "after the divorce, he waited, of course, until I'd ended it, I think... I don't know, but I think that Gavin arranged for Sean to have an accident."

Douglas went very still and she rushed on, "I have no way of knowing if he did it but the police said it was suspicious, the accident. They interviewed me a couple of times, thinking I might have had something to do with it, but they never could prove anything. Gavin was so angry, he hated Sean anyway and when I told him some of the things Sean had said. Well... once, when I was in high school, some boys were talking about me, saying nasty things and Gavin took them on, all five of them. They eventually beat the hell out of Gavin but he did a good deal of damage before they overcame him and, after that, the talk stopped. It was known from then on that I was Gavin Fairfax's sister and no one was to mess with me. It played havoc with my social life, let me tell you." It was a lame joke but she was trying to lighten the very heavy mood.

Douglas's face was no longer blank and he was not amused by her joke. His look was now strangely intense (or more intense than was normal with Douglas) as he stared down at her and she had to tilt her head back to look at him.

She found she was holding her breath.

"So you think, because Webster 'messed with you', Gavin arranged for him to have an accident?" he asked, his voice deceptively calm but underlying it there was hint of an emotion Julia could not put her finger on.

"Yes. I don't know, maybe. It's not entirely out of character for Gavin. He seemed very easygoing but you didn't mess with someone he loved. What the police said, it sounded bad. Sean wasn't beloved by all, so it could have been others, but Gavin could be, well, he protected Mom and me our whole lives as the man of the family after our father left, even when he was a little boy. So I wouldn't put it past him to protect me like that, get vengeance for me. Sean wasn't hurt too badly, he survived. It was just a warning." She hoped to make it seem not as bad as it sounded. "We're close," she went on. "It was only the three of us, we all took care of each other. So, Gavin took care of me and now... now I'm taking care of his children," she finished on a shrug and hoped he understood. She wanted desperately to get away from him, wanted to escape his bizarre intensity, wanted to stop talking about Sean.

"Gavin didn't arrange for Webster to have an accident," Douglas announced firmly, surprising her with his words.

"How do you know?"

"Because I did," he told her bluntly without a hint of hesitation.

Julia gasped and her eyes rounded in disbelief.

Then she cried, "*What?*"

"He was an ass," was all he said to explain.

She stared at him, stunned, then whispered, "You? *You* did it?"

"I may do it again," he muttered as if to himself.

"But why? Why did you do it?" She ignored his last comment.

"He was an ass," Douglas repeated.

"Did Gavin ask you to?"

"No."

Then it dawned on her.

"Tamsin," she breathed.

He moved closer to her but she didn't notice. She was too astounded by his incredible announcement.

"She told me," Julia explained, "long after Sean was gone. She told me he made a pass at her, a rather unpleasant pass. She told you too, didn't she?"

It was then Julia realised how close he was to her. If she moved, her breasts would brush against his chest. She started to feel a rising panic, both because of his unpredictable mood and of her body's acute response to his closeness.

"What would he say to you?" he asked, abruptly changing the subject and she faltered.

"What?" she blinked, not following.

"Webster. What would he say to you?"

"Why do you want to know?"

And why *did* he want to know? Not only was it none of his business but she couldn't imagine he'd care.

"Just tell me," he demanded.

"I don't want to, I don't like thinking about it."

To her further shock, his hands came up, both of them. Gently resting on either side of her jaw, he held her face and Julia's body went still.

Douglas rarely touched her, he rarely touched *anyone*, and he'd certainly never touched her like this.

"Tell me." His voice was now cajoling, his face close. She couldn't keep up with him, the ominous Douglas, the gentle Douglas, the fierce Douglas, the coaxing Douglas, when it always used to be just... *Douglas*.

God, her head was spinning with it.

She took a shaky breath and then another one to calm down.

Maybe if she explained, he'd trust her. Maybe he'd finish this idiot game and they could live in some kind of détente, he would leave her alone and they could simply raise the children. Maybe if he understood her and her bond with Gavin a little bit (even though she doubted he had a like bond with anyone), he'd give her the benefit of the doubt. And maybe, if she told him, he'd move away from her so she could think straight, get control of her emotions and her body, which were both betraying her. Her stomach was warm and melty and that feeling was travelling relentlessly south.

"It was crazy, he was insane," she said on a quiet rush. "I couldn't do anything right. He didn't like the way I dressed, he didn't like how I styled my hair. I ate too much, talked too much or said stupid things. We'd have a dinner party and he'd yell at me about how I prepared the dessert. I'd go to the grocery store and I didn't buy the right kind of coffee even though it was the coffee he'd always liked. I don't know, it was everything and it was nothing." His thumbs were now gently stroking her jaw, she felt his touch vibrantly and she bit her lip to try not to react to it. "It doesn't matter now," she whispered. "It was a long time ago."

"He was a fool," Douglas murmured and his words caused the melty feeling to radiate throughout her entire body.

"He was a lot of things," Julia agreed, her voice shaky. "Now could you –?"

"How did you feel?" he interrupted her. "About the accident?"

"I…" Now that she knew he was behind it, what could she say? It scared her that he was capable of it but she'd accepted it from Gavin, even though she never really knew for sure. He was only doing the same for his own sister. But understanding he was capable of that type of violence, violence he inflicted on behalf of his sister, it drew her and repelled her at the same time.

"I was beyond caring at that point," she lied. She wasn't beyond caring then and she wasn't beyond caring now.

She had felt a guilty satisfaction that Sean had a modicum of pain, that maybe someone somewhere had wanted to hurt him and did. As much as she knew it was wrong, she also knew that something had long since died in her, something Sean killed, a hope for a life of love and happiness spent with a wonderful man. Because of that, Julia felt somewhere, in the deepest, darkest regions of her heart, that Sean deserved it.

One thumb moved from her jaw, to slide gently across her bottom lip, in doing so making her lip tingle. Douglas's face was completely illuminated by the moon and she watched as his eyes followed his movement and she trembled, a delicious feeling she could not control moving through her body as her thoughts ravaged her mind.

"And now?" he asked, sounding like he very much cared about her answer.

"Now?" Julia whispered.

"Yes. Now. How do you feel?"

"You mean, now that I know you did it?" she inquired, her teeth bit her bottom lip again to stop it from trembling and she accidentally nipped his thumb. She just stopped herself from apologising but he ignored it except his eyes moved back to her mouth, his gaze directed there making both her lips tingle.

With his hands holding her face, she couldn't look away and he didn't answer her question.

"You wasted your energy. Sean wasn't worth it," she replied, trying to make her tone hard to change the mood.

Although her words were true, how she really felt was floored. Mostly because he was so nonchalant about it, being responsible for another person's misfortune. But also the depth of feeling such an act showed that he had for his sister, she didn't know Douglas had that depth of feeling in him for anyone.

"Julia." His tone held a gentle warning that said he didn't believe her.

She closed her eyes and licked her lips, pressing them together. Then, for reasons unknown to her, she whispered her darkest secret, "He wasn't worth it but he deserved it."

Douglas's only response was to tighten his hands on her jaw and she felt somehow that response, however slight, was significant.

"And have you recovered from his behaviour?" His soft words caused her eyes to flutter open.

She stared at him, wondering what this was all about and tiring of true confessions.

Enough, she thought, really was enough.

"Why do you want to know this?" she asked, her voice sounding slightly curt.

"Just answer me."

"No. Okay? No," she snapped, tore her head away from his hands and leaned away from him, arching her back against the desk to do so. "I haven't recovered. You don't recover from something like that. I learned my lesson. I'm better off without him, without anyone," she admitted with rancour.

"I see. This is why you didn't remarry."

"Yes," Julia replied, exposing bitterness deep in that one word. "This", how he put it, was why she didn't do anything since Sean, no boyfriends, no lovers, no nothing. Sean had worked hard to teach her a lesson about men and added to that was her father's betrayal of her mother. Between the two of them, she learned that lesson well. There were very few Gavin Fairfaxes in the world, indeed, only one and he'd been her brother and now he was gone.

Again, they were in territory that was none of his business and it was decidedly ticking... her... off.

"If you must know, and apparently you do, yes," she informed him. "I won't remarry and if by some miracle I do, it will be to a pudgy, short, bald man who worships the ground I walk on and doesn't mind cleaning the bathroom."

With that statement, Douglas threw back his head and roared with laughter as if this situation was of such comedic proportions as to delight all mankind.

This shocked her so much, Julia jumped.

Firstly, it was *not* an amusing moment and secondly, she'd *never* heard him laugh.

Perhaps a chuckle here and there but out and out laughter?

Never.

When he was finished he leaned into her and she was forced to arch further away. She couldn't escape him, however, because, to her disbelief, his arms slid around her and he pulled her into his body.

"Douglas," her voice was low, her pulse leaping madly, "what are you doing?"

"I'm going to kiss you," he replied evenly as if this was the most natural thing in the world. As if he hadn't just gone from accusing her of whatever it was he was accusing her of to demanding she bare her most personal, painful and illicit secrets.

His breath smelled pleasantly of whisky and his hard body warmed her and that was a heady combination.

"Oh no you aren't." She shook her head, tried to twist her body away and pushed against his chest all at the same time. These actions had no result except his arms tightened.

"Yes," he whispered, his head was descending, "I am."

With superhuman effort, she pulled free and slid to the side, retreating by walking backwards towards the door.

"Listen," she pleaded, "I don't know what game you're playing but I don't want to play it with you. I've got enough to worry about without you doing... whatever it is you're doing. So can you just stop it and let me be?"

"No," was his answer and he followed her, advancing as she retreated.

"Why?" Julia cried, her voice rising. "Why on earth are you doing this?" Then she stopped and squared up against him, aggravated beyond caring. "It's unnecessary. I'm not a gold-digging, crazy woman, okay? I'm just going to raise those kids, get a job, live my life and when Ruby moves on, I'm going to go away. That's it. Period. The end. I don't have my eyes on your fortune. I'm just here to grant my brother's dying wish and I don't need you making it more difficult for me than it already is."

He'd stopped too but he didn't say a word.

"*Okay?*" she prompted on a near shout.

"No," he said again.

"Why?" she threw her hands up in agitation. "What are you getting out of this?"

She asked and she really wanted to know. He started walking towards her again and Julia started retreating again, step for step. What he didn't do was answer.

"Okay, play your games." She gave in but she did it with her heart beating faster. "See if I care, I'm going to bed," she announced to finish and turned to walk away.

"Excellent idea," he returned immediately, his insinuation as shocking as it was clear.

"Alone!" she spat over her shoulder.

"Julia, we need to talk."

"Not now we don't and I'm not sure we ever do!" She whirled around and faced him. "I'm fed up with you lot. You leave me with your *mother* who has all the warmth of a Siberian winter. You don't call. You don't give a good goddamn about those children. You show up accusing me of... whatever," she threw one arm out, dramatically, "you kiss me for no reason, stalk me around your study. Fine, okay, I get it. I'm some kind of game to you. Apparently your life is so boring you've run out of challenges so you have to play with humans in order to find amusement. Go for it. See if I care. You obviously don't know how stubborn I am so have at it. You won't win."

And with that, Julia turned to leave.

"I think I will," Douglas said to her back.

"Think again, I'm a lot stronger than I look," she announced as she made her way to the door, hoping she was right. "If I can take on an asshole like Sean and emerge unscathed... well, virtually so, then you're a pussycat."

"I wouldn't underestimate me," he warned.

She thought of something, stopped at the door, turned back to face him and put her chin up.

"One rule," Julia declared.

"No rules," Douglas replied.

"One rule," she ignored him, "whatever it is you're after, you don't drag the children into it."

He didn't even think, just inclined his arrogant head in agreement.

"Good. Let the games begin," she declared sarcastically.

And before he could reply, she left, trying not to look like she was fleeing. Her heart was racing, her head was aching and she was scared to death. As she walked, she felt the arctic draught around her feet and looked down.

It wasn't an invisible draught this time but looked like wisps of fog gathering around her ankles. She picked up the pace but it stayed with her, detached from her ankles and floated ahead. Julia watched in dread as it approached her bedroom door but then it slid past, towards the chapel, disappearing around the corner. She ran into her room, slammed the door and, for good measure, threw the bolt home.

"Dear Lord, what have I gotten myself into?" she asked the room.

The scratching at the window was her only reply.

9

JULIA'S NEW POSITION

The next morning, Douglas arrived to an empty breakfast table. Julia had gone with Carter to take the children to school. Avoiding him no doubt.

Knowing this almost made him smile.

After breakfast, he holed himself in his study, catching up with e-mails and telephone calls he'd not been able to return while he was away with Nick. His mother arrived home with the usual fuss and fanfare and he kept his door closed. Monique knew from experience that meant he did not wish to be disturbed. For hours, he heard nothing more, Julia, Ruby nor Carter returned home. Julia would have to come through the front door, of course, the family never used anything but the front door. To do that, she'd have to pass his study.

Then it struck him that, being Julia, perhaps she didn't use the front door.

Finally, impatient to set his plan into action, he went to find her.

Mrs. Kilpatrick was in the dining room using a foul-smelling, lemon-scented balm to polish the already exceptionally high sheen of the dining room table.

"Sir," she muttered, not looking at him.

"Mrs. Kilpatrick," he replied as greeting, intending to pass her as usual and go straight to Julia's rooms.

Then he heard, "Lady Ashton got home not two hours ago."

Mrs. Kilpatrick addressing him caused him to stop in surprise. He turned back to her, saw her eyes on him were hesitant and inclined his head as a gesture of gratitude at her unnecessary bit of news.

"Miss Julia…" she said loudly when he started to walk away.

He stopped walking and turned towards her again.

"Is at the supermarket," she finished hurriedly.

He regarded her inquisitively.

Mrs. Kilpatrick had been in his life for as long as he could remember. She excelled at her job, never complained, was immensely loyal to his house and her work and, for all of that, he respected her.

Even so, except for when she reported the household finances to him on a quarterly basis, he wasn't certain she'd ever spoken more than a few words to him of her own free will.

"Is that so?" he replied in an effort to be polite and he swore he saw her gulp. He couldn't imagine what was wrong with her though he didn't give this much thought as he had other thoughts on his mind and he started back towards his study.

Then he stopped and saw Carter outside surveying the fountain as if something was wrong with it.

If Carter was outside, how was Julia at the market?

"Tell me, Mrs. Kilpatrick, did Miss Fairfax get her driver's license while I was away?" he asked courteously, glancing in her direction again.

She nodded. "She certainly did, sir. Pleased as pie, 'Freedom!' She said. 'Relief!'"

Misinterpreting what the woman wanted him to understand, and amused at her description of Julia's reaction, he thought she wished to report that Julia had taken a car.

"So, she's out in one of my cars, is she?" he prompted.

She surprised him by shaking her head. "No sir. She walked."

"Walked?" He'd never been to a grocery store but he'd driven by them and he knew the closest one was in town and that was at least three miles away. Furthermore, why didn't she simply ask Carter to get her what she wanted from the market? "Why would she walk?"

"She's begun to like the excursions, sir. She takes Ruby. They both come in with cheeks pink and healthy," Mrs. Kilpatrick answered.

Douglas crossed his arms on his chest.

"Mrs. Kilpatrick. I have things to do," he explained impatiently, his tone telling her in no uncertain terms she was wasting his time and she should get to the point.

And Douglas was impatient because he was annoyed. This was obviously Julia's way of telling him she was not going to use his staff and that she was going to do her bit to contribute to the household by purchasing groceries since he wasn't going to allow her to pay her way.

"Sorry sir," Mrs. Kilpatrick bent to her task and he couldn't help but think she looked scared to death. This annoyed him all the more.

He expected his staff to respect him, to be quiet and go about their duties but he never expected, or to this point received, fear. He knew the staff were anxious around his mother but they'd never appeared that way with him.

"It's just," she went on, interrupting his thoughts, her voice so quiet he could barely hear her and it held both a tremor of fear and, if his hearing didn't deceive him, a note of anger, "those children need something decent in their bellies, something they like to eat. And Lady Ashton won't allow me to add anything to the grocery list or Carter to buy anything more. It's a long way for Miss Julia and little Ruby to go, carrying back bags and all, especially when it's raining. And since Lady Ashton forbid them to use Carter unless she gave her *express* permission, then they had to walk all last week. I thought that they'd get to use a car, seeing as Miss Julia has a license now and she was so excited about it. But today, Lady Ashton said now she couldn't use a car unless she gave her *express* –"

"Thank you, Mrs. Kilpatrick," Douglas cut her off, turned away and walked toward his study, his jaw set, his gait determined. The annoyance was escalating to an extraordinary feeling the like of which he had not felt for a very long time.

Then he turned back and called down the hall. "Mrs. Kilpatrick," her head shot up and her hand flew to her throat in fear, "tell Carter to go fetch them. When he gets back, tell him I want to see him."

"Yes sir!" she replied and walked swiftly towards the front door. As she passed him, he could tell she was holding back a smile.

For his part, Douglas found nothing to smile about.

His phone was ringing when he walked into the study. He strode to his desk, jerked it angrily out of the cradle and answered curtly, "Yes?"

"Oh no, sounds like you're having a bad day," Oliver Forsythe returned.

"I'm hoping it'll get better," Douglas ground out as he sat, turned in his chair and stared out the window, thinking of Julia and little Ruby tramping out there in the cold and mud, heaving carrier bags of groceries home all because of his *bloody* mother.

"I'm afraid I'm calling to tell you it's going to get worse. Charlie had a conversation with Julia this morning and now she's..." the other line buzzed and Douglas swivelled in his chair to look down at the phone while Oliver finished, "on the warpath. She told me she was going to call you."

"I don't think she's wasted any time. The other line is going."

"Good luck, mate," Oliver replied, his tone amused, and rang off.

Douglas hit the button to connect to the other line and before he could speak, Charlotte exploded, "Douglas, have you lost your mind?"

"Hello Charlotte," he responded evenly to her irate voice.

"Don't you, 'Hello Charlotte' me. Do you know where Jewel is right now?"

He wondered vaguely when Julia had become "Jewel" to Charlotte and he felt a bizarre twist of jealousy slice through his gut.

"The supermarket?" Douglas ventured.

"Do you know how she got there?" she yelled.

"She walked. Listen Charlotte, I just got home last night –" for some reason, far beyond him, he felt compelled to explain. Even though his feeling the need to explain was a rather spectacular event, Charlotte ignored him and broke in angrily.

"And that's another thing, you're gone too much. Not only have you left Jewel like a lamb at the slaughter that is Monique, you're never home. I called this morning to tell her I have some friends who are trustees at a faltering charity and they need some quick, and cheap, as in free, consultation. With a little work bringing her up to speed, and Sam could do the research for her, Jewel could have helped them. It would have been a great way for her to get some experience, start to network, learn the ways in a different country. But, *no...*" she drew out the last word sarcastically, "she doesn't trust Monique with the children and doesn't want to ask more of your staff, so she refuses to leave the children behind and won't do it."

He had barely processed her speech when she went on, telling him of Monique's little "tea party" and something about "lollipop girls" and how Monique told Lizzie she was overweight. His brain conjured an image of the girl with her sunken cheeks and bruised eyes and his jaw tightened again.

"Enough, Charlotte," Douglas interrupted her curtly. "I get your point."

"You'd better because it isn't fair on her, putting up with all of that and dealing with her homesickness and her and the children's grief. I didn't expect much of you, and, doubtlessly, neither did Tammy, but I expected more than this." Before he could reply to that cutting remark, she said, "I'll see you on Thanksgiving," and the phone went dead in his hand.

He replaced the receiver and stared at the phone. As Charlotte and Mrs. Kilpatrick's words started to penetrate, he felt a slow, unfamiliar, but not in the slightest indecipherable, burn begin.

"Darling! You're home! How lovely."

He looked up from the phone and saw his mother in the doorway.

Monique had very bad timing.

Douglas didn't like what he was feeling. He had, for many years, guarded against feeling anything at all. He'd had to or he would have been crushed by his father's tirades. But now the thoughts were racing through his mind and anger was boiling at his gut.

While he'd been away, he thought a great deal about Julia.

Once he made up his mind about something, he didn't often turn back. He was intent on starting his strategy to win her around to his way of thinking, of making her his wife and then, or before (if he was successful) taking her to his bed.

But he'd allowed himself to think of that kiss. That extraordinary kiss in the dining room and just how easily she responded to it. Sean Webster had been a wealthy man of position; it wouldn't be the first time Julia had found herself a good catch. Douglas was definitely her type if Webster was anything to go by.

And Douglas had allowed himself to believe from his vast experience of human behaviour that no one did something for nothing. Especially if that something required a great sacrifice that altered their entire life and their future.

And he had limitless knowledge of conniving women who put on a great show for the ultimate goal, which was him.

So he berated himself for his quick decision to make her his wife, which would be exactly what she wanted. He talked himself into believing the worst of her and then decided to confront her with it. He'd been thrilled she'd given him that opportunity quickly by appearing so fortuitously in his study last night. He intended to trip her up, make her expose herself and then he intended to kick her out.

He had not expected how their conversation would turn. He had not expected for her to admit to sustaining the same abuse from Webster as he himself had endured from his father.

And lastly, he had not expected his intense reaction to it.

When she said the word "hurt" in that awful voice as if it was dredged up from her very soul, he knew it corresponded to a feeling long since buried deep in the pit of his own.

Rage and sorrow for another human being, he found, did not mix well. Julia had never let on, not once, to the extent of Webster's callousness. She had always put on a brave face.

He found, to his surprise, that he wanted to do something about it, to take away her pain, her bitterness, to make her happy.

Her face had been in shadow but her words were enough. She was either the best actress in the world or she was innately damaged. Her proclamation that she'd next marry a balding short man who would clean the bathroom was said with such force, he thought she believed it.

He then decided immediately to resume his strategy. She would *not* next marry a short, balding man unless he himself started to lose his hair and shrink.

And not only would he never, but she would also never again clean a bathroom.

He faced his mother with his temper close to the surface.

"Mother," he said tersely by way of greeting, "you've been busy while I was away."

Her step faltered when she caught site of the unusual look on his face but she persevered. "Well yes, I was just at the spa and –"

"I didn't mean the spa. I meant Julia."

Her eyes narrowed. "Of what, exactly, are you accusing me? Did she –?"

"Julia didn't say a word," he informed her and realised it was true.

Julia had been angry last night and said something about his mother being as warm as Siberia but that was the extent of it. After Mrs. Kilpatrick and Charlotte's descriptions of his mother's behaviour, he was a little surprised that Julia didn't throw that in his face, especially when she was angry.

"Well," Monique sat in a chair across from his desk, completely composed except her eyes flashed maliciously. "She's insufferable. I cannot imagine what drove Tamsin to torture me in her death. It is, frankly, too much to take to force her poor, grasping, *American*," she said the word with all the xenophobia she felt, "sister-in-law on us. It is simply *too much!*"

"Unka Douglas," Ruby screamed from the doorway.

Douglas looked up to see Ruby racing across the room toward him and Julia standing in the doorway, her face pale beneath the rosy blush on her cheeks, acquired, no doubt, from being outside. Her posture was rigid, her eyes angry. She was wearing a pair of her faded, snug-fitting jeans, an item in her wardrobe of which he was beginning to be rather fond. The jeans ended in a pair of scuffed, old cowboy boots. She had on a thermal shirt with little pink dots printed on it, over that a Western-style denim shirt that buttoned part of the way up with pearl snaps and a thin, pink, downy vest over it all. Her hair was pulled back from her face in a ponytail at the crown of her head and her gorgeous face was free of makeup.

Ruby interrupted his perusal of Julia by jumping up, he caught her in his arms, lifting her into his lap and she threw her own arms around him, giving him a big, sloppy kiss on the cheek.

"Hello Ruby," Douglas murmured when he caught her eyes.

"We just went to the supermarket," Ruby yelled.

"Did you?" he asked but his eyes moved to Julia.

Monique didn't bother to turn and her face remained a frozen mask.

"Yes, we're going to make choca-chip cookies today!" Ruby shouted.

"I'll bet you are," Monique muttered scathingly and at that, Julia spoke.

"Come on Ruby, let's get washed up and make those cookies." Her voice betrayed nothing to Ruby as she extended her arm but her movements were jerky and Douglas knew she was angry and he knew this was because she'd heard his mother's words.

Douglas leaned forward, put Ruby on her feet and the little girl rushed back toward Julia. Julia didn't say a word to either Douglas or Monique. She just took Ruby's hand and walked stiffly away.

"Charming. I've been gone for days and she doesn't even say hello," Monique noted, her tone ugly and she ignored the fact that she not only hadn't greeted her grandchildren's aunt, she also had not greeted her grandchild, nor, Douglas realised something very telling, did Ruby even look at her grandmother.

He sat back in his chair, put his elbows on its arms, steepled his fingers and rested his chin on them. Then he regarded his mother coldly and, as usual, quickly made his decision.

"Mother, I don't believe we've had an important conversation," he declared with deceptive calm.

"Yes, dear?" she asked, her eyebrows going up, her face the picture of innocence. He reacted rather negatively to this familiar faux expression.

"I think," he started, "you need to be aware of my thoughts on the matter of Julia and the children."

"And what are those, darling?" She was the picture of motherly love and concern. For years he'd ignored it but now it made bile rise up the back of his throat.

"Julia is now a member of this family, *not* a member of staff, *not* a guest, though you haven't treated her as such. She will be afforded all the power and protection that means."

All motherly love gone in a flash, her voice now had an edge when Monique demanded, "Perhaps you should make yourself *perfectly* clear."

"It means that Julia's position here, as co-guardian to Tamsin's children, is elevated above yours," he retorted bluntly and heard her gasp.

"I cannot believe you'd –" she began.

"Believe it," Douglas cut her off. "If you don't like it, you can move to the dower house in Clevedon or I'll find you a place in London." Her eyes widened in fury but unaffected, Douglas carried on. "Now, do I make myself *perfectly* clear?"

"I cannot believe you'd chose that... that... *woman* over me!"

He didn't bother to reply.

Then her face changed, the outrage melting to venom. "I see. I see very well. You are, of course, welcome to her. She'll suck you dry, as she did with Sean, but –"

"That'll do," Douglas declared with such finality her head jerked. She stared at him a moment, her eyes working then she nodded slowly and rose from her chair in order to leave.

She moved to the door but stopped and paused for a parting shot. "I cannot believe I've raised such a cold-hearted son who'd put his mother out in favour of a money grubbing schemer."

"Can't you? As I remember, you didn't particularly care to raise Tamsin or me at all. Both of us you ignored and for my part you left me in the hands of a vicious and abusive father."

Again she let out an outraged gasp, this quite genuine as he'd brought up a subject that they had never discussed.

Not ever.

"I'll not have you talk about your father in that way!" Monique snapped.

"Mother, in case you hadn't noticed, he's been dead for years. He can't hear you defend him and then offer you a diamond necklace for your efforts."

She blew air out of her nostrils at this effrontery and then, without a word, whirled on her heel and left.

Douglas stared at the door for long moments after she left. He was furious at the conversation and cursing himself, his mother and Julia who was inadvertently responsible after bringing up all his old demons last night during their conversation. Demons he had methodically locked away. Demons he did not want to, *would not*, face.

It was high time he had the conversation he'd been meaning to have with Julia since this morning.

With determination, he got up and went to the kitchen to do just that.

10

THE PROPOSAL

They were elbow deep in cookie dough, three baking sheets sitting on the vast kitchen table half-filled with sloppy balls. Ruby was on her knees on the bench, her fingers a mess, slipping Carter, who was sitting across from her doing a crossword puzzle, pieces of dough (while consuming much of it herself) nearly as fast as Julia could put them on the sheets.

"It would be nice, Ruby-girl, if your brother and sister had some cookies when they got home from school," Julia admonished but her tone was teasing.

After she said this, with confusion Julia noticed Carter stiffen and he glanced swiftly down at his crossword puzzle, all the smiles and winks he'd been passing Ruby erased from his face.

"Carter."

Julia jumped and turned around to see Douglas stroll arrogantly in the kitchen. She cursed him silently, prowling around like a cat. How a big man like him could be so damn quiet, she'd never know.

Then her mind stilled and she stared at him in wonder. He had a face like thunder and she'd never seen such an expression from Douglas. She was used to either bland or indifferent, and lately, appreciative, but thunderous was new to her and it was both frightening and awe-inspiring.

"Sir?" Carter asked, dropping his crossword and jumping up from the bench, again showing an agility of a much younger man.

Douglas came to a halt next to Julia and declared, "It has come to my attention that I should make some explanations about your priorities."

Julia held her breath. She didn't know why but there was an underlying edge of fury in Douglas's tone that was making her highly uncomfortable. She did not want, nor did she want Ruby, to witness Douglas abuse Carter in the way that Monique freely abused the staff.

However, there was no escape.

Douglas continued. "My mother has led you to believe that you needed her permission in regards to Miss Fairfax using your services."

Julia and Ruby both looked from Douglas to Carter.

Carter just nodded.

Julia and Ruby looked back to Douglas.

"I apologise for that confusion," Douglas went on.

Again, Julia and Ruby's eyes slid back to Carter, whose jaw, they witnessed, dropped as this heretofore unheard phrase came from Douglas's lips. They turned back to Douglas when he continued speaking.

"Miss Fairfax, not only when she's doing something for or with the children, but *at all times,* has priority when you're assessing your workload. Understood?"

It was Julia's turn to have Carter's gaze on her face and *her* jaw dropped.

"Furthermore," everyone looked back to Douglas, "she's to have free use of the Audi TT, the Aston Martin and the Range Rover. Make certain she has easy access to each set of keys."

"Yes sir," Carter replied brightly.

Douglas turned his attention to Julia.

"I'd like a word." It was phrased as a request but certainly wasn't one.

She felt her stomach flip at the fury that still lay in his eyes. She didn't know if this stomach flip was fear or something else because in this mood he was both enormously frightening and perversely magnetic.

"Um... I'm making cookies," she ventured hesitantly.

"This won't take long." He turned to leave and Julia instantly decided it best not to fan the flames of that temper. She threw the spoon in the bowl and wiped her hands on the apron tied around her waist then tore at its strings to take it off.

She tossed it on the table while indicating Ruby. "Carter, do you mind?"

"Don't worry, lass, I'll watch her," Carter assured her.

Julia smiled at Carter and tousled Ruby's hair before she hurried after Douglas and saw he was headed to the study. After last night, and the time before, she didn't have a lot of good memories of conversations with Douglas in the study so she called after him.

"Could we...?" At her voice, he halted abruptly and turned to her, raising a haughty brow. "Not the study," she said, her voice timid and she cursed herself. Though, she had to admit, he *was* scaring her. What *he* had to be angry about (*she*, surely, was the one who should be angry after what she'd heard Monique say earlier), she didn't know but at that moment, she didn't want to find out.

"Fine," he clipped, changed his direction and walked back through the dining room, passing her, and he turned right at the door at the end of the room.

Toward her rooms.

"Wait..." she called but he kept going. She thought, hoped, that he intended to go to the chapel instead but he turned right again, pushing open the door to her room and she heard a frightened chirp from Veronika.

"Leave us," he commanded brusquely and, as Julia turned into her own room, she saw Veronika, her face a mask of fear, hurry out.

At witnessing Veronika's expression, Julia's own fear was subsiding, giving way to anger.

"What on earth?" she snapped when she entered her room and closed the door with a slam.

"It has come to my attention that I'll be having guests at Thanksgiving," he announced, looking about her room.

He picked up a framed photo from the writing desk that showed Julia with some friends at Margarita Mayhem Night. He gave it a hard glance and then put it down. She watched him do this and saw his movements were rough with rage.

"Yes," Julia replied, jutting up her chin and steeling herself for a forthcoming tirade, "I'm an American and those kids are half-American and we'll be celebrating Thanksgiving. Don't worry, I'll buy and prepare the food, and serve it, so you won't feel a hiccup in the strict Sommersgate regimen."

"In future," he stated smoothly, "I would like for you to inform me of these things in plenty of time for me to rearrange my schedule so that I can be free to attend."

Her mouth dropped open again and then she snapped it shut.

"Of course," she whispered, surprised. That was the last thing she expected to hear.

"Charlotte informs me you have the opportunity of an unpaid consultancy," he went on.

She looked at him warily. He was angry about something, what, she didn't know. However, all the things he said belied his apparent wrath.

"Yes," Julia agreed carefully, drawing out the word longer than necessary.

"Take it," he ordered. "Veronika can use the extra money. I'll increase her pay to cover any added duties."

Julia clenched her teeth together in an effort not to allow her jaw to go slack again.

She watched him as he turned, surprised he knew any personal information about any of his staff much less an underling like Veronika. He walked across to the mantel and picked up another photo. This was of her and Gavin when they were children; she had her arms wrapped around Gavin's neck and her leg thrown over his lap. He stared at it a moment and then set it down, his face impassive.

"I heard what your mother said," Julia told him, summoning up all her courage to confront him. His head came up and he looked at her, his face betraying nothing.

"I know you did."

"If you want me to go, I'll go. I'll be happy to go. I just want to take the kids with me. All you have to do is sign over custody –"

"No," he said flatly and Julia tensed.

"Douglas, I know neither you nor your mother have any interest in the children and both my mother and I will be able to give them a happy, healthy upbringing in Indiana. We can somehow circumvent the will that says they have to be raised at Sommersgate."

"I said, no."

It was her turn to shake with fury.

"Why?" Julia asked on a cry. "Why when you obviously don't care? When you're more interested in games than your nieces and nephew? When your mother can't stand the sight of me?"

"Because it's what Tamsin wanted," Douglas answered.

"Tamsin wouldn't have wanted this!" Julia retorted angrily.

For some reason, he smiled. It wasn't a grin but an all-out, white-flash of teeth against tanned, handsome face smile. Just as quickly as a snap, his fury was gone and he was smiling at her. It was unnerving and it only proved to heighten of her own temper.

"Do you want to tell me what's going on?" she demanded hotly.

She thought he'd refuse but instead he said, "Yes, Julia, I'd very much like to tell you what's going on."

But then he said no more.

And she wasn't sure she wanted to hear what he had to say at all.

She stared at him and he stared back.

"Well?" she snapped, sick to death of his staring contests and curious beyond what she knew was healthy.

"This is what's going on," he stated and started back across the room toward her.

When he was halfway to her, she put her hand up. "I... I'd like you to stay where you are," she stammered and he slowed his determined gait but he did not stop.

"I told Monique that she could either live with you cordially or move out."

This was so shocking, Julia gasped. He kept moving toward her but she no longer cared.

"You did?" she asked in disbelief.

He didn't affirm but moved relentlessly forward and didn't stop until her still raised arm with its upturned hand hit the hard wall of his chest.

"She won't trouble you anymore and if she does, you're to phone me immediately and I'll deal with it."

Julia swallowed and nodded, too afraid to say a word, his eyes were so dark indigo, they appeared black.

At that moment, she almost felt sorry for Monique.

Almost.

"I... uh, thank you," she finally broke the silence.

"Don't thank me, I'm not through yet."

She nodded again, stupidly, the heat of his body seeping through her hand.

"As for Tamsin's wishes, I intend to carry them out to the letter. There was a reason she wanted you here, you and your delectable body and your enticing perfume and your legs that go on forever." She was stunned by his words and could barely process them before he went on. "My sister was a romantic and she cared for us both. She had very specific intentions for this little arrangement she created and I've no doubt she talked Gavin around to her way of thinking."

He was exerting pressure on her hand and she was finding she needed more and more of her strength to keep him at arm's length.

"What... what way of thinking was that?" Julia spluttered, thinking, from his words, that he'd gone mad, utterly and completely insane.

What he said next proved she was right.

"She wanted me to marry you and I'm going to do it."

Julia's entire body froze.

Then she shouted, "*What?*"

Her arm failed and Douglas took advantage. He moved the rest of the way and she retreated until she felt the heel of her foot hit the wall. She was caught and he moved close.

"It's the perfect solution to this mess," he informed her calmly. It registered that he'd referred to her as a "mess" and her eyes flashed but before she could say a word, he continued. "You'll have the protection of my name and thus status over my mother, the children will have a stable family unit, you'll have freedom to live and work in this country as long as you please and –"

"Why?" she cried, the word filled with anger and confusion.

"Why?" he asked calmly, as if he asked women he barely knew to marry him every day.

"Yes, *why?* I don't love you, you don't love me. What if you found someone else and you and I were married, what would you do then?"

"I wouldn't. You wouldn't. I'll have my solicitors draw up a contract. We'd stay married while the children are underage. When Ruby is old enough to leave the house and doesn't need our guardianship anymore, you can decide to move on if you wish. I'll be certain throughout our marriage that you have a generous allowance and when, or if, you left, I would give you healthy settlement. So healthy, you wouldn't need a pension. In the meantime, you can work, if you like, and –"

She could just *move on?*

"Marriage?" she whispered, her eyes narrowed. "Have you lost your mind?"

He shook his head and she stared at him in disbelief, casting around for anything that would get this crazy scheme out of his head.

"So what do you do when you..." she stopped, flustered, then started again, "need to see to your needs? Or when I do for that matter? You just ignore my lovers and I ignore yours?"

"There'll be no lovers," he announced implacably, almost forcefully, his hands furthering the point by coming to grip her upper arms firmly.

"A platonic marriage of convenience with no release?" She couldn't believe they were having this conversation. She couldn't believe *he* of all people was making this suggestion. He was a known womaniser, even a celebrated one.

"I never said the marriage would be platonic, Julia."

At that, she jumped away with a surprised yelp and slammed against the wall.

Trapped, she could do nothing but stare at him in astonishment.

"You're saying you want to marry me, *marry me.* As in a real, full-blown, consummated union of the souls?"

"There'll be a union but I cannot guarantee it'll be of souls," he replied and she gaped at him open-mouthed.

Then she snapped her mouth shut.

"No," she shook her head, unable to cope with this latest announcement, "no way, no."

"May I ask why?" he queried calmly.

"Because it... is... *insane*," Julia enunciated her words carefully then she demanded, "Step back."

"No," he replied and her panic rose. "You'll have a good life, I promise you that," he vowed softly, changing tactics, his voice was now coaxing. "Anything you want, you'll have. Command of this house, control of the children. We'll offer all of this to William as my heir or we could make our own –"

"Children?" she asked, her voice a high-pitched squeak.

"If you wish," he replied as if it mattered less to him than... her mind raced but she couldn't think what mattered to him at all.

"This is nuts, insane, crazy. Absolutely beyond –"

"I'm not insane, Julia. I'm a busy man who has assumed a terrible responsibility I'd rather not have. Not because I don't care about those children but because my responsibility for them means my sister is dead."

That shut Julia up and she stared at him in wonder. It was the first time he'd ever spoken of it with any emotion. His dark eyes were darker, if that could be possible, and blazing.

"God," she breathed, "you're doing this for Tamsin."

"Not just for Tamsin, no."

"Then why?" she asked, incredulous and curious at the same time.

"Because I need a wife and because you'll make a good one."

She stared at him in open-faced shock at *that* unlikely pronouncement.

Then she gathered control of herself and declared, "I've tried marriage before and I'm here to tell you that I am *not* good at it."

"You were fine, it was the bastard you chose who wasn't good at it," he informed her like he was their long-term marriage counsellor and could make such a judgement.

She tried another tactic. "Okay, then I don't *want* to be good at it. I don't *want* to be married to you or... or anyone!"

He leaned in, put his hand up on the wall at the side of her head and when he spoke his voice was low and smooth. "Then I'll have to persuade you to change your mind."

She knew exactly what he meant.

Again, she narrowed her eyes. "Don't you dare!"

"Do you think I can't?"

"Of course you can't," she scoffed.

Mistake.

Big, big mistake.

Because it was then, Douglas kissed her. Pressing his body full against hers and with nowhere to run, no way to get away, she was forced to endure.

And she *had to* endure. She had to prove she was immune to him. She had to prove that the morning in the dining room was a fluke.

But the heat shimmered through his body to hers, her breasts were pressed against his hard chest, his mouth was teasing, tempting.

Dear Lord.

Julia managed to keep her mouth resolutely shut and tried to think of things that were very unsexy. She thought of the doodle art he patronised for the gallery and that was a good start. Pleased with herself, she stiffened her body in resistance.

Douglas, unfortunately, was not deterred. His arms, which had slid around her, pulled her from the wall and moulded her to him, breasts against chest; soft, yielding hips against hard, straining ones. One arm held her firmly about the waist while the other hand slid down, softly, gently, over her bottom.

His hand at her bottom felt good. Oh God. *Too* good.

As tingles shot across her skin, she thought harder about the doodles then her mind flashed to him handing her a glass of champagne. Then to him sitting in the Bentley and talking about her perfume. Then to him holding her face gently in his hands and stroking her jaw and bottom lip while she told her tale of woe last night. Her resolve quickly flagged as the tingles matured to delicious tremors.

She groaned in despair, low in her throat, and pressed her hands against his chest, pushing him away while his teeth nibbled at her lips in an illicit and enticing way, his one wayward hand had moved up her side and was now stroking, slowly, achingly slowly, against the side of her breast.

"Stop it!" she finally cried, turning her face away but he didn't stop. He was relentless. His mouth trailed down her cheek to her neck.

This was big mistake number two. The skin of Julia's neck was sensitive. As he dragged his lips, whisper-soft, along her neck to nip at her earlobe she felt shivers shoot through her body. Her breasts swelled against her will, straining against his chest and she wriggled against him to get away from his mouth. Her stomach was melting, her legs were going weak and his heat was penetrating her body everywhere it touched.

"Kiss me," he urged in her ear, his deep voice like velvet and a fresh shudder tore through her.

"No," she denied, her breath coming fast.

"Kiss me once and I'll leave you alone," he promised, his head coming up to look at her.

She felt a flash of hope. "Now and forever, no more talk about marriage, no more of these... episodes?" She pressed him verbally as she pushed against his chest.

He grinned, then rubbed his lips back and forth against her firmly closed ones and she longed to stop that intimate caress by pressing her lips to his.

"No," he finally stopped his torture to reply against her mouth.

She dug deep into the last reserves of her strength. "Then no, I won't kiss you, now or –"

His hand, which had been stroking the side of her breast quickly lowered, going under her denim shirt, under her thermal t-shirt and up her belly.

"What are you...?" she breathed against his mouth, trying to sound in control but everywhere he touched sent a path a fire, her muscles contracting as his hand caressed its way from her belly upwards, the whole time he watched her face, his eyes heavy-lidded.

"Please don't," she begged on a whisper, not caring how weak she sounded because she knew she couldn't endure much more.

This was Douglas, handsome, compelling Douglas and she'd had a crush on him since the moment she laid eyes on him.

Not to mention, it had been a long time for her, a dry spell, an enormous dry spell and it was like not eating for months and then being shown to a five-star, gourmet banquet. Douglas, so close, pressed against her, his hand working wonders, was the banquet and she, unfortunately, felt like gorging herself.

His hand cupped her breast over her bra, his thumb rubbing against her nipple and Julia instantly melted. She closed her eyes and moaned low in her throat, the workings of his thumb shooting dizzying shafts of pleasure from her nipple downward through her belly straight between her legs.

She bit her lip in an effort at control just as she clutched at his shirt.

"Stop it," Julia whispered, her eyes flying open to see the satisfaction on his face.

He didn't stop, he nibbled at her lips and they parted in a silent gasp as his thumb caught at the top edge of her bra, pulling the cup down roughly and it carried on with its earlier work, this time with no barrier, skin against skin.

Oh my, but that feels nice, Julia thought but out loud she whimpered as the pleasure intensified.

"Kiss me." It was a demand this time, rumbling out from deep in his chest.

"No," she denied him, how she did it, she didn't know as she was nearly at her end.

At her denial, Douglas parted her legs with his knee, pulling her towards him, the heat of his thigh like fire on the insides of hers even through her jeans. His thumb ceased rubbing only to be immediately replaced by both thumb and forefinger providing more excruciatingly lush pleasure. Her head fell back and, against her volition, her back arched pressing her breast more deeply into his hand.

She raised her head and stared at him with angry, passion-filled eyes. "You bastard," she breathed and he chuckled low in his throat.

"Kiss me," he commanded again.

And she did. She couldn't help herself. She wrapped her arms around his neck, slid herself up his thigh and opened her mouth under his.

She touched her tongue to his, her stomach somersaulted and then plummeted. His fingers righted her bra, his hand moved away from her breast and his arms slid around her, holding her so tightly it took her breath away. His mouth was demanding and insistent and she gave him everything he asked for and then more.

And she gloried in doing it.

Then, finally, in one move of pure strength and willpower, she tore away. Sliding to the side she quickly put five feet between them.

"I think…" she said, her voice husky, her eyes flashing, her breath coming in halting gasps, "I hate you."

"Not words on which to start a lasting engagement, so I'll focus on your actions instead." His voice was also lusciously husky and his breath heavy but his face was set and determined.

He walked forward, she stood her ground and she would have scratched his eyes out if he reached for her (or, at least, she told herself she would).

He didn't, instead he lifted his hand and just ran his thumb across her swollen bottom lip while she held herself frozen.

To her surprise, he murmured simply, "I'll make you happy."

"From current behaviour," she snapped in return, "I find that impossible to believe."

He smiled at her, that devastating smile then he leaned forward, brushed her lips with his, pulled away and walked out the door.

She stared at it in disgust, grabbed a pillow off the bed and threw it at the door. Then another one and then another, until they all sat on the floor behind the door and she sat on the bed with her head in her hands and her mind blank to everything but the memory of his beautiful, mind-shattering touch.

❧ 11 ❧

THE MISTRESS

Julia stood surveying herself in the three-way mirror. She wore a pair of wide-legged black trousers that hugged her low on her hips and a skin-tight camisole, the hem of which only just reached the waist-band of her trousers. Over that she wore a see-through black blouse with satin edging at the buttons, collar and cuffs. She'd put in her diamond studs and tied a black velvet ribbon tight around her throat. She kept her hair long but used a blow dryer to straighten its waves. The finishing touch was a pair of silver, strappy sandals, the straps across her coral varnished toes were braided and the heel was stacked in a high, thin, black wedge.

An hour ago Charlotte and Oliver arrived for the Thanksgiving cele-brations which were to take place tomorrow. Sam followed twenty minutes later. Tonight they were going to have a light repast in prepara-tion for the gorge-fest that was going to take place the next day.

Even Monique had condescended to join them, more than likely because Charlie and Oliver were coming.

Monique had been on her best behaviour the last two weeks since Douglas's return. Although she hadn't been around much to behave any way at all with her whirlwind of brunches, lunches, dinner parties and manicure appointments. When she was around, she kept to herself, not even bothering Douglas and completely ignoring Julia and the children.

Douglas, as well, had been on his best behaviour.

After his bizarre and maybe even unhinged proposal of marriage, Julia had steeled herself for the sexual onslaught that she thought would begin after she pulled herself together enough to leave her rooms to help finish the cookies. Instead, he had been the perfect gentleman, cordial, thoughtful and even, if it could be believed, friendly.

She didn't trust him one bit, mostly because she suspected he was unhinged due to his out-of-the-blue marriage proposal which proved, to Julia, that Douglas Ashton was completely and utterly *mad.*

He, on the other hand, was around far more often then he used to be, which she felt under the circumstances, was most perverse.

He was at the breakfast table every morning and was home every night. She knew he went into the office and even took quick day trips to meetings elsewhere in the UK and on the Continent. He might not make tea or supper or Ruby's bedtime but he was at least home to say goodnight to Willie and Lizzie.

But he didn't kiss Julia, stalk her around any rooms, say anything outrageous, mention a word to the children, press a heavy, antique, heirloom engagement ring on her finger or any behaviour of the like.

And Julia was immensely relieved (and secretly disquieted) by his behaviour. Even so, she did not let her guard down.

Julia watched and noticed that the children were responding to Douglas being home, Monique being mostly absent and Julia having charge of their care. They clearly enjoyed a settled regime that was far less strict and a house that also included the presence of their uncle.

The day after his proposal, Douglas had asked Sam to arrange an appointment for them at his bank to open an account for her. He'd met her there, already in the manager's office waiting for her when she arrived. She completed forms and put up with the manager's oily gushing to Douglas *and* herself.

The whole while Douglas sat back, one foot casually resting on the other knee, one arm possessively (she knew exactly his meaning this time) draped across her chair, watching her as if witnessing the completion of forms was the height of entertainment (which meant completing the forms was far more gruelling than it needed to be).

When they were finished and standing on the pavement outside the bank, he asked her if she'd like to go for a drink.

"No thank you, I need to get home to the children." Her voice was filled with acid-fuelled politeness.

"Julia, they won't spontaneously combust if you're gone for a few hours."

She'd given him a narrow look and stalked to where Carter was waiting for her beside the Bentley.

Like the gentleman he was apparently wanting her to believe him to be, he let her go.

The only glitch in his charade was the one time Douglas *did* come home in time for tea. After dinner, when the children went off to their homework, computer games and television, Julia had settled on the couch in the grand entry in front of a roaring fire that Carter had made. She was reading through some paperwork Charlie had sent her on charity organisations in the UK in preparation for the consultancy she would begin the next week. To her surprise, and under her distrustful eye, Douglas joined her. He had not changed out of his suit but had taken off his tie and jacket and loosened the collar of his deep green, finely-tailored shirt. He carried with him a book instead of work. Not any book, of course not, instead it was a Russian novel, printed in Russian no less.

She surreptitiously watched him read it for awhile and determined that he did, indeed read Russian. This shocked her but she was busy ignoring him, and doing very well at it, so could not, or more to the point *would not*, allow herself to comment (as she very much wanted to do).

Ruby was the first to break their hesitant peace, storming in with a loud complaint that Lizzie was watching a programme different from the one that Ruby wanted to watch.

"Ruby, you don't need to shout. Uncle Douglas and I can hear you perfectly," Julia told her niece firmly but kindly. "And I thought we agreed it was Lizzie's night to choose what was on the telly."

Ruby flounced away, seemingly accepting her fate but clearly unhappy about it.

Next it was Lizzie's turn. She wanted something to eat.

"You don't have to ask, honey," Julia explained. "Do you want some help?"

"No, I'm okay," Lizzie replied and slunk toward the kitchen, still in the depths of her despair but Julia had little time to respond to it when Willie arrived.

"Ruby just walked in and changed the programme," he shouted angrily. "I was watching it and she said you told her –"

Julia started to rise but Douglas lithely beat her to it.

"I'll take care of it," he declared to her stunned surprise.

Willie stalked off with Douglas trying to match his uncle's ground eating strides.

Julia gave it ten minutes then she went in search of them, her assumption being that Douglas would need some kind of assistance.

Willie and Lizzie were alone, eating potato chips in the lounge, watching television.

Douglas and Ruby were not there. Nor were they in the study or kitchen. They couldn't have gone to the drawing room without her noticing them but she did use the back hall to check the billiards room, morning room and finally the library. No luck.

She climbed the stone staircase, her steps muffled by the deep-pile, rich burgundy runner and she found them in Ruby's room.

Douglas was seated on the floor, his back to the wall, his long, muscular legs stretched out in front of him and crossed at the ankles.

Ruby lay beside him on her back, her head on his thigh, her legs cocked with one foot resting on her other knee while she listened with rapt attention to him reading her a story, her eyes gazing dreamily at the ceiling.

Julia silently registered this shocking scene and crept quietly away before either of them saw her. She didn't like what the sight of that scene made her think *or* feel so she tamped down any thoughts and definitely all feelings and went back to her work.

Douglas joined her some time later and informed her Ruby was in bed, asleep.

"Thank you," Julia replied with a brief inclination of her head and a curt tone.

He didn't respond, just settled back with his book, the picture of patience and good will. It made her want to grit her teeth.

Shortly after, she called to the other two to come and give them kisses goodnight and, once Willie and Lizzie had accomplished this chore, Julia allowed them time to prepare for bed before she rose to go to Lizzie's room.

"Where are you going?" Douglas asked, his eyes warm on her which made her knees go weak (a reaction she firmly ignored).

"I need to tuck Lizzie in. I do it every night," Julia replied, ignoring his soft gaze.

She watched as Douglas got to his feet.

"I'll do it," he told her, surprising her, and turned to walk away. Then, after only a step, he turned back and asked, "How, exactly, *do* I do it?"

She forced down a smile at his disgruntled expression, too pleased that he was going to make an effort with Lizzie to be angry and she calmly explained.

He nodded but didn't move.

"Yes?" she prompted.

"*Why* am I doing it? She's twelve years old."

"Because Gavin did it," Julia explained quietly.

His face changed almost imperceptibly and she expected him to refuse. However, to her relief and gratitude (which Julia felt but did not express), he nodded again and left.

She didn't creep up to see it, didn't think she could bear it and instead she escaped to her own room and refused to allow herself to think about it or, indeed, anything at all.

The night hadn't, thankfully, repeated itself since. Julia couldn't have borne up against that gentle of an onslaught. She had to trust that this was a genuine effort on his part and not Douglas using the children to get to her and thus breaking their only rule.

However, it had caused a slight change in Lizzie's behaviour as she seemed to have a bit more bounce in her step from that night onward. Julia never asked her about it but vowed that even if nothing went right for her and Douglas, she would always be thankful for his one night of kindness.

Julia turned to her dressing table and picked up her perfume. Since that day when Douglas told her (not *asked* her, *told* her), he was going to marry her, she hadn't used her normal scent. She told herself she wasn't using it because she didn't want to run out. Instead she put on the expensive French perfume her mother bought her every Christmas. It was a leftover from Sean, who used to buy it for her and she loved it so much she still used it occasionally even though it reminded her of her hated ex-husband.

And, Julia decided, she could use reminding of rotten, selfish men who did whatever vile thing they had to do to get what they wanted.

Everyone was to gather in the library for drinks before dinner and when she arrived, Douglas, Sam and Oliver were there as were all the children.

"You look pretty!" Ruby shouted and Julia stopped to bend down and kiss the top of her head as Ruby ogled her shoes. "I *love* your shoes," she drawled out the word "love" dramatically, giving it about five syllables and Julia laughed.

"You can have them when I'm done with them, Ruby-girl," Julia promised her niece.

"Wicked!" she shouted Willie's favourite word and the next thing she knew, Douglas was pressing a martini in her hand.

"'Pretty' is not the word I would use," he said in her ear and she flashed him a false courteous smile. "You smell lovely, something new?" he inquired lazily, his amused grin telling her that he was on to her game.

"I'm not surprised you like it. Sean used to buy it for me. He *loved* it. It seems you two have things in common," she drawled cattily and walked quickly away.

But when she made her escape and caught his eye, Julia saw he was watching her and she could tell that he was not happy. She tried to tell herself she didn't care but she knew that comparing him to Sean was out of line and she felt uncomfortably like a screaming bitch, mostly because she'd acted like one. It was something Monique would say. Perhaps they were playing games but she'd never been one to fight anything but fair.

"When's this feast being laid out?" Charlie, upon entering, greeted the entire room, making the children giggle. "I've heard about these American holidays and I haven't eaten for a week in preparation."

And this started a night that was surprisingly and welcomingly full of laughter and teasing. Even Monique slipped only once, confiding in a stage whisper to Charlie, "Ruby. I don't know what possessed them. Such a *common* name."

Before Charlie, who looked as if she'd just eaten something foul, or Julia, who was about ready to jump out of her chair, could reply, Douglas did.

"Obviously, Mother, you're unaware that it's a family name on both sides. I believe it's Julia's grandmother and also some distant ancestor of Father's who shared the name."

Monique's eyes cut toward her son, glittering quickly with ire but then she shook it off and again ignored the rest of the table in order to act the lavish hostess to an indifferent Oliver and openly beleaguered Charlotte.

Julia shot Douglas a grateful look but he ignored it, most likely still angry at her earlier comment and she had to admit, he was entitled to it.

After dinner, Monique didn't retire to the billiards room with them because the children did.

Once there, Charlie and Julia walked directly to the couch in front of the warm fire. Avoiding the rug of dead tiger hide lying on the floor in front of it (complete with head), they tucked their feet underneath them, settling in to finish the evening drinking wine and gossiping.

The children, Sam and the men engaged in boisterous games of snooker behind them with the mortifying heads of dozens of dead stags staring blankly over their heads. Julia liked this room, albeit not the dead animal pieces hanging on the walls or lying on the floor. Unlike most of the house, it was snug and welcoming, inviting you to stay awhile. Someone had long since disposed of the billiard table and replaced it with snooker and they were at it until it was time for Ruby to go to bed.

"I'll take her up," Sam offered. "I'm dead on my feet and don't often get a break." She slid a comical look of accusation at Douglas who completely ignored her comment except to raise one, arrogant brow and his lack of response that nevertheless included a response made everyone else laugh.

It didn't make Julia laugh. Instead, it made Julia's inebriated mind fill with thoughts of just how sexy he looked with that one brow raised.

Lizzie and Willie were allowed to stay up later than normal due to the holiday and loudly protested when the time was nigh for their beds.

And Julia found it difficult to insist they go. Lizzie, that night, had allowed her grief to crack and, although it was a slow process, it eventually ruptured during the snooker games with her uncle. Surreptitiously glancing their way, Julia had seen both of them teaming up against the others and she couldn't help but feel immense relief that Douglas was making more overtures to their niece. She saw him encourage her and even lift her gorgeous hair off her cheek to tuck it tenderly behind her ear.

Upon seeing that, Julia could almost have kissed him, if she was in such a mood, which she, of course, was *not*.

But she had to insist they went to bed mainly because they'd be bears the next morning. And when Julia's insistence was met with the children's denials, Douglas insisted.

This, of course, worked and Lizzie and Willie called goodnights and slunk from the room.

"All right then," Charlie started, rising from the couch when they had the room to themselves, "it's time for me to wipe the floor with you."

Charlie and Julia had been steadily drinking for the last several hours. Julia had a martini before dinner and, since then, so many glasses of red wine, she lost count.

When she rose to join her friend, she felt light-headed and realised, belatedly, that she was a little drunk.

This made her giggle to herself until she noticed Douglas's eyes on her and *that* sobered her immediately.

She made her way gingerly to the snooker table as Oliver and Charlie argued about the teams. Apparently Charlie was an accomplished snooker player and also, clearly, quite competitive. Julia ignored them and Douglas and sipped distractedly at her wine. All she hoped was that she wasn't on Douglas's team.

"That's settled then, boys against girls," Charlie announced to Julia's relief. "Jewel, do you know how to play snooker?"

"No," Julia replied truthfully. "You should have asked me before you chose teams. I won't be any help."

"Never mind," Charlie replied airily.

"It's kind of like pool," Oliver supplied helpfully.

"I'm rubbish at pool too," Julia explained on a grin. "But I'll give anything a go."

"Come over here, girl," Charlie beckoned. "I've got a strategy."

Julia approached, Charlie whispered her outrageous strategy and Julia laughed out loud when she heard it, even though she knew she'd never carry out her part in it.

The "boys" won the toss and Douglas broke. Julia had no idea how to play snooker but it looked like it wasn't such a good break, the balls barely moved except one red one fell into the pocket.

Her face must have betrayed her thoughts because Oliver leaned over and said, "Not exactly like pool. That was a damned good break."

Douglas went ahead and accomplished a bunch of "potting" of balls while Charlotte bugged her eyes out at Julia, wanting Julia to start the strategy. Saving her from disappointing her friend, Douglas missed a difficult shot and Charlie was up, showing she was nearly as good as Douglas... just not quite.

When it was Oliver's turn, Charlie commenced her "strategy" and she was shameless, sidling up to him as he made his shot and distracting him with her hand on his bottom at the last minute, making the ball fly wide.

"It's going to be like that, is it?" Oliver reared up and towered over her in mock severity.

"Whatever do you mean?" Charlotte asked, her hands out to her sides and eyes wide with sham innocence.

Julia moved to the table, did her best to line up her shot with Charlie's coaching and missed by a mile.

"You'll get it next time, tiger," Oliver teased and Julia grinned at him but Charlie reproached him good-naturedly.

"Don't be condescending, darling, it doesn't suit you."

Douglas started again, ignoring the witty repartee and in no time he was on another roll when Charlie came over to Julia and pushed her into Douglas. Tipsy, she couldn't right herself before she fell forward and nudged his hip, jarring him and making him send the ball flying in the wrong direction.

He slowly rose and turned to her. She prepared herself for an unpleasant confrontation but instead he simply lowered his cue and looked at her with heavy-lidded eyes.

"I'm sure you can think of some better way to distract me," he goaded, his eyes challenging her.

Her stomach flipped at the look in his eye.

"I'm sure she can!" Charlie took up the gauntlet for her with glee and Julia nearly groaned. She bugged her eyes out at Charlie who just bugged hers right back.

At that point, the game descended into total farce. Oliver destroyed Charlie's shots, Charlie destroyed Oliver's shots and when it was Julia's turn, Douglas approached a tense Julia, murmuring about "coaching" her.

"I think I should help my own teammate, thank-you-very-much," Charlie barged her way forward, slipped against Julia, who had lined up her shot, sending the cue flying into the ball, which went off in a wild trajectory across the table. Julia was too occupied to notice what happened to her wayward shot as Charlie falling into her sent her back-wards, straight into Douglas. One strong arm closed around her waist to steady her and she immediately became aware of his warm body behind her.

"That's her shot!" Oliver crowed.

"It is not! It was a mistake. She tripped." Charlie went off to argue with her husband and Julia pulled herself firmly, albeit it tipsily, away from Douglas's arm.

Therefore, she stumbled again, cursing the drink as his hand shot out to steady her.

"I'm fine," she said and thanked the Lord above there were no words to slur in that statement. Then she turned and he dropped his hand.

"I can see that," he replied, amusement dripping from every word.

She lifted narrowed eyes to him.

Douglas was *amused?*

"Are you making fun of me?" Julia asked.

He didn't answer, he simply lifted a brow.

"I hate it when you lift that brow," she outright lied. "It's so *superior.*"

"That's apt, especially in snooker," Douglas returned.

"We'll see about that!" she snapped, this time accepting his challenge herself.

It was his turn and as he lined up his shot, she got in front of him, as close to him as she dared, and looked down on him as he bent over the table.

"Oo, that looks like a difficult one," she remarked in a sugary-sweet tone with false wide-eyed wonder. "Do you really think you'll make it?"

He lifted his head to gaze at her levelly over his shoulder, turned back and, within a split second, potted the ball.

Oliver hooted, clapped and then shouted, "Well done, mate!"

Julia wanted to stamp her foot in frustration.

Charlie was having the time of her life.

"Don't give up!" she cheered from across the room.

Douglas chose his next shot and, with a lot of wine-fuelled courage and Charlie's urging, she sidled up next to Douglas as he leaned over the table. She bent over behind him and, as he pulled the cue back, she screwed up her courage, leaned in deeper and blew in his ear.

The shot flew wide and she straightened quickly, jumping up and down and clapping her hands as Charlie came over and gave her a whirling, girlie hug.

But her joy faded when Charlie released her and Julia saw the set look in Douglas's eye.

The gloves, Julia knew immediately, were off. She shivered at the knowledge but she was unsure if her shiver was of dread or anticipation.

Oliver practically tackled Charlie the moment before she took her shot. Charlie yanked Oliver's cue clean away from him before he took his. And as Julia lined up hers, Charlie coaching her, she concentrated on what Charlie was saying and not what Douglas was doing. She didn't know where he was, couldn't see him at all and became so flustered, she jumped several inches when his body settled in behind, beside and above her, surrounding her, it seemed, *everywhere.* She looked over her shoulder at him as his hands covered hers on the cue.

"Let me," he whispered in her ear, "show you how it's done." Crack went her cue and she potted the ball.

Charlie shouted with glee.

Oliver groaned. "You aren't supposed to help them!"

Shot after shot, Douglas showed her which to take, helped her line them up and leaned over her, his body warm against hers, his arms around her helping her hold the cue and snapping it against the ball as she (well he, really), potted the rest of the balls on the table.

Charlotte was in throes of ecstasy at "winning" and it was so infectious, even Julia started jumping up and down. Charlie and Julia hugged. Charlie hugged Douglas for helping and then she hugged Oliver for good measure. Swept up in it all and having had way too much to drink, Julia hugged Douglas and kissed him on the cheek.

Not one to miss an opportunity, his arms came quickly around her and, grinning down at her, he muttered, "You can do better than that."

Having such a good time for the first time in months, and more than slightly tipsy, she lost herself and without hesitation threw her arms around his neck and kissed him smack on the lips.

He leaned into the kiss and made what she intended to be a quick peck something more. Not much but it was harder, longer and more meaningful. Her head shot back when it was over but he didn't drop his arms.

"That's not fair," she whispered.

"Who said I play fair?" he whispered back.

She became aware that the joviality had left the room and she broke free of Douglas's arms to see Charlie watching her speculatively and Oliver pretending he didn't notice anything.

"Time for bed, we girls have cooking to do tomorrow." Charlie, thankfully, waded into the silence. "Goodnight you two," she said, the couple came forward and hugs were exchanged.

However, Oliver's was strange and when Julia looked up into his hazel eyes she realised Charlie wasn't the only one who was speculating about what she saw.

They walked out together, Charlie and Oliver ahead of Douglas and Julia.

Julia stopped in the hall behind the morning room. She would carry on down the back hall while Douglas and the rest went through the morning room and lounge to get to the stairwell.

The other couple went on and she turned to Douglas. "Goodnight."

He caught her wrist when she started away and pulled her back.

"Don't I get a goodnight kiss?" he asked and his tone, (dare she believe it?) was almost *playful*.

"No," she answered immediately, all of a sudden not in the mood to be playful, all of a sudden sober as a nun and reminded she was *not* treading cautiously.

He chuckled and pulled her closer anyway. Completely ignoring her change of mood and her answer to his question, he dipped his head and swept his lips against hers.

"You're," she couldn't think of what to say, "too much," she finished on a hiss.

"Thank you." His tone was sarcastic and Julia realised that now *his* mood had changed. He inclined his head, dropped her wrist and started to walk away.

She stopped him by calling his name.

At her call, without hesitation, he turned back.

She bit her lip as she watched him, took in a breath through her nostrils and let her lip go on an exhale.

"That comment, earlier tonight, about Sean was uncalled for," she admitted. "I'm sorry, you're nothing like him."

He watched her for a second then repeated, "Thank you," but this time he meant it.

Then, without another word, he walked away.

Julia was in her room, taking off her shoes and trying (with difficulty and not a great deal of success) not to think of the events of the night and just how much she enjoyed them (from start to finish, except, of course, her catty comment) when she heard it. Or, more to the point, since it was nearly always there, *didn't* hear it.

The scratching was gone.

She lifted her head as she dropped the second shoe and looked at the window, the draperies closed on it. She'd only lit the bedside lamp when she entered, not having the energy to light more.

That was when she felt it, the draught at her ankles, and she looked down, pulling her feet up on the bed. She saw the misty fog swirling and then it moved away, where the window scratching always took place and Julia watched the mist in frozen, horrified fascination.

It rose off the floor and she stared as it took form, swirling around as it shaped itself slowly into the body of a beautiful, young woman dressed in a flowing, empire waist gown, its misty, shredded ends streaming round her like they were alive.

Julia stared in open-mouthed terror when the ghost said something, her mouth moving but nothing coming out. Julia found herself leaning forward as if to hear and then without warning, the spectre shot forward, right toward Julia.

Julia let out a frightened, muted scream but she wasted no time. She leapt off the bed and ran to the door. Yanking it open, she tore down the hall and only when she was well into the dining room did she allow herself to look back to see... nothing.

But it was too late, she'd looked behind her so she wasn't looking where she was going and she slammed straight into a solid barrier. A *human* barrier. A human barrier that grunted in surprise. A human barrier whose arms came around her like vices.

They both fell to the (thankfully thickly carpeted) dining room floor. He on his back with nothing to break his fall, Julia right on top of him.

She pulled herself up, one hand on the floor, the other on his chest and saw through the darkness it was Douglas.

"What the hell... are you... doing?" he asked, his voice winded and irate.

"A ghost. I saw the ghost of The Mistress. In my room!" She was lying fully on top of him but she was looking back over her shoulder.

She felt hands grab her waist tightly and she was flipped expertly on her back, this time Douglas on top.

"What are you doing?" she cried hysterically from her new, unexpected position.

"I need to... *breathe*," he forced out and took a deep breath and then a second one. "You knocked the wind out of me and your weight wasn't helping."

"I saw the ghost of The Mistress," Julia repeated, looking up into his shadowed face and ignoring his justified complaints because, well... there a haunting was afoot!

"There is no ghost of The Mistress, it's just a myth," Douglas replied calmly, his breath returned to normal.

"I saw her," Julia snapped in the face of his calm, slapping his bicep with her hand to express her annoyance (and also anxiety). "She formed from a mist, right in my room!"

He looked over his shoulder then back at her. "No ghost and no mist," he declared.

Tentatively, Julia lifted her head to look over his shoulder, grabbing them both with her hands for leverage. Like Douglas, she saw nothing.

"I swear I saw her," she whispered unsteadily, lowering her back to the ground.

"You're drunk."

"I am not drunk!" she hissed (even though she kind of was) as she let go of his shoulders and slapped his bicep again.

"The Mistress doesn't show herself anyway. She's always just there."

Her eyes rounded at his words. "You know about this? The draughts, the whispers... the screams?" she asked him, her tone accusatory, as it bloody well should be.

"Of course, I've lived here all my life," Douglas answered. "I've never seen it, felt it or heard it but I know about it."

Julia gasped then snapped, "That first night I was here, you made me think I was a crazy person."

"If you believe in ghosts, you *are* a crazy person," he replied.

She started to squirm out from under him but he pulled her back.

"Let me up," she demanded.

He hesitated only a moment then knifed away from her, lithely got to his feet and bent over, grabbed her hand and pulled her effortlessly to her own.

"I take back my apology," she informed him angrily. "You're a jerk."

She couldn't see his smile but she heard it in his voice. "And you're mad."

"I know what I saw," she told him haughtily.

"Would you like to show me?"

"I can't go back there!" Her voice was edgy with fear and she didn't care one whit. "Maybe she's waiting."

"You could come with me to my room," he suggested smoothly. "The inn's full tonight, but I have a big bed, plenty of room for the both of us."

"You're impossible," she hissed in return.

"And you're adorable," he replied instantly, his tone warm and teasing.

Julia gaped because Douglas Ashton had just called her *adorable*.

Not to mention Douglas playful *and* warm *and* teasing, all in one night? It was too much to take. And, try as she might, she couldn't stop the warm tingles that his easy, sweet compliment gave her.

"Fine, I'll go back," she announced and walked by him, deciding her best bet was to ignore the whole thing but when he didn't move she turned back and demanded, "Well? Are you coming?"

"Are you inviting me to your room?" he returned.

"Of course, you have to make sure it's safe."

"Protect you from a ghost?" he asked incredulously and she was certain, even though she couldn't see it, he'd raised that damned brow.

"Yes!"

He regarded her for a moment then chuckled but did not move.

She sighed angrily.

"Well?" she prompted.

He hesitated only briefly.

"Lead on fair damsel," Douglas muttered, Julia saw his shadowed arm gesture for her to move forward and she was too frightened to utter another angry rejoinder. She walked on and, at her door, she stopped.

"You go first," she whispered.

He spared her a glance then walked through and surveyed the room while she stayed at the door.

"No ghosts," he called to her.

"Did you check by the window?" she called back.

"Julia," he replied with patience that was strained but in an amused way, "there are no ghosts in your room."

She walked in hesitantly and when she saw the room was clear of spooky spectres, she moved around in order to turn on every light she could all the while he watched her. She was trembling and edgy and expected to see the apparition at any moment.

When she got near Douglas, he caught her arm with his hand to stop her and he dipped his head to look closely at her.

"You really are frightened," he stated softly.

"I told you!" she cried. "I saw it! She was standing... floating... forming, whatever! Right over there!" Julia pointed at the corner. "And what's more, The Master scratches at the window every night. I hear him and I saw *him* once too."

"Who told you this story?" Douglas asked, his voice and face now beginning to betray anger.

"No one, I saw him and heard him and felt her. I asked Mrs. K..." She stopped when his head tipped back and his eyes moved to the ceiling.

After a few seconds, his gaze locked on hers. "Mrs. Kilpatrick told Tamsin these stories too when she was a little girl. Tamsin believed them all her life, just like you do now."

"Well, Tamsin didn't tell *me*. Neither did you. But I saw or felt them both and I know Ruby does as well and so does Veronika."

"It's an old ghost story. Someone puts it in your mind and you see it."

"So," she stood with hands on her hips, "there was no old baron who died trying to get in this house while his wife was locked inside and mysteriously strangled?"

"That story is true," he admitted.

"See!" Julia threw up her arms, dislodging his hand.

When it was clear she wasn't going to listen to him or calm down, he grabbed her and pulled her into the safety and warmth of his strong arms and, Julia had to admit, she felt exactly that. Warmth and safety. *Intense* warmth and safety.

Oh dear.

"Julia, listen to me," Douglas ordered quietly when she automatically relaxed in his arms. "You're safe here. Nothing is going to happen to you."

She stared into his eyes and they were so serious and so grave, she believed him.

"Promise?" she asked on a whisper, sounding childish but she didn't care because, bottom line, *she'd just seen a ghost!* Douglas nodded and then something occurred to her. "What were you doing in the dining room?"

He smiled and his arms tightened. "Coming to see how sorry you were about your comment earlier this evening,"

It was such an audacious thing to say and do, and the night had been so pleasant, she threw back her head and laughed, then tilted it forward and rested her forehead against his chest. After she caught her breath, she looked at him and noticed he was grinning down at her.

That grin warmed her even more and made her stomach clench pleasantly.

Even so, she informed him, "I'm not *that* sorry."

"I figured not." He was still smiling.

She realised belatedly that this had gone on long enough. She stiffened in his arms, pulled away and said, "I'm okay now, Douglas, you can leave. But... um, thank you."

He didn't try to reach for her again and she fought against a strong sense of disappointment she knew she shouldn't have.

"Are you going to send my electricity bill even higher by sleeping with all these lights on?" he asked.

"Of course not," she lied without remorse.

He stared at her a moment and nodded again.

Then he carried on with his unusual sweet Douglas behaviour which meant his hand came up and he cupped the back of her head. Bringing her forward, he kissed her forehead. It was a strange and, she had to admit, gorgeously intimate gesture that made her feel something deeper than warmth. It was sweeter and it was also very, very frightening.

Then he walked away and she had to fight again to tamp down more disappointment as she watched him go.

The door closed behind him and she was forced to acknowledge, against her better judgement, even if it was only in her own mind, that she had a wonderful evening that night (apart from the ghost, of course) and Douglas had contributed to that wonderful evening, more than a little.

She washed her face, slathered on her moisturiser, put on stretchy pair of black pyjama bottoms and a plum-coloured tank top and slid into bed, keeping every light burning.

She was just settling down with her book when her door opened and she jumped a mile.

It was Douglas.

"What on earth do you think you're doing?" she cried, pulling her covers up to her neck.

He still had on his deep tan corduroys and black turtleneck and he lifted his book to show her as he went around the room, turning off all the lights but the floor lamp in the turret.

She watched as he settled in one of the chairs there, rested his feet on the ottoman, opened his book and, eyes on the pages, he murmured, "Go to sleep, Julia."

She stared at him dumbfounded because he knew she was frightened and, in knowing, did something about it.

Julia felt her stomach clench, again not unpleasantly, as she watched Douglas read.

Then, not one to look a gift horse in the mouth, she set aside her own book, cuddled into the pillows and, for once, did exactly as he commanded.

❦   12   ❧

THANKSGIVING

Douglas felt the smart, strategic thing to do was leave her room before she woke.

What he wanted to do was take off his clothes and join her in bed.

He didn't often ignore his instincts when it came to strategy thus, as hard as it was, sometime after he heard her breath even, he turned out the light and sought his own bed.

He didn't, however, do this before he silently approached her and watched her sleep. Pulling her heavy, soft hair away from her face to bear witness to the fact that Julia was just as beautiful unconscious as she was when she was conscious. *Then* he turned out the light and went to his rooms.

Breakfast, they had been told in advance, was the beginning of the festival of food that Thanksgiving Thursday would be. Julia was up and in the kitchens by the time he finished his morning run and arrived at the breakfast table, Oliver, Sam, Monique and Ruby already there. Just as he was taking his seat at the head of the table, Charlie wandered in from the kitchen, looking harassed, wearing an apron and sporting a smudge of flour on her face as she announced, "The girl is a lunatic. The entire Black Watch couldn't eat all that food."

Just then, Veronika shooed in a tired Lizzie and Will while Mrs.

Kilpatrick and Julia brought in stacks of pancakes, platters of scrambled eggs, bacon and sausages, hash browns, jugs of syrup and, in the middle of the table, Julia set down an enormous coffee cake.

"Dig in, folks," Julia announced, taking what had naturally, over the weeks, become her place at Douglas's left side while Monique sat across from her on his right (the table was far too long for Douglas to take the head and Monique to take the foot).

Douglas saw his mother stare at all the food in disgust but everyone tore into it like they'd been starved for months, especially the children.

"Tell us the story of Thanksgiving, Auntie Jewel."

This, Douglas heard with surprise, came from Lizzie.

He'd taken special care with Lizzie, not because *he* wanted to, but because Julia wished it. It wasn't the easiest task he'd undertaken, facing the grieving twelve year old image of his sister, the sister who, at that age (especially at that age) was the only one who fought his losing corner.

But Lizzie had responded to him immediately and he found she was not at all like his cheerful, bright-eyed, romantic sister.

The depth of pain and feeling in her eyes matched what he saw in her aunt's and *that* he found, albeit contradictorily, was far easier to handle.

Furthermore, he came to the uneasy realisation that he enjoyed her response and, watching the despair that clung to her like an aura slowly disappear, further was pleased to know he had a hand in it.

"The true Thanksgiving story is hogwash," Julia told the stunned table. "Something about pilgrims and Indians and bounty. I don't know. It's all perverse considering the pilgrims most likely murdered the Indians after supper."

Monique gasped in outraged horror (something she seemed to be doing a lot lately and, Douglas thought cynically, had nearly perfected). Ruby, however, giggled excitedly. Will muttered, "Wicked," not at his aunt's words but that she was so blunt at telling the truth and, more than likely, outraging his grandmother for whom, Douglas had grown to understand, none of the children cared much (and he didn't blame them).

"Thanksgiving is just a day to be thankful, for your family, your friends, who..." Julia went on, turning to Charlotte, "are the family you choose for yourself." Julia took in the table at large and continued. "The food is just celebration. This afternoon, when we get dinner," she told the children, "you'll all need to think of something you're thankful for and if you feel like it, you can tell the whole table."

"I know what I'm thankful for!" Ruby shouted.

"I know I'd be thankful if you'd quit shouting," Lizzie pit in and at that, Julia turned her startled, pleased eyes to Douglas.

When she did, he felt his chest tightening at her bright-eyed look and he had to stop himself from touching her flushed cheek. The scene which would ensue from a gesture such as that as witnessed by Monique would kill the moment and, Douglas found, he very much liked the moment.

Further, he didn't want the children aware of his plans until Julia had firmly agreed to them. He'd promised Julia that.

Tearing his gaze away from Julia, Douglas saw Ruby poke her tongue out and Lizzie.

"Not at the table, Ruby," Douglas warned automatically, sounding to his own ears like the doting but strict father-figure.

Before he could react to this unwelcome thought, however, Julia shot him another pleased look, her green eyes melting from bright to tender. His chest constricted further and he used every ounce of willpower to ignore it even as he noticed Charlotte give Oliver a meaningful look and Sam hiding her grin by shoving a fork full of coffee cake in her mouth.

"Sorry Unka Douglas but can I say what I'm thankful for?" Ruby asked politely, at a decibel level that was still loud but didn't shake the windows.

"Please do," he invited.

She screwed her face up with her big announcement and then broke out into a crooked smile, "I forget!"

Everyone burst out laughing and Douglas watched Julia. The exhaustion that had been etching her features since she arrived was gone, the light was back in her eyes. Her glance fluttered to his yet again but this time she turned away and busied herself with filling her plate.

"We're not eating again until three or four so you better fill up now," Julia told the crowd, acting the kind and efficient hostess and making Monique's dark expression turn black.

Julia didn't have to encourage anyone, all plates were piled high, except Monique, who had a small bit of eggs and a rasher of bacon.

Regardless of her expression, Monique was being uncharacteristically well-behaved and Douglas didn't trust it. She had something up her sleeve and Douglas was keen to give Julia her Thanksgiving weekend. Having friends and family around her seemed to delight and relax her and he planned to take best advantage of that.

Last night, he'd seen a serious thawing of the icy reserve Julia had been showing him since he announced his intentions.

He still couldn't credit the moment when she'd leaned over him, her breasts brushing his back, and blew in his ear. He'd nearly grabbed her, thrown her over his shoulder and carried her to his bed like a caveman.

He'd never had such an acute and uncontrolled reaction before, *to anything*, much less a woman.

He knew she was more than slightly inebriated at the time but he had never worried too much about the ethics of his tactics, just as long as, in the end, he got what he wanted.

However, unfortunately, he knew it was too soon and Julia would have been furious at such an action perpetrated in front of Charlotte and Oliver, so he kept control of himself, but only just barely.

And Douglas was more and more determined to get what he wanted, for a variety of reasons.

In a short time, Julia had a remarkable effect on everything around her and thus everything around *him*.

Sommersgate itself had changed. It was more welcoming than he'd ever felt it. The staff were more cheerful, even smiling openly to each other, Julia, the children and even him (they were still dour-faced and smile-less when Monique made an appearance). Last night, entertaining friends, the house felt normal. Although he'd never really known normal but he knew that Sommersgate felt no longer cold and forbidding but instead warm and even welcoming.

Douglas cleared these thoughts. He'd never believed what many of the staff, local myth, and even Tamsin thought as the house having its own personality.

What he did believe was that Julia thought that she had truly seen a ghost last night. As hilariously adorable as she was in her fright (and she was, indeed, adorable), it was clear she believed thoroughly in the myth that shrouded Sommersgate. To Douglas's way of thinking, this was only to his fortune. He was pleased she saw The Mistress last night and hoped the ghost would return and drive her, again, straight into his arms.

He just hoped the next time she ran into him, they were closer to *his* bed.

The breakfast manfully consumed with still enough left over for another group of their size to eat until they were satiated, everyone filed away from the table. Sam and Charlie headed to the kitchen and Oliver and Douglas were off to the stables when Douglas saw Carter.

Monique was drifting toward the morning room and Julia was seeing to the children when Douglas called out to the man.

"The shrubbery around Miss Fair..." he stopped himself and thought of how the staff addressed her less formally, "Miss Julia's windows needs cutting back. Please see to it."

Carter simply nodded but Douglas caught the look of disdain on Monique's face and the look of pleasure on Julia's.

Everyone but the women spent the day pleasantly occupied however they saw fit. After breakfast, the children followed Oliver and Douglas to the stables, they all saddled horses and took a morning ride, Ruby seated in front of Douglas, Willie and Lizzie on their own mounts.

When they returned, the children came and went from the kitchen. Charlie and Sam would emerge for a rest but Julia was firmly entrenched in her cooking and Douglas didn't see her the entire day.

At three, Veronika moved through the house timidly to tell people that supper would be served in forty-five minutes. At the allotted time, Douglas and Oliver met Charlotte at the bottom of the stairwell. Charlotte had changed from casual clothes into a fetching black dress.

"Did it really take you three and Veronika *and* Mrs. K to make Thanksgiving dinner?" Oliver asked his wife after he'd kissed her cheek.

"No, but we didn't make *a* Thanksgiving dinner, we made *two* Thanksgiving dinners," Charlotte answered.

"For God's sake, why?" Oliver breathed, likely still recovering from the breakfast orgy.

"Julia made one for the staff. While we sit down to eat the one Mrs. K and Ronnie made for us, they'll sit down and eat one Julia and the rest of us made for them. 'No one,'" Charlotte drawled in a husky, American accent, teasingly mimicking Julia's voice, "'Misses out on Thanksgiving.'"

Charlotte turned her face to Douglas to see how he'd react to this news but he kept his expression bland. He knew his friends were speculating about Julia and himself but he had no idea if Charlotte would be an ally or an enemy. She knew too much of his history, especially with women, and she'd formed a close bond with Julia in a short time. He had decided to tread carefully with her.

Douglas, did, however, have a reaction. Nearly all of his friends growing up had servants and many of them had long-standing staff who had effectively become members of their family. Monique and Maxwell Ashton did *not* share this affectionate bent. Although Douglas himself had never known a time when Mr. and Mrs. Kilpatrick had not been in his life, he knew nothing about them and never asked, first because it wouldn't have been allowed by his parents and then as pure habit. Yet in a matter of weeks, Julia had made deep inroads into entrenching his servants into the family unit.

No more was said as, just then, the children clamoured down the stairwell followed by Julia who was walking beside Sam, both of them laughing at something.

At the sight of her, Douglas took a swift intake of breath.

Julia was wearing a soft, cream, knit sweater dress that covered nearly every inch of flesh, from its deep, cowl-neck all the way down to her wrists with the figure-skimming skirt swinging gracefully around her ankles. It didn't matter that it covered every bit of her. Everywhere, the material fit snugly, lovingly accentuating every lush curve. She'd fastened a gold, link belt tantalisingly low on her hips and had dozens of golden bangles on both her wrists. And her feet were encased in a pair of tan cowboy boots.

"You might not want to ogle my new best friend," Charlotte hissed in a playfully irate voice and Douglas, unusually, started. He swiftly shuttered his blatant reaction, his head swung to his friend but he saw Charlie was admonishing Oliver who turned sheepish eyes to his wife.

As Julia and Sam made it to the bottom of the stairwell, the children already rushing to the dining room, Douglas moved forward, intent on one thing.

Dinner may get cold and his careful strategy might be damned but he was going to slip her somewhere so he could privately show her exactly how much he liked her dress. Privately and thoroughly, until she was in no doubt about his particularly strong, insistent feelings about that... *fucking*... dress.

Julia lifted her eyes to his and Douglas saw hers became startled as she read his unconcealed intent and, at that moment, with her green eyes on him, that dress on her, he didn't give a good goddamn that she could read him so easily.

However, just then there was a bustle of activity down the hall and Monique came gliding out of the library.

"How delightful, my friend is just in time. Now, another Thanksgiving tradition, a family reunion."

Douglas ignored his mother but Julia's eyes followed Monique.

He arrived at her side and bent to whisper in her ear, "If I may have a private word before dinner?"

"What?" she asked distractedly, not looking at him, but instead she continued gazing down the hall and he saw her face pale as she breathed, "Oh."

Douglas followed her eyes and saw what made her pale. In confusion, he stared at a tall, familiar-looking man with greying blond hair and faded blue eyes.

Then he heard Julia whisper, "My God, it's my Dad."

At her words, Douglas's vision exploded in a white-hot blaze of fury.

❧ ❧ ❧

Monique was escorting into the stairwell, and fawning over, Dr. Trevor Fairfax, Julia's father.

Dear Lord in heaven, Julia thought and then she felt the room reel and she was almost certain she was going to faint even though she'd never done such a ridiculous thing in her entire life.

"I didn't want to say anything because Dr. Fairfax didn't know if he could make it but here he is! Isn't this an extraordinary surprise? A family reunion!" Monique announced with malevolent delight.

The room was still spinning and in a desperate effort to steady herself, Julia focused on Douglas. Looking at him from under her lashes, she saw to her distracted surprise that he was staring at her father, not blandly, but thin-lipped, his scar frighteningly defined and a muscle worked angrily in his hard jaw.

Monique continued with her announcement and Julia swung her dazed eyes to the woman. "I know, Julia, that this will be a big surprise for you. But I *do* hope it's a welcome one. I've had many heartfelt conversations with your father, who was understandably upset about Gavin, and, of course, that no one saw fit to invite him to his own son's funeral."

At any other time Julia would have laughed out loud at the thought of the heartless Monique having a heartfelt *anything*.

However nothing at that moment was even the slightest bit funny.

She didn't even dignify Monique's second pronouncement with a thought. Of course her father hadn't been invited to Gavin's funeral. It was Trevor Fairfax's choice not to be a part of their lives. Julia herself hadn't seen her father since her college graduation when he handed her a tiny cardboard box that held a pair of earrings made of paste and some metal that turned green within a few weeks. He had walked away from her then, feeling his duty done, and she'd never seen or heard from him again.

And she liked it that way.

"Julia." Her father came forward, his smooth, cultured voice, grating across her skin like sandpaper. His blue eyes, eyes so much like Gavin's, moved over her face with worried care. To her disbelief, he pulled her rapidly stiffening body into his arms. "I was so sorry to hear about Gavin."

"Children!" Monique called and Julia jumped while still suffering her father's embrace. "We have a surprise for you."

Julia uttered a panicked noise and her father released her, his hands on her shoulders slid down to hold her firmly by her upper arms. They had to look, for all intents and purposes, like the happily reunited father and daughter and this thought made Julia want to scream.

For some reason she could not fathom, her eyes searched for Douglas, but he was no longer at her side. She didn't want the kids to be involved in this, yet somehow in those vital seconds, she had been rendered speechless.

Sam, Oliver and Charlie were staring at the scene openly, obviously bemused by this highly-charged turn in the so recently convivial state of affairs.

The children had entered the room and were watching in silent confusion. Before Julia could pull herself together, she realised Douglas had moved toward them.

"Lizzie, take your brother and sister into the kitchen." His deep voice ordered then Julia saw Mrs. K bustle up the long room. "Mrs. Kilpatrick, please take the children to the kitchen."

"What's happening?" Mrs. K, who normally would not say a word in response to any command of Douglas's (except "Yes, Lord Ashton"), took one look at Julia's stricken face and her own became a mask of concern.

Julia finally found her voice.

"Please," she implored and Mrs. K became all business. She quickly hustled the children out, pulling the dining room doors closed behind her.

Julia heard Ruby's shout, "Who's that man?" and Julia's eyes closed in despair as she pulled herself free of her father's hands.

"Julia, my dear, I know this is a surprise. I was stunned to get your mother's letter telling me what happened to Gavin. So young, so full of life." Her father was speaking to her and when she opened her eyes, she couldn't meet his, couldn't get a handle on her careening thoughts. His words were so inane, the kind of thing you'd say about someone you didn't know.

But then, he *didn't* know Gavin.

She caught Monique in her line of vision, the other woman's face alight with vicious glee while she stood taking in the scene. After fifteen years, Monique knew that Trevor Fairfax had no place in his first family's life and still she contacted him, invited him there, *on Thanksgiving.*

Julia's bewildered panic began to give way to anger. She felt rather than saw Douglas position himself behind her, *very close* behind her. So close, she could feel the heat from his body. For some reason, this emboldened her.

"So full of life?" she whispered, as if to herself, emotions surging through her and she lifted her eyes to her father's. Gavin would have likely looked like him, if he'd been given a few more decades, and that thought drove away all vestiges of panic and replaced them with blinding fury.

The likes of Trevor Fairfax, who could cheat on his wife and turn his back on his children, rarely seeing them, never paying child support, never giving them a kind word or a loving touch, could live happily into his sixties. But a good man like Gavin, who was full of love and fun and enjoyed life to its fullest, didn't even make it to forty years of age.

At that thought, Julia's rage exploded.

"How do you know what he was full of?" she snapped. "You hadn't seen him in fifteen years, hadn't sent a single Christmas card, hadn't looked upon his children or ever met his beautiful wife! He could have been dying of cancer at the time of the accident, brought low with diabetes, had his legs crushed in a freak accident involving a tree," she declared wildly, her voice rising.

She felt Douglas's hand touch the small of her back and feeling it there gave her even more courage.

"What are you doing here?" she demanded hotly.

"Julia, I don't think..." Monique started a reprimand but surprisingly it was Trevor who interrupted her.

With a look at his audience, his eyes showing nothing but polite irritation at her outburst, the very soul of the patient father, Trevor asked, "Perhaps we can have some privacy?"

"Yes, perhaps we should *all* go to the kitchen," Charlotte offered quietly from somewhere behind Julia.

"*No!*" Julia cried, panicked, wanting her friends around her, feeling she couldn't face this loathsome man alone, not without Patricia there, *not* without Gavin there. Tears began to fill her eyes, tears she resolutely refused to shed.

Douglas moved even closer. "Oliver, please take the women into the dining room and begin the meal." His voice rumbled, so close, it sent vibrations down her back and her head twisted, her eyes flying to his.

Don't leave me, she silently begged.

Douglas spared her only a glance before he said, "We'll go into the library."

She saw that Douglas's eyes were blank, gone was the anger she had seen in his face earlier, gone was the teasing man she was with last night. Now, it was pure Douglas, unaffected and calm.

Even in the face of that, she felt a sense of relief that he said the word, "we".

The others bustled quickly into the dining room, closing the door behind them as Douglas swung out his arm toward the library, cordially inviting them to move forward, the picture of the gracious host.

Trevor hesitated. "Could I speak with my daughter alone?"

Without hesitation, Douglas said simply, "No."

It was said in his usual authoritative tone that brooked no argument. After uttering that one word, Douglas pressed his hand into Julia's back, gently forcing her forward before she could see her father's response and before her father could respond at all.

She preceded both men into the room, Douglas stopping considerately to allow Trevor to go in front of him and then turning to close the doors behind him.

Julia walked to the ceiling-high windows and surveyed the gardens. Although she knew in their full bloom they could be beautiful, now the formal and regimented beds had been put to sleep for the winter. They were nothing but borders and large circles of overturned dirt with enormous empty urns in the middle surrounded by still-green lawns. They were terraced with magnificent balustrades that led into a small, natural wooded area that gave way to graceful rolling fields where chocolate-faced, round, woolly sheep grazed. The sun was already beginning to set on this beautiful pastoral scene and the day, whose weather had veered from hazy to bright, was fading.

Julia saw none of that, her mind turning in circles and she had begun to shake.

She was shaking because her father was there, pretending to feel a grief there was no way on God's green earth he could feel.

She was shaking because she knew Monique hated her enough to do this to her, on a special day, a *holiday*, for goodness sakes. It was never pleasant to acknowledge that someone hated you that much, especially someone with whom you were forced to live.

And she was shaking because even if Douglas was with her (and she was thankful that he was and she wasn't going to try to process why, she just was), she still felt somehow alone. Thousands of miles away from her wise and dramatic mother who would know exactly what to say. And forever away from her beloved brother who would have known exactly what to do.

And she was just Julia, the weakest of the lot, and she wasn't sure she had the strength to face this.

"Julia, you must know, regardless of our estrangement, it came as a great shock –" her father began but she turned and levelled her gaze at him, the look in her eye causing him to stop speaking.

He'd walked into the room and was standing not five feet from her, his face earnest, his eyes warm.

Her lip curled.

"Estrangement?" she broke in, her voice shaking. "What a convenient word. I thought it was called 'abandonment'."

Trevor's head jerked in response as if she'd physically struck a blow.

"Of course," Julia continued, ignoring her father, anger spurring her on. She turned her attention from her father to Douglas, who was standing with his shoulders against the doors and his arms crossed on his chest, regarding her with that bland expression on his face. "I may not have full command of the English language. *I* was born in a small town in Indiana to a mother whose parents were farmers, as were their parents before them. We're just simple folk." Her eyes swung back to her father. "*I* was not born to privilege. *My* mother was not heiress to a popcorn fortune who came complete with a trust fund, a five bedroom mansion and a fourth generation membership to the country club. *My* father was, of course, a well-known surgeon but *I* never saw him. He didn't send *me* to private school and violin lessons and pay for college and graduate school. So perhaps *I* have it wrong. I suppose the genteel way is to refer to it as 'estrangement' but where I come from, we call 'em as we see 'em and we'd call it *'abandonment'*." Her eyes swung back to Douglas. "What do you think, Douglas?"

"Julia, is this really necessary?" her father asked before Douglas could answer (not that he was going to answer). "I came to make amends, when things like this happen, you realise –"

It was then Julia completely lost control, her vision exploding into fireworks of fury. Her fists clenched and her body tensed from the top of her head to the tips of her toes.

She leaned forward stiffly from the waist and hissed, "Make amends? You can *never* make amends. Even if I was to spend the next fifteen years telling you, you will never know what a good man your son was. You will never have the chance to meet the glorious woman he chose for his bride. You will never have her joy and light shine down on you. You're too late."

"I know that, Julia," Trevor replied, his voice conciliatory. He began to walk forward and she threw her arm up to fend him off. It registered somewhere in her brain that Douglas had pushed away from the doors when father started to approach daughter but Julia was too overcome to think about what that meant.

"So now, because I have a little bit of my brother in me, I'm going to let you have Thanksgiving dinner with your grandchildren. Not for your sake, but for theirs," Julia went on. "Their parents just died and I don't want anything disturbing what, up until now, was perhaps their first lovely day in months. And afterwards, you're going to go back to your wife and family and never darken our door again."

At the mention of his second family, his face grew pale and his carefully controlled expression faltered.

"Felicia's left me, Julia." His voice cracked on this admission and instead of Julia feeling an ounce of compassion, which she saw his eyes beseeching her for, it all became blazingly clear why he was there.

If his wife had left him then now *he* was alone, only now would he come back into her life. Not of his own accord, but because, perhaps, he had no one else.

She didn't care. She could not believe his selfishness, it took her breath away. But he wasn't finished.

"My children, they're all…" He didn't complete that thought and she didn't wonder at it. None of her half sisters or brother had ever made any advances to her or Gavin either. "And then I heard about Gavin and I just had to –"

She advanced on him, taking two swift strides and barely registering his wince and recoil at her quick, furious charge. She realised then how old he looked, how faded and defeated, his handsomeness nothing but a memory.

Gavin would have *never* looked like that. *Never.*

She jolted to a halt.

"If you have problems, they're *your* problems. We, Mom, Gavin and I, had problems too but we managed to sort through them without *you!* There was the time when Mom had nineteen cents in the bank and you hadn't paid child support and we had no toilet paper, where were *you* when Gavin had to break open his piggy bank so we could go to the store? There was the time when Gavin won All-County in football and all the other boys stood on the stage with their fathers and Mom had to be at work and my brother had to stand there alone, where were you then?" She hurled every word at him like a spear. "So, now you can take my offer and then you can go away and I swear to all that is holy, if you ever approach my mother, I'll hunt you down and –"

"I believe," Douglas cut in firmly, quieting her with his calm words, "dinner is getting cold. I would imagine the children are missing their aunt and likely becoming concerned." Both father and daughter swung to Douglas who was now standing several feet from the doorway. "If Julia has anything more to say after supper, perhaps she can do so then. Now it's important to get back to the children."

Julia was still shaking but she took a deep breath while she watched Douglas. He looked completely unperturbed at this turn of events and she tried to suck some of his energy from across the room.

"Of course," she agreed with a stiff nod, because he was right, she should be thinking of the children. "Father, would you like to meet your grandchildren?" she inquired, but her tone was barely civil, making these lovely words sound nearly threatening.

He simply nodded, looking back and forth between Douglas and Julia.

She took another breath and motioned with her arm to the door. Trevor started to exit the room and she followed him, her movements jerky. As she passed Douglas, he caught her hand and pulled on it gently to stop her.

"You have to get control of yourself," he told her from between his teeth. "You can't let the children see you like this."

"And how do you propose I do that?" Julia flashed back. *He* may be able to stand cold and controlled in the face of just about anything but *she* wasn't built like that.

Douglas turned.

"Dr. Fairfax," he called to the older man and her father, already in the hall, stopped. "If you'll give me a moment with Julia?"

Trevor looked relieved, obviously believing that he had an ally in Douglas as he had in Monique and therefore he nodded gratefully.

Julia also wondered where Douglas stood on all this drama and decided that it was likely exactly where Douglas always stood, casually removed.

"Please close the doors and wait for us in the hall," Douglas requested. "And please do not approach the children until Julia and I are there to make introductions."

Trevor nodded again before he closed the doors behind him and Douglas pulled Julia back to the windows where his gentle tug on her hand made her halt.

He turned her to face him but didn't let go over her hand.

"I can't believe this is happening," she muttered under her breath, her body still shaking, resolving to worry about Douglas some other time.

"Julia, you lose your temper, you let him see he can affect you and you give him power. You cannot give him power. You need to control yourself," Douglas informed her, like it was as easy as that.

"He *does* have power!" she burst out. "He's my father. He'll always be my father."

It was all too much, losing Gavin and Tammy, losing her old life, playing this game with Douglas and now *this*. She didn't have the strength, never had, Sean had shown her that.

She lifted a hand and raked her fingers with agitation through her hair.

"He's never been your father," Douglas stated and her entire body jerked at his pronouncement, her arm dropping listlessly, because, in his statement's exquisite simplicity, she realised he was right.

She stared at him, stunned with the knowledge shared eloquently, through five little words, that Douglas didn't stand casually removed, not from her but instead, from Dr. Trevor Fairfax. Gone was the fury she'd seen the moment her father entered the hall. Douglas gave Trevor Fairfax nothing and this was because he was *worth* nothing to Douglas except his casual indifference. And telling her this, showing her, Douglas was indicating this was how she should also behave.

The tears she'd pushed back sprang to her eyes. She pulled her hand from his and swung away, putting distance between them as she fought back her emotions and tried to find the strength to follow his lead. She stopped, her back to Douglas and pressed the fingers of both of her hands to her mouth.

Douglas didn't follow her and she used the moment of semi-privacy to battle for control.

"You know, I don't really miss him," Gavin said once when they were talking about their father. "Whenever we had to go to his house for the weekend, I always couldn't wait to get home to Mom."

Tamsin had kissed the top of her husband's head.

"Yeah, Gav," Julia had agreed quietly, "I know."

"I was glad when he stopped coming to pick us up for visits," Gavin had muttered. "It was a relief."

Then Gavin looked up at them and laughed off the sad thoughts he was expressing aloud and the sadder ones that underlay them. Julia never knew if it was actually a relief or if her brother was trying to convince himself. Had he wished he'd had a father? Had he wished he'd not grown up in a house full of women? Had he needed some male guidance?

She'd never asked and now she'd never know. What she *did* know was that Gavin worked every moment of every day to be a good father to his children, a shining example and, furthermore, an excellent, attentive, loving husband to his wife.

For Julia's part, she'd always wanted a Daddy, someone to make her feel like a princess just as she'd witnessed her own father treated his other two daughters. She'd wanted that kind of love and devotion, to be the beautiful darling, the girl who could do no wrong in her Daddy's eyes. And she never gave up hoping for that, hoping that one day he'd be that kind of Dad. And then came the day he gave her the cheap cardboard box filled with cheaper earrings after she had struggled her way through four years of university, working as a tutor, and left with a staggering amount of student loans which he, not once, offered to assist her with. That day, she had given up hope.

She thought about those earrings, which she kept until just over a month ago, finding them when she packed up her house. Before she moved to England she had thrown them in the trash.

Douglas was right, he had *never* been her father.

She straightened her shoulders and drew air into her nostrils, her head tilting back with the effort. She released it from her mouth and turned to Douglas.

Not one tear had been shed.

"I'm ready," she told him, her voice, surprising her, was strong.

He assessed her as she walked toward him but when she went to pass him, he took her hand. They walked together, hand in hand, as if it was the most natural thing in the world. Even though she knew it was weak, knew she shouldn't allow it, she needed his hand in hers. She might not have made it across the room without it.

When he stopped to open the door, he turned to her.

"Well done," he whispered, the indifferent expression gone from his eyes and now clear, undiluted admiration was shining in them.

She felt every bone in her body turn to jelly and it was an immense effort of will simply to stay standing.

She should have nodded casually as if there was no question she could master the situation. But instead the corners of her lips tilted up ever-so-slightly at the look in his eyes that made her stomach clench, not with desire but with pride.

She dipped her head, slightly flustered, and whispered, "Thank you."

She felt Douglas's hand squeeze hers then he opened the door.

❧ ❧ ❧

Five hours later, with a huge dose of Charlie's experienced flair, coupled with Julia's determined grace, a bit of Sam's hilarious energy and even shades of Monique's cultured charm, Thanksgiving Day did not become the disaster for which it seemed to be destined.

The children were hesitantly accepting of their grandfather, although both Elizabeth and William seemed far more reluctant than Ruby, undoubtedly they'd heard their parents talk. They looked constantly at Julia *and* Douglas. Julia would give them reassuring smiles; Douglas took Julia's lead (but not so far as to smile, just communicating non-verbally that all was well).

Trevor acted the benevolent grandfather but seemed to be more interested in dancing attendance upon Monique.

Now, the children in bed, Douglas felt the need for pretence was gone.

He had known his mother was up to something and he resolved to deal with her later. He knew exactly what he intended to do to punish her for today's antics. He would not, however, do it in front of guests.

As for Trevor Fairfax, *that* matter would need to be dealt with immediately.

Julia's words about Gavin needing to smash open his piggy bank so her family could have the bare necessities made his gut clench. And the new knowledge that the proud, easy-going man he knew as his brother-in-law, who showered steady devotion on his family, at one time stood alone on a stage without a parent to support him, made him understand with a clarity he never had before why Tamsin had fallen so deeply in love with her husband. Patricia Fairfax was clearly a remarkable woman to make up for so much and nurture her family the way she did.

Douglas watched Julia and marvelled at her strength of will to control her emotions, to sit in a room and have dinner with her errant father. Douglas found her behaviour stunning.

But now it was high time his soon-to-be wife was allowed to relax and enjoy her fucking holiday.

They were all in the formal drawing room finishing a nightcap. Julia's father seemed happy enough, sitting and conversing and even, Douglas noted to his disgust, discreetly flirting with Monique.

For Julia's sake, Douglas had been nursing a slow burn for five hours and he was coming to the end of his patience with it. It was her father, her issue and he had to allow her to deal with it in her way (with his guidance, of course), even though he very much wanted to eject the man the minute he realised who he was.

But it was her battle. And Julia had, after a valiant struggle, handled it quite splendidly. If she had turned to Douglas and told him to get rid of her father, he would have done so, without hesitation. But she didn't and that too, he thought, was not only her prerogative and it was also honourable.

However, when Monique finally moved away to refresh her drink, Douglas was finished with allowing Julia to have her honourable way.

He strode over to Trevor and said under his breath in a tone that could not be ignored nor misunderstood, "I think, Dr. Fairfax, it's time for you to leave."

Trevor turned astonished eyes to Douglas, clearly having been lulled into relaxing in his very plush surroundings. Even though Julia said barely a dozen words to him since dinner, Monique had been expending a great deal of energy making him feel welcome.

The older man read Douglas's face and was smart enough to nod.

Douglas wasted no time in announcing his guest's imminent departure. Farewells were quickly and not-so-cordially exchanged (Charlotte, Oliver and Sam had correctly surmised Julia and Douglas's mood and behaved accordingly).

Douglas and Julia, joined by Monique, walked Trevor to the front door where Carter (at Douglas's behest) had been waiting with the Bentley for the last half an hour. When Douglas ordered Carter to the front, Carter informed him that Trevor arrived in a taxi. Where Trevor now was going, Douglas neither knew nor cared.

Monique gave him a fond good-bye, pleased that it seemed she'd gotten away with her spitefulness. Julia just stood with her arms crossed on her chest and didn't say a word.

Douglas, tone and manner civil, shook the man's hand and then said in a cordial voice, "Just so we understand about this evening, Dr. Fairfax, you are not to return to this house or approach Julia, the children or Patricia unless one of them expresses the desire to communicate with you."

Unnerved by Douglas's belying manner and words, Trevor blinked and stammered, "I... I –"

Douglas released his hand.

Monique, of course, was *not* at a loss for words. "Douglas! How could you? Trevor and I have, these past weeks, formed a lovely friendship." She turned to Trevor. "If *I* wish to see you, you are always welcome at Sommers –"

Douglas didn't allow her to finish.

"If you invite him into my house without Julia's consent, you will find yourself no longer living in it," he stated inflexibly.

It was Monique's turn to stammer, this time not in astonishment but in outrage and Douglas heard Julia's surprised gasp.

Douglas ignored his mother and Julia and turned back to Trevor. "Did I make myself understood?"

Douglas didn't wait for his answer and began to walk away, offering his arm to Julia who walked forward woodenly, her face partially in shadows, her breath shallow. She placed her hand in the crook his elbow and he tucked it firmly in his side.

Julia didn't offer her father a good-bye.

"Sir," Carter called, "I thought you'd like to know, a somewhat urgent call came about five minutes ago. I explained you'd ring him back."

Douglas felt his irritation escalate. *Now* was exactly not the time for this. He needed to talk to Julia, he wished to see if she was all right. He certainly didn't need to leave her alone with his mother, and then, of course, there were the children to consider

His eyes met Carter's.

Fucking hell. He would have to have a word with Mrs. Kilpatrick.

His mind moving swiftly through the problems this new turn of events caused, he strode by Carter but said over his shoulder, "I'll phone him immediately."

Julia seemed oblivious to the entire exchange.

When they arrived inside the hall, leaving Monique to make her apologies or explanations to Trevor, Douglas closed the heavy door behind them.

When he finally caught sight of Julia's face in the lights of the hall, he felt his breath catch. Her eyes were shining with gratitude. Gratitude he would have liked very much to have the time to translate into something else.

She licked her lips and came forward, placing her hand on his chest, she leaned close to him.

"Thank you," she whispered for the second time that day and the strength of feeling underlying her tone was his undoing.

He pulled her roughly in his arms and pressed a hard kiss on her lips, catching her gasp against his mouth. His body immediately responded, beginning to tense, his hands on the soft material of her dress itching for more of her, the smell of her scent (she'd worn the one he preferred that day) surrounding him.

For his own sanity, he let her go just as abruptly as he grabbed hold of her.

She stood swaying gently, her eyes blinking at him and he settled his hands on either side of her jaw and moved in as close as he dared in an effort to retain control.

"I have to go, something important, I don't know when I'll be back," he told her.

She blinked again. "Okay," she muttered, drawing out the "O" dazedly.

He felt a smile come to his face at the bedazzled look in her eye, inordinately pleased that he could do that with one kiss.

As a reward and against his better judgement, he gave her another one, pulling her forward using gentle pressure on her face. Their bodies didn't touch, just their lips and their tongues. He spent longer on her, used more care, teasing her, tasting her, feeling his blood stir, his already tense body tightening hungrily.

The moment he heard the sexy little moan he was getting used to, the one that came from the back of her throat that heralded the moment she would give in and move to deepen the kiss, he forced himself to let her go.

And without looking back, he walked away.

13

THE INCIDENT

Mrs. K put the finishing touches on the grocery list that included the ingredients for a bakewell tart, an apple crumble and a variety of other bits and pieces that she would have made for her own children if she and Roddy had ever decided to have any. Sommersgate House had always been their child, hers the house and her husband's the grounds. As it turned out, there wouldn't have been time for anyone else.

She heard her before she saw Julia come in the back split farm door to the kitchen, a way that Tamsin had sometimes used, Douglas never used and Julia nearly always used. She was wearing a pair of slate grey pants, a pale, dusky-blue blouse with feminine tucks down the front and a winter-white tailored blazer. The finishing touch was a pair of navy pumps with a big silver oval affixed to the toe and a heel that was dangerous in two ways, it was way too high and it was way too thin. Miss Julia strode in like she was wearing slippers.

"Hey Mrs. K," she greeted with a small wave of her slim black brief-case and a bright smile.

"How was work?" Mrs. K asked and Miss Julia threw herself at a bench at the table while Mrs. K flipped the switch on the kettle.

"That place is a mess!" Julia answered with contradictory delight in her tone. "But the staff is great and dedicated and I think we can turn it around. Where's Ruby-girl?"

"Veronika's taken her to the petting zoo. Coffee?"

"I'd kill for some coffee," Julia replied, a grateful smile on her face.

Mrs. K returned her smile. Mrs. K hadn't smiled so much in a very long time, in fact, never, and she knew exactly why.

Before he left after what Miss Julia cheekily described as "The Thanksgiving Fiasco", Lord Ashton had given the edict to all the staff that orders were now to be taken from Miss Julia. Miss Julia, he stated firmly, had the running of the house. This not only came from Lord Ashton's lips, he'd even scrawled a note to confirm his wishes in writing. Upon seeing it, Lady Ashton's face had turned white as a sheet, her lips thinning to invisibility. She said not a word, left the room and shortly after, left the house to go to Kensington.

For her part, Miss Julia looked rather stunned and, fighting for composure, simply said, "I figure, Mrs. K, you know what you're doing so you probably should just get on with doing it."

And with that, everything had changed. Mrs. K never had the full run of the house and she was having the time of her life.

Mrs. K almost felt like finding the awful woman she'd worked for most of her life and thanking her for bringing Julia's dreadful father (Julia had, of course, confided the whole story to Mrs. K and Ronnie over coffee) back on the scene. Her actions had triggered a great deal of change, or, Mrs. K had to admit, had solidified the changes that were already taking place. Also, with Monique gone, to Mrs. K's way of thinking, things could finally progress a lot more smoothly in another quarter if Lord Ashton would just come home.

She was a little surprised at the turn of events. Mrs. K thought that it would be Julia who had to win over Douglas but it appeared that it was happening the other way around. This made Mrs. K's hope blossom as she knew Douglas Ashton always won, no matter what he attempted.

After Thanksgiving, Lady Ashton left first thing in the morning, Carter stuffing her and the seven Louis Vuitton cases (that Veronika methodically packed) in the Bentley. Even after all these years, Mrs. Kilpatrick didn't mind seeing her go. That woman had never been very nice to her staff or to her children. To Mrs. K's way of thinking, she deserved everything she got, especially for orchestrating that nasty turn with Miss Julia and Gavin's father.

Charlotte, Sam and Julia went out shopping with Ruby, Oliver went out on the rounds with Roddy and Lizzie and Willie went back to school and nary a word was said about Lady Ashton or Dr. Fairfax. Though everyone was far more relaxed and at ease. Sam, Charlotte and Oliver finally left on Sunday morning after spending a lovely weekend at Sommersgate.

Monday arrived and Miss Julia went in to Bristol to start her new job. She was supposed to work Monday through Thursday from ten o'clock until two. But she didn't arrive home until well after three even though it was only a fifteen minute drive to Bristol. Mrs. K glanced at the clock, it was nearly four and the children would soon be home.

"Anything exciting happen today?" Julia asked as the kettle burbled.

Mrs. K wanted to tell her that everything exciting had happened that day because nothing had happened without Lady Ashton to please. Mrs. K felt a sense of such deep relief, she didn't exactly know how to handle it. She did not keep an eye out for every speck of dust, every slight smudge on window, mirror or the sheen on the banisters or tables. She didn't have a pile of laundry to inspect to make certain they were fresh smelling and stain and wrinkle free. She didn't have to mentally calculate every calorie in every dish she was making. And she didn't have to calm Veronika's nerves every time she saw the girl, who was also adjusting to this new feeling at Sommersgate with rapid ease.

All they had to look forward to was Miss Julia's smiling face coming in the backdoor, a quick gossip over a fresh cuppa, the children's rushing about when they got home and the rest of the time nothing but peace.

Even the house seemed to be settling into this new regime. The days were getting shorter but at Sommersgate the evening shadows were receding. The weather was becoming chill but in the house the draughts and cold were disappearing. In the evening, when it always seemed so dark, in the house, the edge was off the night. Shadows lost their menace. Rather than seeming alive and frightful, as they always had done, they just became shadows of this piece of furniture or that shape of a tree hit by the moonlight.

Even The Master and The Mistress had been silent. Not even Ruby saw or felt them anymore, Mrs. K knew because she'd asked the girl.

"No, nothing exciting," she answered and Carter walked in just then with a nod and grabbed the grocery list and one of Mrs. K's homemade scones. "Make it quick, I want to get that crumble ready for tea."

"Aye, aye, captain," Carter grumbled but he did it genially while Mrs. K poured the water into the freshly ground coffee in the cafetière.

"I was reading about The Master and Mistress last night," Julia told her as she got up to grab mugs, sugar bowl, teaspoons and the jug of milk out of the fridge. "There are a couple books about the Barony in the library and in one, there's quite a bit about them."

Mrs. K pressed down the cafetière.

"Learn anything?" she asked as she sat down at the bench across the table from Julia, something she'd done every day this week so far, something she'd never have done, ever, with Douglas or Monique Ashton. But then, both of them rarely came into the kitchen.

"Their names, Archibald or 'Archie' as he was known and get this..." she paused for effect, "Ruby! I bet that's why Tamsin named Ruby-girl that."

Mrs. K nodded, looking fondly at the other woman's glowing face. "It's likely. Miss Tamsin was taken with that story, always was from the first moment she saw The Master and felt his lady."

Julia took a sip of her coffee. "Did you know there are portraits of the two of them amongst the others in the stairwell?"

Mrs. K leaned forward in a small rush of excitement because she *didn't* know. In all her years there, she'd never had the time to go sorting through the Sommersgate library (nor did she wish to get caught) to find information about the ghosts.

"Which ones?" she asked.

"Come on, I'll show you," Julia invited conspiratorially, grabbed her mug, they went out to the stairway, walked up to the landing and Julia pointed, "Those two."

Mrs. K stared at two paintings she'd seen nearly all her life, even twice, in that time, had ordered taken down and cleaned.

They stood alone, the only portraits on the wall at the landing, while all the other walls were stuffed full of them, higgledy-piggledy arranged to get as many in the space allowed. They were also the grandest of them all, twice as big as any other painting. The man stood tall, looking a bit like Douglas, or at least he had a similar way about him even if the features were only a touch the same. The woman was dark-haired, fair skinned and lovely. He looked arrogant and haughty. She looked, as Mrs. K always thought, happy. She had a bit of what Mrs. K thought of as a Mona Lisa smile, as if she was content and had a secret.

"That portrait, according to one of the books, was finished only two weeks before her death," Julia mentioned, indicating Lady Ruby Ashton's portrait. "She doesn't look like a woman who had an unhappy marriage, do you think?"

Mrs. K considered it. "I always thought, of all these portraits with their grim faces that she looked the happiest."

At that point, Mrs. K and Julia could talk no more as the kids rushed through loudly, their voices ringing happily through the halls. Another change that Mrs. K welcomed but also caused great relief for it said the children too were adjusting to the changes Julia Fairfax was causing and, Lord knew, those beautiful children needed, finally, to adjust.

It was time for their homework and for her to start dinner and hopefully a quick apple crumble.

But later, when she walked around to put the house to bed, Mrs. K found Julia again on the landing looking up at Lady Ruby with a wondering gaze.

❧ ❧ ❧

Julia sat at her writing desk going through her lists. Or, she was supposed to be going through her lists, but instead, she was thinking about *him*.

He'd done it again, left without a word or warning and now it had been a week since Douglas left.

This time, however, he'd called. Just once, but he'd called. Last night, when the kids were asleep, Ronnie and Mrs. K gone, the phone rang.

For a second, she didn't know what to do. She was told by Mrs. K

195

that the staff answered the phone unless it was in the study. In the study, no one touched it except Douglas. There was a complicated system of inter-comming via the phone, which meant you had to memorise which number rang to which person (which meant the phone rang everywhere with a specific ring that the member of staff knew meant them) or room. One was Mrs. K, two Carter, three rang only in the kitchen, four was Veronika and it went on.

Patricia always phoned when the kids were awake and not out at one of their scheduled classes so she could talk to them as well, so if it was her mother, it was an emergency.

Late Thanksgiving evening, her mother had the full briefing about Trevor Fairfax and Monique (not to mention Douglas's actions, which elicited a "You're *joking!* Well, well, who knew the boy had it in him?" and Julia thought only Patricia Fairfax would refer to Lord Douglas Ashton as "the boy"). Patricia had made her usual threats of arriving at Sommersgate House imminently to save the day and had been talked down by Julia at the last minute.

If it wasn't Patricia, then who would be calling, Julia couldn't imagine and how she should answer the phone, she didn't know.

She was in her room, the phone on her writing desk (which could be called by dialling number nine) ringing insistently. She grabbed it nervously and said, "Sommersgate House," as she suspected the staff would do.

"Julia?" It was Douglas.

She felt a rush of warmth in her belly at the sound of his deep voice and just stopped from letting out a little, happy sigh.

Then she shook some sense into herself. What was wrong with her? For goodness sake, he'd just said her name!

She tried to make her voice sound detached when she replied, "Douglas. Where are you?"

She assessed her tone and thought it sounded aloof and was somewhat pleased with it.

"How are the children?" He, she noticed, didn't answer her question.

"Fine, in bed, asleep. It's late, is something wrong?" It wasn't late, it was nine thirty but she was trying to strike a mood.

There was noise in the background, people talking, just one or two and then they were muffled. When the muffling was gone, she could hear no more voices.

"Nothing wrong," he replied belatedly and didn't deign to explain the delay in answer.

"Then why are you calling?"

"Did you start your consultancy?"

She wanted to growl with frustration. Again, he didn't answer her.

"Yes, I did –" Before she could finish, he went on.

"How is it?"

"It's good, fine. They're in a pretty serious muddle but we think we can pull them through without any loss of staff," she answered, trying to be short and to the point but really she wanted to talk about it. In fact, she was dying to talk about it. It was something entirely different than what she was used to doing and even though it was all familiar, everything was new. It was like starting from the beginning but instead of it being frustrating, it was a fascinating challenge and she was loving every minute of it.

But she didn't tell him that (as much as she wanted to), instead she said, "I'm fine, the children are fine, the house is fine, everything is fine. When are you coming home?"

There was another pause, this one felt heavy with meaning but she couldn't put her finger on what that meaning was.

"Home?" he asked and his voice was strangely husky.

Julia reacted to the strange tone in his voice and queried, "Are you all right?" And she couldn't, even though she wanted to, completely hide the concern.

"No," he answered, to her surprise and further to her surprise, continued. "I'm shattered and things aren't going well here."

"Is there..." she didn't know why she said what she did, but she felt compelled at this unprecedented sharing of feelings and his announcement of being "shattered". The very idea of Douglas shattered was incomprehensible. "Anything I can do?"

Again, he didn't answer her question. "I'll be back sometime during the weekend."

"Okay," was the only way she could think to reply.

"Sleep well," he bid in a strangely gentle and equally strangely sweet, low tone and then he rang off without letting her say a word. Julia had stared at the receiver in her hand and only then became aware that her legs were trembling.

But that was then, and now it was the next night, much, much later than nine thirty and Julia was making lists. Tomorrow she wasn't supposed to go to work but she'd been looking through the charity's budgets for the last few years and she'd hit on a few places they could cut back so she thought she'd go in for a couple of hours. She was also making lists of Christmas presents she wanted to buy. And she was also delaying when she would go to sleep because to sleep was to dream and to dream was to dream of Douglas and she didn't want to dream of Douglas anymore because she liked it too much.

She'd never dreamed so much in her life. Before Sommersgate, she would have the odd nightmare or wake up with a strange feeling and vaguely remember some images. Every once in awhile she'd recall dreaming of disjointed events that made no sense but weren't entirely unpleasant.

But now her dreams were vivid and they were always about Douglas. Not things that had happened, not memories, but fantasy scenarios. Full-blown, romantic-movie-type fantasy scenarios that were ridiculous in the extreme but, at the same time, very much *not*.

Douglas walking toward her smiling, lifting her off her feet and whirling her around with his face in her neck whispering words she never could really hear. Or chasing her through the house, but not threateningly, playfully. She'd always be running from him, throwing smiles over her shoulder and laughing right before he caught her and pushed her against the wall and kissed her until she was dazed and shaking.

And then there were the ones where they were in bed. After those, Julia would wake up smouldering, her breath uneven, her body tingling.

She should let it go and enjoy it, since she wouldn't allow herself to enjoy it in real life. It didn't hurt to dream. But it was different, dreaming about movie stars or daydreaming about attractive acquaintances you know you'd never make any advances to, they were safe, because you didn't live with them or see them all the time.

Dreaming about Douglas wasn't safe. It was very *unsafe* because she could get mixed up, she could allow her defences to go down and then where would she be?

And where *would* she be? Married to a man who didn't love her, who said she could just move on when Ruby was gone, just... like... that. A man who could have any woman he wanted and would most likely go looking for them once he tired of Julia. He said there would be fidelity but she'd known him long enough (and she knew men-at-large well enough) to know that wasn't likely. And why did he want Julia in the first place? It just didn't make sense.

The problem was, she was beginning to *like* him. She was seeing things about him that she thought were funny or sweet or kind or (the worst) damned sexy.

Douglas and all these things (except the last) were incomprehensible.

She shook her head again. She could like him but if she found herself sleeping with him, married to him, *attached* to him, then he could find his way into her heart and break it and she was simply not going to let that happen. Not again.

She had been glad, at first, that Douglas was gone. Her defences had gone down and she'd allowed herself to enjoy his presence a bit too much. Now she had time to get them back up again and she felt strong enough for him to come home. She would allow herself to like him, even for them to become friends, but the rest, well, the rest she had to put a stop to it.

It was on that thought that she heard the scratching and her head shot up.

The Master was back!

He'd been gone for days, no scratching, no nothing. Mrs. K said that even Ruby had not seen him. The Mistress also seemed to disappear. Mrs. K, Ronnie and Julia had spent some time that day over coffee speculating about this absence, deciding Sommersgate itself felt more settled with Monique gone. But now, the scratching had returned.

She got up from the desk and wondered if he'd show himself, wondered if he'd come through the glass at her, wondered what he'd do if she said, "Archie, don't be a naughty boy, just go away."

She tentatively pulled back the draperies and looked for the spectre.

No shimmering Archie but, instead, there were headlights in the drive and what she could see with some alarm through the darkness were two men. One short and he was helping a stumbling tall one towards the front door, a tall man who looked, she peered closely, her nose nearly pressed against the glass, exactly like Douglas.

Feeling a sense of unexplained urgency, she turned around and fled her room. She met them in the long entry hall that led to the stairwell and what she saw through the darkness cut only by a small side lamp on a table made her skid to a halt.

Douglas was lurching awkwardly and had his arm around the short man who was holding him up. The other man's arm was held out straight in front of him, pointing *a gun... at Julia.*

Her heart skipped a frantic beat and she threw her hands up in a reflex response that was the universal sign language for *Don't shoot!*

"It's okay, Nick," Douglas muttered, "she's my wife."

"You're *what?*" the man asked, his head jerking around to look at Douglas as he dropped his gun arm.

"I'm not his wife!" Julia cried.

"You're going to be," Douglas returned.

"No... I... am... *not,*" Julia retorted.

"He's delirious," the man named Nick put in.

"*I'll* say he's delirious!" Julia responded.

Nick decided their bizarre discussion was at an end. "No, woman, I mean, he's really delirious. He's been shot."

Julia gasped, her heart skipping eleven frantic beats and then seemingly shuddering to a halt.

"Be quiet," Nick warned. "I need to get him up to his room without being seen or heard."

They were moving forward and she noticed that Douglas's left arm was hanging limply at his side.

It was at this time she also noticed the wet looking stain on his coat.

Julia's hand flew to her mouth, her heart kick started to drill in her chest as her eyes darted around the hall.

"My room," she stated urgently, thinking quickly and Nick looked at her mutely. "You'll wake the children. They can't see him like this, take him to my room. It's out of the way." Then she ordered, "Follow me."

She started ahead but obviously Nick hesitated because she heard Douglas's deep voice say, "Follow her."

They got Douglas to her room and Julia ran to the draperies she left open, closing them as Nick deposited Douglas on her bed.

She hustled to the bathroom and grabbed every towel she could see then back and saw Douglas gingerly stripping off a black, long-sleeved t-shirt. Nick already had Douglas's overcoat off and had thrown it on the floor.

She saw the blood on his back, the bullet hole below his shoulder and rushed forward.

"Holy crap," she whispered.

"That doesn't sound too bad," Douglas noted sardonically. "I would say this was at least a 'fucking hell' moment.

"Don't joke!" Julia snapped. "How on earth did you get shot?"

Nick and Douglas looked at each other as Julia began obsessively to lay towel after towel on the pillows as if their smoothed absorbing layer would make the difference and all would become right again in the world. She then pushed Douglas back against them gently, handing him a clean hand towel to press against the wound.

Neither man, she noted, answered.

She decided to let that go and announced, "I'm calling the police."

Douglas caught her arm in a surprisingly firm, almost painful grip.

"No police," he declared implacably.

"No police?" Julia asked, feeling her brows shoot up. "But you've been shot!"

"No police," Douglas repeated.

"Listen, the doc is coming to fix him up," Nick put in. "We'll be okay now, can you go and find somewhere else to sleep?"

"Sleep?" she asked incredulously, like she'd just walk out on this scene and lay herself down on some fluffy pillows and calmly go to sleep. Was he *mad?*

She looked in Douglas's eyes and then her gaze dropped down to his wound. There was blood all over his chest... his very well-muscled chest, she noted vaguely. But the wound looked like it was no longer bleeding.

"We need to make sure he doesn't lose any more blood," Julia tried to pretend like she knew what she was doing, which she most certainly did *not*. "When's the doctor coming?" she demanded to know from Nick.

"Girl, you need to leave this to me," Nick returned, obviously losing patience.

She stood up to her full height, which, in bare feet, was five foot nine, at least two inches taller than him.

"When, I asked you," she stated, her voice straining for calm and authoritative (and she felt she didn't do half-badly), "is the doctor going to be here?"

Nick glanced at Douglas and Julia followed his gaze.

Douglas was lounging against the towel covered pillows holding the hand towel pressed firmly against the wound. He looked for all the world as if he was watching an only slightly entertaining play. When it became apparent that something was required of him, he just shrugged his good shoulder and Nick started to say something but Julia whirled on Douglas.

"You have two choices, Douglas Ashton," she told him sharply, her temper flaring out-of-control. "Your first choice is to tell me when I can expect a doctor to arrive and your second choice is that I will first phone the police and second phone my mother so she can tell me how to treat you. You are not going to quietly bleed to death on my bed!"

"Calm yourself, Julia, I'm fine. It's a flesh wound," Douglas returned.

"It's a fucking gunshot wound!" she shouted.

"Calm yourself!" Douglas roared in a voice she'd never heard before. He reared up and then gritted his teeth in pain and Julia stepped back, partially in fear, partially in surprise.

She'd seen his face of thunder and been awed and, maybe, a little thrilled by it. But that roar was something else. It was the roar of a man that expected to be obeyed, who was *entitled* to be obeyed and who didn't, wouldn't, maybe even *couldn't* abide it when he wasn't. It was his right, not only by birth and by accumulation but also because, she sensed, he'd earned it.

She took a deep breath and considered his ridiculous command to calm herself when he was lying on her bed bleeding from a gunshot wound. Regardless of his title, station or whatever else, she decided to ignore it. And it took every ounce of courage she possessed because this man, who could go from bland and unmoved to seductive lover to roaring aristocrat to dangerous, predatory deity, scared the living daylights out of her.

Still, none of that changed the fact that Douglas was *bleeding* from a *gunshot wound* on her *bed.*

"Nick, go get the whisky from his study and the first aid kit that's in the kitchen," Julia ordered and when Nick didn't move she whirled on him. "Go!"

Nick glanced at Douglas who obviously gave him the go ahead because Nick left the room.

"Lay back, relax, when he gets back, I'll, well, I don't know what I'll do but I'll figure out something," she told Douglas.

Douglas was watching her and she watched him right back, steeling herself against his glittering, intense eyes whose depths she couldn't read.

Obviously unable to win one of his staring contests, she finally asked, "Are you in pain?"

"Not when I don't move."

"Then don't move."

"Good advice."

Julia stopped staring at him and started glaring at him and Douglas just accepted her glare. Nick arrived back and just to do something, she grabbed the whisky decanter and gave it to Douglas.

"Drink," Julia commanded and Douglas gratefully lifted the decanter to his lips.

"Doesn't alcohol thin the blood?" Nick asked.

Like lightning, Julia jumped forward and snatched the decanter from Douglas's grasp.

"Get her out of here, Nick, before I kill her," Douglas said through gritted teeth, his angry eyes gleaming darkly at her.

"I'm not going anywhere," Julia boldly declared and cut her eyes to Nick who was advancing on her. "You touch me, I'll scream bloody murder. Just try me."

Nick stopped.

Douglas sighed.

"I'm cleaning the wound," Julia announced into the void.

"Well, Doug, that sounds like a good idea, doesn't it?" Nick asked, sounding like he was trying to placate a wounded beast so he could draw out a thorn. She'd never heard anyone but Tamsin call him Doug and she wondered who this Nick character was. He looked rough and, regardless of his height, he looked like a man you wouldn't mess with. Lastly, he was also obviously trusted implicitly by Douglas.

Douglas didn't reply.

She searched through the first aid kit and found only minuscule cleansing wipes that were smaller by half than your average handi-wipe.

"What," she turned slowly and showed the wipe to the men, "am I supposed to do with *this?*" Without waiting for an answer, she turned back to the kit, rifling through it. "Don't you have any rubbing alcohol, any hydrogen peroxide? This kit is a joke."

"She's trying to kill me, Nick. She wants me dead so she can take the children back to America."

Julia whirled around "Rubbing alcohol won't kill..." but she stopped when Douglas's head shot up.

"Doctor," Douglas muttered and Nick immediately left the room to fetch the doctor.

Julia and Douglas surveyed each other like opponents on a battlefield.

Julia broke the silence. "Douglas, is there something you want to share with me?"

"Not now, Julia."

"I'll tell you something for nothing," she said, her anger taking over her nerves and making her lapse into the Midwestern twang her mother tried for years to breed out of them. "If you die, I'm going to kill you."

To her shock, her idiotic threat made him grin. What he thought was worth grinning about in this grim situation, she could not imagine. Furthermore, she had to steal herself against just how devilishly sexy his damn grins made him, gunshot wounds or not. Before she could respond to the wickedly handsome look on his face, the doctor was at the door.

Julia watched as he inspected the wound then looked up and spoke to Nick and Julia.

"One of you stay to help me, the other one, leave us."

"I'll do it," Julia immediately offered.

"No!" both Douglas and Nick shouted.

"You're outvoted, luv," the doctor said kindly and Julia, without a fight so the doctor could see to Douglas without delay, left.

Instead of going toward the house, where the kids might hear or see her, she went to the chapel.

The chapel, as it was unused nearly all the time, was unheated. She hadn't put on her robe or slippers and only had on a pair of thin, knit, mint green, drawstring pyjama bottoms and matching lace-trimmed camisole.

She paced through the darkness to keep herself warm and she counted to keep her mind busy. She did *not* want to think of what her life had become. She did *not* want to list in her mind the many reasons her life had descended into sheer, unadulterated madness.

But as the minutes ticked by, her control slipped and she started listing. She couldn't help it, it was habit.

There was Monique, the Super Bitch, out there somewhere, Julia knew, conniving to make Julia's life a living hell. There was Douglas, lying on her bed with a gunshot wound in his shoulder. That same Douglas who wanted her to marry him for what had to be nefarious reasons and kept kissing her for no reason at all. There were the ghosts of separated lovers haunting this creepy old house. Then there was the house itself, spooky beyond belief and…

"Doc's done," Nick said from behind her, making her jump.

She rushed through the chapel, down the hall and back into her room.

Douglas was lounging back on her pillows and the bloody towels, shirt and overcoat had disappeared. His chest was cleaned of blood and his shoulder was wrapped expertly in bandages.

"Are you his intended?" the doctor asked her.

"What?" she forced her gaze away from Douglas who had his eyes closed and seemed to be sleeping.

"His intended? He said you were getting married," the doctor explained.

Thinking that he may not tell her important information if she said no, she said, "Yes."

Douglas's eyes opened and he grinned again.

She wanted to stamp her foot in frustration but she forced herself to turn calmly to the doctor. "How is he?"

"He's fine. Didn't hit anything major and went clean through. I'll want to have a scan of it tomorrow but he needs rest tonight. No moving the shoulder. I've given him something for the pain." He looked at Douglas. "I'll see you tomorrow."

He clasped his case closed and Nick left with him.

Julia stared down at Douglas suddenly deflated and overcome with relief that everything was going to be okay. *Not* relieved that he'd shown up in the middle of the night with a gunshot wound, a wound which somehow didn't send him into shock and a wound which he would not allow her to phone the police to report, but *that* particular discussion would have to wait for tomorrow.

"Well, now that I know you're okay, I'll go upstairs and sleep," she announced.

"Why don't you sleep here?" Douglas suggested, his voice slightly slurred making her think the painkiller was working.

"As comfortable as that chaise lounge is, I don't want to sleep on it." She was grabbing her slippers and robe but she heard him pat the bed.

"No, not there, here." He was watching her, his eyes half-shut and she had to admit, he looked unbelievably sexy. He had a *very* nice chest, well-defined abs and she just noticed the snug black jeans...

She tore her gaze away. "I'll find a bed upstairs, there're plenty."

"No," Douglas returned. "Mother keeps them unmade. Doesn't like the sheets gathering dust. Only made up for guests. The children will hear you if you make up a bed."

"Then you stay down here and I'll sleep in *your* bed."

His eyes went from half-shut to fully-open, regarding her sharply. "Julia, you don't sleep in that bed until I'm in it with you."

Her stomach flipped at his words, his tone *and* his look.

To hide her fluster, she said with false bravado, "Well, at this point,

I'm not entirely certain what you'll do about it considering the... shape... you're..."

She trailed off as he stood up and stalked, absolutely *stalked*, toward her.

He didn't stop until he was towering over her.

"If I have to, I'll open this wound and carry you back down, or join you up there. Your choice."

She stood there, stunned.

"I'll find a couch," she offered.

"Julia, I'm tired, I've been shot, for Christ's sake, just get into the bed."

"Why?" she asked shakily.

"Because I want you to. Because I need something warm and soft and alive beside me tonight. Something that smells good and feels good. After what I've seen..." he stopped when her eyes widened in curiosity at his words. It was then the shutters closed over his features, he gave up and turned away from her. "Forget it, find your couch."

She stood there and stared at him as he fell back on her bed and closed his eyes.

And she couldn't help but wonder, what exactly *had* he seen? What on earth could make Douglas Ashton's renowned composure slip?

Pulling herself from her thoughts, Julia went around turning off the lights and making up her mind (or making up excuses, depending on how you looked at it).

It wouldn't hurt, just tonight; he'd had a painkiller which *eventually* should kick in.

And he'd been shot, for goodness sake.

And he needed human companionship and gone so far as to admit it. She couldn't say no as she knew exactly how that felt.

She decided tomorrow she could go back to being aloof and unaffected by him.

Tonight, she was going to give Douglas what he wanted.

Just this once.

She climbed into bed cautiously and no sooner had she begun to lay back, his arm shot out and pulled her closer.

Then he hissed, "Bloody hell, your hands are like ice."

Hastily she explained, "I was in the chapel, I didn't want to children to hear me pacing. It was cold."

"Get under the covers," he ordered and she jumped out of bed as he rolled off the other side. He carefully took off his boots as she ran to put on a pair of socks so her feet wouldn't freeze him, returned and got under the covers where he already was.

Just as before, the minute she lay her body down, he pulled it towards him. The way they were laying she had no choice but to rest one hand on his chest and her cheek on his good shoulder. She felt his muscles tense at the coldness of her hands but he said nothing.

She felt like a fool.

"I'm sorry my hands are cold," she whispered.

He made a noise that sounded a lot like a grunt.

Then, silence.

She tried to relax and couldn't.

So she asked, "Where's Nick?"

Another grunt and no further reply so she assumed Nick wasn't coming back.

She waited another moment.

"Who *is* Nick, by the way?" she inquired, not able to stop herself.

"Julia, if you don't shut up, I'll be forced to shut you up and although I have a feeling we both would very much enjoy what I have in mind, it might cause me to bleed to death. So, I'm asking you please, just be quiet and go to sleep."

"Okay," she relented, too terrified to say anything else.

"And don't be scared of me," he demanded in that tone that again said he expected her to obey even though his demand was impossibly ridiculous.

"Okay," she repeated meekly, trying to get him to relax as she could tell by the muscles flexing under her hands that he wasn't. "Goodnight. I'm glad you're okay," she whispered.

At that, he pulled her closer.

And, much sooner than she ever expected, she fell into a dreamless sleep.

14

FIRE AND ICE

Douglas awoke in an empty bed, moving his head to the side to see Julia was gone. He looked at the clock and it was seven forty-five. The children would have left for school and he was wondering where the hell she was when he heard the shower.

He felt his body involuntarily relax.

The painkiller hadn't started working until after Julia had fallen asleep. He could tell when she finally dropped off and the tenseness went out of her body, the weight of her settling against his side.

He very much enjoyed that feeling.

He awoke sometime in the night to feel that Julia had settled in quite well. The freezing cold hand she'd laid tentatively on his chest was now a warm arm that draped across his abdomen. Her face was snuggled deeper into his shoulder and she'd crooked her leg, the knee settled just under his groin, her calf falling between his legs. Her body was remarkably warm in sleep and he found her heat strangely comforting.

Hearing the shower stop, he tested his shoulder cautiously and winced at the pain. He should get up and leave but none of the staff knew he was home and he didn't relish exiting Julia's room first thing in the morning, bare-chested and wrapped in bandages.

She strode into the room wearing her long, lilac cashmere robe and wrapped around her hair was a towel that had obviously been confiscated from another bathroom. Douglas's mother was particular about the colour coordination of towels and Julia had used all of hers on him last night.

She walked straight to the desk, the front of the robe parting to accommodate her stride showing a shapely length of leg. She hadn't noticed he was awake so he took advantage of this opportunity to observe her.

Douglas watched as she stood by the desk and reached down. He could tell by her movements that she was using the touchpad on her laptop and was clicking through something. She stopped, leaned over the screen to have a better look and smiled softly. He felt his chest tighten at the smile, an instantaneous reaction the cause of which he felt it best to ignore.

One of the many reactions he'd been having to Julia lately that he felt it best to ignore.

She sat down to give whatever it was her attention, crossing her legs to the side of the desk and the robe fell away, exposing them fully to his gaze. Her fingers flew over the keyboard with astonishing speed but before she was finished the handle on the door rattled. He watched her head shoot up then she exited the chair and flew across the room.

She caught the door as it was opening and whispered, "Ronnie..."

Douglas heard his maid murmuring and Julia responded quietly, "I got up a little late... didn't get a shower before breakfast. I'm sorry, can you come back later? I'll find you, okay?"

He heard the affirmative noise from Veronika, Julia closed the door and turned toward the bed. He saw her head peeping around the draperies and closed his eyes, feigning sleep. When he heard her move off, he opened them again.

He watched her stroll down the hall of her dressing room. She sorted through some drawers and he saw her pull out a wisp of white.

This was when any chivalrous man would either close his eyes or let her know he was awake.

Douglas, however, was not the kind of man to let chivalry stand in the way of seizing an opportunity.

She bent down to step into her underwear, her back to him, the robe hiding anything but a brief flash of leg, which, Douglas thought, was damned disappointing.

At that point, he found himself tiring of the game and wanting her attention instead. He rolled cautiously out of bed, walked silently across the room and stood in the doorway to her dressing room, leaning his good shoulder against the door jam.

"Good morning, Julia."

She let out a small, stifled scream and whirled around, her hand flying to the opening of her robe.

"You're awake," she noted the obvious.

He crossed his arms on his chest and winced. She noticed his grimace and came forward.

"How are you feeling?" she asked gently, her eyes were on his bandages.

How *was* he feeling?

That was an excellent question.

His shoulder was burning with pain but that he could handle.

His feelings about last night were quite a bit different.

She'd been extraordinary. Throughout her performance he didn't know whether to order Nick from the room and throw her on the bed or strangle her.

In his life, only one woman had ever even attempted to care for him and that woman was his sister. His mother had never bothered. He'd never had another woman who cared for anything other than his money, his title, the enjoyment he could give them in bed or the number of photographs she could appear in at his side.

While they were growing up, Tamsin had been just like an angry lioness protecting her cub, albeit she was a powerless one.

Last night, he watched Julia do the same, but she wasn't powerless. She was dazzling and formidable, bent on controlling the situation and looking after him, even when she had no idea what she was doing and even when he ordered her not to.

Her behaviour only served to strengthen his resolve to have her as his wife. Outside of that, he wouldn't allow himself to contemplate.

"It hurts like hell," he answered her question.

He watched with no small amount of fascination as her eyes melted and she closed the space between them.

"I'm sorry," she said, her voice low and gentle.

"I'll survive," he told her, his tone just as soft.

She looked in his eyes and hers became startled as realisation dawned that they were sharing a tender moment. Douglas watched, registering a vague sense of disappointment when the guard went up and Julia carefully controlled her features.

"Well, never fear," she stated airily, the moment lost, she was moving back into the dressing room and waving her arm for emphasis, "Carter had a quiet little chat with me this morning and apparently your friend Nick called him. You have a doctor's appointment today at nine. Carter is going to bring some clothes down for you and he'll be taking you."

She stopped abruptly and turned around slowly, the melting look in her eyes now long gone. She glanced around the room, down at herself and then up at him.

"You seem bright-eyed this morning," she commented warily.

"I've been awake for ten minutes." He watched her eyes widen in angry amazement. "Maybe fifteen," he allowed.

She stood there a moment, shocked speechless and then she smiled.

"You cad!" she cried, her voice filled with humour.

Her unusual word choice almost made him smile.

"Cad?" he asked.

"Yes, 'cad'," she replied. "I'm practising not cursing. I don't want to pass any foul words to the children."

She pulled the towel off her head and whipped her hair around while she grabbed her comb. He found her reaction to his spying on her while she put on her underwear bizarre in the extreme.

"You aren't angry." It was a statement, rather than a question and she turned to him.

Then she looked in the mirror as she pulled the comb firmly through her hair.

"Oh, yes, Douglas Ashton, I'm angry. Although I find I can't make room to be even angrier at you now that you've taken the liberty to spy on me while I put on panties. I'm already angry enough that, when you arrived home last night, not only had you been shot but your companion was pointing a gun at me." Julia's eyes moved from her reflection to Douglas. "Not that I would mind nocturnal visits from gunshot victims or having firearms mistakenly levelled at me in dark hallways…" she paused, straightened and skewered him with a look, "if I lived in some war-torn, third-world country and you were a rebel fighting for our freedom against the nasty federales!"

She took a breath and continued staring at him. He was having some difficulty dealing with the intimate sensation he felt whenever he heard her say the word "home". Not to mention trying to keep his face straight at her dramatic tirade.

When he made no response, she went on.

"So, I hope you'll allow me to vent my anger at today's antics some other time."

"Certainly." He inclined his head, still trying hard not to smile.

At that, she threw her comb at him. He ducked, the quick movement sending a jolt of pain through his shoulder as the comb went flying over his head.

Apparently, she wasn't finished.

"To start, do you want to explain last night?" She put one hand on jutted hip, her eyes flashing.

"No," he responded.

"That's not going to do," she fired back.

"It's going to have to," he replied calmly, because it was the truth. He watched as her eyes blazed. "Julia, there are some things you can't know."

"That's not good enough," she retorted, walking toward him angrily. "In case you don't remember, even though I can't imagine you forgetting because I keep reminding you, but you're also responsible for three other human beings on this earth. Whatever you're doing that puts your life in danger has to stop. They've lost enough; I'm not going to let them lose *you!*"

He watched her eyes flare and she had ended her tirade by using one long, slim finger to poke him painfully in the chest.

She needn't have used her physical exclamation point; he felt each word like a blow. An odd feeling stole over him, a feeling that he vaguely identified as guilt.

Julia continued. "Furthermore, what if one of the children had happened on you last night instead of me? I can imagine the years of therapy that would ensue at having a gun pointed at one of them or seeing their uncle bleeding and delirious."

"I wasn't delirious," he felt it important to point out, although this conversation was beginning to be very uncomfortable, mainly because she was right.

"It doesn't matter! Whatever it is you do with your life now affects the lives of three other people and you can add me to that list because if something happened to you, *I* would be left with *your mother!* And if that, whatever it is, happens to bring danger into this house, I have something to say about it and guns are frankly unacceptable in a house where there are children."

He shifted uncomfortably.

"Point taken," Douglas allowed, staring directly in her eyes and not believing his own words. He wasn't in the habit of *being* wrong, must less admitting he was. Although this wasn't an admission, it was the closest he would get.

She simply kept staring at him like she was a schoolmarm and he was a disobedient student.

"It won't happen again," he bit out.

"See that it doesn't," she demanded and he nearly burst out laughing when she ruined her well-expressed diatribe by whirling dramatically away and searching in vain on her dressing table for something. "Now where's my damned comb?"

"I believe you threw it at me," he informed her helpfully.

She strode back in the direction she came.

"You're not funny," she snapped as she walked by him.

"I'm not trying to be," he replied in all seriousness.

"Good." The word was clipped and he wondered how she'd feel if he kissed her. From the angry line of her back he assessed that wasn't the brightest strategic move at that particular moment. Still, she was magnificent and he longed to do it.

"Who's Nick?" she asked, tearing her retrieved comb through her hair and interrupting his pleasant reverie.

"Nick's a friend."

She eyed him, her brows raised, doing a bloody good impersonation of him.

Douglas decided to elaborate. "Let's just say Nick's a sort of... bodyguard."

"If that's the case, you need a new one," she replied glibly and tramped back into the dressing room.

Sensing his setting-down was complete, he sought to change the subject.

"May I use your phone?" he asked courteously.

"Be my guest, it is *your* phone we're talking about," she replied, obviously not feeling less angry after her rant and Douglas was glad of it. He had to admit he was enjoying this. Julia was deeply amusing when she was in a pique.

He went to the writing desk and picked up the phone, punching in Sam's number. There was a knock at the door and he watched as Julia strode back through, opening it and taking some clothing from Carter. She closed the door and tossed the clothes on the bed before sauntering angrily back into the dressing room. He was enjoying just watching Julia, even if she was angry (in fact, *especially* when she was angry), as he listened to the phone ring. He dropped his eyes and saw the e-mail she'd been writing.

Joe, you're a darling, what would I do without you...

He didn't read any further as he felt his stomach clench and his lips thin in an angry line.

Who the bloody hell was Joe?

Sam answered and he spoke curtly to her, "I'm out of commission for a few days. I'll be in my office at Sommersgate."

"You okay?" Sam asked, her voice filled with concern but he put down the phone on her question and read further.

You can't imagine how much I needed a smile. Things could be better here...

"What are you doing?" Julia asked, back in the room and looking at him in disbelief.

Douglas lifted his eyes to her.

"Who's Joe?" he asked in return.

Her eyes went from his to her computer and they narrowed.

Then Julia flew to the laptop and slammed the top shut before looking back at him and demanding, "Are you reading my e-mail?"

"Who's Joe?" Douglas asked again.

"You're impossible," she announced in a voice that said, eloquently, that she meant it.

It was his turn to raise an eyebrow but he did this instead of throwing the laptop across the room, which was, for some absurd reason, precisely what he wished to do.

"Joe," she started, exuding wounded patience when she realised he wouldn't let it go, "is a friend. An assistant coach for the Indianapolis Colts who was instrumental in getting a number of players to do a fundraiser for us last year."

"And what is he to you?" Douglas asked, his voice very level, so level it had an edge.

"I told you, he's my friend," she retorted.

"What kind of *friend?*" That edge was now dangerous.

Julia threw up her hands in exasperation.

"The kind of friend who helped me offer more scholarship money to students from disadvantaged backgrounds who wanted to be nurses!" she replied, angrily. "The kind of friend who also happens to be married to my best friend from high school, Molly, since he got her pregnant at eighteen when the condom broke. The kind of friend who didn't realise he was in love with his wife and family until their son was diagnosed with leukaemia and I spent six months making lasagne and tuna casseroles for them so they'd remember to eat while their boy had treatment. The kind of friend who paid me back by helping me score a *major* point at work by convincing a bunch of big jocks to use their big hearts to help some aspiring nurses rather than the kids they preferred to raise money for. That kind of friend. Would you like to know more? I don't know his shoe size but I could ask Molly."

Douglas immediately relaxed and then tensed again as he contemplated his reaction.

Julia was staring at him, her expression brooding.

"I don't know what to make of you," she finally admitted.

"I think I've explained quite clearly what you can make of me and what my intentions are of making you. There'll be no 'Joes' in your future," Douglas declared. He knew he was being irrational but he was in no mood to be anything else and, furthermore, he didn't bloody well care.

At that announcement, she gaped at him, a study of angry astonishment, just as there was a tap on the door.

"Yes?" he called as he moved around her and toward his folded clothes on the bed.

Carter looked around the edge of the door.

"Sir?" Carter asked.

"Give me a minute to dress," Douglas ordered and Carter retreated, closing the door.

His hand went to the waistband of his jeans and Julia cried, "You aren't changing in here!"

Douglas carried on with what he was doing because he knew if he didn't get dressed and out of that room he might not be responsible for what he did do.

And this was even more absurd. It had been so long that he'd been in complete control of his thoughts and actions that he found it inconceivable that now, he was not.

Nevertheless, he was not.

She watched him, eyes wide, for only a brief moment before she forced out an exaggerated sigh, stomped to the dressing room and slammed the door.

And he was left with a mental list of things not to think about and not a clue how to get his own bloody shirt on.

❦ ❦ ❦

When Douglas arrived back from his doctor's appointment much later, which had included some minor, on the spot surgery for which he only allowed a local anaesthetic and refused the doctor's demands that he spend the night at hospital for observation, Julia was gone.

"At work," Mrs. Kilpatrick informed him in a nasally voice, her eyes red and running, "she should be back around four." She glanced at his arm in its sling. "Are you... okay, sir?" She sounded ill-at-ease with her own question.

"I'm fine," Douglas started to walk away then turned back. "Are you ill?" he asked and found himself uncomfortable with the personal question. He couldn't remember Mrs. Kilpatrick ever being sick, not, he had to admit, that he would have noticed if she was or was not.

Mrs. Kilpatrick looked stunned at his question.

"Why... no," she said then she belied her words with a succession of three quick sneezes. "Just a head cold," she wheezed when she was done.

Too exhausted to pursue it, Douglas let her be. He wanted to go to his study to catch up on work but was too tired for that as well. Instead, he went to his room, took a painkiller and went to bed.

He woke several hours later feeling slightly better but also acutely feeling the pain in his arm.

And he was hungry.

He walked down the stairs in search of food and heard Julia's voice coming from the lounge. He turned to the right, rounded the corner and saw her standing in the room addressing the children who were all sprawled on the sofas watching television.

"I've asked Mrs. Kilpatrick to go home, she's unwell, so it's Chip Shop Night," she announced.

The room rang with the children's boisterous response to this piece of news and Douglas saw Julia smile.

"Uncle Douglas!" Lizzie called as her eyes found him and her face turned worried when she took in his sling. She got up and then sat back down immediately, visibly unsure of what to do or how to behave.

"Unka Douglas," Ruby shouted. Never unsure of how to behave, his youngest niece ran toward him, hell bent for leather, but Julia caught her about the waist and swung her back.

"Uncle Douglas has been hurt, you must go gently," she warned and Ruby's eyes widened. Douglas watched and noted that Julia was avoiding his gaze.

When Julia let her go, Ruby approached more cautiously and gave his legs a hug. He patted her affectionately on the head in return.

"What happened?" Willie was standing now and his eyes were on the sling. They, too, were worried.

"Nothing," Douglas replied, "It was an..." He was about to say "accident" but stopped himself. "Nothing," he repeated. "I'm fine."

At the children's reactions to his injury, Julia's words of the morning came back to him and so did the feelings of guilt.

Julia spared him a quick (and amusing) "I-told-you-so" glance but Ruby was talking. "Auntie Jewel has the best thing for an owie, don't you Auntie Jewel?"

"What's that, Ruby?" Douglas asked, more out of politeness than curiosity.

"I hurt my elbow," she showed him by jutting out her bent elbow and pointing to a spot that still was a bit pink, "right there and it felt a lot better when Auntie Jewel kissed it. She said her kisses have magical powers."

Julia's face paled and Douglas nearly laughed at her horrified expression.

"I bet they do," he murmured in response to Ruby.

"You should kiss his owie," Ruby declared authoritatively to Julia.

Julia blanched and Douglas grinned.

She recovered quickly. "Maybe later, I've got to get your supper. Orders please," Julia stated, firmly closing the subject on any kissing of Douglas's "owie".

"I'll come with!" Willie offered.

"Me too!" Ruby jumped up and down.

"We'll all go, get your coats," Julia announced as the children scattered.

"Do I get to go too?" Douglas asked as she approached the door. He was standing in its frame and had moved aside to allow the children to race through but he resumed his position when she came near him.

"No, not enough room in the car," she lied. The Range Rover would easily hold them all. He smiled and she gave him a disgruntled look. "Anyway, you should be resting. What did the doctor say?"

"I'm fine," he replied simply and she looked at him closely, narrowing her eyes.

She decided to let it go but he could tell it cost her and he grinned again.

Then she asked, "Do you want something from the chip shop?"

What Douglas wanted was a nice, juicy steak, cooked rare, potatoes dauphenois, asparagus smothered in hollandaise sauce and a huge glass of full-bodied, dry, red wine. Then he wanted to sleep for three days, preferably with Julia's furnace-like body pressed to his side.

What he did not want was fish and chips.

"Yes, of course," he said.

"What do you want?" she asked.

He wasn't sure what to say. He'd never actually been to a chip shop. He figured his choices were either chips or fish and chips.

"Whatever you're having," he answered.

For a moment, Julia regarded him curiously.

She opened her mouth to say something when they both heard Nick's voice. "How you doin', mate?"

Nick was strutting toward them and with some disappointment Douglas had to turn away from Julia toward his friend.

He was tired of telling everyone he was fine so he didn't say anything at all. Nick was used to him and didn't mind not getting a response. What Nick could see was Douglas alive, breathing and standing and that was good enough for him.

"All right, Jules?" Nick asked and Julia gaze moved to him but her brows rose at the familiar use of her name.

Nick had a habit of either shortening someone's name, if he liked them, or giving them a nickname, if he didn't like them, usually something foul. Clearly, somewhere in their short acquaintance, Julia had passed the Nick Test.

Apparently, she accepted his shortened name and his silent offer of camaraderie after the tense night they all shared for she responded, "Yes, all right Nick." Then she looked from Nick to Douglas and back again. Douglas had no idea what was going around in her head but he found he would give half his fortune to gain this knowledge. Fortunately, before he could make that asinine offer, Julia continued speaking. "I'm going to the chip shop. Are you going to be here for awhile?" she asked Nick.

"Don't know," Nick replied, rocking back on his heels and crossing his arms on his chest.

"Well I do, you'll have dinner with us," Julia returned firmly. "What do you want from the chippie?"

The chippie? Douglas thought and glanced at her, suddenly realising she was adapting quite well to her new environment. They didn't have chip shops in America, at least not on every market street as they did in England. If they did, Douglas doubted they called them by the shortened "chippie".

Then he realised she'd pulled off a nice manoeuvre. Company would mean she would have less chance of being alone with him.

This time he only nearly grinned. She was good.

"Battered sausage for me, make that two and don't let them skimp on the chips," Nick ordered, breaking into Douglas's thoughts.

Julia nodded and left and he and Nick watched her walk away. She was wearing a pair of snug-fitting, fawn-coloured corduroys, a skin-tight black turtleneck and her spike-heeled boots. Douglas decided his second most favourite pieces of her wardrobe were her corduroys.

Or maybe it was her boots.

"Phwoar, mate. You can pick 'em. Fire and ice in that one, more fire than ice, lucky for you." Douglas turned to his friend and noticed that he was avidly staring at the space where they'd last seen Julia. Nick looked at Douglas, an approving gleam was in his eyes. "You really going to marry her?"

"Yes," Douglas replied.

"Good luck, mate, that one's gonna be a handful."

"Precisely," Douglas returned and Nick threw his head back and laughed with deep appreciation.

Douglas ignored him. "We need to talk."

There was still mirth in Nick's eyes when he said, "I figured that. Wasn't keen on the events of last night, was she?"

"Not particularly, no."

Douglas walked into the lounge and Nick followed while talking. "Been telling you, since your sister died and those kids came here, that you should quit the work."

Douglas nodded and sat down. Until he was seated he didn't realise how badly he needed to do it.

"You gotta take it easy, mate," Nick noted softly, his words held grave meaning.

"I need you to move into the Gate House. I'll ask Mrs. Kilpatrick to have someone come in and clean it for you. No one's been there in awhile."

Nick nodded, no discussion required, he knew what Douglas was asking.

"One thing, though. You seem determined you're gonna marry her," Nick was back to the subject of Julia, "but she doesn't seem to agree."

Douglas should have told him to mind his own business but he was still tired, hungry and his shoulder ached. He closed his eyes and pinched the bridge of his nose with his thumb and forefinger before, uncharacteristically, he shared.

"She needs a bit of convincing."

Nick whistled. "There's a woman out there who needs to be convinced to marry *you?*" he asked, clearly amazed.

"Apparently."

Nick laughed again before saying, "I like her even more."

And even though he'd never sought anyone's approval, never asked for it, not since he'd given up searching for it from his father, he looked at his friend, who was his "bodyguard", his comrade and his partner-in-crime, and said with feeling, "Good."

❧ ❧ ❧

Chaos ensued when Julia and the children arrived home, the children flying around and setting the table, introductions to Nick were seen to in short order and Lizzie prepared drinks, pouring the men's bitters into chilled beer glasses.

As they settled in, Julia was still dumping fish and chips onto Ruby's plate when Lizzie slid into the seat to Douglas's left, glancing at him under her lashes. This left the seat to his right, the seat relegated to the lady of Sommersgate House, open for Julia. He didn't react to what was, he assumed, his niece's gentle matchmaking but was pleased to find he might have a surprising ally.

When Julia turned to take her seat, she stopped and stared. Lizzie immediately began forking huge pieces of fish into her mouth.

Yes, Douglas thought, *a surprising ally.*

Julia stiffly took the seat to his right, not looking at anyone and also not eating much of her meal.

Douglas found that he liked the food, although it was not a nice steak, it was, at least, filling, in a greasy way. He also liked the company. Julia fell easily into the role of hostess, going out of her way to include Nick and the children in the discussion and making Nick at ease.

Not that Nick wasn't already at ease, in fact, Nick was enjoying himself tremendously. He was also enjoying the children, telling jokes that made them laugh. Julia eventually allowed her stiffness to recede and laughed along with them.

Douglas watched this scene with a sense of fascination, thinking, soon, this scenario, strange to him and something he'd never experienced before, was to be his life. Every night, sitting and talking with the children, laughing, eating. Afterwards there would be… whatever it was that families did after supper.

Then it would be Julia and him, alone, in his bedroom. Julia, perhaps, pulling a brush through her hair and striding around in nothing but her dressing gown.

Later, Julia in his bed, wearing nothing at all.

Something stirred deep within him, something he'd never felt, not once in his entire life. Something that was both alarming and soothing. Something, for his sanity, he firmly set aside.

The kids finished and Douglas allowed them to leave the table, taking all the plates and cutlery to put in the dishwasher. Julia went with them but came back carrying two more cans of bitter and another can of cider for herself.

"You got a job or do you look after the kids?" Nick asked as he popped open his bitter, ignoring the glass and drinking it straight from the can.

Julia had reseated herself, informally folding one leg underneath her on the chair and leaning forward to put her elbow on the table.

She poured her cider while she spoke. "I'm volunteering at a charity in Bristol."

"Yeah? You like it?" Nick asked, genuinely interested.

Douglas watched, now captivated, as Nick's simple question turned on a switch in Julia and she lit up. Forgetting to be stiff and aloof, she started to talk.

"I was a little worried, starting something new. I was at my old job in The States for over a decade, but it's better than I expected, far better..." Her eyes were alight, passion in her words as she carried on.

Douglas sat back and watched her silently while she poured out information that normally would have had Nick nodding in his chair. Instead, her fervour was catching and even Nick found himself making up questions to keep her talking.

And Douglas was struck by two things. First, she was very clever, knowledgeable and accomplished and second, her work wasn't just work, it was a calling and she loved it. There was something extraordinary in that, he'd never met anyone who had truly found their passion.

She seemed to realise she was monopolising the conversation and her eyes slid to her empty cider glass. "I'll shut up now. I've got to be boring you."

"Not at all," Douglas assured her quietly, her gaze flew to him and he had the unflattering impression that she'd forgotten he was even there.

"Okay," she whispered, making a decision and rising. "I've got to get the kids to bed. It's past Ruby's bedtime and she's a bear in the morning if she doesn't have her full night's sleep. Nick, lovely of you to stay." She nodded to a smiling Nick and then she quickly exited the room.

Again, both Nick and Douglas watched her leave and, finally, Nick asked, "Once I'm in your Gate House, can I come to dinner every night?"

Douglas turned to his friend. "No."

Nick chuckled, taking no offense. "Didn't 'spect so. Wouldn't want to share her myself."

Nick left shortly after and Douglas went in search of Julia. She was in the lounge, drawing the draperies.

He stood watching her, liking the way she took care of his home, liking more the way she took care of his friend and even more the way she took care of the children but mostly the way, last night, she took care of him.

When she turned and saw him, she jumped.

"Don't do that," she snapped, but her voice was breathy.

"What?" he asked.

"Sneak up on me," she explained.

"I didn't sneak up on you," he told her truthfully.

"You glide around like a cat, it's bizarre. No man of your size should be so quiet." She walked from the room, sliding by him, giving him as wide a berth as possible and went into the dining room.

Douglas followed her.

"We need to talk," he told her as she gathered all the glasses from the table and turned to go to the kitchen.

"It's late, you need your rest." She walked away, thinking that was that and leaving him where he was. He heard distant rumbles in the kitchen as she tidied.

He thought of his options, made a quick assessment of them and then walked to her room. He turned on the lights and eased himself into the chair in the turret. He was shattered but determined to have this talk, even if Julia was just as determined to avoid it.

She came in not five minutes later and jumped again when she saw him.

"What are you doing here?" Again the breathy snap, this time with wide eyes.

"As I said, we need to talk."

She studied him.

He waited.

"Douglas," she finally said, her tone now beyond weary, "I didn't get enough sleep last night. I'm exhausted, you need to recuperate, let's talk later, okay?"

"No," he replied.

She crossed her arms on her chest, regarded him for another moment and then gave in with ill-grace. "Well then, say what you have to say."

He opened his mouth to begin but she interrupted.

"No, I think I want to go first."

He closed his mouth and lifted a brow.

"I think..." she started and stopped. "No, that isn't right. I thank you for…" she stopped again and then looked away, emitting a frustrated noise that Douglas decided was bloody adorable then she started again. "Your attention *and* your stated intentions are very nice and I appreciate them. I… I'm honoured," she stammered.

He watched her, not saying a word and not finding her adorable any longer mainly because he did *not* like that she considered his intention to marry her "very nice".

"But," she shifted uncomfortably and then looked at him before suddenly and exasperatedly bursting out, "quit staring at me like that!"

"Like what?"

"Like… like that!" she retorted, with a jerk of her head toward him, clearly thinking her words were an explanation (which they were not).

He lifted his good hand, palm up.

"Oh forget it, forget the chat too, I'm tired," she snapped.

"Julia." He stood, deciding it was time to take control of the conversation. She whirled on him and he expected another one of her brilliant tirades, a pouring forth of one of her lists. But instead her shoulders drooped, she turned her head to the side and she pulled a shaking hand through her hair.

"I can't believe you've been shot," she whispered. "What on earth are you doing that puts you in the way of a bullet? What is it that the police can't be involved?" He walked toward her and she turned her face to him. "I want to be your friend, Douglas. I think I could be happy here, with the kids, in this house, having a challenging job. If you would just help a little and be my friend." Her voice was aching and he felt an odd, unfamiliar feeling of tenderness as he stopped before her. "But I can't let myself like you if I think something's going to happen to you. I have to protect myself, protect the children."

She was suffering from a hint of post-traumatic stress, he imagined, and he moved closer to her, gathering her warm body in his one good arm.

She leaned away, arching her back against his arm and looking up at him.

"I talked with Nick today," he explained quietly.

He felt a hint of gratification when her eyes flared with hope. "Yes?"

"Yes," he assured her and saw, as well as felt, the relief flood through her as she realised what he was saying. He felt the strange stirring again at the thought of doing something of which she so obviously approved.

"I'm glad. For us and for you too," she whispered.

"Now," he said, setting that topic aside, "about your being my friend."

She nodded her head. "I'd really like that, Douglas."

"I would too." His gaze dropped to her lips and he watched the tips come up in a happy smile.

"I'm so glad," she breathed, more relief, so much it made her tense body relax against his. "This is going to work so well, I promise," she stated brightly, obviously misinterpreting what he said.

"Julia." She was pushing against his arm trying to get away; he tightened it and swept her against his body. He felt her soft breasts press against his arm in the sling and the warmth of her body and he liked both.

"Oh," she muttered, lifting her head again to look at him. "What?" She was still straining against his arm and it was causing pain in his opposite shoulder.

"Stop trying to pull away, it's hurting me," he told her and she immediately stilled.

They watched each other for awhile and then she gave into her curiosity and asked, "Is there something more?"

Douglas noted her tone was slightly strained.

"It's about us being friends."

"Yes?"

"I'd be delighted to be your friend," he told her.

"I... I thought we'd established that. I'll be delighted to be your friend too."

He nodded.

So did she, but hers was jerky and unsure.

"But I also intend to be your husband." Her body stiffened again and she started to pull away but glanced at his sling and stopped then her eyes flew to his in fear.

Douglas ignored her look, determined to move to the next phase in his strategy and went on. "Julia, I intend to be your lover." With Julia's soft warmth pressed so close, he could smell her. Both the feel of her and her scent made his body begin to tighten in an intensely pleasant way so that, when he spoke, his voice deepened, became hungry, as he, again, made his intentions clear but this time, he made them *clearer*. "I intend to sleep in sheets that smell of tangerines and jasmine. I intend to have your naked body squirming under mine. I intend to touch you everywhere with my hands and my mouth. I intend to memorise the taste of you, to make you call my name while I'm moving inside you, to make you so excited you beg me to let you come..."

"Stop it," she whispered but her voice was husky, her frame had softened, moulding to his and, in her eyes, there was a mixture of warmth and panic.

Progress.

Now, Douglas thought, *to make myself perfectly clear.*

"I'll do whatever I have to do. Even break our rule," he promised, thinking about Lizzie.

The warmth in her eyes gave way to the panic.

"You wouldn't!" she gasped.

"I would," he assured her bluntly and her eyes widened then narrowed.

"That's low," she accused.

"I get what I want," he vowed. "I'm a patient man but my patience is running out."

"Why do you want to marry me? Be my lover?" Her voice rose hysterically. "Douglas, it's mad!"

He stared at her quizzically. Could she not know her effect on him, on Nick, on Oliver, on men in general?

The thought was ludicrous, all women knew. They knew it and they used it.

All of them.

"Don't ask ridiculous questions," he clipped, his voice impatient. "It doesn't suit you."

Her mouth fell open and then snapped shut.

Suddenly, she dropped her head and exerted gentle pressure on his arm.

"Okay, fine, you've made your point. No truce, no compromise, the battle still rages." She was talking quietly but sarcastically. He could not read her mood, couldn't see her face but something in her tone made him let her go.

She quickly took several steps away.

"You should know," she said when she looked at him, her face carefully controlled but her eyes were still glittering with something he could not read, "that there will be consequences to all of this. I doubt you'll understand it, that it will even penetrate that reserve of yours, but it will happen."

He had no idea what she meant and when he started to ask she shook her head.

She moved toward the dressing room. "Please, just go. For tonight, let me be the winner."

Without looking back, she entered the dressing room and closed the door behind her.

After a moment of gazing at the door, he did as she asked and left.

On his way back to his rooms, he found himself thinking that, even though she said his leaving would make her the "winner", he knew by her words, her tone, the line of her body as she walked away that she was wrong, he had won.

Not just tonight, but eventually, he knew that she understood that he'd be the ultimate victor.

And somehow, instead of making him satisfied, it made him vaguely uneasy.

❧ 15 ❧

THE EMERALD

The next three weeks were bedlam.

Mrs. K got the flu and Ronnie and Julia became acutely aware of just how much Sommersgate depended on her when they tried to make it run as efficiently as its housekeeper, and failed.

Furthermore, Julia and Ronnie weren't about to let Mrs. K suffer without constant vigilance (Mr. K admitting he was hopeless playing nursemaid) so they took turns running up the hill through the wood to the Groundskeeper's Cottage to make certain she was fed, watered and medicated.

Adding to this, Douglas informed Veronika that Nick was going to move into the Gate House as soon as possible. The Gate House hadn't been touched in over three years. So Veronika and Julia had to find someone they trusted to clean it and give it a fresh coat of paint. Both women refused to bother Mrs. K for her contacts, which, Mr. K explained "she keeps in her head". Hiring a cleaning team and decorator was far more difficult than expected and Nick was forced to stay in Sommersgate House in the interim. This meant one more mouth to feed for Julia (who took over the cooking after one look at Veronika's borsht) and one more bed to make for Veronika (who always made the beds).

It was the Christmas season and all that was Christmas, decorating, shopping, wrapping, baking, cards and the kids with a variety of parties to attend. Julia had to get her presents bought, wrapped and mailed to The States. She also wanted to be certain the children, in this first Christmas without their parents, felt loved and cared for so she danced attendance on them especially.

Julia's personal shipping came from home, boxes and boxes of clothes and shoes, mementos, photos and things of Gavin's that she and Patricia wanted the children to have. Most of it was to go directly into storage but as Mrs. K controlled all storage issues in the house and she was unavailable for two weeks and catching up on backlog when she came back. The result was that Julia's rooms were a mess.

Through all this, Julia was working longer hours than she promised, scouring through budgets, creating reports and writing business plans.

To her surprise, Douglas had retreated completely. There were no more insane conversations filled with marriage proposals and salacious innuendo.

Not that the last conversation was innuendo at all.

He had been quite clear, concise and detailed about everything he wanted.

Indeed, he'd been *crystal* clear, *perfectly* concise and *exceptionally* detailed.

Just the thought of it made Julia blush and, sometimes, squirm (but, she had to admit, most times she thought of it, she'd shiver, in a *good* way).

And she thought about it a lot.

Too much.

In fact, all the time.

There had been times when he could have, and in the past would have, made some kind of advance, but he didn't.

Making matters worse, it seemed that Lizzie was throwing herself into a matchmaking role. If Douglas walked into the lounge while the children and Julia were watching television and Lizzie was sitting next to Julia, Lizzie would shoot to her feet and call out to him, "Uncle Douglas, sit here." Or if they were out to dinner or all getting into the Bentley, she'd boss Ruby and Willie so Julia would have no choice but to slide into the booth or car next to Douglas or else make a scene. Or if Julia was talking about anything at all, Lizzie would declare, "Uncle Douglas is good at that," or "*You* should ask Uncle Douglas, *he's* the expert!"

Douglas didn't seem to be the slightest bit aware of Lizzie's endeavours, though that didn't stop her from trying. Julia knew that Lizzie was trying to recreate the loving family she once had and even if this would ultimately lead to nothing, it was far better than her despondency so Julia's heart went out to the girl, so much so she couldn't bring herself to disabuse her niece of her notions.

In the meantime, Douglas took them to London to fulfil his promise to Ruby and so they could go Christmas shopping. Monique had (thankfully) been in Paris. While they were there, Charlie helped Julia find a gown for Tamsin's charity ball.

Douglas even spent time with them during this trip but all the while he was an utter gentleman. He often took Julia's elbow or put his hand in the small of her back to guide her but that was it.

However, sometimes, when she would talk to him on a crowded pavement or in a store, she noticed that he'd lean down to hear her and his eyes would be so warm and intimate, just looking into their dark depths made her belly melt. In those seconds, she believed he was still up to his tricks. But they were just seconds and nothing would come of it.

They had been photographed in London twice by the paparazzi and both times it had been in the papers (which was something else Julia didn't need as it was sure to set Monique stewing). One time, it was late in the afternoon, outside Harrods, while they were waiting to get into the Bentley. Ruby was exhausted and Douglas had picked her up and was carrying her as if she weighed no more than a doll. He'd had his sling removed the week before and behaved as if nothing had ever happened, including heaving Ruby around. The little girl had put her head on his shoulder and her arms around his neck. While holding Ruby, Douglas put his hand on the small of Julia's back to guide her just as she was herding the other two children into the car.

Lord Ashton out shopping with his new family including stylish sister-in-law, Ms. Julia Fairfax, the caption had read.

She'd clipped the picture for reasons she wouldn't allow herself the time or energy to consider (though Julia had to admit to liking the adjective "stylish" being attached to her). In the picture, he looked so handsome and devoted to his "new family" that if she gave herself a moment, she would have talked herself into believing what the picture looked like what it showed.

They were also photographed in Bristol when he took them all out to a South American restaurant for dinner. This, too, was printed in the paper. Willie had said something funny and Julia had lost herself for a moment, grabbed Douglas's upper arm and laughed. All three children were giggling and even Douglas was smiling.

Lord Douglas Ashton, now familiarly accompanied by Ms. Julia Fairfax and their nieces and nephew, that caption had read.

She'd clipped that one too and kept it in the upper drawer of her writing desk with the other as well as the one from the night at the gallery, which she also, for some reason, couldn't allow herself to part with.

While recuperating, Douglas was home all the time but after a few days, he'd fallen into his earlier pattern of being at the breakfast table, going out during the day and returning home, now usually by suppertime.

Through all of that, no brazen advances.

He was spending more time with the children, taking Lizzie and Willie out to ride the horses, answering questions about their home-work, sharing the responsibility of getting Ruby to bed, taking them all out to dinner, ferrying them to parties, wading in to handle arguments. All of this he did with natural skill, innate fairness and extraordinary negotiating ability and, again, if Julia allowed herself to think about it, she knew she would be undone.

So, she didn't think about it.

But he had retreated.

Julia knew it.

She knew it because, just the night before, Julia had approached Douglas in his study. He was reading through some documents, striking things out boldly with his Mont Blanc pen and writing things in the margins. The children were in bed and she and Douglas were alone.

She hadn't knocked before going in, simply walked up to his desk.

His head came up when he caught sight of her movement and she knew she'd startled him. It had always felt like he felt her very presence in a room, even if he hadn't seen her, not only since she'd moved there but before, all those times she visited. Something about knowing he'd dismissed her so thoroughly made something inside her die. She hated to admit it, but the fact was, it was true.

"Julia," he muttered, putting his pen down, her name on his lips sending unwanted pleasant shivers across her skin.

She pushed these thoughts to the back of her mind.

"I wanted to ask a favour." Julia had stopped in front of his desk, she was holding her business plan for the charity and he looked at it.

"Another list?"

This was said without humour or teasing, just polite curiosity. It made her even more nervous, both about asking him what she was going to ask him and about the fact that if he was going to go back to his insolent ways, now would be his golden opportunity. And she had no idea how she would respond, most especially if he *didn't*.

"I've written a business plan," Julia informed him.

He quirked an eyebrow.

Anxiously, she continued. "I'm going to present it to the trustees after Christmas and I wondered if... well, if you had time, could have a look?"

She extended the plan to him and he automatically reached out and took it.

She held her breath but he did nothing but nod. Then he set her plan atop a pile of other papers and looked back down at his own.

That was it.

She didn't move, frozen to the spot, disappointment so keen it felt like a pain in her chest.

When he realised she hadn't left, he looked up again.

"Is there something else?" he inquired politely.

Was there something else?

Yes, there bloody well was! Part of her mind cried.

"No, nothing," she replied and tried her damnedest to saunter casually from the room.

Now, she was being primped and primed to go to Tamsin's ball.

Sam had hired a stylist and makeup artist for her. It was unnecessary; somewhere in her heart she knew the only person she wished to impress was unimpressible.

He'd taken her at her word three weeks ago. He knew what she meant that night in her bedroom. If he persisted in his flirtation and got what he wanted, he'd have an unwanted attachment on his hands, a lovesick, heartsick albatross and he'd thought better of it so he'd cast her aside.

It was for the best, she knew.

At least it was better now with Douglas being around for the children.

As for Julia, the logical part of her brain reminded her it was safer this way, certainly her heart was safer and she knew she should be happy. She even tried to be happy.

But she was anything but happy.

"That's it, you're done," Sylvie, the hair stylist, announced, pulling Julia from her dismal thoughts. "*Magnifique!*"

Rosie, the makeup artist, handed her a tube of lipstick and a blush compact. "For touch ups," she explained.

Julia looked at herself in the three-way mirror and pulled in a breath.

Magnifique was right.

"Girls, you're miracle workers," she told them.

They looked at her and then at each other in surprise.

"You shine a perfect diamond, it only glitters a bit more," Sylvie replied.

Julia laughed at her remark as if it was hilarious and stared at herself in the mirror.

She was wearing a green velvet grown made by Charlie's most favourite new English designer known only as "Gregory" (*with* the quotes). The velvet was of such a dark, rich green it appeared to be black with only a sheen of colour. It was sleeveless with a low-cut, v-neck. It had no back at all, falling in an elegant, dramatic and slightly risqué drape just under the small of her back with only one thin strip of velvet that held the sides together under her shoulder blades. It moulded her body snugly, the skirt falling straight with a generous kick-pleat at the knees in the back leading down to a small train. She wore long, black, fitted, satin gloves and black satin, stiletto-heeled pumps. She'd put on her "essence" and the pair of emerald cut emerald studs that her mother had given her when she graduated from college. She felt the dress needed no other adornment and anyway, she didn't have any to do it justice.

Sylvie had swept up her hair and pulled it back from her face softly and whirled and twirled it in dozens upon dozens of different curls pinned to the back of her head. Rosie's makeup was not subtle, it was dramatic and glamorous and Julia felt just like a movie star.

Gazing at herself, Julia was beginning to look forward to the evening.

"Whoops, we're late and so are you," Sylvie noted, glancing at her watch.

She hugged them both (to their surprise), dropped her new lipstick and compact into her jet-beaded evening bag and took out generous tips to give them both.

"No, we're covered," Rosie said, holding up her hands.

"Then Merry Christmas," Julia replied and firmly pressed the notes in both their hands.

The girls packed up their things and left as Julia squirted one more spray in her cleavage, grabbed her wrap (this made from black velvet and lined in green-black satin) and threw it around her shoulders to allow it to settle in the crooks of her elbows. Then she scuttled out to see Veronika loitering in the hallway.

"I thought you'd gone home!" Julia cried.

Veronika stared, her mouth agape.

"Are you okay?" Julia asked, concerned when Veronika didn't speak, just kept staring.

"I waited... to see..." Veronika paused then exclaimed, "You are movie star!"

Julia giggled and struck a pose. "I know, didn't they do a great job on my hair and makeup?"

Ronnie continued to stare at her and then said firmly, "No," she pointed at Julia, "*you* look just like movie star."

Julia's giggle died at the earnest look in the girl's eyes, she pulled her close and hugged her.

In her ear, Julia whispered a heartfelt, "Oh Ronnie, thank you."

It was just the boost of confidence that she needed.

Ronnie hugged her back tightly, pulled away and gave her a brief smile before disappearing toward the kitchen.

The children were at Mr. and Mrs. Kilpatrick's for the evening; Julia rounded the door to the dining room and saw Douglas through the opposite doorway standing in the hall at the end, looking unbelievably attractive in a well-cut tuxedo. His dark, overlong hair brushed at his collar and something about the fact that he always seemed to be so impeccably turned-out, so in control of everything, yet always seemed to need a haircut was endearing to her.

If she were his wife, she could remind him to get a haircut.

That tugged at her heartstrings too but she refused to allow herself to dwell on it.

He was scowling at his watch and she was slightly surprised. She hadn't seen his scowl in awhile or his grin or smile or his hilarious arrogance. He'd been reserved, remote, expressionless, the same old Douglas.

That thought started to drag at her budding excitement and, hiding her disappointment, she tilted her head down to adjust her glove and called out, "Sorry, sorry, I'm ready."

The glove was tangled at the back of her arm so she stopped to give it a good tug and, once it was smoothly pulled into place, she looked up to see the old Douglas, scowl gone, he simply regarded her coolly. He showed no reaction to her transformation and she realised he had most likely spent considerable time waiting for women far more glamorous than herself.

Julia instantly deflated like she was an overblown balloon that had been pricked by a pin. She stopped in front of him and tipped her head questioningly.

"Ready?" She hoped she sounded distracted instead of disappointed.

"Not quite," he replied and pulled a thin, black velvet box from the inside breast pocket of his tuxedo jacket.

She watched in mute stupefaction as he opened it and she glimpsed a stunning emerald cut emerald, ten times the size of her studs, set without further ornamentation and suspended from what looked like a simple platinum chain.

He pulled it out of the box without any ado and moved to stand behind her. She saw the emerald dangle before her eyes for a moment and then felt it settle heavily on her chest, resting just above her breasts. She then felt his hands make light work of clasping it at the back of her neck, his fingers brushing her faintly there, causing a delicious, dual tremor, one that slid down her spine, the other up into her scalp.

The whole time he worked at her neck, Julia opened and closed her mouth, words tumbling into her head but her brain would not engage with her mouth to let them out. Her skin tingled where his fingers touched and the hairs raised with acute awareness down her neck, back and arms.

He came around her side and threw the box carelessly on a table in the hallway.

"Now we can go," he stated casually, as if he hadn't just clasped an expensive jewel around her neck, and offered her his arm.

She didn't move to take it.

"What's wrong?" he asked, looking down at her and barely masking his impatience.

"The..." she stopped.

What's wrong? She repeated his words in her head incredulously. He'd just put what was an incredibly expensive emerald around her neck, for goodness sakes!

"The necklace," she finally explained, touching the stone lightly with the tips of her fingers. Her voice sounded strained to her own ears.

"It's nothing, an early Christmas present," he replied tersely, the subject obviously closed and even more obviously meaningless to him, as if he gave enormous, precious jewels to women all the time, which he probably did. "We're late, there'll be traffic enough as it is."

He offered her his arm again and she took it, still mentally reeling.

Then Julia walked out to the Bentley at Douglas's side thinking that she might be the only woman on earth who could have a perfect emerald affixed around her neck and still consider her brief feelings of the excitement for the night were well and truly dead.

❧ ❧ ❧

Three hours later, she was no longer feeling the same.

This was because of Charlie, who was determined to show her a good time and because of six glasses of champagne, which would make *anyone* start to relax.

"All I can say is, forget about him!" Charlie declared and then blew out a stream of smoke. They were on a terrace and hiding from Oliver. Charlie had quit smoking over Thanksgiving but was now what she called, "Christmas-stress-smoking".

Julia had thrown caution to the wind and, after glass of champagne number four, had confided in her new friend about Douglas, the marriage proposal, everything.

Charlie, at first, had stared at her in dazed disbelief and then she'd muttered triumphantly, "I *knew* it!" After that, she'd hugged Julia and shouted, "Hurrah!" so loudly that everyone around them turned to stare.

After glass of champagne number six, Julia had gotten around to explaining how it all ended and the way it was now. In response, Charlie had grabbed her and two more glasses of champagne and pulled her out to the terrace.

"There are men who would kill for you in there!" she announced, extravagantly gesturing back to the ballroom. "If he doesn't want you, find one who does!"

Julia giggled before declaring, "Hardly. And anyway, it's not that easy. I live with him, remember?"

"It's just that easy!" Charlie decided, but her eyes were glittering with something Julia couldn't quite make out. "He doesn't care, so be it. He wants to live in his shell, he's welcome to it. But *you* live *your* life." Charlie came forward and linked her arm through Julia's, saying firmly, "Let's go."

Charlie smashed out her cigarette in a thoughtfully provided ashtray and pulled Julia back into the crush of the ball.

Julia and Douglas had arrived three hours ago to the flashbulbs and shouts of the paparazzi, but now they were shouting *her* name too. She held on to his arm for dear life, doing her best to keep a slight smile pinned to her face (it wouldn't do to have her picture flashed across the newspapers looking like a deer caught in headlights or worse). They'd also had to stand for photos for the society papers and magazines as they were not only representatives of Tamsin and Gavin, who were being memorialised in the programme, but Douglas was the largest benefactor of the event.

Then, that was it. Charlie and Oliver had come in from London for the evening and found them. Charlie swept her away for a round of introductions and Charlie-induced fun. Julia hadn't seen Douglas again except in the crowd every once in awhile. The strange thing was, every time she caught sight of him, he was looking directly at her. Still no expression on his face but she found his constant stare highly disconcerting.

Now, Charlie determinedly pushed through the crush and just as determinedly sought out, nailed down and introduced Julia to every available (and some not-so-available) man of Julia's age (and some a bit younger than Julia's age). It was impossible not to laugh at Charlie's outrageousness or, indeed, participate in it herself, enjoying every moment as the harmless diversion it was. Diversion was good, Julia needed diversion and Charlie, she was realising, gave the best diversion there was to give.

So, she thought, as she sipped her seventh glass of champagne, she'd have a great time and Douglas could stand there and glower and scowl with Oliver, who was also glowering and scowling...

Julia stopped laughing at something her male companion was saying, which was what she was doing when she caught sight of Douglas and she swiftly averted her gaze, a feeling of dread seeping through her.

"Charlie," Julia said, her voice low with warning, rudely ignoring the man at her side as a chill ran up her spine.

Charlie threw back her head and roared with laughter at something a rather handsome man of somewhat average height was saying to her.

Julia felt a pair of eyes, maybe two, boring hotly into her back. She hazarded a peek and then turned quickly away again at what she saw.

It was true, she wasn't seeing things. Douglas was glowering, scowling and now, she could say, *glaring* at her and Charlie.

"Charlie." She grabbed her friend's arm and pulled her away from the man she was laughing with. "Excuse me, I just need a quiet word," she explained awkwardly to the man.

"What's wrong?" Charlie asked, immediately registering Julia's discomfiture.

"Um, don't look now but I think your husband may be a bit peeved and Douglas looks..." she glanced back and then away again as his eyes drilled into hers. "Fit to be tied," she finished lamely.

Charlie whirled around and gave them a bold, anxiety-free stare. "Well, well, well," she said, "the beast awakens. About bloody time."

Julia's mouth dropped open and, because she was acutely aware of being the recipient of censorious glare from across the room, she snapped it shut again before asking, "What do you mean?"

"No time to explain, call me tomorrow. And remember, *you owe me,*" Charlie said mysteriously, leaned forward, kissed her cheek and then disappeared.

Julia had no time to react or to do anything because the next thing she knew, her hand was taken in a firm, almost painful grip and she heard an iron-edged, velvet-cloaked, deep voice growl in her ear, "We're going."

That's when she knew she was in trouble.

16

JULIA'S REALISATION

Douglas Ashton, Baron Blackbourne, was *not* happy.

"I'll kill her." These were Douglas's thoughts but they were uttered by his friend, Oliver, who was standing at his side.

For the last half an hour, Oliver and Douglas had witnessed a display of womanly wiles so practised and successful that Douglas had no doubt his phone would be ringing off the hook tomorrow.

Which meant, tonight, after he was finished with Julia, *thoroughly* finished with her, he was going to leave her exhausted, naked body in his bed and then throw every phone in the whole damned, bloody house in the bin.

Jealousy, and he knew exactly what the feeling was, there was not a thing vague about it, was eating at him. A fine, red film of fury had long since glazed his vision. The only thing that stopped him from striding across the room and dragging her from the building was the scene he knew it would cause.

He'd spent the last three weeks calmly, he thought, patiently, he felt, waiting for her to come to him. He thought, if he allowed her some space, she'd come around to his way of thinking. If he let her have a moment to think, to settle in, she'd stop being so bloody-minded and realise she wanted him.

He'd been wrong.

His usually precise strategy had been spectacularly inaccurate. She'd been blithely unaware of him the entire time. Only once or twice he caught her looking at him with what he thought, even so far as fucking *hoped*, was longing, but nothing came of it. She was impossibly busy, always doing something for her charity, for the kids, nursing an ailing Mrs. Kilpatrick, setting a big bowl of spaghetti and meat sauce in front of a grinning Nick, decorating the damned Christmas tree.

The only time he felt as if he was making any headway was when she'd brought her business plan to him last night. She looked devastated when he'd set it aside without comment and gone back to his work. He thought his actions would make her react, finally (and verbally).

They did not.

The truth was, he'd been inordinately pleased she'd asked him, even trusted him to read it and he'd reached for it the moment she left the room.

That was then, this was now.

If she felt she could flirt, under his nose, with practically every man in the room, it was time for Douglas to disabuse her of that notion.

He'd only made his decision when he caught her eye and she blinked at him, her laughter at something the idiot at her side was saying dying on her face.

He realised that she knew he was displeased and that satisfied him immensely. He watched as, in the next moments, she glanced anxiously at him a couple of times and grabbed Charlotte.

"If you'll excuse me, Oliver, I think I'll call it a night," Douglas muttered to his friend, deciding quickly to make his move before Julia had any chance to make hers.

"Capital idea," Oliver muttered right back.

Douglas's angry, ground-eating strides went unfettered by the crowd as they parted to accommodate him. In reality, they had no choice; he would have simply run them over.

In no time at all he had hold of Julia's hand. She was looking away to where Charlotte had escaped and he leaned forward and told her simply, "We're going."

Her frightened eyes flew to his face but he didn't hesitate. He had her at the cloakroom within moments. He tossed her wrap to her, pulled her out the front door and practically threw her in the back of the Bentley that Carter had, thankfully, parked close to the front steps.

Then they were away into the night.

She waited a few minutes before she spoke. "Is... um, Douglas?" she hesitated. "Is there something wrong?"

He didn't even attempt to mask his reaction to her as he had been doing, painstakingly, for the past three weeks.

He turned burning eyes to hers.

"Wrong?" he inquired, his voice steely.

The passing streetlights illuminated his face and she shrunk away from him but said, "Yes. Wrong."

"Why would you think something's wrong?" With effort, he tore his eyes from her.

He couldn't look at her in that exquisite dress without tearing it off her equally exquisite body. He imagined Carter, who was now practically like her favoured uncle, would find something amiss in such an action.

When he'd first seen her earlier that night standing in the dining room wearing that remarkable dress and calmly adjusting her glove, he'd nearly lost all control.

He had never, in his entire life, been so enamoured of clothing the way he was of Julia's... entire... *fucking*... wardrobe. It took everything in his power to compose his face and regard her blandly when she finally deigned to give him her attention.

She laughed, breaking into his thoughts, he heard the anxiety in the sound and he was unreasonably glad of it.

"Well, we practically ran out of there," Julia stated nervously. "I didn't get a chance to say good-bye."

She stopped when his head swung around to regard her. "Who, may I ask, of all the many people you met tonight, would you have liked to wish a good evening?"

She didn't answer for a few moments.

Then she surmised accurately, "Something *is* wrong."

Douglas didn't reply.

Fifteen very long minutes later, when the air in the back of the

Bentley was so thick Douglas felt it hard to breathe, they glided to a halt in the drive of Sommersgate.

In an attempt at escape, Julia grabbed hold of the door handle before Carter could make it around.

Quick as lightning, Douglas caught her upper arm.

"I think not," he bit out, his voice holding a warning.

She froze and stared at him, caught like a startled doe in the burning heat of his gaze.

When Carter opened the door, she grabbed her opportunity and scrambled out. Douglas followed her swiftly, nodded sharply to Carter and bid him a curt goodnight.

He didn't wait for Carter to reply but stalked behind Julia, who had made some headway, already had heaved the front door open and was in the house. However, in those deliciously erotic heels, she was no match for him and he caught her arm again as she was turning into the dining room, heading toward her rooms.

Her cautious gaze captured his.

"Drink?" he inquired, his tone barely civil.

"No, thank you," she replied, her words polite, her voice tight. "I think I'll just go to bed."

"Excellent idea," Douglas agreed and, not letting go, he slid his hand down her arm, capturing hers, and pulled her towards the stairs.

"What? Where are you...? Let go of me!" she burst out, tugging at her hand in his.

"No," he returned, feeling her hand trying to pull from his, he stopped and yanked her forward. Caught off guard at this quick change and off balance at the jerk of his hand, she stumbled into him and his arms locked around her.

"What's the matter with you?" she cried, her anxiety gone and the spirit and fire he was used to was beginning to light her eyes.

He watched her with smug satisfaction, enjoying her eyes sparkling. He much preferred her this way, the fire rather than the ice. Her fire would make this vastly more enjoyable.

She watched him back. When she was done waiting, she pushed against his chest. "Let me go!"

He pulled her closer to him, his arms tightening; her soft body had no choice but to yield to his hard one.

"No." Her eyes rounded in anger but he carried on. "I'm not going to let you go, Julia. I thought I explained that to you. My patience has finally run out. I warned you."

And that was when he kissed her.

It was not a tender kiss. He meant to devour her, he meant to punish her, he meant to let her know, in no uncertain terms, how he felt about watching her flirt with male after male right under his nose. He'd told her he wanted her to take his name, his hand in marriage and her body to his bed. He'd made himself perfectly clear on those particular subjects. He was not a man to be trifled with and he already considered her *his*. The kiss was meant to teach her that all-important lesson.

She tore her lips from his.

"What was *that?*" she snapped in disgust, wiping her mouth on the back of her gloved hand.

"*That* was a lesson. *This* is a promise," he replied on a growl.

And he kissed her again, at the same time he forced her backward until she hit the stone wall of the stairwell. She let out a small cry of protest but he relentlessly pressed her into the wall, pressed his body into hers, feeling the glorious heat of her seep through his clothes. His mouth was hard and demanding but this time with hungry passion, not anger. His hands went behind her, both of them aiming low, one sliding over the velvet at her bottom outside her gown. The other did exactly what he'd been imagining since he'd seen the unbelievably sexy dip in the back of her dress. It delved in and rounded over her buttock then he pulled her tightly against his groin.

He counted on her melting as she did practically every time he touched her but he thought it would take some coaxing. He didn't expect the minute his hand touched her bottom, with only the thin, lacy barrier of her underwear between his hand and her skin that she would react the way she did.

He heard her moan, deep in her throat, the sound nearly guttural with need. Her back arched, her mouth opened and her tongue darted between his lips.

He felt the blood rush to his head, through his veins and to his cock, heating his body to a fever as her hands went under his dinner jacket, tearing at his shirt, pulling it free of his trousers. Then he felt them, encased in their soft satin, gliding across the skin of his back, his sides, roaming everywhere, trailing fire.

While his tongue played with hers, she made a soft mew that he could swear he felt to his very soul and then he felt her nails, made less harsh through her gloves, drag down his back.

"God, I want you," he growled against her lips, his one hand still cupping her soft, generous ass, his other hand pulling brutally at the material at her shoulder, the strap at the back tore free and the bodice fell to catch where his chest pressed against her breasts.

He registered her nodding mutely as he pulled away to watch the material fall further down, exposing her spectacular breasts to his view. With his hand on her buttock and the other arm now tightened at her back, he lifted her up to the tips of her toes while his head descended and he captured one perfect nipple between his lips. He dragged his teeth across it and felt it stiffen against his lips at the same time he felt his body tighten with a nearly overwhelming need and he heard a hungry moan escape Julia's lips.

Her hands went to his hair, her fingers sliding into it, holding his head fast. He heard her breath catch then her body shuddered so deliciously, it communicated itself to him and the shudder tore through his as well. His lips closed on her nipple and drew it in sharply and she cried out in desire, the sound so primitive, he felt it straight into his bones.

He swiftly moved his mouth to hers, hungry to swallow the end of her cry, sucking her tongue into his mouth when she was done, just like he'd done to her nipple. When he became cognizant that she was pressing her body against his with need, her arms wrapped around his neck with longing, he tore his mouth away.

"Do you want me?" His voice was rough with passion, foreign to his own ears. He'd never felt this kind of desire, this desperate need in his entire life.

He was holding his breath, waiting for her reply, for some reason he knew his future depended on her answer.

Julia was silent.

His hand tightened on her ass.

"Do you want me?" he growled against her mouth.

"Yes, Douglas, I want you," Julia breathed.

And then, abruptly, he bent double, picked her up and, just like a bloody, fucking caveman, Douglas threw her over his shoulder and carried her to his bed.

❧ ❧ ❧

Julia woke up sometime in the night, her naked limbs tangled with Douglas's.

She wouldn't be able to move without disturbing him and, for the time being, she wanted to relish in the delicious moment of closeness. She wanted to take this precious time to savour what they had shared only hours, or maybe it had only been just moments, before.

He had carried her up to the bedroom, not in his arms like a doting lover, but in a fireman's hold like a marauding Viking.

Not until he had her through his personal sitting room and in his bedroom did he put her down or more to the point throw her down, right in the middle of the bed. He didn't utter a sound, not even a grunt of effort.

Some sanity had returned at that point and her hands flew up to adjust the fallen neckline of her dress while he turned on the light at the bedside table.

"Don't," he barked when he saw her movements and, at the sound of his rough voice, her hands stilled, holding the bodice in place over her breasts as she struggled into a semi-reclining position.

He was staring at her and she was immobile in the face of his blazing eyes. She watched him in fascinated silence as he shrugged off his jacket and threw it on the floor. His hands moved and he yanked at his tie viciously. In one tug, it came loose and he threw it to join his jacket. Then he went to work on the buttons on his shirt.

"Douglas…" Julia was trying for a conciliatory tone, she was half-mad with wanting him, half-sane enough to realise her own fear. She sought control of the situation, time to think. He was furious, she knew, even though she wasn't entirely certain why, and a fury the strength of his was a frightening thing.

But it was also something else.

It was magnetic.

She wanted this, she was forced to admit. She was no fool and she tried never to fool herself.

At the same time she was terrified of it.

He wasn't helping her, looking at her as if he would be hanged in the morning and she was his last meal.

He had the last button undone on his shirt then his arm reached out abruptly, grabbed her by the waist and jerked her to her feet in front of him.

"Who chose this dress?" he asked, his hands sliding down her sides slowly.

"Charlie," she answered nervously.

"Remind me to thank her," he remarked right before he bunched the material at her hips and savagely pulled it up over her head, forcing her arms up with it. In a split second it, too, fell on the pile with his tie and his jacket.

His hands settled on her waist, the heat of them searing her bare skin and making her shiver as he roughly pushed her a couple of inches away from his body, holding her suspended, for she would surely never have been able to stand on her own at that angle.

Rather than cover herself, her arms fluttered down to her sides and she watched helplessly as his eyes drifted over her hungrily. She was wearing nothing but her black gloves, a pair of black, lace edged, garter-less stockings, black lace underwear, her pumps and his emerald.

"Jesus," he murmured, looked in her eyes again and she could have drowned in the depths of his, they had turned to ink.

He pulled her in his arms, her bare skin crushed against the edges of his partially opened shirt and she barely had time to savour that sensation before she was falling backwards, one of his arms around her waist, the other one thrown out to control their fall. Her back no sooner hit the bed when he was gone, pulling away from her, his hand reaching for her panties.

"Douglas, we need to slow down." This was going too quickly for her, she needed to think, she needed her clothes, she needed...

"Slow is not an option," he declared as he pulled the lace expertly down her legs and it too joined the pile of clothing.

She gasped at the quickness of his action but his body covered hers before she could think or move and she became aware that he was still nearly fully clothed while she was nearly naked. She felt exposed and vulnerable.

This, she didn't like.

He kissed her again and all such thoughts flew right out the window. Her body ignited as if the time between the white-hot passion of the stairwell and now had simply melted away.

He sucked her tongue into his mouth and she took the opportunity to explore it boldly. His hands were all over her, her hands roamed over him. Her skin tingled where he touched it and she moaned low in her throat.

He pulled his mouth away. "Take off your bloody gloves," he commanded and, for once, she obeyed happily, shakily removing her gloves and flinging them wherever they would land.

The minute her bare hands touched the skin of his back under his shirt, there was no time to think, there was only time to feel. She felt his mouth on hers, on her neck, at the base of her throat. She felt the edge of his teeth drag against her nipple then pull it hungrily in his mouth then move to the other, only to do the same thing. She felt his hands roaming the skin of her sides, her bottom, her hips, her belly, against the silk of her stockings and then up, between her legs.

"Oh!" she cried, as he found her with his thumb, a fleeting, joyous pressure that sent her neck arching back and her mouth opening in a silent groan of pleasure. Then it was gone, only to be replaced with one, long finger sliding slowly inside her.

Her breath dragged out of her while his finger moved and his thumb again found its spot. She started panting, actually *panting*, as her stomach clutched and then dropped away and she pressed her hips urgently against his hand.

It was her turn to touch him, her hands insistently roaming, her mouth at his neck and throat, her tongue darting out to taste the salt of his skin against the hard muscle as she rode his hand like a madwoman.

She was close, the pressure was building, she felt she only had to reach for it and the wild joy he was promising would be hers.

"Do you want me?" His mouth was at her ear but his finger had slid away, his thumb disappeared.

"Yes!" She didn't hesitate, wanting it all back, wanting it immediately and willing to do anything to get it.

His hand was still gone and she arched her back, her breath ragged, her fingers desperately running down his arm to find his hand and pull it back to where it was. But this was thwarted, Douglas captured her hand in his and pulled her arm over her head, his body settling on hers as he caught her other wrist and imprisoned both over her head in one of his hands.

Then she felt him yanking at his trousers, then parting her legs and settling between them and, finally, she felt him there, just at the edge and not moving any closer.

She wanted him closer. She *needed* him closer.

She needed him inside her.

She realised her eyes were closed when they flew open and she saw him watching her, his indigo gaze boring into hers.

"Douglas," she whispered and the minute she uttered his name, he slammed into her with a heady ferocity that she welcomed without question. Her hips lifted to receive him, her legs moved to open herself to him, one wrapped around his hip, the other curling around the back of his thigh.

He let go of her wrists and both of his hands went to pull her hips boldly upward to meet his thrusts, deepening them, his open lips on hers, receiving her moans in his mouth, every once in awhile his tongue shooting out to duel with her own.

She'd never, not once, climaxed simply with a man inside her but she felt it building now, felt her muscles tensing with anticipation, her legs tightening, her fingers clawing, her mouth searching... and then he was gone. His body completely still, he was suspended where she could feel the promise of him but she didn't have him.

She arched against him in desperation, pressed her hips down, sought him soundlessly and through all this he withheld from her.

She bit her bottom lip, her nails dragging down his back and when she could take it no more, when she thought she would likely die if she didn't feel him inside her again, she pressed her mouth against his, looked into his dark eyes and begged, "Please."

Hearing that word, he drove into her violently, burying himself to the hilt inside her, and she exploded, her entire body tensed, wrapping him fiercely in her limbs as if she would never let go and she went completely still. Except her mouth, which emitted a prolonged moan that eloquently informed him of the profound pleasure tearing relentlessly through her body.

He'd joined her moments later and she registered it with contented feminine knowledge but was still too immersed in the residual shudders and tingles of her own climax to watch. Then she felt the weight of his body settle against hers.

Her response was to tighten her arms and legs.

They lay there, still joined, his heavy weight pressing her into his soft bed while her mind fought for control over her body, and lost.

It had never, ever, been this good. She hadn't even imagined it could be, not in her wildest dreams. She felt an intoxication that had nothing to do with seven glasses of champagne and no matter how hard her common sense struggled to remind her that this was a frightening risk, she delighted in it.

Douglas lifted his head and looked at her. She didn't know what to say so, for once, she said nothing at all.

"Do not ever flirt with another man in front of me," he growled so ferociously his command throbbed through both of their bodies.

She blinked at him in surprise.

So *that* was why he was angry.

She lifted a palm and laid it gently against his cheek. "Douglas, if this is my punishment for flirting, I'm afraid I'm going to have to do it more often."

He didn't move.

"In fact," she went on, "I may do it all the time. I might start flirting with Nick," she informed him and his arms stole around her, his weight bearing heavily on her. "And even Carter," she breathed, because his body on hers was taking her breath away, in more ways than one. "You're crushing me," she whispered softly in his ear.

She no sooner said it than she lost his arms and *him* as he pulled out of her and away, dropping to the side, half-on her, half-off, lifting himself on his elbow to look down at her.

She may have been teasing but she saw that he was not amused.

He watched her and then asked bluntly, "Are you going to marry me?"

His eyes were intense and she didn't know whether to laugh or cry.

She wanted to say something flippant.

She wanted to rush home to the safety of Indiana, her old house, her old job, her old life, her old grocery store where she knew where the cake mixes were, but she understood now that it was all too late.

"Yes," was her simple reply.

There was no crowing in victory. Douglas simply rolled into her, gathering her in his arms and he kissed her. Gone was the passion and urgency and in its place was complete and surprising tenderness which left her a different kind of breathless.

Then he carefully pulled away and, nearly reverently, swept off her shoes and stockings, righted her body on the bed and pulled her under the sheets. He discarded the rest of his clothes and met her there, pulling her back into his arms.

She wanted to talk to him, for him to reassure her, for something to be said that would be a hallmark of this momentous occasion.

Instead, she asked teasingly, "So, you liked the dress?"

His response, "It's obvious you think this is incredibly amusing but allow me to educate you. Men do not like to be teased."

He was lying on his back and had pressed her against his side and she'd laid her head on his shoulder.

"I gathered that," Julia mumbled, his hand drifted to her bottom and he may have been about to give her a smack but she didn't feel it because the intensity of her climax suddenly stole over her and she drifted to sleep.

Now, she was awake and she needed the bathroom, she needed a moment to herself, she needed a moment to think.

She shifted slightly and his arms tightened.

"Douglas," she whispered, not knowing if he was awake or asleep, "I need to use your bathroom."

Apparently he was awake for his arms loosened. She slid out of them and rolled off the bed.

Not entirely comfortable with ambling around his still-lit bedroom completely nude with him half-asleep, or not (she'd learned *that* lesson the night of the gunshot wound), she grabbed the closest thing at hand, which was his shirt. She shrugged it on, avoiding looking at him and scurried to one of the two doors she could see, hoping it led to the bathroom.

Thankfully, it did.

As with his bedroom, it was decorated in deep chocolate browns, dusky blues and sharp chartreuses. She quickly went about her business and, at the basin, after washing her hands, she stared at herself in the mirror.

She nearly laughed out loud.

Her hair hadn't moved. It was still twisted in its elegant coils as if she hadn't just been thoroughly satisfied by a rapacious baron.

She'd just lifted her hands to begin to release her hair from its pins when the door flew open.

She jumped.

"What are you doing?" Julia demanded, staring in the mirror at Douglas standing behind her in his glorious nakedness, his lean, muscled body nonchalantly exposed to her eyes, which were shining in disbelief at his intrusion. Her arms were lifted and her hands were stilled in the process of taking the hairpins out of her the hair at the back of her head.

He looked at her, also through the mirror. "You were taking a long time."

"What? Did you think I was going to crawl out the window?"

He walked forward and stopped. She felt the heat of his naked body against her back, his eyes still on hers in the mirror and his hands settled on her waist.

"Honestly?" he asked.

She nodded.

"I wouldn't put it past you."

She couldn't help herself, she burst out laughing.

When she finished, she noticed he was still watching her in the mirror, no amusement in *his* eyes.

She was wearing his shirt which was unbuttoned and only partially gaping, exposing very little except the winking emerald that still lay against her chest and a one inch expanse of skin from chest, between breasts, down her midriff and belly to below. His eyes dropped to follow the opening as her hands began to pull out the pins.

"I need to take down my hair," she explained her delay as his deep blue eyes rose to meet hers in the mirror.

Douglas surprised her when his hands lifted and pushed hers aside. He then further stunned her by working his fingers into her hair, gently seeking out hairpins and pulling them free, tossing them heedlessly in the sink.

Her arms fell and she grabbed the edge of the sink in an effort not to relax against him, which was what she desperately wanted to do. Her chin dropped to give him better access and she spied the emerald at her neck.

"How did you know?" she asked.

"Know what?" His deep voice rumbled behind her, causing her to shiver.

"About the emerald, how did you know it would be perfect?" Her voice was quiet.

His reply came immediately. "I asked Charlotte. She told me the colour you intended to wear and about the emeralds your mother gave you. So I found something to match."

At the pronouncement of that bit of thoughtfulness, her fingers tightened spasmodically against the edge of the basin as something stole through her, starting at her belly and this time, heading north, straight to her heart.

She was falling in love with him.

Dear God, she was falling in love with Douglas Ashton.

In fact, Julia thought hysterically, she may have started falling in love with him the moment she met him.

But what she knew for certain was that she was falling deeply, madly, *stupidly* in love with him now.

She was falling in love with how good he was with the children and the reason he watched over them (and her) because of his heretofore unknown bond with his sister.

She was falling in love with how he warned off her father and how he protected her against Monique.

She was falling in love with the way he helped her learn snooker, didn't make her feel a fool when she'd seen The Mistress and sat with her in her room until she fell asleep.

And she was falling in love with the way he made her feel when he looked at her (and was already in love with the way he made her feel with his mouth and hands and body).

His fingers worked carefully in her hair but her body stiffened against the knowledge stealing into her heart.

For the second time she was going to marry a man she loved. This time, she knew in advance the heartbreak it would bring. This time she knew that there would be a day when his eye would wander, when he'd grow tired of what they shared earlier that evening even though she'd live for it.

Her father had left her mother. Sean's behaviour had forced Julia to leave him. And Douglas, Douglas would be no different. He was just Douglas. A man of means who got what he wanted, when he wanted it and, when he was satisfied, he'd be gone.

And it was then she realised she couldn't do it. She'd agreed to it but she couldn't go through with it.

He finished finding pins and his fingers slid against her scalp, running gently through her hair to it ends, then they dropped, stealing around her waist until he was holding her loosely there. She lifted her eyes to the mirror, first to look at herself (worrying that her hair would be a crazed, Medusa-styled mess but instead it was just a mass of curls) then to catch his eyes.

"Better?" His eyes warm, he asked his question softly, that one quiet word fastening like a silken shroud around her heart, and she nodded, not trusting her own voice. Not trusting what she might say. Not wanting him to know, *ever*, how she felt. And lastly, not wanting this moment to end because, she knew, it would be their last.

"Good," he said, "come to bed."

She nodded again, too undone with her new knowledge to bristle against his order.

He let her waist go but caught her hand and she followed him, still staggered by her realisation.

She had no idea what she would do, how she would cope but, right then, she was just going to go with it.

"Jewel," Gavin had once said, "you need to take a risk, leave that little farm town and live your life. There's something out there for you, little sister. But you've got to go out and find it."

Tonight, she'd taken a risk.

She'd agreed to marry a wealthy, dangerous, English Baron, who she could easily love, who also happened to own a haunted mansion.

Tomorrow, she'd take it back and most likely regret it for the rest of her life.

But she had no choice. She had to guard her heart. She couldn't go through it again without being destroyed.

He stopped, his back to the side of the bed, turning her to face him. His hands went to her belly and then turned, the backs of his fingers brushing against her as he spread open the shirt. His head descended and his teeth nibbled at her lips.

"I want you," his voice was low and silky, "with this on," he said, his mouth teasing hers and he indicated what he meant by tugging at the shirt.

She took a shuddering breath and mumbled, "Okay."

He found her hand and pulled sharply at it, forcing her to fall with him back on the bed, hooking her at the waist so she fell on top of him.

He kissed her, his right hand delving into her hair to hold her head firmly to his and his left hand pushing the fabric of his shirt away so her naked body was pressed against his. She felt the immense heat of him and revelled in it, allowing it to fire her skin. Then his hands ran down her back, over her bottom and he did an abdominal crunch, his fingers softly sliding down her legs to the backs of her knees.

He pulled his mouth from hers and she found she was already breathing heavily, wanting him again.

"This time," he began and with a forceful jerk he pulled her knees up and she found herself, with a surprised gasp, straddling him. One of his hands moved from her knee and went between their bodies, the other hand went to her waist. "You get to do all the work." His hand on her waist drove her relentlessly down on him and, as he filled her, her teeth caught her lower lip in delicious pleasure, her head rolled back and her back arched.

"I think I can do that," Julia breathed, wishing she sounded more sultry and cosmopolitan but he'd have to make do with just her.

She bent forward again, kissed him softly and it began.

Of course, it didn't end with her on top, not with Douglas. Moments before their climax, he flipped her onto her back and drove into her unrelentingly, this time wrapping her legs around his waist himself, thrusting fiercely as if he wanted to penetrate her very soul, until her teeth bit uncontrollably into his shoulder and, finally, she had no choice but to throw her head back and cry out his name in pure, excruciating, mind-numbing pleasure.

17

THE MORNING AFTER

Douglas woke, felt his arms were empty and the delicious furnace that was Julia's body in sleep was gone.

His eyes opened, he turned his head and saw Julia had pulled away from him some time in the night and was lying a foot away, her back towards him. He turned to his side and lifted himself on his elbow in order to watch her sleep.

She was leaned slightly forward and her chin was tucked into her chest, her arms crooked, hands resting on the pillow in front of her, the side of one palm lightly pressed against her nose. Her face was relaxed, the sleek line of her jaw partially covered by a soft fall of her hair.

There was something about Julia in sleep, something he couldn't quite put his finger on, but it was something he liked.

Watching her, he felt an odd sense of contentment settle over him.

He had won; she had agreed to be his wife.

He always knew he'd win however, he did not count on it taking so damn long.

Nevertheless, the harder the battle, the sweeter the victory.

And victory over Julia was exquisitely sweet.

He pulled the heavy, golden hair away from her neck and kissed her there. She didn't move, not even a twitch, but then, he thought with an inward smile, she was surely exhausted.

Douglas was unbelievably energised.

He rolled off the other side of the bed and caught sight of the clock. Cursing under his breath, he strode to his sitting room, closing the door to the bedroom with a soft click. He picked up the phone and dialled twenty.

Mr. Kilpatrick answered at the Groundskeeper's Cottage after two rings. Douglas could hear in the background what sounded like pandemonium.

The children, it would seem, were either tearing apart the Kilpatrick's home or ripping each other to shreds.

Regardless of the tenor of the noise, there was something both pleasing and distressing about it. This was because Douglas had heard it before, time and again, whenever he'd go to Tamsin and Gavin's home.

He had never heard it at Sommersgate, not before Tamsin and Gavin's deaths, nor after.

Douglas was pleased to hear it again just as he was distressed it had stopped and all the reasons why.

At Mr. Kilpatrick's repeated greeting, Douglas shook off these thoughts and, without introducing himself, started to say, "Can you…" but stopped speaking when another phone was picked up and Mrs. Kilpatrick muttered a distracted hello.

Douglas was forced to start again. "I need you to watch the children for a few more hours."

"Is everything all right?" Mrs. Kilpatrick asked immediately, sounding alarmed.

Douglas found he was at a loss of what to say. He'd never been asked a question when he'd given an instruction. He couldn't say that Julia was ill or Mrs. Kilpatrick would come racing down to the house. He certainly couldn't tell them the truth.

"Miss Julia is," he fought for a diplomatic explanation and found one, "indisposed."

Silence greeted this announcement and then he heard a phone inexplicably clatter down in its cradle. Mr. Kilpatrick assured him the children were safe with them and Douglas rung off.

He returned to the bed, sliding in behind Julia and fitting his body against the silken length of hers while he slid his arm around her waist. He was debating with himself whether to take a moment to relive the extraordinary events of last night or to press his hand between her legs just so that he could hear another of her husky moans. Then, later, he'd coax her to say his name in her sweet, low voice when her limbs were wrapped tight around him and he was buried inside her.

While he was uncommonly undecided, she settled into his body, wiggling her ass into his groin.

Immediately, he chose the latter.

Before he could move though, she mumbled something sleepily into the pillow.

His arm curled tighter around her and his lips sought her ear.

"What?" he whispered and he felt her delicious shiver at the sound of his voice. This made his contentment grow.

He enjoyed his power over her, her response to his merest touch, the sound of his voice, in fact, he exalted in it.

She lifted her chin, nearly bumping his head with hers.

"Wanna kitty," she mumbled.

"What?" Douglas repeated, thinking he hadn't heard her correctly.

"Used to have a kitty, would sleep in on the weekends and he'd curl up right here." Her hand fluttered to her waist then fell to rest on his arm. "Had to put him to sleep a couple of weeks before Gavin died." She took a deep breath and then let it out in a long shuddering sigh. "I miss him."

Her voice was husky with sleep as well as longing for her cat.

She settled further into Douglas and then again whispered softly, "Wanna kitty."

Douglas pulled her deeper into his body.

"I'll get you anything you want," he promised her.

"Just a kitty," she answered and then fell back to sleep.

He'd get her a cat; he'd get her a dozen of them. And a sapphire just like the emerald she still hadn't taken off. And more than likely a ruby. And a fat pearl surrounded by diamonds.

He buried his face in her hair and smelled tangerines and jasmine. He discovered last night she wore the scent between her breasts as well.

He discovered a lot of things last night.

He discovered that when Julia climaxed, the legs she wrapped around him tightened convulsively, drawing him deeper into her body when he thought he couldn't go any deeper. He discovered that she had an incredibly talented tongue. He discovered that, even though he'd become excessively fond of her wardrobe, the sexiest thing he'd seen her wear was his dress shirt.

He also discovered that the sight of her with another man, or, in the case of last night, quite a number of them, turned him into a jealous lunatic.

He'd never felt a fury the like of last night, nor behaved in the way he did. He lost all control. That wasn't just unusual, it was unprecedented.

He didn't regret his behaviour, not in the slightest. The results spoke for themselves. She was there in his arms, in his bed and he intended for that not to change. Soon, she'd have his ring on her finger and she'd take his name. He'd been certain this was what he wanted, but now he realised this decision was absolute.

His hand splayed over her stomach, wondering, as he hadn't used protection (either time), if they'd created a child last night. Something stirred in him at the thought but he brushed it aside. Surely she wouldn't have allowed him to continue if she needed some protection. Not, of course, that he'd given her much choice. However, a clever woman who looked like Julia, and thus received the amount of attention she did (judging from last night), undoubtedly kept herself protected.

At the thought of that attention, his hand shifted upward and he cupped her breast.

There would be no more of that, now she was truly his, and he vowed to himself that would *never* change.

He used the pad of his thumb to stroke her nipple. As he was becoming accustomed, her body immediately responded, her nipple tightening. Most women of his acquaintance acted coy or were overeager or were greedy but not Julia. Julia took everything he was willing to give but she gave everything of herself in return, honestly and openly.

Just then, he heard a noise in the sitting room and his body reflexively tensed, his hand tightening on her breast and Julia grumbled sleepily, her eyes fluttering open, her neck twisting so she could look at him.

He released her breast, put a finger to her lips and lifted his head to listen.

Someone was in the sitting room.

He was out of the bed in flash, pulling on his trousers.

Where the bloody hell was Nick? He thought.

No one should be in the house. No one should be able to get through Nick.

Julia had turned toward him and pulled herself up on her elbow. Her other hand was clutching the covers to her breasts. Her eyes were sleepy and curious and her curls were tumbling around her face and shoulders. He put his finger to his lips this time to keep her silent and she nodded, bemused, as he moved stealthily to the door. If he needed to, he'd find a weapon in the other room and gave the room a mental inventory deciding on his target. If it was one of the children, however, come back for some reason, he certainly didn't need to go tearing into the room with a makeshift weapon raised and threatening.

It was a good decision.

As he yanked open the door, Mrs. Kilpatrick jerked upright, both her hands flying to her face.

"My lord... sir." She stopped and looked crazily around the room as if she was considering diving behind an armchair to hide herself before her eyes came back to him. "Mister Douglas," she finished, using a name for him she'd never used before.

Then she gestured to an extravagant tray that lay on a table. It was filled with plates carrying plain, almond and chocolate croissants, a selection of marmalades and jams sitting in little china bowls, a piece of butter moulded into a fleur de lis, a crystal bowl filled with sliced melon and strawberries, a silver coffeepot and two delicate china cups, two stemmed glasses filled with orange juice, a folded newspaper and even a slim crystal vase holding a single red rose.

"I brought a bit of breakfast. Just croissants and..." she trailed off then started again. "I didn't have a lot of time. I didn't want to disturb you but I thought you might be hungry."

Before he could respond, Julia's shocked voice sounded from behind Douglas.

"Mrs. K!"

Douglas turned to see her standing there, not in her dress or his shirt but, instead, wrapped tightly in his dressing gown.

Mrs. Kilpatrick looked at Julia, she blinked and then, he could swear, the ends of her lips twitched upward.

"Miss Julia, I brought breakfast," Mrs. Kilpatrick told her.

Gone was the stammering, Mrs. K bent and gamely made a few adjustments to the tray, straightening some lace-edged linen serviettes unnecessarily. "It's not much but it'll do in a pinch. Enjoy. Don't worry about the children; Roddy's taken them off to the ice rink. You've got *hours*." She emphasised the last word meaningfully and then threw Douglas an encouraging look that both surprised him and made him want to roar with laughter.

He had the insane urge to walk up to his housekeeper and kiss her cheek. Instead, Douglas said not a word, simply nodded. If he'd opened his mouth to speak, he would surely have laughed.

He did, however, allow himself to grin.

Julia, who had turned scarlet, muttered an embarrassed, "Uh... thank you."

Mrs. Kilpatrick smiled at Julia and Douglas witnessed stark adoration shining in her eyes. It struck him that this woman shared his home for nearly the length of his life and she never looked at him in that way. Julia had been there two months and Mrs. Kilpatrick would have laid down her life for her.

For some reason, this pleased Douglas immensely.

The older woman turned to him and he nodded at her in approval and she slowly, hesitantly, to his disbelief, winked at him.

Then she was gone.

He turned his eyes to Julia, who was staring at the door.

"She must think I'm a tramp, a tart," Julia burst out. "Oh my God, this is terrible!"

"Do you think," Douglas started and Julia turned humiliated eyes to him, "that she would bring you breakfast if she thought you were a tart?"

Julia looked at him, at the breakfast, at the door Mrs. Kilpatrick just exited through, back at Douglas and then she said, "Doesn't she bring all your women breakfast?"

Douglas's lingering grin immediately turned into a scowl.

"No," he replied shortly, walking toward her, "she has not once, in my debauched past, brought breakfast to a woman in this room."

Well certainly not unless he ordered her to do so but Julia didn't need to know that.

Julia ignored his tone and his comment and skirted around him to head toward the breakfast tray.

Douglas sighed. He would not be amused if she was going to begin resisting him again. He crossed his arms on his chest and watched as she sat on the couch in front of the food and reached for the coffeepot.

"Coffee?" she asked, lifting the pot gratuitously and failing to meet his eyes. He nodded and she poured, adding no milk or sugar and walked to him to hand him a cup. He continued to regard her, wondering at her mood, as she made her own, one sugar and a splash of milk. She deposited the pot on the tray, grabbed the cup by its saucer and an almond croissant and headed across the room.

To the door.

"Where are you going?" he demanded to know.

"To my room, to wash my face, brush my teeth, take a shower," she replied, her tone carefully blasé and she continued moving.

"You can do that here," he told her.

She stopped and turned to him, her mouth opening to speak when a knock came at the door.

"Yes?" he called before Julia could utter a word and Mrs. Kilpatrick popped her head around the door.

"Just brought you a couple of things, Miss Julia, toothpaste, your face wash..." she sidled in and stood, carrying a toiletries bag. She looked confused for a moment as Julia's hands were full so she moved to Douglas and, as he had a free hand, gave him the bag. "Thought you might want an easy morning and not have to run all over the house. You've been busy lately, you deserve a break." She stopped at the door, offered them both a cheeky smile and then closed the door softly behind her.

Julia swung widened eyes to his as her jaw dropped and Douglas raised his brow at her.

He could swear he heard her make a growling noise and she retraced her steps, put down her cup and croissant, walked to Douglas, snatched the bag out of his hand and tramped to his bathroom.

She didn't take long and when she came back, fresh faced, her hair pulled back in a messy bundle secured with a clip, he was seated in an armchair, sipping his coffee and reading the paper. Without access to his dressing gown, he had shrugged on his dress shirt to ward off the slight chill in the room but hadn't bothered buttoning it.

It smelled of her perfume and he decided he liked that.

Very much.

She sat on the couch and reached for her coffee, her movements jerky, her face duelling between bemused and mutinous.

"Is something wrong?" Douglas inquired, wondering how long courtesy would require for him to give her to have her breakfast before he dragged her back into the bedroom.

Or perhaps, he would have her on the couch.

Julia interrupted his pleasant reverie.

"Well, she might have brought your other women breakfast," she continued doggedly with the idea of his "other women", "but she probably didn't bring them toothpaste." Julia looked from her coffee to him and then grabbed the croissant. "It would seem she approves!" she exclaimed as if this idea was impossible.

"Firstly, there are no other women." When Julia looked like she would interrupt, he added, "Anymore. And secondly, yes, I would say her behaviour indicates approval. Why is that hard to believe?"

Julia took a bite of croissant and contemplated this piece of news while she chewed. She did not, however, answer.

He folded the paper and tossed it on the table.

She jumped.

He sighed again at her reaction before he said, "Julia. We need to talk."

She swallowed the bite of croissant as if it had the heft and width of an anvil. "About what?"

"About last night," he replied.

"What about it?" she asked, giving him a sidelong glance.

"You agreed to marry me."

At that, she paled and faced him head on.

"You *do* remember agreeing to marry me?" he demanded, his eyes narrowing.

"Of course!"

He felt his body relax and hadn't realised he'd tensed in preparation for her response.

However, there was something wrong, she was acting cagey and guarded. Or, more cagey and guarded than normal.

Her last husband hadn't handled her well, to say the least, and Douglas forced himself to move cautiously.

"Come here," he commanded gently.

She hesitated, her eyes darting around looking for escape. He leaned forward, pulled her coffee cup out of her hand and set it in its saucer and then divested her of her croissant. Then he grabbed her hand and tugged lightly. She rose to her feet with a deep, ungracious sigh and stepped the two paces toward him. He opened his legs and positioned her until she was standing between them, staring down at him, his hand still holding hers.

"Is something bothering you?" he asked softly.

Something dark crossed her eyes and she shook her head, then nodded, then ended with moving her head in a circle that encompassed both.

Douglas waited patiently.

"I... well, I wasn't exactly prepared for what happened last night," she admitted.

The realisation dawned on him what she was referring to and he felt a strange sensation that was part expectation, part hope and part triumph.

"Are you using birth control?" he queried.

Her body jerked.

"What?" she breathed then her hand ripped out of his and flew to her mouth as her eyes grew wide. "Oh my God."

Apparently, he realised, she was not referring to *that* kind of preparation.

He stood which brought him to within an inch of her. He was pleased to note that she didn't try to move away. He slid his hands around her waist, settling them loosely at the small of her back, enjoying this casual intimacy tremendously. "If you weren't talking about contraception..."

Her face cleared and she lifted her hand and waved it blithely between their two faces, nearly knocking him on the nose.

"Not to worry," she proclaimed. "Sean and I tried to have children for years and couldn't. He went to get checked and they found nothing wrong with him. So, obviously, it was me who was unable to conceive. Sean didn't want to go through all the rigmarole of the infertility clinic..." she didn't finish but heaved another sigh, though he didn't know if it was of relief or resignation.

Douglas continued to stare at her.

"Did they find something wrong with you?" he asked, his voice quiet, finding himself far more interested in her answer than he would have imagined himself to be.

"Sean told me I didn't need to check, he was okay and –" she started to explain.

Douglas felt his mouth tighten. "You didn't get checked?"

"No, I –"

"Did it occur to you that he might be lying?"

She blinked up at him. "Of course not, why would he do such a thing?"

That was an excellent question.

However, there were more questions as to Sean Webster's behaviour.

Such as, why would he torment and disparage a vital and intelligent woman? And why, when he had her love and devotion, would he abuse it? And lastly, why, when he had her legally bound to him, would he let her go?

Douglas knew the way men like Webster worked, he knew it intimately because his father was one. Sean Webster was not the type of man to admit to any failing. He preferred other people feeling they were inferior, even going so far as making them feel that way, rather than admit something was wrong with himself.

"Even Sean wouldn't be that cruel," she scoffed.

He watched her silently and gave her time to think it through. He saw the warring of emotions on her face, careening from disbelief to apprehension.

"Dear God," she breathed and started to tremble. She shut her eyes tight and whispered, "I'm such a fool."

His hands pressed in and he drew her nearer to him while she began to shake her head from side to side in denial. He felt an astonishingly strong sense of anger on her behalf. He would like to get his hands around Webster's throat and squeeze.

She lifted her dazed eyes to his.

"What'll we do?" she asked and Douglas didn't answer, he just looked at her. Julia carried on. "If... I mean, last night?"

"It's unlikely we conceived last night, if we did, we'll worry about it when it happens," Douglas assured her.

It was all the same to him except that perhaps the existence of a child would make it a certainty that she would never leave. At that thought, he fitted her snugly against his body before bending his head to brush his lips against hers.

When he drew away, he watched Julia lean back against his arm, her eyes wide with something he couldn't identify, something immensely tender and phenomenally raw. He'd never seen the like of it and the sight made his arms tense protectively around her while a feeling he could not place sliced through his gut.

He also felt a near overwhelming need to possess her, though he always felt that way, but somehow, just then, it was different.

Last night it had been a driving need to brand her as his, to bend her to his will, but now it had gentled. He had no intention of making her squirm under him, of withholding himself until he heard her whisper his name, of making her beg him for release. What he had planned for her this morning was entirely different.

But he knew he couldn't take her now and the only way to respond to her acceptance of this newly realised cruel deception was again to brush his lips against her parted ones.

"Maybe," he whispered, "we should try again." He lifted one hand

and exerted pressure between her shoulder blades to press her torso back to his body but she resisted.

She had masked the look in her eyes and he found that, even though he had only encountered it a moment ago, he wanted it back.

Her response was to pull out of his arms, stepping away and walking to the window. She stood there staring out at the fields and wrapped her arms around her body protectively.

Another man might have given her a moment of contemplation but he didn't want Julia to have a time to think.

Julia, Douglas decided, thought way too much.

He followed her and stood behind her, seeing her reflection in the window. With his left hand, he pulled her hair from the right side of her neck. He bent his head to drag his lips lazily from the soft spot behind ear to where her graceful neck met her shoulder while his left hand stole around her waist and pulled her against his body.

"Douglas," she whispered, her voice trembling with something he mistakenly thought was desire.

Without lifting his lips, his eyes caught hers in the reflection of the window, his right hand came up to her shoulder and he slowly pulled the dressing gown aside, his lips trailing its progress, his other arm drawing her incredible warmth deeper into his body. He noticed as her glowing, faultless skin became exposed at her chest and he felt the acute response of his body when he saw she was still wearing his emerald. His eyes dropped as the lapel of the dressing gown swept across her breast and caught against her nipple.

"I need you to promise me something," she interrupted his progress by speaking and his hand stilled at the fervent tone in her voice as his eyes lifted back to the reflection of hers in the window.

With her body against his, the smell of her in his nostrils, the taste of her at his lips and his knowledge of what was going to happen in his bed in a few moments time, he almost told her he'd promise her anything.

Of course, he did not.

"That depends." His hand slid up from her waist to just under her breast. His lips ascended her shoulder again, up her neck and behind her ear, a delectably sensitive area he discovered last night.

As he expected, she shivered. Also as he expected, she ignored her reaction.

"I want to talk about our, um... my agreeing to marry you."

He'd anticipated something like this. She thought too much. It probably had something to do with the children. She was excessively careful with them. Not to mention, she had an exceptionally strong sense of self-preservation, he'd been living that nightmare for two months. He wasn't going to give her the opportunity to build an exit strategy. If today's behaviour was any indication, Mrs. Kilpatrick might set fire to Julia's room and he couldn't imagine what antics the self-styled matchmaker Lizzie would get up to.

"Yes?" He ran his tongue up the side of her neck and playfully nipped her earlobe, his body gladly absorbing the shudder that his action induced.

He was becoming impatient. Mrs. Kilpatrick said hours and all the things he wanted to do to her would take much longer than that.

Definitely months

Probably years.

"Promise you won't get angry with me," Julia said.

He couldn't imagine anything she could say at that moment would make him angry with her. Douglas didn't, however, answer. He simply waited.

"I'm not going to marry you."

Except that.

"*What?*" he exploded, his arm tightening reflexively about her body, his head coming up with a jerk.

"I'm not going to marry you," she repeated.

"You bloody well are," he growled.

She shook her head and tried to pull away, succeeding in putting inches of space between them. He wrenched her back and his other arm went around her to hold her more firmly.

"Douglas, let me go."

"I believe I've answered that request more often than I've cared to," he clipped into her ear.

"You don't understand!" she cried, her eyes on his in the window.

"Explain it to me," he bit out.

She pushed against his arm. "Please, give me some space."

His arms loosened with a motive, the minute she moved away, he swung her around and yanked her back against his body, facing him then his arms closed back around her roughly.

"Douglas!"

"Talk!" His voiced cracked in the room like a thunderclap and he watched her clouded eyes clear as she became angry.

"I don't want to marry you!" she burst out.

"You must be joking," he snapped derisively.

Her eyes widened in angry apprehension.

"You aren't entirely irresistible," she informed him.

"Would you like me to prove you wrong?" It was a threat and his tone dangerous.

"No, not that," she evaded, knowing exactly what he meant and not stupid enough to deny it. Her eyes moved left to right and back at him. "That was... lovely."

"*Lovely?*" His voice was scathing. "You describe last night as *lovely?*"

"It was good," she stopped at his narrowed eyes. "Very good." His arms tightened. "Okay, it was wonderful. All right?" She was losing her composure, he saw she was both frightened and angry and he didn't care.

"So, explain to me how I'm resistible, would you?" he demanded.

"You have to give me a moment to let me think."

"I don't have to do anything."

"Fine," she snapped, "you're cold –"

"I was hot enough for you last night."

"I'm not talking about last night!" She stamped her foot in frustration and, at any other time, he would have found that adorable.

Now, he did not.

"Stop interrupting me," she ordered.

"Go on," he allowed, his strained patience showing as he spoke through clenched teeth.

"I've done this before, this marriage thing and let me tell you it is *not* all that it's cracked up to be."

If he thought he couldn't get angrier, he was wrong.

"I'm not Webster," he growled.

"I know that!" she shouted. "I didn't say you were and you're interrupting again."

He snapped his mouth shut and glared at her with glittering eyes.

"I can't do it again, I can't. I won't! It's too damned hard!" she burst out. "You get mixed up, you lose yourself. I won't lose myself again, Douglas. I can't and I won't."

He stared at her.

There had been very little in Douglas Ashton's life that he ever wanted. Most of it he could obtain, the rest of it, a loving mother and father, his sister back from the dead, was unobtainable.

At that moment, he found himself wanting something.

And what he wanted was for Julia to lose herself with him.

He wanted this stubborn, tempestuous Julia Fairfax to disappear and an acquiescent, but still tempestuous, Julia Ashton to take her place. He wanted to brand her with his name and shackle her with his ring.

Did she not understand that was a good thing?

He used a particularly heavy weapon in his arsenal. "And what if you got pregnant last night?"

She gasped and her tense body stilled. He jostled her in his arms, giving her a none-too-gentle shake.

She came out of her surprise. "I'll worry about it if it happens."

"You'll damn well marry me if it happens!" he roared and she reared back against his arm.

He could not believe in all his years, all his experience, all the women before her, that he was reduced to ordering a woman to marry him.

"Of course!" she blurted.

"Jesus, Julia, don't you know I'll make you happy?" The words should have been beautiful but instead they were rough with anger.

"Douglas," she used words that stung, "what do you know of making anyone happy?"

He felt those words like a kick to the stomach and he immediately let her go and stepped back.

He wouldn't have expected that attack from Julia.

His mother, probably, his father, definitely, but not Julia.

They watched each other across the short expanse that separated them like warriors on a battlefield.

Finally, she seemed to realise the cruelty behind her words and she made a move toward him but stopped herself.

"I'm only protecting myself," she whispered. When he made no response she continued. "You won't want to hurt me but you will. They always do." Her words were filled with a strange mixture of wisdom and bitterness.

He looked at her and realised his mistake.

Weeks ago it occurred to him that she was innately damaged, not only by her ex-husband's treatment but at the hands of her father.

But again, he'd been wrong.

He'd never been wrong so many times in his bloody, fucking life as he was with Julia.

She wasn't innately damaged.

She was destroyed.

His challenge was far bigger than he expected. To have her, he'd have to gather the shattered pieces of her and put them back together.

He vaguely noticed she was speaking. "It'll take some time but we'll get passed this..."

He heard her talking but he wasn't listening.

Instead he was thinking exactly how very much he liked a challenge.

"I'm not the others, Julia." He cut her off and she just looked at him. "I'll simply have to prove it to you," he declared.

Her mouth opened slightly but no words came out. He didn't wait for a reply; he walked toward his bedroom to take a shower.

"Don't you ever give up?" Her exasperated voice sounded from behind him.

His answer was to close the door.

18

ALONE

Julia heard the beeping in her room after she came out of the shower.

After that scene with Douglas, she was shaken and frightened half out of her mind. She wanted to pack and leave but couldn't because of the children. Wouldn't, because of her promise to Tammy and Gav.

She was stuck in a nightmare.

And it was all her own damned fault.

She saw her evening bag lying on the bed. She must have left it in the Bentley and Carter found it. She opened it to find that her mobile was telling her she had a missed call.

Or, to be precise, eleven.

And all from Charlie.

She was considering turning it off when it sounded in her hand.

She jumped, nearly dropping it and before she could think what she was doing, she flipped it open and put it to her ear.

"Thank God, Jewel! I've been worried sick, I thought he'd killed you!" Charlie shrieked and any other time Julia would have laughed at her dramatics.

"I'm all right," Julia lied, not wanting to talk to Charlie, not wanting to talk to anyone.

Charlie failed to read her mood. "You just *have* to tell me what happened! Oliver spent the entire drive home to London, two hours, mind, lecturing me about interfering so I hope it's good."

"Charlie..." Julia started and then she couldn't stop herself, she burst into tears.

Seconds before she wanted nothing but solitude and the time to plan her defence against whatever barrage on her senses and emotions would next come from Douglas. But now she strode to the chaise lounge and collapsed on it, unburdening herself entirely, honestly (and somewhat explicitly), to her friend.

When she finally finished, Charlie was silent.

Julia sniffed and wiped her eyes on the sleeve of her robe "Charlie? Are you there?"

"I'm here," Charlie stated, uncharacteristically quiet.

"I think I need –" Julia started but Charlie interrupted her.

"What you need, Jewel, is to marry Douglas."

"*What?*" Julia gasped.

"Listen to me, darling," Charlie demanded urgently before Julia could get a word in edgewise, "you may never get Douglas to love you; he just isn't built like that. I don't know why but he isn't. I have to tell you, though, what you have from him is more than I've ever seen him give *anyone*."

Julia palpably felt these words go through her and was holding the phone to her ear like she intended to graft it there.

She searched desperately for excuses to defend her heart against the words it wanted to hear. "Charlie, I can't settle for that. And anyway love turns to –"

"No, Jewel, not always, in fact, mostly never. You've had tremendously bad luck. I know you had some tough experiences but no matter what Douglas is, and he's a lot of things," she noted with her usual bluntness, "he isn't the type of man who would hurt you."

"How do you know?" Julia was thinking about the accident Douglas had ordered Sean to have, the gunshot wound he never explained, the two years when he'd disappeared. She remembered his words, *"Because I need something warm and soft and alive beside me tonight. Something that smells good and feels good. After what I've seen..."*

He had secrets, dark ones.

She had no idea what he was capable of and she figured Charlie didn't either.

"Because he'd never hurt Tammy and to hurt you would hurt Tammy. He had great respect for Gavin too."

Oh God. She had a point there.

"Charlie –" Julia tried to interject.

"Honestly, Jewel, don't you understand from what you've just told me that even not having it all with Douglas is a damn sight better than *anything* you'd get from anyone else?"

Julia was struck silent at Charlie's stunning proclamation. And before she let the truth of it edge into her mind, she shut it out completely.

"Think about it," Charlie urged. "I'll call you later," and she hung up.

Miserable, Julia spent (hiding, she knew), the whole day in her rooms. She kept her mind obsessively busy by wrapping presents and making unnecessary lists and when the children came home, they rushed in to say hello and out again because Douglas was taking them horseback riding.

She wasn't alone in the room, she knew. The Mistress was there with her, freezing her ankles, trying to tell her something Julia couldn't understand, probably didn't want to understand. Julia did her best to ignore her and she finally went away.

Much later, when the sun was setting, to her amazement, Julia saw The Master, clear as day, pacing, agitated, back and forth in front of Julia's windows.

Julia shut the curtains.

When she became used to the impossibility of living with two ghosts, she did not know and she didn't have the energy to worry about it.

It was Veronika's shift at the house and Julia let her go early. She made a big vat of Texas chilli for dinner, spending the entire time she cooked mentally preparing for any upcoming confrontation with Douglas at supper.

The children screamed in, still jazzed from a day of physical activity and she met them in the hallway. She was wiping her hands on a dish-towel as the kids started to scatter this way and that. Out of the corner of her eye, she saw Douglas saunter in but didn't acknowledge him.

"Everyone get cleaned up. Dinner is in half an hour," she announced.

The kids raced up the stairs and Julia turned to see Douglas standing in the hallway watching her, his arms crossed on his chest and his feet planted apart.

He looked exactly what he was, lord of the manor, master of all he surveyed. With that sexy scar on his lip and that even sexier glint in his eye, instead of looking like a man who was born to it, he looked like a man who had seized it.

This thrilled her, annoyed her and scared the living daylights out of her all at the same time.

He wore a soft suede jacket the colour of clay and a forest green turtleneck over faded blue jeans and boots. Slap a cowboy hat on his head and he was the *GQ* version of the damned Marlboro Man.

"Dinner is in half an hour," she repeated tersely.

"I heard you," he replied.

She walked away, hoping that he wouldn't follow her.

He didn't.

Then she hoped for the disappointment that came from him *not* following her would go away.

It didn't either.

❦ ❦ ❦

"And he sits the best horse *ever*," Lizzie enthused with the fervour of a zealot.

Everyone was sitting around the huge dining room table eating dinner. Even though Julia loved chilli, she found she wasn't hungry. This was probably because she was *extremely* aware that Douglas was sitting to her left side. Every time she looked at his hands, she thought of what they could do to her body. Every time she looked at his face, her eyes dropped to his lips and then she thought about what *they* could do (and, as if he could read her mind, those lips twitched at the corners which then made her want to crash the nearest, undoubtedly priceless vase over his head).

Since their return that afternoon, she had gone from worrying about what Douglas would do next to worrying about what *she* would do if she was pregnant. Then she started to get angry about what Sean had likely done. Now, she was frustrated at Lizzie who seemed to want to convince Julia that Douglas was, at any moment, going to walk calmly outside and fly, such were his superhuman powers.

"He's going to teach me to play polo," Willie said through a mouthful of chilli.

Et tu, Willie? Julia thought, her eyes rolling to the ceiling.

"I'm gonna play polo too!" Ruby shouted, not wanting to be left out.

"Do you know how to ride, Julia?" Douglas asked, his deep baritone rumbling over her like a caress.

She ignored the caress and answered the question. "No."

"You do too!" Lizzie accused. "We all went riding at Pokagon State Park."

Julia watched the girl closely to see if there would be any negative response to a verbally acknowledged memory that involved her parents. None of the children seemed to notice and she allowed her quick bout of tenseness to subside.

Julia swept a glance passed Douglas who was looking at her with what appeared, to her stunned disbelief, to be smugness.

She turned her attention to her chilli, pretending to go about the business of actually eating it when she'd only been able to manage two mouthfuls and she stirred it around.

"Lizzie-babe, I hardly think some cowboy getting me up on a two hundred year old horse by pushing me up with a shove on my behind and then riding it docilely in a line with ten other people for half an hour constitutes as 'knowing how to ride'."

"Yeah, that was funny. Even in the line, you nearly fell off," Willie added then turned to inform Douglas, "She didn't take her hands off the pommel the entire time. The cowboy guy eventually had to ride beside her the whole way."

Another glance showed that Douglas no longer looked smug, he looked annoyed.

Willie, now a veritable font of information, told Douglas, "And she walked around for the rest of the day like she had a tree between her legs."

Julia gritted her teeth.

Douglas grinned.

"What's for pudding?" Ruby screeched and Julia could have kissed her youngest niece for changing the subject even if Julia wasn't certain she'd ever stop the ringing in her ears.

"All right, everyone," Julia ordered, "plates rinsed and in the washer."

She managed dessert without too much of an effort and Douglas thankfully disappeared for the rest of the evening, leaving her to take care of the kids and then hurry to her own room in an attempt to avoid him.

Even though it was early, she prepared for bed. In a gesture toward confidence-building, she pulled on her favourite nightie, a short, spaghetti-strapped, strawberry-coloured cotton wisp of material with little embroidered peach flowers and peach lace around the hem and neckline.

She tried to read but all she could do was think.

So she quit reading and turned off the light and tried to sleep.

Still, all she could do was think.

She wasn't falling in love with Douglas Ashton.

Julia was in love with him.

In fact, there was a very good possibility she'd been in love with him for fifteen years.

She probably even married Sean because he reminded her of Douglas (she decided it was a good idea to blame Douglas for her first marriage fiasco, it helped her stay focused).

She was in love with Douglas and forced to live with him for, at least, the next twelve years of her life. What on earth she had done to deserve this dastardly end, she did not know. And, if the last two months were anything to go by, she didn't think she would make it for another two months let alone more than a decade.

If he didn't leave her alone, she wouldn't be able to resist him.

And she *had* to resist him. No matter what Charlie said, Lizzie wanted or even Mrs. K apparently hoped for, she had long since vowed to herself she was never going to let another man like Douglas into her heart. He wasn't Sean, she knew, and he wasn't her father either.

But he wasn't Gavin.

Gavin had loved his wife with a powerful distraction that was unlike anything Julia had ever seen and definitely nothing she'd ever known. When he married Tamsin and he said his vows, he nearly shouted the roof off the Cathedral, he was so proud to say them. Any other man would have looked the fool, but not Gav, and Julia knew every woman's heart in that church melted because that's what happened to her own.

Julia wanted a man like that and if she couldn't have it (which she knew she couldn't), then she wanted no man at all.

She was self-sufficient and capable and didn't mind being alone.

But she was tired of her loneliness, tired of fending for herself, tired of not having anyone to talk to her about her day or help her if the car had a flat tire.

She wanted to be cared for and protected; she admitted to herself this was true.

But she wanted it with devotion and in the meantime (which would be for always) she knew she could take care of herself.

She had no other choice.

It was easy for Charlie to tell her to settle, she had Oliver and he blatantly worshipped the ground Charlie walked on. He might do it sometimes with exasperation at her crazy antics, but he did it and would do it, for all time.

Julia was a game to Douglas, he made that perfectly clear. He'd had dozens, maybe scores, it could even be *hundreds* of women for all she knew. She was just one in the long queue and, more than likely, not the last one.

Once he'd conquered her, he'd move on.

That was what she feared, that was what she would have to avoid, that was why she could not let him win. Because she knew that if she let him see what was in her heart and he couldn't reciprocate it, then she would be lost. He would go on with his life and she would be left picking up the pieces. Again. By herself. She doubted he'd be cruel, but was thoughtless indifference any less unkind than outright abuse?

She finally fell into a fitful sleep and dreamed of Douglas, one of those vivid dreams, so realistic it was almost like it could actually be happening. Now, with the intimate knowledge of what it was like to be with Douglas, the dream was all the more intense.

He was behind her, his hard body pressed the length of her. His mouth was at the back of her neck then behind her ear then he was nipping her earlobe with his straight, white teeth. His hands were all over her, hot and strong, one stroking tantalisingly at the underside of her breast while the other one slid underneath her to wrap around and cup her between her legs. A finger idly stroked her there, deliciously teasing.

She pressed back into him; she had no need to protect herself from a dream. She wiggled her behind into his groin and heard a low groan which caused a shudder to pass through her and a flush of heat to spiral from her stomach downwards where a glorious ache had begun.

The hand between her legs changed position, coming up to cup a breast while his free hand pressed into her underwear, his knee forced itself between her legs from behind just enough to part them and give him better access.

Then his finger slid inside her.

Her head tilted back and she whimpered low while lush sensations shot out across her body from between her legs. At the same time the pad of his thumb stroked across her nipple and his finger disappeared from between her legs, only to come back as two, filling her more completely. His thumb found just the perfect spot between her legs and she started to move, nestling her bottom into his lap at the same time pressing into his fingers. Her hand found his arm, sliding down, holding his and feeling it while he tormented her.

The minute her hand found his, his body moved slightly, his mouth came to her ear and she heard him say in a husky voice, "Julia."

Though it was not Dream Douglas saying her name, it was Real Douglas.

Her eyes flew open but it was too late, her body had betrayed her, she couldn't stop moving, pressing against him, using her hand to encourage him. The ache was building to fever pitch, he was pressing, stroking, soon, she knew, it would be over, she could feel it coming and she wanted it more than breath.

But knowing he was there, she wanted *him*, not his hand and even as her body begged him to bring her to climax by pressing against his, she tried to turn toward him.

His arms tensed immediately, holding her in place against him but still away from him.

"No, Julia. This is for you."

"I want…" she whispered but it was too late, the sensations overcame her words and with a small cry, her back arched, her pelvis ground into his hand and the pleasure tore through her violently and when the first wave ended, his hand continued its work and to her shocked outcry of, "Oh!" (which didn't half do it justice), the second wave began. Somewhere in her dazzling double climax, her dazed mind noted she felt Douglas smile against her neck.

When the luscious tension ebbed out of her body, his hands slid away, his lips drifted across her shoulder and he disappeared.

As in, he left the room.

She lay there, her body spent, her mind still full of hazy cobwebs of desire.

And she lay there, satisfied, but alone.

She wanted to forget it, to ignore it, go to sleep and worry about it tomorrow. She wanted to think of it as another crazy day in a life full of crazy days since moving to England.

But she couldn't.

And because she couldn't, instead of bursting into tears of frustration (and longing) Julia began fuming.

Then her ruminating anger turned to fury.

She whipped the covers off the bed and the minute she did, Archie started scratching at the window and The Mistress slid arcticly through her ankles.

"Oh, bugger off!" she seethed and distractedly she noticed the scratching stopped immediately and the draught melted away.

In the darkness, she paced the room once then twice then went to the door, wrenching it open only to whirl around and pace the room again. She tried to calm herself, tried to figure out why she was so furious, because it wasn't all that surprising, she wouldn't put anything passed Douglas.

Then she knew.

"I mean, how *dare* he?" she muttered to no one.

He was playing with her, toying with her, he *knew* exactly what he could do to her and he was using *her own body* against her.

He didn't fight fair.

Well, she thought, *two could play at that game.*

With long, angry strides, she exited her room and went to his, half-blinded by fury, feeling as if her head would explode.

Not wanting to wake the children, she carefully opened the door to his sitting room and just as carefully closed it with a noiseless click.

The sitting room was dark but the door was open to his bedroom and a soft light came from there. She crossed the sitting room quickly and surged into his bedroom.

She'd caught him fresh from the shower, walking across the room rubbing his wet hair with a towel while another towel was wrapped around his waist. She noted that there were still droplets of moisture on his broad shoulders.

He halted the moment he saw her.

"Julia," he said warily catching the look in her eye. His hands holding the towel dropped.

"Tomorrow, I'm leaving. I'm moving home to America and I'm taking the children with me," she announced and she watched, with not a small amount of fear, as his face grew hard.

"The hell you are," he replied, wariness obliterated and instant rage in its place.

"Watch me," she retorted and turned on her heel, whirling around but before she got to the door, he was there, quick and quiet as a cat, and he slammed it shut right in front of her. She felt the whoosh of air as it whipped closed.

She jolted to a stop and then turned to him.

"I'm leaving," she repeated.

"You leave, you leave the children behind." His eyes were glowing dangerously but she ignored it.

"You promised you wouldn't bring the children into it." She threw in his face.

"I lied," he stated calmly.

She pursed her lips, her fury a tempest behind her eyes.

Then, she hissed, "I hate you."

"No you don't."

"Oh yes, Douglas, I do," she assured him.

At that, he advanced on her and she could no longer ignore the look in his eyes, their dark blue turning midnight. His lips had tightened and the scar came out in bold relief, making him even more menacing.

She retreated.

"You can't make me stay," she said, her anger melting into bravado.

He quirked an eyebrow, tossing the towel he was holding to the side. "No?"

He took it as a challenge that she should have been smart enough not to throw at him but she wasn't feeling in the mood to be smart.

"And I'll take the children with me, you'll have to fight me for custody," she threatened as he kept at her and she continued to retreat, walking backwards. He was quickly closing in on her, barely a step away.

"I'll do it," he warned. "I'm far richer than you and they're British citizens, I doubt international law would smile upon kidnapping."

"It wouldn't be kidnapping, I have custody!"

"It would if Baron Blackbourne says it was."

"You wouldn't do that!" she burst out.

"Try me," he snarled and she reared back, coming to the end of her retreat when her knees hit something soft and solid and she toppled backwards onto the bed.

"Well done, darling," he drawled.

She started to scramble away, thinking what a fool she was for retreating *toward* the bed but he swiftly caught her ankle and yanked her effortlessly back across the comforter. She yelped and twirled and then watched as, with a rough jerk, he pulled the towel away at his hips.

"Don't touch me!" she snapped.

He loomed over her. "When I'm done, I'll have you begging me, you'll press your wet, tight –"

"No!" She shoved at him.

It was too late. He was there, he was driven, he was furious and he was going to have exactly what he wanted and there was nothing Julia could do about it.

To her extreme humiliation, she melted within moments of his mouth landing on hers, his hands on her body and his hardness against her. He seemed to be everywhere and her body wanted him, her heart wanted him, it was only her mind that wouldn't allow her to have him.

And she kissed him back, nipped his shoulder with her teeth and licked away the moisture there. She gasped in his ear and ran her nails up his spine. He left her long enough to tear her underwear down her legs and then he was back, she opened her legs to welcome him and he was gliding inside her. He was fully ready for her and she was long since ready for him.

She arched her back and neck and knew he had won.

But, throughout it all, silently, she was crying.

His mouth took hers again in a brutal kiss while his hips pounded into her and she gloried in it at the same time her grief was engulfed by his passion. He tore his lips away and her breath gave a stuttered hitch from the soundless weeping but he didn't notice. He slid his cheek down hers, slammed his groin into her and her neck arched with delight and despair at the pleasure of just how deep he was.

She wanted to hold him there forever.

It was then his head came up and his body stilled.

She tensed.

"Julia?" His voice was hoarse and as he looked down on her she turned her head to the side in a futile attempt to hide the tears on her face.

His hand came up to her cheek and gently moved her face to look at him. His thumb found the tears that were sliding down the sides of her eyes into her hair. He stroked her there, trailing a wet line of tears down her cheekbone to her lips so she tasted their saltiness.

"Julia," he muttered, his voice thick.

"It's okay," she told him, her voice shaky, her hips moving because he was still buried inside her. His body tightened, his muscles stiffening under her hands. "Really, Douglas, it's okay. You win, for tonight, you win," she whispered.

His forehead dropped to rest on hers, the length of his nose pressing against hers and he closed his eyes as if he was in pain.

"It doesn't have to be like this." He was moving again, gently, sliding in and out with sweet, agonising slowness.

"I bring out the worst in people," Julia admitted haltingly, "especially men."

He groaned, low and deep and it sounded like there was pain mixed with his pleasure. He kissed her, not with brutal passion but this time tenderly, a kiss like none she'd had from him before, a kiss that made something bud inside of her, awaken and start to grow.

Then his lips broke away, they trailed down her cheek, her jaw and he buried his face in her neck, the whole time, making gentle love to her.

"What am I going to do with you?" His voice sounded disgruntled in her ear.

"Whatever you want."

This brought another croaky moan from him, his arms wrapping around her, his hands lifting her hips to receive him.

Her neck arched again as her body melted further into his, wrapping itself tightly around him, *everywhere.*

"Why do you want to go?" His voice was still at her ear and she shuddered, loving the depth of it, his accent, he had such a beautiful voice.

"You came down and... did what you did in my room and then you left me alone." Her arms tightened around him and she whispered, "Douglas, I'm so tired of being alone." She pressed her hips against him and he ground his against her.

"You don't have to be alone."

"I'm always alone." Her voice was an ache.

His hips were moving faster, pressing harder, she melted further into him, tightened around him.

"Julia," his breath was shallow, "I'll not let you go." He drove into her, not gentle now, his heat was overwhelming her and her head reared up, her face burying itself in his neck.

"You have to," she whispered into his ear, knowing he was struggling, knowing that she was close but he wanted her to finish before him. "Let go, sweetheart," she urged but he held back, moving faster, driving deeper and she went closer. "Douglas," she breathed and he gave it to her, her lips opened against his skin where she moaned as the pleasure rippled through her.

Julia came down, dropping her head to the bed and Douglas lifted his, his eyes locked with hers and she held her breath at the look in their dark depths before he rammed into her hard, twice, and then his head jerked back and she saw the chords and veins standing out in his neck as he climaxed inside her.

For some reason, she thought watching Douglas lose control while he was buried inside her was the most beautiful sight she ever beheld and she allowed herself to glory in the fact that she could give that to him, the fierce, powerful, handsome Douglas Ashton.

She lifted her head to run her tongue along his neck as she slid her fingers in his thick hair.

He collapsed on top of her, his weight pressing her into the bed and she welcomed it, holding him tight to her with all four limbs. His breath was coming fast then but after it slowed, he shifted himself so that he wasn't fully resting on her but he didn't move away.

His lips brushed hers, feather light.

"I didn't mean to hurt you; I meant to give you something." He was talking about before, in her room and she knew it was the closest she'd get to an apology. She nodded and his hands came back to her face, rubbing the place where the tears had been.

"If you ever leave," his voice had changed from soft to harsh, "I'll find you and bring you back."

She felt her stomach lurch and she didn't know if it was with fear or happiness.

She made no reply, there didn't need to be one with that kind of promise. She simply stared at him.

He moved suddenly, reaching out to his side and jerking down the covers. He rolled them both towards the pillows, finally disengaging from her. Then he carefully righted their position on the bed, settled her at his side and yanked the covers back over them.

"I can't sleep here, Douglas, the children –"

"If you leave," he repeated, "I'll find you and bring you back."

She didn't know what else to say because she knew he'd be true to his promise.

It was a Douglas she'd never known before. She'd been used to his calm but now she'd heard him roar, she heard him tease and she'd heard such harshness in his tone that it felt like it was both shredding her heart and mending it at the same time.

After what happened that night, she didn't know what tomorrow would bring. But she fell asleep with her body held closely against his side, her head on his chest, all the while thinking of his forehead pressed to hers and that unbelievably tender kiss.

19

CHRISTMAS

Julia found out quickly that Douglas's next line of attack would be what could only be described as a "tender onslaught" mixed with "not-so-tender onslaught" both of which were very effective even if she'd be damned if she'd let him know it.

It started the very next morning after the night he'd made love to her.

He woke her by running a finger lightly down her spine, her eyelids fluttered open to see him sitting on the side of the bed watching her with sexy, hooded eyes.

He was fully dressed wearing a grey suit with a vermillion shirt and a matching vermillion tie that had grey and blue designs patterned on it.

"What time is it?" she grumbled sleepily.

He bent and kissed her shoulder. "Time enough for you to get to your own bed before the children wake," he muttered against her skin.

That got her attention. She whirled and sat bolt upright and in a frenzy, threw the covers back. Dodging his body, she jumped out of the bed. She located her panties, tugged them on quickly and, without a backward glance, began to dart out of the room.

It occurred to her belatedly she should mark the occasion with something, lest he get the wrong idea. She stopped halfway to the door and turned back.

"Don't read anything into last night, that was last night and now is... well, now," she finished lamely.

He stood slowly and surveyed her with a curiously intense expression.

"Nothing's changed," she warned.

He watched her a moment and then the intensity faded from his eyes and warmth filled them.

Warmth from Douglas was something else Julia wasn't used to and something she found excruciatingly hard to resist.

When he spoke, his voice was amused, "I figured that."

She ignored his warmth, his tone, gave one curt nod and escaped.

He was gone most of the day on business. It was the day before Christmas Eve and the children were already beginning to let their excitement override their common sense. It took all her time to finish up her Christmas chores, break up their arguments and deal with what would essentially be three days without Mrs. K (who would be coming for Christmas dinner, but as a guest).

Douglas arrived home for supper and joined them, having shed his jacket and tie. Then, after the pudding dishes were whisked away by Mrs. K, Julia settled in the lounge with the children to watch a Christmas DVD when Douglas strolled in, holding a sheaf of typed papers that had black scrawling all over them.

She looked closely at the papers and saw it was her business plan.

His eyes met hers. "If you have a moment, Julia, I'd like to discuss this with you."

She stared at the papers, unable to mask her horror.

"You've marked all over it," she whispered.

"Ten minutes," he said, his tone gentle.

From the marks she figured it would take ten hours but like a doomed man heading to the gallows, she followed him to his study.

He sat at his desk and she stood opposite.

"It'll be hard for you to see from there," he commented, quirking an arrogant brow.

She glared at him, already beside herself with curiosity that was mingled with hesitation warring with the feeling that she did not want to spend any more time alone with him than was absolutely necessary.

She didn't trust him, not one bit.

But curiosity won out and with an undignified sigh, she walked around the desk and stood at his side.

He immediately began to explain his notes, using his Mont Blanc pen to indicate bold scratching and what they meant to her passages, patiently explaining what he wrote and why.

She found, against her will, that she was fascinated by what he had to say. He was very clever, thorough and intuitive. Despite herself, she leaned forward, bending at the hips to rest her elbows on his desk.

Finally, unable to hide her enthusiasm, she became fully engrossed, leaned into him, grabbed the pen out of his hand and started to write her own notes around his as he talked. Their heads were bent together over the document barely an inch apart.

When they came to the last page, she underlined (twice) a particularly salient concluding point and, lost in the pleasure of the work, turned her head to smile at him.

"This is brilliant," she complimented him, unable to stop herself.

"It was very good before I started," he replied, his eyes hooded but her mind was still fully consumed by the document.

"Thank you," she replied, dismissing a compliment that, since it came from Douglas (who she knew had a very astute head for business), was very dear indeed.

Before she could turn her head away, he caught her chin in his hand and leaned forward, pressing his lips against hers in sweet, but hard, kiss.

Her body instantly froze but she had no time to have any further reaction as a sound came from the door.

Julia tore her chin out of his hand and shot upright.

Lizzie was standing at the door.

"Sorry," their niece started to retreat then came back in a rush of two steps, a tentative grin settling on her face. She grabbed the door-knob and declared helpfully, "I'll just close the –"

"Lizzie-babe, there's no need," Julia said but the door already closed with a snap.

In a dither (an actual *dither*), Julia grabbed the papers and started to move away. She halted, twirled and stammered, "Um, thanks Douglas... for this... it's good."

He had come to his feet and was watching her, his eyes actually dancing mischievously.

Dancing. *Mischievously.*

At his expression, she wanted to scream or throw herself into his arms. Instead she forced herself to start to leave again and noticed she still had his pen so she rushed back and held it out to him.

"Keep it," he said, not looking at the pen, instead looking in her eyes.

"But it's an expensive pen."

He shrugged. "I have others."

She ignored him, placed it carefully on the desk and fled the room.

The next day, Christmas Eve, she had no time to worry about Douglas as she was too worried about the children. Tammy and Gav always made Christmas a very special day for the kids and Julia wanted to be on her guard just in case they lapsed into the same melancholy that she felt edging every moment of her day.

They seemed to cope well with Willie and even Lizzie doing their best to stay jolly and Patricia helped by calling and making everyone laugh. They sat around most of the day, watching Christmas DVDs and eating. Julia made them homemade pizza for dinner, Douglas joined them finally and they all ate the pizza while watching Gavin's favourite movie, *White Christmas.*

It took a great deal of time settling them into bed and Julia didn't want to start her Santa preparations until she was certain that Ruby was well asleep. The girl got up three times, coming down to check things out, rubbing her eyes in pretence and saying she was thirsty, she heard a noise and then trying the thirsty route again. The final time, Douglas came out of his study and took her up himself, which was a stroke of pure genius as Ruby was unlikely to leave a bed that Douglas firmly tucked her into.

Finally safe to start, Julia began collecting the extra Christmas presents, stocking stuffers and the boxes her mother had sent that she had hidden in her rooms and Mrs. K had secreted away in various places in the house. She thought about preparing Christmas herself but it would take forever and she had a long day tomorrow. Surely the children would be up early and she had a lot of cooking to do as she had invited Mr. and Mrs. K, Ronnie and Nick to Christmas Dinner (Carter had gone to his daughter's place in Devon for the holiday).

Douglas had not said a word about his servants being invited to dinner, merely nodded his head when she suggested it and said distractedly, "You've the running of the house, Julia."

Nick had no qualms about it, of course, but the Kilpatricks and Ronnie seemed somewhat shy, although also delighted about the idea.

She went to search for Douglas as he was her only hope of getting the presents sorted and getting to bed at a halfway decent hour. She could not find him anywhere and realised with chagrin that he'd most likely already retired.

With leaded feet, she approached the door to his rooms and then knocked softly, not wanting to awaken the children.

She gasped when it was thrown open almost immediately.

He stood there wearing his jeans and the khaki v-neck sweater he'd worn that day but his feet were bare.

His eyes warmed immediately when he saw her.

"Julia," was all he said.

Not wanting him to get the wrong impression, she rushed in with an explanation. "I was hoping you'd help me play Santa."

His damned eyebrow lifted.

She gave him a mutinous look.

"Ruby still believes and we have to get the stockings stuffed and Santa's presents laid out..." she looked at his feet, "you'll need your shoes."

He looked at his feet then at her and didn't say a word.

She lost her nerve, deciding instantly she could do it alone even if it took all night, and blurted, "It's okay if you don't want to help, I'll do it myself." And she whirled and escaped, going as fast as her feet could take her.

He found her in the back hallway, dragging a huge bag filled with wrapped presents. Without a word, he reached around her and hefted it up as if it weighed no more than a pencil, turned and walked away.

She noticed he was wearing shoes.

She ran to her rooms to get more.

Once they had all the stuff in the library where the tree was and where the children had decided they wanted Christmas, he stood there dubiously eyeing the bags and boxes filled to overflowing and the vast piles of presents already under the tree.

"This is ridiculous," Douglas stated correctly. It looked like Santa and his whole workshop of elves had exploded in the room.

"Mom and I wanted to make sure that –" Julia started to explain as she took the stockings from the mantel.

"I understand," he murmured, interrupting her, and she fell silent because he sounded like he understood, very much.

As she worked, she began to realise he seemed at odds as to what to do. He likely never played Santa before and she gently gave him directions which he carried out without hesitation.

Feeling strange that they were doing this joyful business in complete silence, she asked, "What were your Christmases like?"

"What do you mean?" He was putting an orange in the toe of each stocking.

"Did you have stockings like this or pillowcases at the end of your bed?" she inquired, suddenly very curious about what his childhood was like.

Tamsin never spoke of her childhood, at least not to Julia. Julia knew that Tamsin worked herself into exhaustion putting every ounce of magic into Christmas that she could stuff into it and she figured Tammy was holding up a tradition (even if it was hard to envision Monique stuffing a stocking, it wasn't hard to envision her ordering Mrs. K to do so).

"Neither," Douglas replied and Julia's hand stilled in the process of following him along the stockings tipping into them the American Christmas chocolates her mother had sent.

"Neither?" she stared at him confused.

Douglas didn't answer.

Julia tried again. "Did you open your presents Christmas Eve or Christmas morning?"

Finished with the oranges, he started to sort the presents in a box marked "Stocking Stuffers".

"We received our present at dinner."

His tone invited no further questioning but she was too stunned by this strange piece of information to let it slide. What did he mean, "present", in singular, and whoever heard of a child getting one present at dinner?

Thinking he didn't understand her question, she clarified, "No, I mean when you were children."

He continued his work, seeming engrossed in it.

"At dinner," was all he said.

An uneasy feeling stole through her. Even Monique (who was, thankfully, taking the holiday with friends in Munich) could not be so cold as to give her children one present at Christmas dinner.

She pressed on. "What was your favourite present ever?"

"My father gave me some stock in Microsoft. I made a fortune on it."

She gasped, she couldn't stop herself. "When you were a child, your parents gave you stock for your Christmas present?"

Douglas shrugged, completely calm, he began to stuff the sorted presents in the stockings. "Every year. Practical and long-lasting."

These words slammed into Julia like sledgehammers.

Christmas presents were not meant to be practical and long-lasting. They were meant to be impractical and no parent was allowed to get angry if the child broke them or lost interest in them before New Year's. It was Christmas Law.

She had no idea if those sentiments were Douglas's, his mother's or his father's.

Julia had met Douglas's father, a charming man who was always absently kind to Julia and who adored his daughter obviously. Julia always felt that Tamsin hadn't returned his adoration. That, for some reason, there was an intangible unpleasantness underlying this and she was always too uncomfortable (considering her own relationship with her father) to ask her sister-in-law about it.

For Douglas's part, he and his father seemed to tolerate each other but were obviously not close. Julia had always put it down to Douglas's reserve and what she thought was the way of aristocratic families. She'd never much thought of it. Maxwell Ashton had been a far sight friendlier than Monique but he had died a few years after Tammy and Gav's wedding and Julia had never really come to know him.

Julia was no longer working, just watching Douglas as he went about this new business diligently. She realised with surprise, rising alarm and a sense of tenderness, that Douglas Ashton, Baron Blackbourne was uncomfortable.

She moved toward him and gently took the stocking he was stuffing away.

"Can you lay the presents in that bag under the tree?" she asked quietly, avoiding his eyes because she knew if she looked at him the jig would be up. He'd know how she felt immediately. She was certain her heart was in her eyes. She continued, making her voice soft. "And then, I'm afraid, you're going to have to eat the mince pie and have a go at that sherry." She indicated Santa's treat. "I'll have Rudolf's carrot."

"I'm not sure you gave yourself the best end of that deal," he commented, his voice bland.

She flashed a too-brilliant smile at him, a smile meant to hide her unease, and said, "We Americans are not overly fond of mince pies and sherry, or at least *this* American isn't."

He gave her an assessing look and she turned her attention quickly to completing the stockings and started to babble. "How people think Santa can drink sherry at every house and not bumble around drunkenly, giving out the wrong presents and tipping over the tree, is beyond me."

"You think only the sherry consumption aspect of the concept of Father Christmas is hard to believe?"

She dumped talcum powder into the bottom of the discarded stocking stuffer box. "Oh yes," she replied, too brightly, "magic can explain a lot of things but if *I* had thousands of glasses of sherry, Christmas would be a mess and I'm not just talking about leaving the wrong presents for the wrong child under the tree."

She heard him chuckle and felt an enormous sense of relief that his awkwardness was gone and she'd been the one to manage the Herculean feat of dispelling it.

She straightened from the box, turned to him and watched him down the sherry in one gulp, the strong muscles in his neck moving in a way that, watching them, she found herself spellbound.

"Julia?" he queried when he had long since completed his gastronomical act as Santa and she just continued to stare.

She jumped then, intent on hiding her reaction, she cried with false lightness, "Okay! One last bit. Step in this box and then you have to stamp the powder around the carpet."

He looked at her as if she'd gone mad.

"It'll look like Santa got snow all over the floor," she explained then ordered, "Be sure to walk over to the plate with the goodies."

"Julia, that's powder," Douglas pointed out the obvious.

"A four year old won't know that."

"I think Ruby is far more perceptive than that. There's rarely snow in Somerset."

Julia walked up to him and, for reasons unknown, perhaps because of how she felt about hearing that he received stock certificates for Christmas as a child (which she still could not quite wrap her mind around), she lightly put her hand on his chest and said, "A child will see past powder and weather patterns when it comes to the magic of Christmas. Trust me. I've had enough Christmas mornings with those children that I know."

He looked down at her hand on his chest, his eyes warming and she quickly pulled away.

Dutifully, he stomped in the box and around the carpet and she tried not to laugh because he looked positively disgruntled. In a perfect world, she'd giggle at him, tease him and then kiss him for doing it regardless of his distaste for the act. But now, she just walked over to Rudolf's carrot and munched away, trying to pretend she didn't notice anything at all.

When he was finished, she announced they were done and stuffed the bags into the boxes, thanked him for his assistance, bid him an airy goodnight and carried the detritus out of the room, trying, somewhat desperately, (and perhaps not successfully) not to look like she was fleeing.

She figured he'd follow her, knock on her door or slide into bed with her but he didn't do any of those things and she tried to ignore her frustration that he didn't. Julia was thankful that there was no scratching at the windows that evening (apparently both Archie and the Lady Ruby took Christmas Eve off from hauntings) and she found herself quickly falling asleep.

Two hours later, dead asleep, Julia was shaken madly by a bright-eyed Ruby.

"Santa's been here!" she screeched.

Julia winced and looked at the clock. It was just passed two in the morning.

"Ruby-girl," Julia smiled wearily at the little girl's enthusiasm, even at that hour in the morning, and tiredly threw off the covers. She was glad that Ruby had woken her; she'd been too frightened to finish her job as Santa in case she ran into Douglas. Now, she had the time. "You need to help me with something quickly. A special errand Santa left for you and me."

Ruby gasped with delight as Julia got up, pulled on her robe and grabbed another small bag of wrapped presents out of her closet.

Ruby's eyes lit up when she saw the bag of presents and they walked hand-in-hand to the library.

"Santa knows that Uncle Douglas stays up late so he left his stocking stuffers with me and asked if you and I could stuff his stocking when we were sure he was asleep," Julia whispered conspiratorially.

Ruby's eyes rounded happily at the thought of Julia having a conversation with Santa and being pulled into a Santa Task.

"I think he's asleep but I'll go and check," she whispered back, tugging a bit on Julia's hand.

Julia held on to the child's hand more firmly, not wanting an excited Ruby to burst into Douglas's room. "No, something tells me we're safe."

They quickly stuffed his stocking and then Julia had an idea. She carefully selected some gifts from under the tree and with a finger to her lips at Ruby to keep her secret; she ran back to her room and hid them in the closet. She then grabbed the throw off the chaise and went back.

She lay down on her side on the couch, the Christmas tree lights illuminating the room happily and she tucked the child in front of her, pulling the warm throw around them. "We'll just rest here and wait for the others to wake up."

Ruby squirmed excitedly. "I think we should wake them up."

"No, honey, just rest for a bit, I'm sure they'll be up soon. Let me tell you about the story of Christmas, the *real* story of Christmas."

"You mean Jesus?" Ruby asked.

"Yes," Julia answered and began to tell Ruby about Mary and Joseph but never finished as the child's breathing evened out and then Julia snuggled her closer against her chest and belly and she herself fell back to sleep.

She felt like she'd barely closed her eyes when her hair was pulled away from her cheek and gently tucked behind her ear. Her eyes slowly opened and she saw Douglas's face very close to hers. He was fully dressed and kneeling by the couch.

Julia blinked several times and then saw the tree and realised where she was.

It was Christmas, she'd always loved Christmas, any holiday really, and she couldn't help herself from smiling sleepily.

"Merry Christmas," she whispered.

A slow, lazy, devastatingly handsome smile drifted across his face.

"Merry Christmas." His deep, velvety voice rumbled and awakened Ruby who took only a scant second to come fully awake and burst out of Julia's arms to dance around the room.

Julia noticed Willie and Lizzie were both watching from across the room, both barely containing their excitement while still looking on with confusion (Willie) and triumph (Lizzie).

Julia got up immediately, all business.

"No one touch anything," she commanded. "Lizzie, you go put the kettle on. Willie, you run and get the camera, do you know where it is?" He nodded and rushed out. "Right. I'm going to brush my teeth and make myself presentable. Let's go!" Julia clapped her hands and quickly left the room, not allowing herself to spare Douglas a glance.

After she'd washed her face, brushed her teeth and pulled her hair back into a ponytail, she made coffee and then the orgy of Christmas began.

If the children were tormented by their parents not being there,

Julia didn't notice it. They tore into their generous load of presents (and, she noted, it was made doubly generous by Douglas's significant contribution, or more than likely Sam's, but it was the thought that counted).

She noted Douglas's surprise when he realised his stocking had been stuffed somewhere in the night but she ignored it, had to ignore it, or the warm feeling that seemed to be permeating her entire body would get out-of-control.

In fact, she did her best to ignore him altogether and concentrate on the children, sipping her coffee, occasionally taking photos, opening a present here and there and tidying the burgeoning mass of discarded paper, bows and ribbons. Finally, Lizzie put a small, exquisitely wrapped box in her hand and she saw on the card, in the unmistakable, confident handwriting of Douglas, that it was from him.

Her eyes finally met his.

"I thought –" she began, intending to mention the emerald.

"Open it!" Lizzie fairly shouted, almost more curious to see what it held than Julia.

Julia tore into the box carefully and gasped in undisguised pleasure when she found a diamond watch inside.

It was not something hideously ostentatious but so subtle and elegant it could be worn every day. She noticed it was a brand that was often advertised in the most exclusive fashion magazines and she knew it had to cost thousands, maybe tens of thousands of pounds. She felt a lump rise in the back of her throat, not at its worth but that it was absolutely perfect. If she had the money, she would have chosen it for herself. The thoughtfulness and attention to her style took her breath away.

She raised dazed eyes to Douglas's inquisitive ones and was spared any comment when he read her expression and his curiosity turned to a look of such male satisfaction that Julia felt her stomach pitch dangerously.

It was then that Lizzie shoved Julia's present for Douglas in his hands.

Her thrill at her glorious present evaporated and she nearly groaned, wanting to snatch his present away.

It was nowhere near a diamond watch. Not only not in the same ballpark, not even in the same *galaxy*.

Obliging Lizzie, he opened it and Julia closed her eyes in embarrassment as he pulled out a midnight blue tie. It did happen to be very smart tie and the most unbelievably expensive tie she'd ever purchased. She had also purchased it at Harrods which was the most unbelievably posh store in the history of time.

But it was also just a tie.

"You bought him a *tie?*" Lizzie blurted, turning accusing eyes to Julia, obviously disgusted.

"It's a nice tie," Douglas said, gently but sternly, reprimanding Lizzie's outburst.

"It's still a tie," Lizzie wailed, ignoring Douglas's soft rebuke.

Feeling the need to defend herself, and not wanting either Lizzie *or* Douglas to think her ungenerous she explained to the girl, "It matches his eyes." Her own eyes swept to Douglas, wanting him to understand, actually somehow desperate that he would understand. "It exactly matches your eyes."

And it did, especially then, when they darkened and became the exact, inky, midnight blue of the tie. At that look, her stomach didn't just pitch, it plummeted deliciously.

"It does match his eyes!" Ruby squealed and the moment was, thankfully, broken.

There was no time for anything further. Presents unwrapped, Julia left the room (or, more appropriately, escaped) and quickly dressed, cooked and served breakfast. After she cleared away the breakfast dishes, she went to work on the piles of used wrapping paper and arranged the opened presents under the tree while the children had scattered to play with new toys (Ruby), new computer games (Willie) or to try on new clothes (Lizzie) with Douglas called here and there to help assemble something or deal with some computer dilemma. Then Julia was off to begin dinner.

Ronnie arrived at noon, followed closely by Nick and Mr. and Mrs. K. As they were guests at Sommersgate House for the first time ever, they didn't know what to do with themselves (save Nick who leapt into the fray, telling amusing, though somewhat frightening, anecdotes that left Julia to wonder if Douglas had any involvement in them).

For his part, Douglas played the attentive host, pressing drinks into hands and drawing out conversation. The company relaxed, starting to enjoy themselves when the children handed out gifts, including ones they had specifically chosen for each person (causing Mrs. K to dab at her eyes with her hanky and Ronnie to escape the room altogether for fifteen minutes).

Mrs. K finally could stand it no longer and when Julia left the room to check the turkey, she followed, nudged Julia out of the way and took over. Lizzie and Ronnie set the table, giving Julia time to shower and get ready.

Tammy and Gav had been resolutely casual for Christmas so Julia followed suit and put on a pair of her jeans and a bright red, fitted long-sleeved t-shirt that had a square neck so wide, it was cut nearly all the way to her shoulders and sleeves that were intentionally long and she had to bunch them artfully at her wrists. Regardless of the fact that they were too elegant for her outfit, she wore her new watch, her emerald studs and the emerald pendant Douglas had given her.

Sherry had turned to wine and dinner, Christmas crackers (Nick manfully put on his paper crown but Mr. K and Douglas demurred), good food and good company (company that had long-since turned into a makeshift family for the children) made the table downright joyous and Julia was beside herself with delight that she pulled off this first Christmas without Tammy and Gav.

When the flaming pudding was consumed and the trifle was dished out, everyone was drinking coffee and the children were itching to get back to their presents, Julia gave her mumbled apologies, pulled her paper crown off her head, whispered in Ruby's ear and they both left the room hand-in-hand.

In her rooms, Julia unearthed the presents she had put there the night before and gave Ruby careful instructions. They both re-entered the dining room with arms loaded with the last presents of the day. Everyone stared at them in surprise as Ruby, acting as if this was the most important task of her entire life (which it probably was), handed out her gifts to the assemblage and Julia announced while she handed out hers, "Douglas told me last night there was a Christmas tradition in the Ashton family that I thought it appropriate to resurrect. When he was a boy, they had their presents at dinner. So, last night, Ruby and I saved a few and here we are!"

Nick, the Kilpatricks and Ronnie glanced surreptitiously at Douglas and meaningfully amongst themselves as Julia reseated herself next to Douglas.

Ruby handed Douglas his last gift and Julia couldn't stop herself from watching him openly (she had not saved a present for herself as she wanted to watch the others).

His face was a picture of astonishment then his eyes became immediately shuttered.

All the presents Julia saved were from her. For Douglas it was a bottle of Lalique men's cologne. An extraordinary scent that she fell in love with when she smelled it and it was presented in an exquisite bottle with the head of a horse carved intricately in the front.

What it was *not* was a stock certificate.

He took it out of the box and moved it around in his hands as Julia leaned over to him. "I hope you like it. It isn't a diamond watch –"

His eyes lifted to hers and his were blazing so fiercely that her breath went out of her in a rush.

"I don't want a diamond watch," he said, his voice both terse and strangely hoarse, the combination of tone and the look in his eyes made her believe that she'd made him angry.

"The horse reminded me of you... not that you look like a horse..." she explained clumsily but she stopped he stood abruptly.

"Excuse us," he declared to the table at large and Julia noticed that everyone was watching them with avid interest.

To her stunned surprise, he put the cologne on the table, grabbed Julia's hand, pulled her none-too-gently out of her chair and walked out of the room, tugging her along behind him, his strides so long and fast she had to run to keep up with him.

He headed to the study, yanked her inside and slammed the door.

She misread his response and rushed to calm him. "Douglas, I'm so sorry, I wanted to do something –"

He grabbed her and in actions that were violent yet controlled, at the same time strangely gentle, he threw her against the door and pressed his body into hers. His hands came to either side of her jaw, tilting her face to his, his mouth descended and took hers in a kiss that was so devastatingly thorough she was panting when he lifted his head.

His hands cradled her face and, if she wasn't shocked enough at this behaviour; he astounded her further by nudging her nose with his own.

"Marry me." His voice was rough and she felt it like a physical touch.

Her legs, already jelly, nearly came out from under her.

She grasped onto his sweater at his sides to hold herself upright but shook her head, panic beginning to fill her.

This was not a Douglas she knew. This was not an indifferent Douglas. This was not a determined Douglas, bent on having what he wanted. This was an altogether unknown Douglas.

A Douglas she could actually say yes to.

"I was just trying to be nice, I didn't expect this." To her irritation, her voice held a tremble.

"Oh yes you did, you just didn't know it."

"What an extraordinarily arrogant thing to say." She tried to sound waspish but it came out breathless.

He grinned and she moaned a little at the sight of it which made his grin grow to a smile.

"It's going to be *so* fun when I win." His nose nudged hers again, this time playfully (a playful Douglas, too, had once been an altogether unknown entity and she found herself shocked that she was actually getting used to it).

He slid his nose up the side of hers. Then his lips kissed each eyelid in turn and she held her breath, scared of what she'd say or do because his actions were so sweet, so tender, so caring, so strangely *loving*, she couldn't cope.

She tried to break the moment. "Everyone is probably wondering where we are, we have to go back."

"Did you like the watch?" He changed the subject immediately, his body pressing more insistently into hers as his hands moved from her jaws and became arms curved around her and his lips slid from her temple to her ear.

She knew that *he* knew that she liked the watch. He was just being wicked by making her say it out loud.

"It's a lovely watch." It was more than a lovely watch, it was a magnificent watch.

"'Lovely.' That's a word you use to describe a lot of things." His voice was at her ear, causing tingles to slide across her skin.

She knew exactly what he was referring to and she also knew she was being churlish, especially considering the thoughtfulness and generosity of the gift.

He deserved better.

"It's beautiful," she admitted. "I love it."

"How much do you love it?" he asked roughly, invitingly, his breath floated across the sensitive skin behind her ear and she squirmed against him, both pushing him away with her hands at his waist and bunching the fabric of his sweater between her fists to hold him where he was.

"It's perfect," she whispered. "It's me. I would choose it for myself. Sam did a good job with all the gifts today."

This caused his head to jerk up and he narrowed his eyes at her.

"Sam did *not* choose that watch. I did."

"Oh." This came out as a breath and then the thought of him entering a shop, choosing something so immensely splendid, so entirely perfect and purchasing it for her caused her to utter the word, "Wow."

"I suppose 'wow' is a damned, bloody sight better than 'lovely'," he growled.

She blinked at him as she realised, belatedly, his mood had shifted.

"Are you angry?" Her eyes had rounded and for some reason he let her go, stepping back a pace.

"I'm not angry," he said in a voice that belied his words.

"You sound angry."

"I'm *not* angry," he clipped.

"Then what are you?"

He looked for a second uncertain and Julia couldn't believe her eyes.

His eyes became focused and he glared at her. "I'm frustrated."

Julia stared at him for a second before returning, "Well, remind me never to do anything nice for you again. Frustrated was not what I was going for."

And before he could reply, she took her opportunity for escape (something, at that moment, she dearly needed) and quickly exited the room, not looking back.

20

RUBY FINALLY UNDERSTANDS

After leaving Douglas in the study, Julia was of a mind to make the men do the Christmas dishes, *including* and *especially* Douglas. She came to her senses and realised she'd escape him more easily by doing the dishes herself because he rarely stepped foot in the kitchen.

The children talked to Patricia while Ronnie, Mrs. K and Julia scoured the pots and pans.

Julia came to the phone last.

"How's it going?" Patricia asked.

"So far so good," Julia replied.

"They sounded good. Happy. You did a good job Doll Baby."

Julia was silent. She wanted to tell her mother everything but couldn't. Patricia would be there in twenty-four hours raising all kinds of ruckus if she knew even half of what was happening.

"Jewel?" Patricia broke into her thoughts.

"You having an okay Christmas?" Julia queried.

"Your Aunt Doris made the most heavenly cake. It has twelve melted Milky Way bars in it."

"It's not time for dinner there yet, how have you had any cake?"

"I might have sneaked a piece," Patricia admitted.

Normally Julia would have laughed but she was in no mood to laugh.

On a sigh, Julia said, "I miss Aunt Doris. Tell her I love her, will you?"

Patricia was silent.

"Mom?" It was Julia's turn to break into her mother's thoughts.

"Are you going to tell me what's going on?" Her intuitive mother demanded.

No, Julia was most definitely not going to tell her mother what was going on.

"I'm fine, the kids are fine, everything's fine," Julia lied.

"Is Douglas fine?"

Julia felt a shiver go up her spine. Her mother's insight was uncanny. It was almost as if she could read Julia's thoughts.

"Yes, I'm just, we're both..." Julia paused and then continued. "Mom, it isn't the happiest day, if you know what I mean, even though we're all pretending it is."

Patricia, as usual, didn't fall for Julia's evasive manoeuvre.

"What's this about a diamond watch?" Patricia asked.

Julia closed her eyes.

Lizzie.

"It's probably nothing to him." It was definitely not nothing to him and it certainly wasn't nothing to her. "He's rich as Rockefeller, Mom. Richer, even. He was very generous, with *all* of us," Julia explained and hoped it sounded plausible.

Her mother made a "humph" sound that in Julia's vast experience was more a motherly "I-know-you're-not-telling-me-something" humph than "I'm-angry-about-something" humph.

When the phone call was done, in an attempt to keep the light-hearted spirit of the day going, Julia organised a game. Lizzie spread the Monopoly board on the carpet in front of the fire in the library in between the three couches that flanked and faced it. They were making teams and the minute Douglas sauntered in, Lizzie shouted, "Auntie Jewel and Uncle Douglas *have* to be a team!"

Julia's mind wasn't working fast enough to find a way to back out that didn't appear ungracious, so, before she could utter a word, she was saddled with Douglas as her partner.

He, to all appearances, was happy as a clam with these arrangements.

Julia was on the floor, stretched out on her side, her back to the fire, up on her elbow, her head resting in her hand. To her shock (and perhaps everyone else in the room's, except Nick, who smiled slyly), Douglas stretched out behind her.

With all expectant eyes on her, it would have been impolite to change her position and Julia allowed herself a quiet annoyed noise only to hear Douglas chuckle behind her. This made her feel angry enough to emit a louder annoyed noise which, to the assembled crowd's bigger shock, made Douglas burst out laughing.

She decided from that point forward to keep her noises to herself and spent the entire game enduring Douglas moving the pieces and rolling the dice by reaching over her to get to the board (each time, his chest pressing into her back).

After awhile she couldn't stop herself from enjoying the game (as much as she tried). Douglas was competitive and relentless and he preyed mercilessly upon weaker teams which included everyone else playing. Furtively, when she thought Douglas wasn't paying attention, Julia would steal from their bank and slip notes into her opposing team-mates' piles. When she snuck £100 into Ruby and Ronnie's fast-dwindling stack, he leaned close to her ear and whispered softly, "Stop doing that."

She fought the thrill that ran across her skin and twisted her neck to look at him in feigned, wide-eyed innocence, "What?"

He loomed over her, his face so close she took that moment to memorise the shape of the scar on his lip.

"Don't think you can distract me," he warned but she could tell he was teasing (teasing!).

Her eyes moved to his and they were dark as midnight.

"I wouldn't dream of it," she assured him and forced herself to concentrate on the game and not provoke him, mainly because she feared the consequences, not from him but from her own damned body (and heart, if she was perfectly honest with herself).

Unable to help the other players, she and Douglas trounced the rest. She could have been the unhappiest winner in history which made Douglas's now ever present grin all the more pronounced.

Unwilling to start another game or any activity which Lizzie could manipulate into a matchmaker's dream, they moved on to nightcaps. Soon Douglas was carrying a sleeping Ruby, who was so exhausted she didn't wake, to her room. Julia followed and Douglas left her to struggle her sleeping niece's body into a nightgown.

Taking this as their cue, when Julia arrived back downstairs, the others moved to leave and Julia gave them all a tight hug good-bye.

"The best Christmas Sommersgate has had in as long as I've known it, lass," Mr. Kilpatrick said gruffly and Julia awarded him a bright smile that made pink tinge his cheeks.

When it was just family, Julia and Douglas rounded up Lizzie and Willie for bed, walking them into the hall for goodnight kisses.

Once Willie finished his fast-as-lightning kiss on Julia's cheek, he said quietly, "It was a good day, Auntie Jewel."

Instantly, Julia's throat closed. He sounded so like his father that she struggled to keep her face straight and the emotion from showing.

Just like Gavin would do, Willie noticed how hard she'd worked on the day and he commented on it.

"You're a good man, William Fairfax" she told him, mock gravely putting her hand on his shoulder, trying to lighten the mood.

"I know," he replied with a cheeky grin, which was also pure Gavin and made Julia's heart lurch.

Her eyes caught Douglas's to see he was watching them, his expression soft and thoughtful and she was just about to say something, do anything to dispel the moment when they heard a piercing, blood-curdling scream.

Not a ghostly woman's scream.

A child's scream.

Julia's blood turned to ice but before she could move to the stairs, Douglas was there taking them three at a time, leaving Julia, Lizzie and Willie well behind.

By the time she skidded to a halt at Ruby's opened door with Lizzie and Willie at her heels, Douglas was standing in the middle of the room with Ruby in his arms, the child's limbs wrapped around him tightly.

Ruby was crying uncontrollably and through her sobs, Julia heard her say, "I was a good girl, Santa came and everything. I thought if I was a good girl, Mummy and Daddy would come home for Christmas. They said that Mummy and Daddy went far away where I can't see them but I've been shouting..." she hiccupped pitifully, "shouting all the time so they could..." more hiccups, "hear me but they didn't come back. I thought for certain on Christmas they'd come back and know exactly where to find me because I've been *shouting and shouting and shouting!*"

Douglas turned and looked over Ruby's shoulder at Julia. The tears Julia wouldn't allow herself to shed earlier pricked the backs of her eyes and then they were there, falling silently down her face.

Julia stood where she was and reached out blindly to grab Lizzie and Willie's hands. Douglas would have to do this alone; she needed to see to the other two. They moved into her body, pressing themselves to her, she dropped their hands and wrapped an arm around each as she heard Lizzie's soft weeping.

Douglas's hand moved slowly on Ruby's back until her uncontrollable wailing turned to mere sobs and hiccups and then he said in a soft, gentle voice filled with pulsating tenderness, "They can hear you Ruby, they can even see you, they just can't come back," he hesitated a heart-stopping second before saying, "ever."

At that announcement, Ruby's breath hitched and so did Lizzie's.

Douglas turned so his back was to Julia and the children in order that Ruby could see them. He was still cradling her in his arms. "They trusted you to us, sweetheart, we're your family now."

It was then, Julia's breath hitched painfully too, the ache in her chest that she had been enduring for months broke open, searing her soul.

She could take it no longer and rushed forward, pulling the children with her. Once she arrived at Douglas's side, she carefully reached for Ruby. Without comment, Douglas moved the girl into Julia's arms and Ruby slid her body around Julia with such fierceness that it made Julia's broken heart shatter into a million more pieces.

"Shh, Ruby-girl," she hushed her, absorbing the girl's wracking sobs into her body and holding her firmly as she hiccupped wetly into Julia's neck. "We've got you," she promised.

After several long, tense minutes, Ruby finally controlled her emotion and the little girl asked quietly, "Auntie Jewel?"

"Yes, baby?"

"Do you think the man and his lady can see Mummy and Daddy?"

Julia couldn't help herself, her throat emitted a noise of pure grief.

With great effort, she composed herself. "No, Ruby-girl, your Mummy and Daddy are in a much nicer place than Sommersgate."

Ruby's head came up and Julia looked into her tear-streaked eyes.

"There's someplace nicer than Sommersgate?" she asked as if she couldn't imagine it.

Julia nodded and gave her a tremulous smile. "Much, *much* nicer, honey. And they're there."

Ruby studied her aunt for a moment soberly before she laid her cheek on Julia's shoulder and when Julia finally looked at Douglas, Lizzie was holding on to him like she'd never let him go. Her face was pressed into his side and his arms were wrapped tightly around her. Julia watched in fascination as he bent low to kiss Lizzie on the top of her head.

Willie was standing to the side but he moved forward.

"Auntie Jewel, I'll take care of this now," her ten year old nephew said, his hand on Ruby's back indicating he wanted Julia to put the girl down.

Julia looked into her brother Gavin's eyes that just happened to be in an altogether different being's face, and, without a word of protest, she bent down and put Ruby on the floor.

Willie gathered Ruby to him and then gently moved to Lizzie, taking charge of her and leading them all to the bed where he sat them down, one, two, three.

Douglas moved to Julia and Willie raised his eyes to them.

"I'll take care of this now," he repeated.

His meaning was clear, or at least it was to Douglas.

Douglas leaned close to her.

"Julia he wants us to go," he murmured.

"I can't –" Julia started but Douglas wasn't listening. He took her hand firmly and led her out. She resisted but she was no match for Douglas and now was no time to make a scene.

When they were out the door, Douglas closed it. Julia turned on him and opened her mouth to speak but he put his finger to her lips, this tender action effectively silencing her.

Then he pulled her vaguely resisting, stiff body into his arms.

"The three of them need time alone," he stated over the top of her head. "You have to respect Will enough to let him take care of it."

She knew he was right. She hated it, but she knew he was right.

She nodded jerkily against his shoulder and pulled out of his arms. Then, resting her back on the wall next to the door, she slid down to sit on the floor close by just in case they called out to her.

She didn't look at Douglas, she didn't want him to try to talk her out of her silent vigil which she would completely refuse to let go.

He didn't.

He sat next to her, rested his back against the wall, one leg straight, one knee bent, he pulled her close to him with an arm around her and forced her head on his shoulder.

Because she needed to, needed it more than anything in the world at that moment, she relaxed against him and her arms stole around his middle. In return, his other arm curled around her, holding her close.

They didn't speak. She (to her everlasting surprise) didn't burst into a fresh round of tears. She just sat in Douglas's arms for what could have been minutes or hours. Then, when her body was stiff and protesting, as if Douglas knew she could take no more, he lithely surged to his feet and bent over to take her hand and pull her up.

Together, they silently opened the door and snuck into the room which was still lit by Ruby's pink daisy nightlight.

Lizzie and Ruby were lying together in Ruby's bed, tucked up and sleeping.

Willie was asleep in the chair opposite.

"We have to make him more comfortable," Julia whispered to Douglas, the boy's position would mean a crick in his neck tomorrow.

"Leave him," Douglas ordered.

She opened her mouth to disagree but saw Douglas shake his head. "He won't thank us. Julia, darling, you have to let him to do this."

She knew he was right.

And anyway, he'd called her "darling" in his deep, rich voice. She would have done anything he said at that point.

She nodded.

She did, however, grab a pink throw from the end of Ruby's bed and very gently, so as not to disturb him, threw it over Willie's body.

When they'd closed the door again, Julia started to go to her rooms but Douglas caught her hand.

She turned to him and started to speak. "Douglas, tonight, I have to —"

"I know," he interrupted her and lifted his finger to trace a path from her temple slowly down then along her jaw to her chin. He watched his finger as it went and then his eyes shifted to hers. "You did well today." His voice was soft with meaning.

She nodded, not trusting herself to speak, not trusting herself to blurt out that she loved him. She loved it that he called her "darling" and loved it that he called Ruby "sweetheart" and loved it that he held Lizzie tightly in his arms when she needed him.

Most of all, tonight, she loved it that he knew what Willie needed to do.

While she was thinking about how much she loved him, she watched him and his eyes changed, burning with a light she'd never noticed before.

He then did something that completely took her breath away.

He kissed her nose.

And if she had gotten her breath back it would have again been stolen.

Because he turned on his heel and he left, just as she needed him to do.

She went immediately to her room, to her phone and called her mother to tell her about the events of the evening with the children.

And she didn't leave out Douglas's part in it.

21

SWEET ANTICIPATION

The next three weeks found Julia experiencing complete emotional turmoil which she felt was a little incredible considering she already thought she was experiencing the height of emotional turmoil.

Clearly, Douglas realised what Julia had officially termed (in her own mind) "The Tender Onslaught Strategy (with Vague Tendencies Toward Arrogance)" was working beautifully so he kept right on using it.

The press had taken it into their head that Julia and Douglas were a couple and they were speculating wildly about her and Douglas leaving the ball so quickly. Not to mention Douglas was no longer appearing with his rail-thin, twenty-something starlets and models at every social gathering imaginable but instead squiring Julia and the children all over Bristol and Somerset.

Making matters worse, they all travelled to London to attend Charlie and Oliver's Annual New Year's Bash. Julia didn't want to go so soon after Ruby's outburst but she couldn't let Charlie down. Sam arranged for the children to spend the night with her nieces and nephews at her sister's house.

Julia took Veronika, saying she wanted the girl, who had no family close and no friends to speak of, to have a good time. If she admitted it to herself, she was really using her young friend as a shield.

Once in London, she found out Sam (or perhaps Douglas, she wouldn't put it passed him) arranged for Veronika to attend a party with her rather than go with Julia and Douglas to the Forsythes.

This left Julia and Douglas together, alone.

Luckily, the New Year's party was a mad crush and Julia easily lost Douglas. She made certain she didn't drink too much; she needed all her faculties to utilise in her efforts to avoid him. Further, she didn't want to do *anything* to let her guard down.

Christmas night was still fresh in her memory and she knew she was losing ground fast. She decided to nurture her irate frustration at the situation; it was the only thing she had left.

Eventually she found herself alone with Oliver and she decided to take that opportunity to pick his brain, subtly of course, about Douglas's history. Douglas's story about his childhood Christmases still had Julia feeling ill-at-ease. In fact, when she wasn't avoiding Douglas, stewing over him or watching the children like hawks (after the Christmas night disaster), it was all she thought about.

Oliver knew him best and Julia felt that, maybe, he could be a font of information.

After a few questions, diplomatically worded (she thought), Oliver cut eyes to her that were not lit with his usual good-natured light.

"What are your intentions regarding Douglas?" he asked bluntly.

"I... well," she spluttered. *Her* intentions with *Douglas?* She didn't know what to say, so she said, "I'm just curious."

Oliver surveyed her for a moment which probably lasted about a second but the intensity of his eyes made it seem like an hour.

"I'm afraid curiosity isn't good enough, Julia. If you genuinely cared, I would tell you, but since you're just curious..." He let that hang and when Julia said no more, he excused himself and, for some reason, this made Julia feel like an absolute heel.

She was caught in a mad crush of happy, drunken people as the clock struck down to midnight (and it was never fun to be an unhappy, un-drunken person in that kind of situation).

At "five" she felt a warm hand on the small of her back. At "four" it was an arm that wound around her waist. At "three" it was pulling her firmly around. At "two" it was hauling her against a hard body. At "one" another arm joined it to tighten around her. At the strike of midnight, a sexy, scarred mouth descended on hers in a hard, thorough, unmistakably possessive kiss that seemed to last forever and stole her breath away.

Anyone who saw it would have been in no doubt that Julia and Douglas were a couple.

Regardless how good the kiss was or, more to the point, *because* of how good it was, and the point it so publicly made, Julia seethed all the way home.

Monique was still (thankfully) in Munich meaning they were all alone at the Kensington house. As Douglas pulled the parking brake up on the Jag, Julia darted out of the car only to have to stand on the steps to wait for him to let her in the house because she didn't have a key.

I really, she thought, *have to think ahead.*

Her blood pressure, already nearly at brain attack level, ratcheted up a notch.

Douglas politely, though not trying to hide his amusement, allowed her to precede him into the house. She practically ran up the stairs only to hear him chuckle.

She was beginning to detest his chuckle. For fifteen years she rarely heard it and now it seemed to ring in her ears on a daily basis. At the top of the stairs she whirled to wait for him and watched as he took his time ascending like he had all the new year.

"I want you to release a press statement that says we are *not* an item," she demanded irritably when he was four steps away.

He completed his ascension and then stopped several inches from her. Towering over her, he looked down at her, not down the length of his nose, as used to be his wont, but directly at her, eye-to-eye.

"And why," he drawled, "would I do that?"

"Because we're not a couple!" She wanted to stamp her foot at having to point out what she thought was the obvious.

He quirked a brow.

She was a woman prone to dramatics but not to violence.

Not until that moment.

She was saved from doing something she would regret by the door opening below.

Visions of Monique drifting in, wafting malevolence and baring fangs, made Julia's chest tighten painfully.

Instead, from their vantage point at the top of the stairs, they saw Veronika enter on a giggle and then lose her footing and crash to the floor.

Julia and Douglas both descended the stairs rapidly, Douglas (of course) made it to the bottom first. Julia was wearing high-heeled, strappy bronze sandals and couldn't catch herself in time at the bottom and ploughed into Douglas. To steady herself, she grabbed his waist with both hands. Worried about Ronnie, she didn't pull her hands away but she peeked around his body and saw Veronika sprawled on the floor, her legs out in front of her and a loopy grin on her face.

Ronnie slowly lifted a curled hand, thumb extended then jerked it toward herself and said gaily, "Drunk!"

"Oh dear," Julia sighed, releasing Douglas's waist and moving around him. "We need to get her upstairs," she told him, all the time looking down on Veronika.

"Sham's very nie-sh," Veronika slurred to the approaching Julia.

"She's lovely," Julia murmured to her as she bent down beside the girl and heard Douglas join them. "We're going to get you upstairs to bed."

"I am lucky," Ronnie stated while Douglas silently put one shoulder under Ronnie's armpit while his other hand grabbed her wrist and pulled it around his neck, lifting her up to her feet. Through his actions, Ronnie spoke. "To have you," she motioned to Julia with her head, an action that threw her off balance and made her stumble, forcing Douglas to right her, "as friend." She went on. "And *you*," she turned to Douglas as he started walking her towards the stairs, "are hero!" she finished triumphantly.

Julia had no idea what Ronnie was talking about but she had no time to consider it as Ronnie made an unmistakably unpleasant noise.

"Quick, upstairs to the bathroom," she told Douglas urgently.

Douglas didn't hesitate. He reached down and slid an arm around the backs of Ronnie's knees, hefted her up and swiftly moved up the stairs. By the time Julia made it to the door of the bathroom, Veronika was on her knees getting sick in the toilet.

Julia rushed forward passed Douglas to pull the girl's dark hair out of her face and kneeled down to soothe her by stroking her back and murmuring to her. All the while, she did her best not to get sick herself at the sight, the sound and the awful smell.

"I'll leave you to it," Douglas said from the doorway, feeling his part in this current drama was done.

Julia just nodded, thinking, *saved by the drunk Russian girl.*

※ ※ ※

Days later they were back home at Sommersgate and Julia was coming in from running errands, entering by the kitchen door.

"Hey Mrs. K," she greeted the older lady, "I could do with a cuppa. You need a break?"

Mrs. K turned peculiarly sparkling eyes to Julia and opened her mouth to answer when Ruby rushed into the room followed by Lizzie. They were both panting at their mad dash and they, too, had sparkling eyes.

"Auntie Jewel!" Lizzie puffed.

The children had survived the Christmas Night Meltdown valiantly. For several days they were quiet and introspective and Ruby had stopped shouting altogether (and Julia found, knowing the reason behind it, she now missed it). But they were beginning to pull out of it having had a great time with Sam's family. Indeed, Julia had a queer sense that Ruby's breakdown had allowed them all to settle more thoroughly into their new lives and begin to truly come to terms with their loss and start healing.

Right then, they seemed to be lit up with happiness and expectation.

"What's up?" Julia asked, unable to stop a grin from spreading across her face at their jubilation. Ruby scrambled forward and grabbed Julia's hand, giving it a hearty tug. Their excitement was catching and she let out a little laugh. "What's happening?" she inquired again.

"Just come with us," Lizzie ordered bossily, grabbing Julia's other hand and pulling more strongly.

They led Julia to the leather couches of the entryway where Douglas and Willie were standing around the furniture. A fire blazed in the grate and Willie was looking down at something on the floor while Douglas watched Julia approach, his eyes roaming over her appreciatively (as he seemed inclined to do more often than not).

"Will someone tell me what's going on?" Julia blurted, deciding it best to ignore Douglas. If she didn't, she knew her palms would sweat or her knees would buckle or her stomach would do somersaults or, in her weakest moments, all three.

"Look!" Ruby pointed at a strange, plastic box with a handle on top and lots of holes all around.

The kind of box in which you carried a small animal.

Looking at the box, Julia felt her palms start to sweat, her knees begin to get weak and her stomach prepared to do somersaults.

"Look, look, look!" Ruby cried, no longer able to contain herself.

She sprinted forward then dropped to her knees and she fidgeted with the box but Julia already knew.

She knew.

She remembered, somewhat hazily, but she *remembered* muttering to Douglas the morning after their first night together.

Therefore, she knew.

Then Ruby had her prize and turned around, cuddling a fluffy, perfectly white, beautiful, squash-nosed, incredibly adorable Persian kitty in her arms.

"Unka Douglas bought them for you!" Ruby squealed.

Julia's eyes filled with tears. She couldn't help herself; she couldn't have controlled her reaction if she was SuperGirl. She missed her own cat and had never been without an animal for this long in her life. It was better than an emerald (which was pretty fantastic), it was better than a diamond watch (which was absolutely tremendous), it was the best present she'd ever received.

With one quick step forward, she reached out her hands and Ruby easily gave up the kitten to Julia who practically snatched it out of her niece's arms.

She didn't notice Ruby whirl back around as she pulled the kitten up to her face and rubbed it against her cheek.

She turned glistening eyes to Douglas.

She didn't know what to say.

More kittens were produced, two more to be exact.

"Uncle Douglas got one for each of us girls," Lizzie declared cheerfully but Julia only had eyes for Douglas who, for his part, was watching her back with a look of tenderness (albeit a somewhat smug tenderness).

"I'm getting a dog," Willie declared at this point.

Julia opened her mouth and then closed it. She opened it again and then, again, closed it. She brought the kitten down to snuggle him on her chest and shook her head as if to clear it.

"Aren't you going to say something?" Lizzie demanded, eyeing Julia incredulously.

Julia was speechless.

"Sometimes," Willie put in, his words and tone far more mature than they should have been, "there's nothing to say."

🐾 🐾 🐾

The kittens caused havoc in the household, nearly making Ronnie fall down the stairs and giving Mrs. K fits as they scratched at every available surface (including undoubtedly priceless silk rugs). The children ran around playing with them and chasing them, which caused the once silent-as-a-tomb Sommersgate House to ring with happy noise.

That weekend, Julia decided to take a walk to clear her head. She put on her mucky cowboy boots, a pair of jeans, a dusky pink fleece and wrapped a long, pink and lavender-striped scarf around her neck. The day was bright, sunny and bitter cold.

The children had gone to the stables with Douglas to ride. Douglas was spending an extraordinary (for him) amount of time at home and had made a habit of being home on the weekends.

Julia found this most annoying, even though there was once a time, not very long ago, when she demanded that he be at home more.

She tried to avoid them. She *wanted* to avoid them. But she found, as if they had minds of their own, after only fifteen minutes her feet took her toward the stables.

Lizzie and Willie were already in their saddles with Ruby sitting alone on a beautiful, shining chestnut horse. As Julia approached, she watched Douglas swing expertly up in the saddle behind Ruby and her heart did a little flip.

She told her feet to turn left. They refused. She told them to turn right. They, again, refused. Before she could begin to escape, Lizzie saw her.

"Hey, Auntie Jewel!" she shouted.

Douglas had his back to her and, at Lizzie's call, he whirled the animal around expertly so he could watch her arrival.

"Don't mind me," Julia called. "You guys go on. I'm on my way to –"

"You should let Uncle Douglas teach you how to ride," Lizzie suggested, obviously thrilled at her wonderful idea.

Julia sighed. Lizzie was definitely beginning to be a problem.

If she was truthful with herself, which she was being less and less these days, she would have admitted that she wanted to see him. However, she did *not* want a riding lesson. She loved horses, she loved all animals, she just didn't particularly like riding them. She wouldn't have wanted to ride a camel either. Or an elephant. Definitely not a horse.

"That's okay." She was amongst them now, all of them looking down at her. She gently stroked the soft muzzle of Willie's horse (a beautiful grey which Julia knew Gavin liked to ride). "I'm good on my own two feet."

But she heard rather than saw Douglas hit the ground and then Ruby was moved from Douglas's horse to the front of Willie's.

Julia watched in alarm.

"Is that wise?" she asked Douglas.

"He's strong and he's good in the saddle. She'll be fine," Douglas replied with confidence and Julia stiffened as he came toward her. "Now let's see about you."

Julia glanced at Willie whose face was glowing at his uncle's compliment. It almost made her want to give in but then she saw Douglas leading the big chestnut toward her. The horse was bigger than all the others and Julia took a step back.

"They can sense fear," Douglas informed her.

"I know!" she snapped. "I've seen enough cowboy movies. They always say that in the cowboy movies."

Douglas grinned.

She narrowed her eyes at him.

That was when he smiled.

"Oh all right," she gave in, mainly because the children were there and she was trying to retain as much dignity as she could considering she knew she was going to lose it all in mere minutes. "What do I do?"

While she had both feet planted firmly on the ground (thankfully) and Douglas adjusted the stirrups, he patiently and competently explained what she should do. She listened as intently as she could considering how much she loved his voice and what it did to her insides. As this went on, the children cantered around them, giving them a wide berth.

"You ready to go up?" Douglas asked, motioning to the horse with his head.

"As ready as I'll ever be," she grumbled, reaching out as he taught her and taking the reins and the pommel, putting her left foot in the stirrup.

She was pleased she'd heaved herself up to straighten her leg but it all fell apart somehow and she began to fall backward. She didn't go down as Douglas's hand found her bottom and gave her a firm push. She ignored the hot imprint his hand left like a brand on her behind, swung her leg over and forced her foot in the opposite stirrup.

He continued instructing her as he walked her and the horse around in circles, his hand on the horse's halter. She never took her hands off the pommel but did as he said in every other way. When he suggested she take her hands from the saddlehorn, she tried it but immediately felt herself sliding off so she grabbed on again.

"You have to use your legs," he noted.

"You've told me that already, like ten times," Julia muttered.

"Then do it," Douglas suggested good-naturedly.

She tossed him an irritated glance. "If I could, don't you think I would?"

"Julia, I know your legs are far stronger than that." His voice was full of warm familiarity and humour both of which played pleasant havoc with her insides.

Nevertheless, she wanted to clobber him.

She tried harder, did better and he stepped away, allowing her free reign, calling instructions to her. She was actually doing it and was rather pleased with herself when she led the horse in a wide, slow circle then back to Douglas where she successfully pulled the beast to a halt.

"Well done," Douglas complimented her, his eyes shining with admiration, like she'd just won Ascot.

"Don't look at me like that. It's more the horse than me." She didn't like the way his compliment made her feel, all tingly and happy. Well, she *did* like it; she just didn't want to dwell on it. "I can't imagine why someone would do this of their own volition. I'd rather pet him and feed him apples than ride him." She finished, leaning forward and running her hand down the horse's neck.

"Take your feet out of the stirrups," Douglas commanded unexpectedly.

She lurched up and the horse danced sideways at her sudden movement.

The children had wandered further away, Lizzie riding expertly in a gentle gallop while Willie and Ruby were doing a sedate saunter.

"Julia, take your feet out." He was using that tone that brooked no argument and was standing so close to the side of the horse that she felt his heat through her calf. She was certain he would take her foot out himself if she didn't do as he said.

She did as he said.

No sooner had she done it, than he grabbed the saddlehorn in front of her, put his foot in the stirrup, and, in one lithe movement, mounted the horse behind her. Both he and she in the saddle pushed her straight up the pommel as he put his other boot in the stirrup.

He reached around her and grabbed the reins from her unfeeling hands.

"What are you doing? This horse is going to collapse under the weight of us. This is cruelty to animals!" she cried, somewhat hysterically, wanting off, wanting to escape, wanting his lean body *not* to be pressing against hers from her bottom to her shoulder blades.

"Swing your leg to the side and straddle the pommel," he ordered.

"*What?*" she screeched then went on, "No..." Then she realised if she did, she might be able just to hop off so she changed her mind and agreed immediately, "Okay." She swung her right leg to the side so she was straddling the saddlehorn sideways just as he commanded but one of his arms slid around her waist and tightened before she could slide off.

Foiled, she thought.

"I'll show you why people like to ride," he said, his voice low and husky in her ear.

She was staring intently at the ground and therefore saw his leg tighten on the side of the horse and they bolted forward. She yelped, twisted her torso and wrapped her arms around him. As they galloped, with each beat of the horses hooves, she slid closer to Douglas.

"Are you insane?" she shouted over the wind rushing in her ears.

He subtly moved the reins and the horse turned gracefully to the left and she held on tighter. She was face to face with his muscular neck, which was a part of him she especially liked (not that there were parts of him she didn't like). To avoid it, she forced herself to face forward and grab the horse's mane. She tried to be gentle but she knew she was holding on for dear life.

And then, moments later, it swept over her. The realisation that Douglas knew exactly what he was doing and that the horse knew too. Horse and rider were in perfect synchronisation. She felt herself and her fingers relax and began to enjoy it. It was a risk but the risk was so thrilling and they weren't going too fast, they weren't out-of-control, they were safe.

Julia was safe, with Douglas.

Once she relaxed against his body, she understood exactly why he loved to be out on the horse, the wind, the crisp air, the speed, the strong beast between his legs, completely at his command, it was everything that was Douglas. And she began to love it too.

He was rounding Sommersgate and when they were within sight of the stables again, he slowed the horse to a canter then down to a roping amble.

"That wasn't so bad was it?" His voice, again at her ear, asked quietly.

"I suppose not." She knew she sounded surly but her guard was down, he was all around her, she could smell…

Her body tensed.

She could smell the Lalique cologne.

She closed her eyes and sighed.

"I'll buy you a horse." Douglas was either ignoring or oblivious to her warring emotions.

His words snapped her out of it.

"You will not!"

One of his hands captured her wrist and fiddled with the diamond watch, a watch the like that no one should wear for a simple stroll in the countryside.

She stifled a groan.

"You like it when I buy you things," he murmured.

She wished she could move her head so he wasn't speaking in her ear. His voice seemed to rumble through her like a shudder.

"I do not," she retorted sharply, lying through her teeth.

His stubbled cheek slid across hers to move her hair out of the way. They were nearing the stables now and she was glad of it. His rough cheek was pressed against her smooth one and it felt nice, too nice.

"You love it," he whispered.

"You are truly *the* most irritating man I've ever met," she snapped in order to cover the fact that he was absolutely right. He knew it and, worse, she knew it.

He chuckled, the sound so close to her, she felt it in the pit of her belly.

The children were already back to the stables and were dismounting. Douglas pulled his horse to a halt and quickly swung his leg off so he was down before she could jump down. He grabbed her waist and she knew she could not protest in front of the children as he slid her slowly off the horse, the entire way down just inches from his body. It was enough to be meaningful sexually but not explicit, for the children.

She was back to wanting to clobber him.

That or throw her arms around his neck and promise to marry him.

"Irritating," she grouched because it was the only thing she could do.

She was imprisoned between his body and the horse. He lifted her face by placing the side of his gloved fist under her chin. If he was going to say something, it was lost as the children interrupted.

"Now you can come riding with us!" Willie called, having helped Ruby down.

She pulled her chin from Douglas's hand and sidled sideways, away from him *and* his damned horse.

"Great!" she shouted back to Willie, trying to sound more enthusiastic than she was.

Ruby ran toward her. "You and me need horses!"

She took her niece's hand and without a backward glance, started leading her to the house.

"We're a little ways off from that, Ruby-girl," she said loud enough for Douglas to hear and she knew he heard because she could hear his chuckle.

It took every bit of willpower she had not to turn back and, at the very least, poke her tongue out at him.

Instead, she set her shoulders, mentally shook off the warmth that had stolen into her body, ignoring the ice that she knew was melting from around her heart and headed resolutely to the house.

She still had the scent of his cologne in her nostrils and she knew she was losing ground fast.

In fact, she knew she was just plain *losing*.

The problem was, it felt like winning.

❧ ❧ ❧

Douglas was not happy.

In fact, he was angry.

Not at his stubborn, pig-headed bride-to-be or at least not because she was stubborn and pig-headed. That, he found, was actually a rather endearing trait of hers.

True, he would have preferred Julia to be spending her time choosing flower arrangements, drafting wedding invitations and spending long nights squirming under him as he did all of the delicious things he fully intended to do to her. Not spending her time engaging in a head-to-head battle with him for her body, heart and soul. However, he was enjoying the battle, mainly because he knew he was winning and the interim was just sweet anticipation. Anticipation that caused a slow ache that he knew would be magnificently fulfilled once he eventually triumphed.

No, he was angry because of the unknown *Tony*.

And he was further annoyed because of his mother. He'd just put down the phone from talking to her.

She wanted to come home to Sommersgate.

Now was most definitely not the time for Monique's return.

In fact, Douglas had decided, there was never going to be a time for Monique to return.

Unfortunately, when he told this to his mother and, considering the frequency he, Julia and the children needed the Kensington house, informed her as well that she would need to find elsewhere to live, Monique had flown into a rage.

He listened to her tirade without reaction and then said, "Sam will find a few flats for you to look at in London, choose one."

"*A flat?* You want me to live in *a flat?*" she snapped, acting as if he told her he'd find her a nice cardboard box on a relatively safe street corner.

Douglas didn't answer.

"Am I to have any say on this *flat?*" she seethed.

"If you have requirements, call Sam tomorrow morning."

He was finished with the conversation and although she spluttered and raged for several more minutes, he eventually finished the call. Monique, being Monique, would not take his actions without a fight but whatever she did, he knew he could handle.

However, he had bigger things to worry about because, tonight, Julia was out with Tony.

Tony, apparently, was a friend from Indianapolis who was in Bristol for some business.

Tony, apparently, was a beloved acquaintance that had Julia in throes of ecstasy at seeing again.

Tony, definitely, was a man.

It was nearly ten and Julia had left the house at five to meet Tony (the man) for drinks and dinner. Carter had taken her and she was to call when she wanted to come home. The children were all in bed and Douglas felt that any responsible guardian should have long since returned, preferably around six.

Therefore, in Douglas's mind, she was late. Very late. Even unforgivably late.

He was just about to go find Carter, ask where she was and bring her home, kicking and screaming if he had to, when the man himself knocked on the study door.

"Sir?" Carter called.

Douglas's head came up.

"Miss Julia phoned, she's ready to come home. The problem is, the Bentley has a flat tire. It'll be awhile to fix so I wondered if I could use the –"

Instantly, Douglas surged to his feet and stated, "I'll get her."

He grabbed his keys, Carter explained that she was at the South American restaurant that Douglas introduced her to and she'd be waiting on the pavement in twenty minutes.

It took all of his willpower not to speed through the winding roads to Bristol. He did this because the last thing Julia and the children needed was for him to crash his car. Further, if he were to crash his car, he would also miss the opportunity to wring Julia's neck.

Or make her pay in a decidedly more pleasurable way.

He parked his Jag on the double yellow lines outside the restaurant and saw her immediately, standing out on the pavement as she promised. She was wearing a pair of her close-fitting jeans, high-heeled boots and a military-style, cranberry-coloured, velvet jacket. She had a woolly scarf wrapped round and round her neck and a matching fitted cap pulled snug on her head, forcing her thick blonde hair to press lushly around her face.

She also had her arm linked through the arm of a tall, lean, bald man and she was leaning into him like she wanted him to absorb her.

Douglas gritted his teeth and did his best to control the rampaging jealousy he was experiencing as he exited the car and stalked toward them.

Tony was one of those bald men who actually looked good bald, he was expensively dressed and exceptionally groomed.

None of this benefited Douglas's mood.

Julia noticed Douglas approach and, to his shock, her face lit up in a smile.

"Douglas! Yay!" she shouted and pulled away long enough to clap her hands several times, claps that were muted by the wool mittens she wore. Then she stopped abruptly and half-stumbled, half-collapsed into her friend.

Douglas ignored her bizarre behaviour, figuring she was going to try to score a point by rubbing his face in her relationship with this Tony. But as he finally arrived at the couple, she surprised him by immediately disengaging from Tony and linking her arm through Douglas's. She then leaned into him and he had to brace himself as he took on most of her weight.

"Tony, now you get to meet Douglas!" she announced happily as if this was her most fervent wish and then she swung her face to his, her green eyes sparkling. "I've been talking about you."

Douglas didn't know what to say because he had no clue what *she* said.

He regarded the pair warily, uncertain of her mood.

She gestured vaguely between the two men. "Tony, Douglas," then she paused and said, "Douglas, Tony." And then she giggled as if this was tremendously funny.

Tony was smiling indulgently at her and came forward to give Douglas a warm handshake.

"Mojitos," he said in an effort to explain Julia's strange behaviour.

"Ah," was the only way Douglas could reply.

"If you're trying to say I'm drunk, Tony Harrison, then... well, you'd be right!" Julia cried, turned to Douglas, pressed her breasts against his arm and lifted happy eyes to his. "I *love* mojitos."

"I'll have to remember that," Douglas murmured, trying to ignore her soft body and failing miserably.

His comment made Julia giggle which made Tony's grin widen.

"You better get her home, I'll be seeing you," Tony said and Julia jerked awkwardly away from Douglas and lurched back into Tony's arms, hugging him tightly with her arms around his neck.

"I miss you, Tony." Douglas could hear the catch in her voice and, for some reason, it made his chest tighten.

"I miss you too, babe," Tony gave her a firm squeeze and then let her go, guiding her carefully back to Douglas who again felt her clamp onto his arm and lean into him heavily. "You bring her back to Indiana sometime soon, would you?"

Douglas found it somewhat odd, and pleasingly telling, that this man was expecting him to be able to do anything with Julia. He nodded, said his good-byes and started to lead her away.

"Oh, and Douglas," Tony called and Douglas turned back to Tony who was grinning madly at him. "Good call with that kitten," he finished then he tipped up his chin sharply.

For the first time in his life, Douglas found himself in an exchange of meaningful masculine nods with another man. And after this, his earlier bad mood evaporated completely and he felt at peace with the world.

Julia, cheerfully ignoring all this, waved gaily at Tony and hummed happily to herself as she walked somewhat unsteadily to the car and he helped her in. By the time he'd joined her, she was strapped in and babbling enthusiastically.

"I just *love* that place. I'm *so* glad you introduced me to it. You'll take me again soon?" Before he could answer that startling request she cried out, "Oh!" And again, before he could react she asked, apropos of nothing, "Do you know any gay men?"

"Um... no," Douglas replied cautiously, uncertain where she was going with this new topic of conversation and mentally reminding himself to make certain Mrs. K stocked the ingredients for mojitos in the house. He started the car and pulled away, heading toward home.

"I've just had an idea!" she exclaimed brightly. "Tony said he might be here for business once or twice a year, isn't that fabulous?" Again, she gave him no time to respond and carried on. "So, we find him an Englishman and then maybe he'll stay here forever and we can all have barbeques again and Super Bowl parties." He glanced at her only to see her face fall. "You don't have the Super Bowl here, do you?"

He didn't answer, he didn't need to, she reversed her displeasure and happily babbled all the way back to Sommersgate planning Fourth of July outings, fondue parties and what she called "Oscar Nights".

For his part, he was pleased – no, thrilled – to learn that Tony was gay.

When he parked the car in the drive, she got out and did not hurry to the door but waited for him. Further, when he took her hand, thinking she still might need steadying (and because he damned well wanted to), she didn't resist but walked with him, hand-in-hand to the house.

"I'm so glad you came to get me, I hate calling on Carter," she admitted and he found himself slowing their pace, making the walk longer so he could draw out this moment. She would come to her senses soon, her mind would kick in, the walls would come up and he found he was enjoying this too much to let it go.

"Why?" he asked as he pushed the door open and they walked through it together.

"Because it seems so, you know, servant-y."

Douglas laughed quietly, closing the door behind them. "Darling, essentially he *is* a servant."

She gave a faux shudder. "I can't get used to it. To me, we're all just family."

At her words, something inside him shifted and along with it the ache for her intensified, turning into need. This need was so consuming, it blurred his vision, it wiped his thoughts, all that existed in the universe was her scent, her hand holding his and the sound of her voice saying those words that still hung in the air.

Her hand tightened in his as she tugged it gently, pulling him to a halt.

As he looked at her upturned face, he was experiencing something he'd never felt in his life.

He was *dazed*.

Her happy face turned concerned.

"Are you okay?"

"Fine," he answered distractedly.

"Douglas?"

"Hmm?"

She laughed, that sexy laugh she had, low in her throat and he focused on her.

"Why do I have the impression you're looking at me but you aren't *seeing* me?" she teased.

She actually teased.

He felt his body tighten as the yearning intensified.

"I see you," was all he said but what he meant was he saw her everywhere, in his thoughts, in his dreams, in his home, in his car, in his bed, *everywhere*.

She interrupted his preoccupation. "I never properly thanked you for Fred."

"Fred?" He was losing it, losing the thread of the conversation, losing everything with the overwhelming desire to lift her in his arms, shackle her to his bed and do things to her that would force her to agree to bind herself to him legally and in the eyes of the children, her family, her friends and God.

She broke into his thoughts. "The kitten, he finally has a name."

That got his attention.

"You named him *Fred?*"

She giggled. "I didn't name him Fred, Willie did. He and I traded, since I couldn't pick a name, I let Willie name my cat and I get to name his dog when he gets one." She tilted her head adorably. "I'm thinking 'Babykins' is a sweet name for a dog, what do you think?"

"I am not addressing a dog as 'Babykins'," Douglas replied gruffly.

"Babykins it is!" Julia chortled and then, shocking him to his core, she leaned into him, kissed his cheek just like she had her first night at Sommersgate, tugged her hand gently free and headed to her room, humming the whole way.

Leaving him watching her go and knowing that he was quite emphatically done with sweet anticipation.

It was time for victory.

❧ 22 ❧

JULIA DECIDES

Julia had lost.

She spent the entire day after her lovely evening catching up with Tony avoiding Douglas at the same time thinking about him nonstop. She'd even not gone to dinner, feigning a headache (not exactly the most original excuse in the world but she couldn't think of anything better that wouldn't worry the children).

While she was thinking, she realised she knew she'd lost, probably known it for ages but was too stubborn to admit it.

She loved Douglas, loved him as long as she knew him, regardless of how cold, proud and haughty he was (or maybe because of it) and had been fooling herself for fifteen years.

Charlie was right, even if he would never love her, *couldn't* love her and even though she knew one day she'd lose him, the time she had with him would be better than anything she could get from anyone else. She needed to take that risk, even if her happiness was short-lived, at least she'd have it for awhile. Tamsin and Gav hadn't known their joyous lives would be cut so short and they still lived every moment like it was precious.

Julia needed to learn that lesson.

Douglas wasn't just gorgeous, dangerous, mysterious, sexy and rich as Croesus. His voice made her tremble, his hands made her shudder and his mouth made her wild. When he looked at her, she felt the most beautiful woman, not just in the room, not in the world, but in history. Though she knew it wouldn't last, now she felt safe with him, she believed to the depths of her heart that he would always do the best for the children and no matter how it ended; he'd never be deliberately cruel to her.

So she was going to marry him.

And tonight, she was going to tell him.

Her consultancy was done. They were ready to hire an Executive Director and begin to put her and Douglas's business plan in motion. Even though they wanted Julia to apply for the job, she still had no leave to work in the United Kingdom and she didn't think she could take full-time employment for the sake of the children. One of the Trustees offered her another consultancy with another charity he supported, an even smaller organisation. Julia took the job, it would last less than a month but it was something to do.

Today was her last day at work and they'd had a small going away luncheon for her that was very sweet. Julia had made friends with the women there and before she left, they officially invited her to attend their monthly "Girls Night Out" dinner. Julia felt honoured, making friends was another important step in feeling home and conquering homesickness.

It was all falling together for Julia, she was settling into her life in England.

She just had one more thing to do.

She was later arriving at Sommersgate than usual due to stopping by the grocery store on her way, getting steaks, potatoes and anything else she thought Douglas would like (though she had no idea of his favourite foods or if he even had any, but she felt safe as most men seemed to like steak and potatoes).

Julia had a simple plan, she was going to ask Mr. and Mrs. K to watch the kids for the night, she was going to make Douglas dinner, she was going to agree to marry him and then she was going to seduce him.

Or she might do the last two the other way around.

Julia came in the kitchen door carrying her bags and saw Mr. K at the table. He had taken to coming around during their break times every once in awhile to have a cuppa and a gab.

Upon entry, Julia offered him a smile, "Hey Mr. K."

"Julia," he said but didn't meet her eyes and she had the feeling that something was terribly wrong.

She came forward and dropped her bags on the table and saw Mrs. K approaching with an already prepared cafetière of coffee.

One look at the determined set of Mrs. K's face made Julia's entire body tense before she asked, "Mrs. K, is something the matter?"

The older woman set the coffee down, stood back and crossed her arms on her ample bosom.

"We have to talk," Mrs. K announced.

Julia's heart leapt and the blood drained from her face, "Is it the children?"

"No, lass, it isn't the children," Mr. K assured her. "Sit down, luv," he continued gently.

Watching Mrs. K's curiously blank face the entire time, Julia sat on one of the benches.

"Is it Douglas?" she asked quietly, hoping he was all right. It could be him, he'd been shot, for goodness sake, anything could happen if he'd once been shot. He could have vicious, armed villains stalking him everywhere for all she knew.

"Not what you're thinking, no," Mrs. K said, sat down herself and prepared the coffee. "But it is him we want to talk to you about."

Mr. K broke in. "You have to know that what we're about to tell you could –"

"We could get sacked." Mrs. K interrupted abruptly, finishing with the coffee.

"Wha…" Julia's voice cracked and she cleared her throat, feeling her mouth go suddenly dry. Whatever they had to tell her had to be important. They both loved Sommersgate and she thought they would do nothing to put their places there in jeopardy. "What is it?"

Mrs. K didn't hesitate but reached across the table and slid over two framed photographs that used to be in Julia's room, the one of her family at Christmas and the one of her wrapped around Gavin when they were children. "Sorry, luv, I hope you don't mind but I took these out of your room."

Julia shook her head, indicating she didn't mind. She also didn't know what the photos had to do with anything. Scanning the photos she memorised, she tentatively took a sip of her coffee.

"For weeks and weeks, I've been searching and all I could come up with is this," Mrs. K went on, then, she slid something that looked like a piece of paper across the table and when it was in front of Julia, she flipped it over.

It was a photograph, a formal portrait taken of the Ashtons with Monique and Maxwell and a young Douglas (who had to be the same age as Gavin in the other photo) and Tamsin (at the same age as Julia).

They all looked refined, well-bred and very serious.

What they did not look was happy.

The stark difference between Julia's photos and Douglas's photo was undeniable.

"What...?" Julia started to say, confusion marring her features and dread beginning to seep into her bones as she stared in fascination at the handsome but serious-looking boy who used to be Douglas.

"As long as I've been in this house, there has been no love here," Mrs. K announced.

Julia's heart clenched and she had half a mind to flee the room because she knew she didn't want to hear what was going to come next – what she knew from piecing together memories and thoughts; what she knew of Tamsin, Douglas and Monique; what Douglas had said Christmas Eve; and what she'd been denying now for weeks.

But she had to stay, she had to *know*.

"You know Lady Ashton, the way she is with you and her grandchildren, she was no different to her own children, cold, uninterested, self-absorbed, sometimes cruel," Mr. K explained and Julia shuddered at the thought of having a mother like that. Patricia might have been strict but Gavin and Julia always knew her sternness came from love.

"Mister Douglas and Miss Tammy, they were close. I was wrong earlier. There *was* love in this house. Miss Tamsin loved her brother. She loved him like crazy." Mrs. K shook her head. "But it wasn't enough.

Not without a mother who cared and not with a father who abused him," Mrs. K stated quietly.

Julia's body jerked at the words and she felt her blood run cold.

"Abused him?" Julia's voice was a horrified whisper. "Maxwell abused Douglas?"

She frantically tried to picture Maxwell in her mind. He was always friendly, though not overtly so. He was solicitous but not exactly kind. Douglas and he clearly did not enjoy each other's company but they didn't avoid one another. Julia had always thought the way Monique and Maxwell treated their children was just the reserved way of the English, titled, upper-class.

"Aye, lass," Roddy Kilpatrick said. "We wouldn't be telling you this if we didn't think, well, that is to say –"

Mrs. K again butted in. "We know you care but you're holding back. I'm sure you have your reasons, Mister Douglas seems an unfeeling man and maybe he is, though lately..."

Mrs. K trailed off and Mr. K took over. "There's a reason for it, the way he is." He was speaking gently, watching Julia with thoughtful, searching eyes. "And we thought you'd want to know."

She didn't *want* to know, she *had* to know.

Julia spoke around the lump in her throat, her voice croaky. "How did he abuse Douglas?"

The couple looked at each other and Mr. K nodded at Mrs. K to go on. "You saw it most, my love," he prompted quietly.

When Mrs. K turned to Julia, there was wetness in her eyes and Julia's heart went out to her at the same time she braced for what was to come.

"It isn't something you could see, no bruises, no broken bones. In fact, I don't think I could even explain." Mrs. K's hands were resting on the table and they were clenched into fists. Mr. K put his hand on one of his wife's and squeezed. She took a shuddering breath and went on. "Mister Douglas tried so hard to be the best at everything. He never played, never sat around and watched telly, such an intense child. If he was outside with a football, it was because he was practising, driving himself to be the best he could be. If he was inside, he was studying or reading or –"

"It was never good enough for old Lord Ashton," Mr. K broke in and explained what his wife was trying to say and Julia felt a sinking feeling begin in the pit of her stomach, a sinking feeling she remembered well. "Once, before Carter, we had a chauffeur named Hodges. One day, ole Hodges was ill so Lord Ashton asked me to go and pick Douglas up from school for a weekend at home. Didn't go himself, even though he had nothing to do, he asked me to go. When I got there, the boy was waiting for me, telling me his father had mixed up the schedule and there was a rugby match he had to play and asking me politely if I could wait. I like my rugby, so instead of waiting at the car, I snuck around to watch the match." He turned eyes that shone with admiration and a hint of pride to Julia and her sinking stomach tightened uncomfortably. "He was magnificent. Could have played professionally, given time, he was so good. Think the coaches felt the same."

"After he came home," Mrs. K picked up the story, "Lord Ashton started shouting at him for being late. When Mister Douglas explained, Lord Ashton didn't even ask him how it went or if he won, just asked him if he made captain. Douglas hadn't, he wasn't popular with the other boys, seeing as he wasn't outright friendly. It didn't matter that he was the best player on the field, Old Lord Ashton just found the thing he could use to hurt his boy and then he yelled at him, right in the stairwell, in front of all the staff and Tamsin and anyone who was in hearing distance which could have been all the way to town. Yelled and yelled, red in the face and cursing, saying things to the boy... calling him names –"

"Enough," Julia whispered, her stomach in knots, her heart in her throat, tears pricking at her eyes and pain shooting throughout her body. But it was as if Mrs. K didn't hear her, so caught was she in the ugly memories.

"And it wasn't just then, it didn't matter what he did, how he did it, how well he did it, which was always well, mind. He'd yell, scream for hours, saying things no child should hear. Even when he was a young man –"

"Enough," Julia repeated, not thinking she could take anymore because she knew, she *knew*. She was an adult when it happened to her, the mental abuse, the shredding of confidence, the abrasion of the soul, to have it happen to you as a child by your very own father, the thought was unbearable.

Mrs. K continued, seeming to need to get it all out and Julia leaned forward and put out her hands, encompassing both Mr. K and Mrs. K's and squeezing, trying to instil warmth and comfort in the older woman while she dredged up the past.

"He shouldn't hear those things, not from his father, not from anyone but especially not from his father." The tears were falling down her face unheeded. She looked haunted and lost, as if she was somewhere else. Julia couldn't imagine her pain, her feelings of powerlessness, being forced to witness something she could do nothing about. At the thought of it, of what Douglas had endured, she felt her own tears spilling over and Mrs. K continued. "Douglas shut down, day-after-day, year-after-year, slowly he shut down. I'm not surprised, no one could take it. I don't blame him for not allowing himself to feel, to trust and love, because all he felt for years was nothing from his mother and unspeakable..." She gulped, unable to find the word to express herself then she pressed on. "At first he found strength in Miss Tamsin, solace, I think, she tried so hard to be everything to him, his champion. But then even she couldn't penetrate the wall he'd built around himself." At that, Mrs. K straightened and her eyes focused on Julia. "And he was good at everything, *great* at absolutely everything, so he built the best wall anyone could ever build," she said with determined pride as if this was an accomplishment akin to singlehandedly building The Great Wall of China.

They sat there, the three of them, their hands together on the table and looked at each other. Julia and Mrs. K with tears streaming down their cheeks and Mr. K's face red with the effort of not being unmanned in front of the women.

Eventually, Mr. K cleared his throat loudly and said, "What's in the bags?"

Julia wanted to laugh. She wanted to run screaming from the room. She wanted to hunt down Monique Ashton and beat her black and blue, to say a tiny prayer to Tamsin that she hoped her sister would hear to thank her for being the one ray of light in Douglas's dismal life. She wanted to find Douglas, tell him she loved him and do something, anything to erase his pain.

Instead, Julia didn't move, didn't take away her hands but kept looking deeply into Mrs. K's eyes. "Tonight I thought I'd ask you to watch the children and then I'd make dinner for Douglas. Awhile ago, he asked me to marry him and, yesterday, I decided I'd tell him yes."

Mrs. K gasped, her tear-streaked face lighting up.

"Well that's a damned fine piece of news!" Mr. K exclaimed, his expression both shocked and extremely pleased.

Julia smiled at Mr. K then moved her eyes to his wife. Quietly, but firmly, she stated, "I love him. I think I've loved him for years."

Oddly, at her words, Julia sensed something. It seemed the air in the room closed in on them, warming, becoming heavy.

Before Julia could process the change, she saw the tears were coming in earnest now from Mrs. K and then, abruptly, the older woman was all a-flurry. She jumped up and ran around the bench and hauled Julia to her for a bone-jarring hug. Then she let Julia go as suddenly as she grabbed her and turned to the bags, pulling out the goods inside.

"Steak, good, he likes steak," not lifting her head, she ordered her husband, "get Ronnie down here, and Miss Lizzie, too. We have things to do."

Mr. K rolled his eyes at Julia, all the despair of moments before dispelled at Mrs. K's exuberant busyness. He stood to do as he was commanded.

"And I need you to go to the store for some things." Mrs. K was standing, holding a bag of potatoes in one hand and asparagus in the other, looking back and forth between them and one could practically see her mind whirling. Then she turned to stare at Julia. "You go get ready, wash those tears off your face. I'll take care of everything."

"But Mrs. K, I wanted to –" Julia began to say.

"Go," she ordered. "We don't have time for dilly-dallying, Mister Douglas keeps no schedule, he could be home any minute and we need to be ready." When neither Julia nor Mr. K moved she shouted, "Go!"

They jumped to do her bidding.

❧ ❧ ❧

When Julia heard the tires crunching on the drive, she was ready.

While getting ready, she'd allowed herself to think of the Kilpatricks' words and to feel compassion for her soon-to-be fiancé. He would not accept or thank her for her sympathy, even though she, of all people, knew how he felt (which must have been why *he* reacted so strongly when Julia explained what Sean had done to her, a fact that, now that she understood it, made her stomach melt). She knew, though, for the sake of his pride, that she could never let him know that she knew the truth. It tore at her heart, knowing why Douglas was the way he was, but it would always have to be her secret with the Kilpatricks.

After years of abuse as a child, she knew it was unlikely she'd ever break through that wall but he wanted her and by God, he was going to have her. If she only had a week or was lucky enough to have years to show him love and tenderness, she was going to give it to him.

Starting tonight.

She was embarrassed about going on to Douglas, of all people, about being alone.

How selfish she'd been. How stupidly lost she'd been in her own grief and bitterness. She'd always had her mother and Gavin and a big family and loads of friends to love, cherish and look after her. Even here, she had Charlie, Sam, Mr. and Mrs. K, Ronnie and the children.

But Douglas had always been alone. Truly alone.

Julia had carefully prepared, picking her best little black dress (v-necked, sleeveless and backless it fell to her knees and fit her body lovingly) and added her stiletto-heeled, pointed-toed black pumps and Douglas's emerald. She pulled her hair up in a loose bunch and let tendrils fall about her face. She was careful with her makeup (as both hair and makeup would have to survive being significantly mussed if she had anything to do with it).

She was trembling with anticipation as she rushed out of her rooms and down the hall.

She stopped dead in the door to the dining room, staring at the vision before her.

A huge crystal vase sat near the end of the dining room table and it was filled with stunning red roses with spikes of greenery shooting out between the buds. A warm fire was burning in the grate and silver candlestick holders held high, white, tapered candles that had already been lit. The table was covered with a white damask cloth and the finest china, crystal and silver were laid out, only two places, hers and Douglas's. There was a silver bucket of champagne, not opened yet, chilling with a folded linen cloth thrown over the top. Somehow, as it was all set at the head, the enormous table was reduced to being cosy and romantic.

"I've taken care of everything," Mrs. K whispered, Julia started and looked to her right at Mrs. K whose head was poking into the hall from the doorway that led to the kitchen. "I'll serve you but I'll be discreet. Roddy has taken the children to the cottage and Ronnie has already gone home."

Julia nodded, a small, expectant (but slightly anxious) smile on her face.

Mrs. K winked and disappeared.

Julia heard footsteps down the hall, and voices.

She went still and listened.

Voices?

A man's and a woman's.

Julia walked into the room and the voices became more distinct.

Before they could turn the corner to the room, she knew. She knew *both* voices.

All the breath left her body and she realised there was a good possibility she would faint.

Then Monique Ashton and Sean Webster turned the corner and entered the dining room.

23

ARCHIE AND RUBY'S HEARTACHE

Tonight was the night.

Douglas wasn't going to allow her to hide in her rooms like she did last night (even at dinner, she gave the ridiculous excuse of a headache making the children eye each other speculatively throughout the meal).

He was going to ask Mr. and Mrs. Kilpatrick to take the children and he was going to find her, hunt her down if required, and make her agree to marry him using any means necessary.

Everything was in place; there was not a nuance he hadn't considered. He had the ring in his pocket and he had an enormous bouquet of two dozen exquisite white roses in his hand.

He knew about the roses because of Patricia.

While Julia was hiding last night, nursing her "headache", Douglas called her mother. He had never told Julia he'd play fair and drastic times called for drastic measures.

"Douglas, my God, is it the children?" Patricia said upon hearing his voice.

"No," Douglas replied shortly, still not believing he was making such a call. "It's Julia."

"Is she all right?" Patricia's voice was filled with worry.

"She's fine," he assured her calmly, "although I have a problem with her."

Silence.

Douglas did silence very well, this time using it to stall while he contemplated the unpleasant task ahead of him.

Eventually Patricia was forced to ask warily, "What problem?"

Through gritted teeth, still not believing Julia had reduced him to this, Douglas forced out, "I seem to be unable to convince her to marry me."

Silence again, this time the shock was palpable over the phone line.

Then, to his stunned disbelief, she asked, "Even after the kitten?"

Douglas didn't deign to answer.

"The kitten was a crowning achievement." Douglas heard the amusement in his future mother-in-law's voice, forgot that he actually held some regard for the woman and at that moment would cheerfully have wrung her neck.

She continued, oblivious. "Jewel is stubborn as an ox and she doesn't like men all that much, though don't think I blame her, considering. Must admit, though, she does hold on to things a bit."

"A bit," Douglas agreed sardonically.

This caused Patricia to roar with laughter. When she was finished, he could practically hear her wiping her eyes.

"White roses," she said, apropos of nothing.

"Pardon?"

"White roses, she loves them, her favourites. Start with that and then whisk her off to Fiji. She's always said she wouldn't consider that she'd truly lived until she went to Fiji, God only knows why but once that girl gets something in her head, she doesn't let it go." Douglas made no response, he'd lived that nightmare. "And let's face it," Patricia spoke into his silence. "The girl needs a vacation. If you go, I'll come out and see to the children."

It took a moment for the realisation to dawn that Patricia was helping him and he hadn't had to convince her.

"I take it I have your blessing?"

Three months ago, Douglas wouldn't have cared less.

Now, he did.

"Let me tell you something, my boy, you've had my blessing for fifteen years. I saw the way you looked at her all this time, Tammy and Gav did too. Not to mention the way she looked at you. Why do you think you're in this pickle? Tammy would be beside herself with sheer, unadulterated glee. By God, you've taken your sweet time."

He was trying to cope with being called her "boy" and was definitely not willing to think of the rest of what she said.

"You want me to talk to her?" Patricia offered helpfully.

"No," Douglas responded forcefully.

She laughed again and then, after a moment of contemplative silence, she said softly, "She'll make you happy."

He felt something reminiscent of the dazed feeling he'd had in the hall the night before but set it aside and said, "I've been trying to convince her that it will be the other way around."

She gave an uninterpretable "humph" then she demanded, "See that it is."

Now he was walking up the hallway toward the voices in the dining room.

He was looking forward to this. He didn't know what he was looking forward to most, sliding his ring on her finger or taking her to bed while she was wearing it.

He rounded the corner and came to an abrupt halt at what he saw.

The room was set to a romantic glow with softened lighting, a fire burning at the grate and candles on the table. An elegant table, set for two, ready for an intimate dinner. Julia was standing in front of the fire looking ravishing in a stunning black dress with her hair softly pulled up at the crown, tendrils tickling the glowing skin of her neck where his emerald hung.

And Sean Webster was standing opposite her staring at her with earnest intent.

For the second time in his life, Douglas Ashton, Baron Blackbourne, completely lost control.

"What *the fuck* is going on?" he demanded, his voice rumbling with barely controlled rage.

Julia jumped, a reaction that took her dangerously close to the fire.

She didn't seem to notice it, her face snapped toward him and he saw that she was pale.

And her green eyes, usually alight with some emotion, were completely, frighteningly, blank.

"Douglas!" Sean exclaimed, the other man walking toward him beaming. "Good to see you, man." And then he stopped and his gaze shifted to the flowers. He looked from Douglas then turned to Julia and started to ask, "What the –?"

"Julia?" Douglas barked, completely ignoring Webster and she jumped again, taking her closer to the fire, so close she could easily get burned. "Oh, for fuck's sake," Douglas finished tersely and he walked forward, threw the flowers unceremoniously on the table as he passed, grabbed her upper arm and yanked her unresisting body away from the flames.

"Do you want to explain this to me?" he clipped, not taking his hand from her arm.

"I was –" she started to speak and her voice was small in a way he'd never heard before, in a way that, hearing it, made his heart squeeze painfully. She looked up at him and her eyes cleared.

As she gazed at him, he saw raw emotion take the place of the blankness that preceded it. He'd seen that look in her eyes twice before, once after the first time they made love and again, in the hall Christmas night after Ruby's outburst. Both times, seeing it, he'd nearly come undone.

He surveyed the room, his hand gentling on her arm.

Julia wouldn't invite Sean Webster to a cosy, romantic dinner in his dining room.

Julia wouldn't invite Webster anywhere.

Douglas turned to the other man. "What are you doing here?"

"I came to talk to Julia. I heard about Gavin and –" Sean was also surveying the room, Julia's dress and the flowers and the cosy scene finally dawned on him making his face get red. "What are you doing with my wife?" he demanded hotly.

At his words, Douglas, already furious, became incensed.

"She's not *your* wife!" Douglas exploded, "She's going to be *my* wife!"

Webster's eyes rounded and then immediately narrowed. You could see the anger fill his face the second before he masked it.

His gaze moved to Julia and his voice turned urgent, pleading. "Jewel, baby, you have to listen to what I was saying earlier."

Julia shook her arm free of Douglas's hand and he swung back towards her, ready to do battle for her, ready to throw Webster bodily from the house if she wanted him to, *not* ready to let her withdraw.

Instead of retreating into her shell, though, she grabbed Douglas's hand and tugged gently on it.

"This was for you, you know," she said, her voice, still small, was getting stronger. "Mrs. K helped me, and Ronnie and Lizzie."

What he suspected was true. Julia would never strike out at him that way.

Never.

That was when he knew he'd won and he felt the exultation of his victory tear through his entire system.

Unable but also unwilling to control his reaction, Douglas pulled her hand sharply, she fell into his body and his arms shot around her, crushing her to him. Then his mouth came down on hers brutally, victoriously, her head was tilted up to him, ready for it, *inviting* it and he kissed her.

Douglas kissed Julia with the dazed passion that surged through his body, exultant in the triumph at her sweet capitulation. It was hot and wet and delicious and better than he would expect it to be even with all the kisses they'd shared before.

And Julia kissed him back without even the briefest hesitation.

"Excuse me! I'm still in the room!" Webster shouted but neither Douglas nor Julia looked at him.

"Say it," Douglas commanded when he lifted his head.

She smiled, it was tremulous but it was genuine and he felt his body respond to it.

"I want to marry you." Her voice was back, full, low and husky and he kissed her again. He couldn't have stopped it if a freight train was pulling him from the opposite direction. She wrapped her arms around his neck, slid her fingers into his hair, pressed her soft body into his and he groaned his satisfaction into her mouth.

When he let her go, he kept one arm locked around her while he pulled a box out of the breast pocket of his suit jacket.

He flipped it open with his thumb and then ordered, "Give me your hand."

She didn't hesitate but stopped idly playing with the hair at his collar and extended the fingers of her left hand toward him. He let go of her waist, took the ring out of the box and tossed it casually onto the table making her emit a little giggle.

"You're going to ruin the table if you keep throwing things on it," Julia muttered.

Douglas ignored her.

"This is unbelievable," Webster seethed from behind them.

They ignored him.

Douglas slid the diamond, a round, four-carat, perfect solitaire set simply yet elegantly in platinum, on her finger. Then his hand closed around hers and he brought the ring to his lips. He watched her the entire time, heat surging through his body when he saw her lips part in pleasure at first sight of the ring and then she bit her bottom lip when her knuckles made contact with his mouth.

"It's beautiful," she whispered.

He didn't give her a moment to let it soak in, keeping her fingers held firmly in his, he turned on his heel and dragged her across the room.

"Douglas where are we –?" she began.

"Julia you can't –" That was Webster who was pale-faced and tight-lipped and staring at them both like they'd grown two heads.

Douglas walked right by him as if he wasn't there.

He took her to the study, not letting her hand go. He stopped at the side of his desk, jerked at her hand gently and when her body came close to his, he dropped it and drew her up to his side with his arm around her waist.

He picked up the phone and punched in a number.

"Nick?" he waited for a response then continued. "We have an unwanted guest." He looked at the door to see that Webster had trailed behind them and was standing in the doorway of the study looking confused and angry. At Nick's response, Douglas finished. "Yes, he needs to be disposed of."

"I'm leaving," Webster stated but then hesitated, looking at Julia, obviously hoping she'd stop him.

Julia was paying no attention, she was holding her left hand with her right, her head bent, staring down at the ring, her face awash with feminine delight.

Douglas placed the receiver into the cradle and immediately picked it up again, dialling two numbers this time. He watched Webster turn and leave without another word and Douglas completely dismissed the other man from his mind.

When Sam picked up the phone he said simply, "Send out the press release."

Julia's head snapped up and she stared at him as Sam whooped in his ear, "Hurrah!"

"What press release?" Julia asked.

"Does this mean I might get a holiday in this decade?" Sam asked cheekily.

"What press release?" Julia repeated.

"Possibly," Douglas answered Sam and then put down the phone.

"What press release?" Julia's lips had puckered and she was regarding him out of the corners of her eyes.

"The one that's announcing our engagement and subsequent wedding in March at Wells Cathedral."

Her mouth dropped open. "You're joking," she breathed.

"You're not backing out on me again," Douglas retorted.

Julia gasped.

"How long have you had this planned?" she demanded then stopped and blinked. "Wells Cathedral? Tammy and Gav were married there."

"All the Ashtons are married there," Douglas explained, moving her around to face him and sliding his other hand across her waist.

He was about to kiss the partially-stunned, partially-mutinous, partially-amused look off her face when there was a sound at the door. They both swung toward it but Douglas didn't let her go.

He might, he thought, never let her go.

It was Mrs. Kilpatrick. "What's happening? I had to run up to the cottage because Ruby had gotten into a muddle. When I came back to see if you wanted the first course, no one was there."

"Is Ruby all right?" Julia asked, her face turning worried.

"Fine, something about... doesn't matter. Kid stuff," Mrs. Kilpatrick looked from one to the other. "Do you want the first course?"

Douglas opened his mouth to tell her they would be eating later, *much* later, but Julia spoke before him.

"We're getting married," she announced and Douglas could have sworn he heard pride in her voice. His fiancée extended her hand the way any woman shows off her engagement ring and Mrs. K gasped then clapped with unrestrained excitement.

"Congratulations!" she gushed as she dashed forward and, to Douglas's stunned surprise, she hugged them both. Even though he hadn't let go of Julia, Mrs. Kilpatrick's arms extended around both of their bodies and she laid a big, loud kiss on Julia's cheek and then turned shyly to brush her lips against Douglas's cheek as well. "It's about time we had some good news in this house!" She paused as she disengaged. "Do you want the first course?"

"Yes please," Julia said at the same time Douglas said, "Later."

Mrs. Kilpatrick chuckled, shook her head and walked away, pausing at the door to look back at them, her face filled with a happiness Douglas had never witnessed from her before.

When she disappeared, Douglas didn't know which one of them she would obey.

Julia turned toward him again, resting her hands lightly on his chest.

Douglas tilted his chin down to look at her and asked, "What did you have planned for tonight?"

She was fiddling with the lapels of his jacket and he was thinking he quite liked standing there with Julia in his arms idly touching him like she did it every day.

"Well, I was going to cook dinner for you then Mrs. K took over. And then I was going to tell you I wanted to marry you, which I've already done." Her eyes lifted to his and they were dark, nearly jade, and intense and he felt immediately robbed of breath at the depth of feeling in them. "And then I was going to seduce you."

He should have taken that golden opportunity to kiss her but instead he threw his head back and roared with laughter.

The thought of her *seducing* him was just too much. Any seduction she had planned would take a nanosecond to succeed.

"Am I interrupting something?" It was Nick at the door to the study and Douglas kept his head tilted back but instead of amusement, he now looked toward the ceiling in frustration.

Who was next? Carter? Ronnie? The children? Would Charlie and Oliver stop by for an impromptu visit from London?

"All right, Jules?" Nick walked in, completely unfazed by the tender scene he should have noticed unfolding in front of him and completely ignoring the meaningful glare Douglas levelled at him.

"All right, Nick," Julia answered, and snuggled, actually *snuggled* into Douglas's body.

"You are," Douglas said shortly, wanting privacy to reward Julia for the snuggle.

"I am what?" Nick smiled, knowing exactly what Douglas meant and choosing to disregard it.

"Interrupting something," Douglas clarified.

"Ah," Nick muttered and leaned against an armchair, thoroughly unconcerned and looking like he meant to spend the evening there. "So, who am I supposed to dispose of then? The man who just tore out of here in a rental or your mother who left half an hour ago? Did she come back?"

Douglas's body jolted at these words and Julia's head lifted to look at him.

"I'll tell you later," she whispered.

She didn't have to tell him. Monique brought Webster here.

"She's disowned," Douglas stated calmly and Julia shook her head in amusement.

"You can't disown your own mother." Her voice held a smile.

"I can when I give her a generous allowance," Douglas returned.

Julia's body stiffened. "Well, then you *definitely* can't disown her!"

Nick decided his fun was over and made to leave. "I'll leave you to it and keep an eye out."

"You do that," Douglas told his back.

"Nick!" Julia called out to him and then again extended her left arm and wriggled her fingers at the other man. "We're getting married," she announced, this time the pride in her voice was unmistakable and Douglas felt...

He felt...

He had absolutely no idea what he felt as it was something he'd never felt before.

Nick had turned at her call and his face lit up for a brief second before he continued to walk away.

As they just about lost sight of him, he yelled out, "About bloody time!"

This made Julia laugh and Douglas found it an immensely pleasant sensation to have her body shake with laughter while pressed against his.

He dipped his head to hers and kissed the laugh off her lips.

"About that seduction," he murmured against her mouth.

She lifted her hand to touch her fingers lightly against his face, her eyes holding his and, slowly, she smiled.

And that was it, he was seduced.

❧ ❧ ❧

Julia woke some time later feeling deliciously sated. Her body had a languorous feel that was a heady type of exhaustion that had nothing to do with tiredness and everything to do with happiness.

She was tucked up against Douglas's left side, her head on his shoulder, her hand on his chest and his fingers were lazily stroking the area just above her bottom.

"You awake?" she mumbled, her voice husky with sleep.

"Mm," was his answer.

She stretched slowly, arching her back which pressed her torso into his side and her bottom into his hand. He stopped stroking her and his hand flattened against her, smoothing down and around to cup her backside.

She shifted and lifted herself up on her elbow to look down on him.

The draperies were open and moonlight was spilling into his bedroom.

She could see his face in shadowed relief and she allowed herself a moment to think of what a brave man he was. He had survived an abusive childhood and created, all on his own, the masterpiece that lay before her.

She couldn't help herself, she smiled with pride.

"What time is it?" she asked.

"I've no idea," Douglas replied, watching her, his eyes heavy-lidded, his hand moving on her behind.

"Have you slept?" she asked, twisting around to see the clock on his bedside table and noting it was not nearly as late as she expected.

"No," he answered.

Her head swung back to him.

"Why not? You must be exhausted." He had to be after all that had happened that night. *She* was.

"No, Julia, I'm anything but exhausted." And his hand tightened on her bottom.

She let out a little, happy laugh even as her body reacted to his words.

"If this is my future, you'll wear me out in six months, a year tops," she told him.

"I'll take my chances," he returned and Julia noted his voice was throaty, sexy and held a tantalising promise.

She shivered and, like everything else she was feeling, it was a very happy shiver.

Julia lifted her hand from his chest and tentatively touched the small scar on his lip. In all the time it was there, she would never have dared to ask what she was about to ask.

But now, because she was going to be his wife (and felt she had a right to know and this thought thrilled her) she dared. "How did you get this?"

He answered without hesitation, "Knife."

She yanked her hand away with a shocked gasp and she could almost feel the blood drain from her face.

"Knife? You had some crazy lunatic wielding a knife close to your face?" Her body became stiff, she pushed up to a sitting position, dislodging his hand, holding the sheets to her chest and twisted to look down at him. "They could have... I don't believe it! They could have really hurt you!"

"What they did didn't exactly feel good," he muttered, moving to his side and up on his elbow.

"They could have put an eye out!" Her panic was rising as was her drama. "They could have slit your throat! How on earth did you get in a knife fight?"

"That's all over now, Julia." His voice was firm and it gave her a modicum (a very small modicum) of assurance.

The idea of any sharp object hovering near his handsome face, much less slicing into it, made Julia shudder. In an attempt to hide her reaction, she reached out and pushed back a lock of hair that had fallen to his forehead. The minute she took her hand away, the lock fell where it was before. Julia found that endearing and she also found the fact that she had every right to touch him felt splendid. She decided to focus on that rather than envisioning a knife close to his face.

Even so, she felt a point should be made, so she touched his scar again with her finger and said, "Well, I hope they got what was coming to them and *I* don't ever meet whoever they were. You don't carry a knife, do you?"

"No, I've never carried a knife." She could swear his voice held a tinge of amusement.

She was not amused.

"You frighten me sometimes, Douglas," she admitted on a whisper.

At that, he surged up and pulled her into his arms, burying his face in her neck.

"It's all over," he promised and she felt his lips moving against her skin with his words.

She nodded, not trusting herself to speak and forcing herself to believe.

Earlier that night, after he'd asked her to seduce him, he'd taken over (of course) and half-dragged, half-carried her upstairs to his bedroom. They made love, well, not exactly made love, it was too hot, too needy, too urgent, too intense to be described as "making love".

However, the *second* time, they *did* make love. It was slow and sweet and she had the opportunity to explore his body, touch him, tease him, taste him before it became out-of-control, gloriously insistent and demanding.

Glowing and satiated, they lay still joined intimately, her face in his beautifully-muscled, masculine throat and she whispered against the underside of his chin, "I'm hungry."

They dressed slowly, Douglas pulling on a pair of jeans and a burgundy sweater, Julia putting her dress back on. He grabbed another of his sweaters, this one moss green. He yanked it over her head and she swam in it but it would help to keep out the chill and she was touched by his gesture.

They padded down to the kitchen, barefoot and hand-in-hand. The house had been put to sleep for the night and she couldn't believe that at one time she found it frightening and sinister.

Now it was just home.

She knew its corners and its shadows. She knew where the edges of the carpets were and how to avoid the furniture in the dark. She was beginning to realise she loved it there, it was Douglas's and now so was she and thus she belonged at Sommersgate. That sense of belonging made her feel wonderful.

They entered the kitchen and Julia thought she'd have to cook their food.

Instead, they found Mrs. K sitting at the kitchen table, her hands busy with knitting, her eyes trained on a portable television that had been hastily set up, probably by Mr. K.

Mrs. K jumped to her feet when they walked in and ignored Julia's surprised face.

"Are you ready for your first course?" she asked as if it was perfectly natural for her to hang around until late evening, waiting for them to complete their sexual antics and come in search of sustenance.

Douglas grinned a sexy, devilish grin and then said, "Please, if you don't mind Mrs. K."

At that, he turned on his heel and left, dragging Julia with him, not understanding the profound moment he'd just created. But Julia watched her friend from over her shoulder.

Margaret Kilpatrick had never been referred to by Douglas in the familiar of "Mrs. K" as long as Julia knew him. She saw the other woman's face flush with pleasure and Julia felt her stomach melt.

Mrs. K had removed the red roses and in their place was a magnificent display of the white ones Douglas had brought home with him.

Over dinner, she told him about Monique bringing Sean to the house then, after fervently urging Julia to listen to what he had to say, leaving. She told Douglas about Sean telling her he'd made a mistake at letting her go and asking her to move home to America with him. She explained that Sean even said she could bring the children, that she could sue for custody and even went so far as to declare that he'd use all his money and contacts to help her.

Throughout this, Douglas listened patiently, his face betraying nothing.

She did not tell him about her weakness, about being emotionally drained after hearing what the Kilpatricks had told her that afternoon and the feelings of disempowerment in the face of Sean that she couldn't help but allow to creep back. She did not confide in him that she was devastated that Sean was going to ruin her much anticipated plans for the evening. That she was worried about a lifetime of the vicious Monique as her mother-in-law for, to bring both her father and Sean back meant Monique truly and completely detested her and that was *not* a nice feeling. She didn't tell him that she was at a loss of what to do and what to say because she simply had nothing to say, not to Sean. The moment Douglas arrived, she was trying to think of a way to get rid of Sean and not coming up with any answers as she'd already told him to go but he refused.

What she said instead (looking down at the delicious panna cotta that Mrs. K served as a finale) was, "I asked him to go but he refused. I thought it best to shut myself down, let him have his say and hope you'd be home soon. I knew you'd know what to do and, it turns out, I was right." She stopped and smiled at him. "Though I must admit, it was better than I expected." Her smile got bigger. "*Much* better."

At this pronouncement, dessert was definitely over (even though she had several more spoonfuls she very much wanted to consume). Without a word, he rose from his chair, pulled her from hers and led her back to his bedroom.

That time when they made love, it was *very* slow and *very* sweet. He touched her with a reverence that was mind-altering; it felt almost like he was worshipping her. It felt like he was memorising her and she forced him to allow her to do the same. When, at long last, she climaxed, she was sure her body was going to shatter at the pleasure of it and she cried out his name but it was muffled as he absorbed her call into his mouth and then, very shortly after, she did the same for him.

That was when she fell asleep at his side, satiated and happy.

Now, he held her in his bed, what would soon be *their* bed, his mouth on *just the right spot* behind her ear. She lifted her hands and slid her fingers into his thick hair.

"What am I going to do with you?" she whispered into the night.

"Whatever you want," he growled into her ear and she felt a shiver slice through her at her own words of weeks ago being repeated. She shoved his shoulders gently and cocked her head at him, the corners of her lips quirking.

"Anything?" she queried, her eyes dancing.

His mouth twisted in a diabolically sexy grin. "Just know whatever you do you'll suffer the consequences."

She didn't hesitate at his playful threat but pushed him onto his back and then manoeuvred herself to straddle him. Her fingertips danced lightly across his abdomen and she watched as he lifted his arms and linked his fingers behind his head to rest it on his hands

He quirked an eyebrow at her.

At this arrogance, she laughed, she couldn't help herself. She was beginning to adore his arrogance, it was so *Douglas*.

She ran her hands across his muscular chest and leaned forward, pressing her breasts against him and nuzzling his neck.

"I love your neck, your throat," she murmured against his skin, darting her tongue out to lick the length of it. She smelled the cologne she'd given him and trembled. "It's my most favourite part of your body," she admitted.

"Your *most* favourite?" His voice rumbled with desire that was tinged with amusement.

She lifted her head to look at him.

"Well, it's in the top five," she allowed. His body shook with silent laughter and she smiled at him, happier still that she could make him laugh and again tilting her head. "Maybe the top ten."

He took his hands from behind his head and slid them around her waist, tightening there.

She abruptly pulled herself up and reached around to take his hands from her waist and gently forced them across her belly, up her midriff and then over her breasts. With her hands on his, she positioned them there, gently squeezing and using a finger on her right hand to move a finger on his left to scrape across her nipple.

As the sensations shot from her nipple on a heady bee-line straight between her legs, she emitted a low moan, her back arching slightly.

"Jesus," he muttered and heaved quickly upward, pulling his hands from her breasts to slide them down the backs of her thighs and position her legs so they were wrapped around him.

"Douglas!" she cried, feeling his hardness beneath her and his hands moved again, one to her bottom to lift her up and the other between their bodies. "Douglas!" she exclaimed again, this time in surprise as his hands came to her hips and swiftly, forcefully, he impaled her. She uttered a half-gasp, half-groan and immediately wiggled her hips, grinding further into him as he buried his face in her neck.

"I love it that you're always ready for me. So damned wet." His voice rumbled against her neck, vibrating with arousal and she shivered as it slid across her skin and, even though it most likely meant nothing, Julia loved it that Douglas had used the word "love" when mentioning something about her.

"You're being very bad. *I'm* supposed to do whatever I want with *you*," she scolded him with a breathy tease.

"You were taking too damn long," he grumbled even though she'd been in control maybe less than a minute.

Then Douglas kissed her, long and hot.

When he moved his mouth to slide down her cheek to her jaw she shakily said, "I'll see what I can do to speed things up."

And she did.

❦ ❦ ❦

While the lovers moved on the bed, across the floor an arctic draught slid slowly, with melancholy, exiting the room.

It took its journey, a journey it knew well, a journey it took day-after-day, week-after-week, for over a hundred years.

In the study, which had been *his* favourite room, Lady Ruby shifted and formed, becoming the ghostly vision of herself, a vision, until just recently, she only let *him* see. She hovered at the window where, outside, her husband was.

"Is it love?" Archie asked and Ruby nodded, but sadly.

He shook his head, knowing she meant it was there but it was not expressed. *"Why?"*

"Too much pain, they won't admit it."

Ruby and Archie spoke without words, communicating telepathically, their mouths not moving and no ethereal sounds came out.

The only sound either of them could make was the hideous scream she cried whenever she was forced to endure, because of the curse, because of the jealous spurned suitor she had angered and his malevolent mother who knew the ways of magic, to relive her violent demise over and over again. Every few months, sometimes if she was lucky, every few years, it would happen to her again, against her will, at the base of the stairs. The unseen hands closing around her neck and squeezing... squeezing... *squeezing* the life out of her.

"I had hoped..." Lord Archibald Ashton said to his wife, lifting his hand to rest it against the window, a hand he could not force through no matter the millions of times he had tried. Her hand joined his there, separated forever by the glass, separated forever by Sommersgate – a cruel irony for it was the house he built out of love for her.

For his part, he could always see her from the French doors to the entry, see her ghostly form strangled again and again, just like that night. She was always fighting violently against an unseen attacker and he could hear her scream, like he had that terrible night, but he had been held back, now by invisible hands but then, by the men, four of them, and he couldn't save her.

Once left alone, he clawed at the doors, tried to break the glass, did everything he could to get to her lifeless body that lay at the foot of the magnificent stairwell he ordered made for her. He wanted to hold her one more time but it was as if Sommersgate was protected by an impenetrable magical shroud. For hours, chilled through to the bone, his body becoming exhausted, the freezing cold permeated him, making him sluggish, until, he too, felt his life ebb away. Over the years, as it happened time and again, he could see her, no matter how hard he fought, and he was forced to live through it again and again, never succeeding in saving her, never succeeding in getting to his beloved to hold her one last time.

"He does not understand his love for her, she's too proud and stubborn to admit hers and open her heart for what she thinks will only result in pain," Lady Ruby replied and then swiftly moved to reassure her love. *"We have hope, the boy, William. He's like his father. Darling, we just need to wait a few years and he'll bring love to this house. He will free us."*

Archie leaned his forehead against the pane of glass and his beautiful ghost of a wife did the same. *"I did want love for Douglas, he –"*

"And I wanted it for Julia, but you know the curse, they have to admit it, they have to say it aloud to each other, or we will –"

"I know." Even without sound, there was an ache in Archie's words.

"We've done all we can do." Lady Ruby, always placating, always trying to instil hope in him, did it again.

"I miss you," Archie whispered, even though he could see her and speak to her, he could never be with her.

Lady Ruby didn't reply, but misty-white, ghostly tears slid down her cheeks which said all that needed to be said.

24

UNHEEDED WARNINGS

The press release announcing Lord Ashton, Baron Blackbourne would (very shortly) marry Ms. Julia Fairfax, an American and his sister-in-law, was met with shocked surprise.

A photograph was issued with the release, it depicted the couple standing side-by-side, his arm casually (but somehow possessively) wrapped around her waist. She was wearing a stunning (and many men thought, rather sultry) green-black dress and he was wearing a dinner jacket (and many women thought he wore it rather rakishly).

The men of Douglas's set were not surprised that Blackbourne had fallen for the American. They made a handsome couple. If the many photos were anything to go by, she had style and an innate elegance, and, of course, a very nice set of legs. Ashton was known as a man of refined tastes and this choice for a bride further demonstrated that fact. Those few who had actually met her thought she was rather lovely indeed, for an American.

The women of Douglas's set *were* surprised, and slightly gratified, that he had fallen for Julia Fairfax. He was notorious for the not-so-sweet but definitely young things he favoured as partners. That he would chose a *woman*, and not a twenty-something, world-weary, cynical, underfed wannabe said a great deal about the handsome baron. Those few who had actually met her found themselves not-so-surprised that Julia had managed to catch the eye (and the heart) of the renown womaniser.

Monique Ashton was verbosely displeased at the announcement.

Much sooner than she had expected that night she had taken him to Sommersgate in an effort to get him to sweep away the unwanted rubbish that infested her home, Sean Webster had appeared at the door to her room at the Bath Spa Hotel. He had been in an absolute rage and had said some remarkably unpleasant things to her. Indeed, she thought for a moment he might actually strike her. However, the management of the hotel heard the yelling and intervened, ejecting Mr. Webster with great force.

Monique went back to London the next day, already trying to decide her next course of action.

She would soon be finalising details on her new, and, she had to admit (if only to herself), wonderfully expensive and elaborate flat.

Upon arrival in London, Monique saw the splashy headlines about her son and was forced to endure phone call after phone call. Of course, Monique told all of her friends and acquaintances (and some people she was not so friendly with) exactly how she felt about the scheming little American her gullible son had asked to marry him.

Unfortunately, these conversations reached the ears of both Oliver and Charlotte Forsythe, (upon hearing the happy news, the former, extremely pleased for his friend, the latter, hysterically giddy with delight for both Julia and Douglas) which meant they very swiftly reached the ears of Douglas. Per usual, Douglas even-more-swiftly went into action.

Monique's phone rang again only days after the official announcement. It was Douglas's PA, Samantha, a girl Monique had very little time for but had to suffer because she was making arrangements for the new flat.

Upon Monique's curt greeting, the distasteful Samantha said, "I'm calling to inform you that Lord Ashton has reneged on the contract for the flat. He also wishes you to know that your monthly allowance will cease effective immediately."

At this news, Monique was stunned speechless.

Samantha continued. "He will reinstate you, at a quarter of your allowance and will purchase and furnish a flat for you, again, at a quarter of your budget, if you publicly and liberally declare your mistaken impressions of his fiancée and officially announce your approval of the match."

"A quarter?" Monique's voice shook with angry disbelief and just a hint of fear.

"He's instructed me to tell you that you can take it or leave it," Samantha returned.

The tone of the girl's voice left Monique in no doubt she was enjoying this tremendously and Monique shook with humiliated ire.

She had long since gone through the trust funds her parents *and* her husband had left her. The generous allowance her son gave her monthly (and often augmented at her request) was her only source of income.

Furthermore, she'd never worked a day in her life. She certainly couldn't (and wouldn't) start now.

Monique was not a stupid woman (just an evil one), she knew when her son said something, he meant it.

Therefore, she had no choice.

"I'll take it," Monique snapped.

Later, Monique had to get herself a rather unladylike portion of sherry (and brought the bottle with her) as she sat by the phone and started to make her calls.

❧ ❧ ❧

At Sommersgate, the news of the impending nuptials met with mixed reviews. Lizzie was beside herself with delight. Ruby, taking the lead from her sister, was equally thrilled. Nick, Ronnie, Carter and the Kilpatricks were all obviously awash with joy.

Willie didn't quite know what to make of it all.

Formally, in the library, Douglas and Julia sat with the children and announced it the day after they'd agreed to marry. While Lizzie and Ruby danced jubilantly around their aunt and uncle, Willie stepped back, once, twice then fled the room without a word.

Julia was horrified and immediately moved to go to him.

Douglas caught her arm and murmured under his breath, "Let me."

She did but not without pacing at the bottom of the stairs, holding her new kitten Fred (who was not very happy at being held and stroked when he wanted to play and, if possible, scratch the wonderful carpet runner on the stairs which was the perfect height for his little claws).

When Douglas descended the stairs, Julia turned fretful eyes to him. He encompassed her waist with his arms and looked into her eyes.

"Give him time," he said quietly.

These were not the words Julia wanted to hear but she nodded anyway.

Two days later at dinner, the mood had not changed. Lizzie and Ruby and the rest of the household were still ecstatic. Willie was unusually quiet and still undecided.

After the main course was whisked away and the pudding about to arrive, Willie cleared his throat and announced he had something to say.

"Thank you, Uncle Douglas," he started, his young voice sounding solemn, "for asking me to be your best man. But I've thought about it and decided, since Dad isn't here to do it, that I should give Auntie Jewel away instead."

Julia's hand flew to her mouth, her eyes quickly filling with tears slid to Douglas who inclined his head soberly at his nephew, his face communicating he felt this decision wise.

"That is," Willie continued, his eyes on his aunt, "if you want me to, Auntie Jewel."

She didn't trust herself to say more than, "Please."

Taking his cue from his uncle, he inclined his head (somewhat arrogantly, Julia noted with a hint of amused dismay).

Lizzie let out a snort, betraying her attempt to hold back her tears. At the noise, Julia let her emotions go and burst into uncontrollable sobs. Lizzie followed suit and Ruby, never one to be outdone, wailed louder than the two other females even though the four year old wasn't exactly certain why she was crying. Douglas and the newly-anointed Will (who had, that evening at the dinner table, forever lost the youthful "Willie") found themselves thrust into comforting the howling women. Douglas pulled Julia into his arms and then steeled himself when Lizzie threw her entire body weight against them and he included the young girl in his comforting embrace. Will, for his part, patted Ruby's back awkwardly.

Mrs. Kilpatrick walked into this scene carrying pudding and after hearing the story haltingly told by Julia, she joined the caterwaul. So overcome was she, Douglas had to phone Roddy Kilpatrick to come see to his wife.

❦ ❦ ❦

Douglas and Julia's first row came less than twenty-four hours after Julia agreed to the marriage.

Indeed, the morning after.

"I'll ask Veronika to move your things up here today," Douglas murmured against Julia's lips, the water from the shower falling on them, his soapy hands on her body.

She smiled but shook her head, moving her mouth from his, she paused from running her lips across his jawbone to reply, "I don't think so."

Douglas's slippery hands slid over her behind, pulling her wet body closer to his. "I do."

She laughed (probably too aroused to realise the seriousness of Douglas's intent). "I'm not moving up here. The children don't even know we're getting married."

"We'll tell them today."

She nodded her agreement but said, "We have young, impressionable children in the house, we can't carry on like this." She brushed her lips against his. "I'll move up after the wedding."

His hands slid up to tighten around her waist.

"You'll move up today," he ordered, his voice brooking no protest.

Her head jerked back, (probably at his arrogant tone which she immediately changed her mind about and most definitely *did not* adore).

"I will not!" she snapped stubbornly.

He pressed her against the wall of the shower.

367

"Yes," was all he said, his fingers finding spots that would (with any normal female) get her to go along with his plan.

Not Julia.

Still, she gasped (she couldn't help herself).

Then she stated firmly, "No!"

"Yes," he growled, his mouth finding the area behind her ear that he knew would get her to acquiesce.

Unfortunately, Douglas again misjudged his bride-to-be.

"We cannot carry on an illicit affair under the noses of the children," Julia retorted (but her reply lost some of its strength due to its breathy quality).

Douglas, not one to fight fair, lifted her effortlessly, spread her legs, pressed her against the wall and entered her in one fluid movement, his hands on her backside holding her aloft.

Her legs immediately wrapped around him.

"And what, pray, do we do about this..." he pulled out slowly and then surged forward, gratified to hear her moan deep in her throat, "in the meantime?"

She sucked in a shuddering breath.

"You... you're going to have to be..." he moved lazily out and then swiftly in again and she paused to savour it. "Creative," she whispered.

Compromise was reached as Douglas very much liked the sound of that.

And creative he most definitely was.

❧ ❧ ❧

With less than two months to plan the wedding, Julia was forced to create an event that was worthy of the nuptials of Lord Ashton, Baron Blackbourne.

Luckily, she had the worthy assistance of Charlotte Forsythe, Margaret Kilpatrick and Samantha Thornton (and the long-distance support of Patricia Fairfax). Further, being a rather dab hand at lists, Julia was able to get organised and have plans underway in short order.

Douglas, coming home earlier than normal, much earlier, *creatively* earlier (that is to say, hours earlier than the children would arrive home from school and with the knowledge that Veronika had taken Ruby to a movie, this knowledge coming from the fact that he told Veronika to do so and gave her a two fifty pound notes for her troubles) strode down the hall to Julia's room.

What he found upon opening the door was of great surprise as well as a little alarming.

Julia, wearing nothing but a rather fetching pale pink bra and panties that was liberally dosed with delicate black lace was being fondled by a tall, rail-thin, impeccably (if dramatically) attired and immensely effeminate man who, for reasons unknown, had yards of ivory silk wrapped around his own body.

"Douglas!" Julia cried.

"Julia," Douglas responded, his face setting dangerously, his arms crossing on his chest and his stance settling belligerently.

The other man stepped back and brought a fluttering, open palmed hand to his chest.

"Oh my," he drawled upon looking at Douglas.

"This," Julia motioned to the man and then grabbed her cashmere robe and shrugged it on, "is Gregory."

Douglas didn't move, didn't utter a noise, he simply glared.

"Oh my," Gregory repeated, his eyes never leaving Douglas.

"Gregory will be designing my wedding gown," Julia explained, hastily tying the belt of her robe.

Douglas, again, had no response.

Except he quirked a brow.

Julia went on. "He designed the dress I wore to the ball."

This caused a slight softening of Douglas's features.

Very slight.

"*And,*" Julia continued meaningfully, "I'm hoping to introduce him to *Tony* at the wedding."

Douglas digested this information then nodded and, with unmistakable intent, strode toward his soon-to-be wife.

"Gregory, as delightful as it is to meet you," Douglas's voice was even and determined, his arm sliding around Julia, hauling her resisting body to his side, "I do think it might be time for you to have a break from your worthy endeavours and seek some refreshment."

"Douglas!" Julia screeched, her voice high with mortification.

Gregory looked from Julia to Douglas, quickly read Douglas's meaning and asked affably, "How much time do you need?"

"Fifteen minutes," Julia quickly responded.

"Two hours," Douglas said at the same time.

"Two hours it is." Gregory, a romantic at heart, quickly exited, thinking maybe he should return in three.

So he did.

⚜ ⚜ ⚜

Julia was so happy, she could barely contain herself.

Life had most definitely taken a dramatic turn.

She still worried about the future (she couldn't help herself). She also had moments of sorrow that she was not sharing these joyous times with Gavin and Tamsin. Further, she would, approximately six times a day (she started counting), have to stop herself from telling Douglas her feelings and would sometimes nearly let slip that she knew about his childhood (it was appallingly easy to drown in moments of tenderness when she was with him, which was often, *very* often).

Despite all that, Charlie's prediction that even without any avowal of undying love from Douglas, life with him was better than any life she knew before.

And Julia savoured it sweetness.

He was possibly *the* most attentive, *the* most voracious, *the* most generous lover she'd ever had, in bed and out of it.

Indeed, if he were actually to love her, she might expire from the rapture of it because it could scarcely get better than this.

Although, in the deepest regions of her heart (where she had firmly and stubbornly buried it), she wished for that vow of love more than anything in the world.

She was humming to herself as she was getting ready for Valentine's dinner. Douglas was taking her somewhere in Bath and they would be gone the entire evening, not to return until the morning, and she knew (happily) what *that* meant.

Ronnie, who also had a new boyfriend of her own, was home at her bedsit getting ready for her date. Carter was off for the evening. The Kilpatricks had taken the children out for a curry and would be watching them for the night.

Julia had the house to herself.

She had wrapped Douglas's present, no cologne or tie this time, but a pair of gold cufflinks of Gavin's which had also been their grand-father's.

She had Patricia's approval of this gift, indeed, as with everything that had to do with Douglas, she had Patricia's approval, especially after Julia (in a moment of weakness and in deepest confidence) explained the Kilpatrick's story of his childhood.

Julia had the cufflinks cleaned and put in a handmade box of cherry-wood that was lined with black velvet. They had been (except for his wedding ring) Gavin's proudest possession and Julia truly hoped that Will didn't mind that Douglas owned them until such time as nature took its course (in, hopefully, about sixty years) and they came to Will.

She had spent an age getting ready, bathed, lotioned, powdered and made up. She donned her frock, made specifically for the night by Gregory. It was an absolute vision, a swathe of scarlet red satin, strapless and form-fitting, cut at the knees. In the back hem, frothing forth from a deep slit, sprung a dramatic poof of black tulle. She wore it with black, high-heeled sandals with peek-a-boo toes and a daring ankle strap.

It looked like something Marilyn Monroe would wear and Julia loved it.

She was affixing her diamond studs to her ears, her diamond watch to her wrist and had moved from humming to singing Dolly Parton's *I Will Always Love You*.

She couldn't *wait* to give Douglas his present. If she couldn't *tell* him she loved him, she was going to do everything she could to *show* him.

Giving her cheekbones one last swipe of blusher, she felt the draught against her ankles and ceased her singing.

"Well, Lady Ruby, where have *you* been lately?" she asked the draught as if it would answer her.

To her surprise, the icy draught turned polar, freezing her ankles and drifting up her calves. It was so uncomfortable, Julia jumped away from it.

"Now, Lady Ruby, nothing is going to spoil my evening. Run along now and play with the kittens. They could use a good scare," Julia suggested (though, not meaning it), walking swiftly out of her dressing room and into her bedroom to avoid the chill.

The sun had long set but, as Julia had been in the dressing for hours, she had not pulled the drapes. The scratching was there, louder than ever, and she saw that Archie was outside her window. The spectre was scratching frantically with both hands, looking like he desperately wished to come inside. His mouth was moving like he was shouting but no words were coming out.

Julia stared at the vision in horrified silence.

The freeze hit her ankles again, swirling around her calves and thighs and Julia staggered back from the frenzied Master while trying to escape his Mistress.

"What's going on?" Julia breathed.

She felt as if the entire house swayed with motive, as if trying to voice some eerie foreboding.

Then she saw him by the illumination of the outside light.

Nick, running toward the front door. She knew from seeing him that something *was* wrong because he was running hell-bent-for-leather.

Julia's heart leapt into her throat, panic seizing her at remembering another night not long ago when Douglas had come home with Nick, wounded and bleeding.

The draught of Lady Ruby moved, surrounding her, almost squeezing her but she ignored its clear warning, turned on her heel and fled the room, running as best she could on her slim heels towards the front door.

When she arrived, Nick had forced his way through the heavy front doors (doors that only Douglas seemed to have no trouble shifting) and was careening down the hall, motioning to her by flailing his arms.

He shouted, "Run, goddammit, Jules, *run!*"

And then the world tilted, the house darkened ominously, closing in on itself. It felt as if the stone walls flexed inward, the shadows everywhere lengthened, stretching out like claws as a gunshot exploded followed closely by a strange "ping" sound and Nick went down like dead weight, cracking his skull with a sickening thud against the flagstone floor.

Leaving Julia to face three men, all pointing guns at her and speaking what she knew was Russian.

25

THE CURSE

"The Royal Crescent Hotel has confirmed, of course," Sam was saying, "you'll arrive in the suite greeted by champagne and strawberries –"

"Isn't that a bit trite?" Douglas interrupted curtly, wanting everything to be perfect.

"Well, I suppose *you* can call your intended's preferences 'trite' but I would never presume to do so. Patty says Julia loves champagne and strawberries."

His silence was the only indication of his apology and his jaw tightened at Sam's referral to Patricia as "Patty". All the women in his life were becoming the banes of his existence.

They were, he realised, ganging up on him.

Charlotte, Mrs. Kilpatrick, Sam and Patricia called him day after day to check this detail or that detail of the wedding or of that evening's dinner (or tomorrow's) or of his schedule. Or simply to check on *him* to ascertain he'd done nothing to make Julia run screaming into the night and the clutching arms of certain death.

Their lack of faith in him was appalling.

Although, he had to admit, he hadn't handled their courtship to his usual exacting standards. However, she had said yes (rather spectacularly), she was wearing his damned ring (rather proudly), she was sharing his bed (or her bed or the couch in the study or the wall of the billiards room, depending on his level of creativity, a heretofore unknown skill he found, through necessity, he had in abundance).

"If you want to buy a ten foot ice sculpture of the Eiffel Tower and set it up in the bloody garden, I don't care. Your budget for the wedding reception, from now on, is unlimited," he'd informed Mrs. K (somewhat shortly) just that afternoon.

Instead of taking offense, the woman seemed downright jolly.

He'd spent nearly twenty years making a fortune (quadruple fold) and one small wedding and four pushy, nagging women were going to bankrupt him in a single day.

Fortunately, Julia was a calm amidst this storm. With her never ending lists, her capacity to interpret (and control) her mother's dramatics, to find Charlie hilarious and to delegate to Mrs. K and Sam when needed, she was taking all this on with a level head – all the while starting a new consultancy, dealing with the children and giving into a (very) demanding Douglas (though he couldn't help but note that the last seemed to be the most favourite of her tribulations).

"Why on earth don't they phone you with these details?" Douglas found himself grumbling (actually reduced to *grumbling*) the evening before.

They were on the couch in his study. Douglas was sitting at one end looking through some papers. Julia was lying on her back with her feet in his lap, Fred, The Cat (his name had been grandly, yet unnecessarily, lengthened by Ruby) sleeping on her belly and she was reading a book.

"I think they're enjoying torturing you, you haven't exactly been, um," Julia hesitated, Douglas cut his eyes to her and she grinned sheepishly, "*approachable* for the last thirty-eight years."

"I'm not approachable now," he ground out. "I'm considering hiring hit men."

She laughed, the sound throaty and sexy and making him immediately want her. If the children hadn't been in the house watching television in the lounge, he would have taken her.

When he was going to have his fill of her, he didn't know and he was beginning to doubt he ever would. Every time he had her, he wanted more, *needed more*, she was like a fucking drug.

"You wouldn't dare," Julia joked, taking him from his thoughts then her smile drained away as she took in his bland look and arched brow.

He saw a worried expression crossed her face and then he turned away, satisfied at her reaction yet unable to stop his lips from twitching.

She set Fred, The Cat aside and launched herself at him, a playful attack he had no idea how to defend. He'd never *played* with anyone, not even Tamsin.

He wrestled her gently, not wanting to cause her harm but he soon found he didn't have to worry because the whole time, she was giggling herself silly. He couldn't help but recognise the strange feeling coursing through him (mingled tantalisingly with desire) was enjoyment.

She ended the tussle on her back, Douglas on top, Julia's arms pulled over her head with his hand holding her wrists. She was still laughing, her body shaking under him while he smiled down at her, revelling in the pleasure of her happiness and that it was Douglas who was giving it to her.

"You're just too funny, sweetheart," she giggled. "I just love..." she stopped, gulped then gave a short, strange, uncomfortable chortle of laughter before finishing, "love your sense of humour."

Her words sounded forced and wrong and his body stilled when he heard them but then she lifted her head and kissed him and he could think of nothing else.

This time, it was Sam who broke into his thoughts.

"The room will be littered, their word, not mine, *littered* with white roses." Sam was continuing to tell him his plans for Valentine's evening. "They'll serve your dinner at nine in the room."

"Right. Thanks," Douglas replied, no longer listening to her, preferring to think back to what happened on the couch and what it might mean.

After a lengthy hesitation, Sam asked, "What did you just say?"

"Right," Douglas repeated distractedly.

"Then you said, 'thanks'." Her voice was somehow breathy with pleasure and he realised he'd never thanked her before.

Jesus, had he always been such an unfeeling bastard?

Bloody hell, he had.

A feeling stole over him that he now recognised. Guilt.

"You did a good job, you always do," he offered this statement like a throwaway comment, immediately uncomfortable with the conversation. "Are we done?" His voice was now curt.

"Yes," Sam answered.

"Good." Douglas almost wished her enjoyment of her Valentine's Day but stopped himself. She might have a coronary and he had a wedding to plan and less than a month to do it and he needed her not to be recovering in a hospital bed.

He disconnected the call as usual, without a good-bye.

His anticipation for the night was palpable. He could nearly feel Julia's limbs around him, the smell of her in his nostrils, the taste of her in his mouth. He'd bought her rubies for tonight, a necklace and earrings to match the dress that Gregory had confided to him (or, more accurately, to Sam) was red. It was an extravagant present, a necklace set with seven oval rubies surrounded by diamonds and diamond-ensconced rubies suspended from diamonds starting at the stud of each earring. Considering her reaction to his other presents, he was most definitely looking forward to giving her the jewels.

Douglas may have been avoiding feeling anything for most of his life but he wasn't unaware that the last several months, and especially the last several weeks, he was unable to continue in this vein. He knew his emotions were no longer under his fierce control but he had little cause for alarm regarding this development considering that he recognised the dazed feeling he was having (albeit unfamiliarly) was happiness.

He was not surprised, Julia was a good woman. She was a beautiful and stylish woman. She was a gratifyingly responsive, adventurous and demonstrative lover. She was kind and thoughtful and had worked miracles with three grieving children, a household of once distant, now familial staff and the tightening of his own meagre band of friends.

Sommersgate, cold, formal, even monstrous throughout his childhood, rang with laughter, shared confidences, constant hilarity (most of which was instigated by one or all three of the kittens or children or both) and happiness.

Lost in these thoughts, he turned through the gates of his ancestral home.

So lost in his thoughts, when he turned into the long drive of Sommersgate, he nearly didn't notice the Gate House, normally lit warningly against intruders, now was completely dark and frighteningly quiet.

But he did notice.

And he put his foot down on the brake, stopping the car and turned his head to stare.

Nick was not going anywhere tonight. Nick had left "the job" with Douglas and had taken up his position (now officially) as Douglas's (but more importantly Julia's and the children's) bodyguard.

The rules were, if Douglas was not at the house and Julia or the children were, so was Nick.

And as Douglas was arriving to pick up his fiancée, Nick should have been at the Gate House.

Even if he was at the main house, his lights should be blazing.

That was the deal; those were the rules, that was how Douglas knew everything was okay when he came home.

Therefore, Douglas had to assume that things were *not* okay.

His stomach clenched and his chest tightened, he snapped the word "Sam" into the dark void around him and the car phone started dialling.

"Yes boss?" Her voice was perky.

"Call the police," he had started the Jag crawling forward through the mile of parkland that fronted the estate and he turned off his lights. "Tell them to get to Sommersgate but to proceed with caution. I don't know the situation yet and I'm going in, I won't report back. Then call the SIS, you know who to speak to, tell him the same thing."

She was all business, although her voice betrayed worry. "Check."

Then Sam hung up on him.

He forced himself slowly (and thus quietly) to glide the Jag toward his home, toward Julia.

He had no weapon. He had no idea of the time that had elapsed from when the trouble (he was certain there was trouble) started to now. He had no idea if the children, Ronnie and the Kilpatricks had already left the house. He had no idea if Nick had managed to get her to safety.

He had not noticed Nick's car at the Gate House so maybe he'd succeeded in reaching her but didn't have time yet to phone and report in.

This thought was made moot when Douglas saw Nick's car careened off the road a quarter of a mile away from the house, slammed into another car, Nick's interior light blazing and its driver's side door hanging open.

"Fucking hell," Douglas bit out.

It took every bit of willpower not to gun the motor but he knew he couldn't go charging in, he couldn't warn them of his approach. He needed surprise on his side.

He slid forward, his teeth clenched, his hands biting into the steering wheel, his eyes vigilantly scanning the landscape and was assaulted by visions of Julia's dead body lying in a pool of blood, a pool of *his* making because *he* wanted a bigger challenge. *He* had been bored with his life. *He* needed a more interesting way to pass the damned time.

He rolled passed the silent and dark Groundskeeper's Cottage, hoping that meant the Kilpatricks had already taken the children to the curry house. Then he slid slowly down the slope and around the chapel. He stopped before he got to the gravelled drive, pulling the emergency brake and turning off the car, the Jag on the gravel would make too much noise. He exited the car, fleet of foot and silent as a cat. He crouched low, keeping to the edges of the wide arc of light illuminating the outside of the house coming from both the lights from Julia's rooms (the drapes, disturbingly, not drawn) and the outside light.

He stayed close to the side of the house, inching forward and, chancing a glance around the corner of the portico, finally seeing the front door slightly ajar.

Ready for him.

Waiting for him.

He knew a trap lay inside.

He didn't hesitate because inside, hopefully still alive, was Julia. And he'd rather get his brains blown out than allow her to experience another minute of the terror she was undoubtedly experiencing.

The moment he quietly slipped into his lifelong home, he knew something was wrong. Not just the danger that lurked there but the house.

Something was very wrong with the whole, damned house.

He'd taken three strides forward, ignoring the alien feeling of Sommersgate, when a voice speaking in Russian told him to stop.

The cold steel of a gun was pointed to his temple.

Without hesitation, and quick as lightning, Douglas's head jerked back. His left hand shot up, grabbing the gunman's wrist in a powerful grip. The man fired a reactionary shot but it went wide.

Swinging around with all his bodyweight and using instinct and years of practice to guide him, he slammed the palm of his hand into the man's septum, forcing it into the back of his brain, causing him to die instantly.

Douglas felt no remorse. He knew who these men were and what they did. That swift a death was an act of mercy. He deserved far worse for the devastation he caused to hundreds of lives.

The Russian fell to the ground; Douglas took his gun, strangely a six shooter revolver rather than a semi-automatic, and swiftly checked its load. Three shots had already been fired which made Douglas's chest clutch painfully. Forcing himself to remain focused, he felt the dead man's body for any further weapons and discovered a knife strapped to his ankle. He removed it and tucked it in the back of his belt.

Julia would not be pleased about the knife but he'd deal with that later.

If, pray God, he had the chance.

He quickly divested himself of his suit jacket, throwing it aside and did the same with his tie. He moved forward, unbuttoning the buttons at his throat and saw that a light was shining into the stairwell from the drawing room. It barely illuminated a prone human form that was lying at the side of the hall.

With a vague sense of concern he wouldn't allow to form fully, Douglas moved silently forward then crouched beside who he recognised as Nick. Noticing the blood on his back, Douglas put out his fingers to check and found his friend had a strong pulse.

But Nick was out cold.

Douglas didn't have time to pay his friend more attention. Hoping the pulse would remain steady; Douglas straightened and walked slowly forward, listening carefully.

The house was utterly silent but somehow he felt almost as if it was alert and watching him take each step.

As he entered the grand stairwell, the drawing room came into view.

And so did Julia.

She stood at the back of a couch facing the door and there was a man standing beside her holding a gun to her temple. She was wearing, as usual, a stylishly sexy dress.

She looked magnificent.

He forced himself to walk slowly, even casually, toward the door, his footsteps sounding preternaturally loud on the stone.

The Russian had seen him and started talking. It was one of the men, as Douglas guessed, who'd been after Veronika. He knew at the time he should have never shown himself to them.

He had his orders, he was too public a figure, it wasn't his job. His job was that he gathered (in a variety of ways) information but he was not to make contact with the criminals.

But he couldn't stand by and watch them beating Ronnie nor could he allow them to force her into a life that was no life at all.

Now, he'd pay for that mistake.

God, *Ronnie*. He hoped they hadn't found her first.

As he came forward, he sought to allay Julia's fears with his eyes but as the Russian talked on, making grandiose and threatening statements about taking something that wasn't his, Douglas finally took in Julia's face.

And he was stunned at what he saw.

Julia, his bride-to-be, looked annoyed.

Not frightened as he assumed she'd be, or, more accurately, terrified out of her mind.

No, she looked *annoyed*.

She looked like he'd kept her waiting and they were going to miss their booking at a restaurant she particularly wished to sample. *Not* like she was being held at gunpoint in the drawing room of her own home by a vile Russian who dealt in white slavery.

If she had checked her watch and tapped her toe, Douglas wouldn't have been surprised.

And in that moment, he knew.

She trusted him. She *believed* in him. She *knew*, without any doubt, that he would know what to do, that he would save her, make their home safe again.

All she had to do was wait.

He felt this knowledge hit him like a physical blow.

Tamsin had believed in him, but she was his sister.

No one else had. Not anyone in his life.

No one.

Except Julia.

Memories of her slid by in seconds, her blowing in his ear at the snooker table; telling him of Sean's abuse in the study; giving him her Christmas present at dinner; wriggling her engagement ring at Nick proudly; wrapping her legs around Douglas's waist passionately, protectively, lovingly while he was inside her.

"What am I going to do with you?" he'd asked.

"Whatever you want," was her reply.

Bloody hell, he loved her.

He came to within a foot of the doorway and her eyes shifted quickly and meaningfully to the side of it, telling him there was another man behind it.

Douglas didn't react.

He just smiled.

The Russian was still talking, threatening, his voice getting panicky because Douglas hadn't dropped his gun as asked.

Douglas ignored him.

In an even, calm voice he said simply, "I love you, Julia."

Her face changed, even from across the expanse he saw her eyes darken and that raw, tender look came about her and he knew what it meant.

Finally he understood.

"Oh Douglas," she replied, her sweet, husky voice shaking, not with fear but with feeling. "Sweetheart, I love you too."

And then it all happened at once.

The house rumbled, the windows flexed in dangerously then out like the house was about to implode.

Julia jerked her head back at the same time she jammed her elbow into her attacker's ribs, drawing a confused yowl from the man. She threw herself over the back of the couch and the last Douglas saw of her was a flash of black netting and her legs ending in two high-heeled black sandals disappearing behind the couch.

Douglas wasted no time; he aimed at her attacker, fired and cursed.

He caught the man in the shoulder but didn't bring him down.

The door flew toward him and he was ready for it. He caught it with his forearm, violently throwing it back with all his weight and strength. He heard an "oomph" of pain come from behind the door but ignored it.

The lights flashed, off and on, then again and again. The chandeliers were swaying dangerously, their crystals tinkling.

A shot was fired at Douglas by the Russian that held Julia but it was wide and Douglas aimed another shot at him and caught him in the thigh but, before the man dropped to the floor, Julia had re-emerged from her position, holding aloft a Waterford vase that Douglas knew was one of his mother and father's wedding presents. She hurled it at the Russian and it smashed against the side of his head causing him to grunt and hit the floor with a heavy thud.

The lights were still flashing, not only in the drawing room but behind him as well and likely everywhere in the house. The walls were creaking as if Sommersgate was about to crumble in on itself.

Douglas had no time to worry about the bizarre disintegration of his ancestral home. The other man stepped wide from the door, his gun raised but Douglas caught his wrist, needing to drop his own gun to do so. The man managed to squeeze off a shot which caught Douglas, stinging his upper, left arm.

As Douglas grappled with the man, an otherworldly moan drifted ominously through the house and then another missile, this time a heavy glass paperweight, flew through the air, hitting his opponent on the side of the neck, making him squawk in angry pain.

"Stop throwing things!" Douglas ordered Julia, his hands full with the man who was fighting both a terror of Douglas, the unknown of

Julia and her priceless glass bombs and a house gone mad. "You could hit *me*."

"I'm not going to hit you! I played softball for seven years!" she retorted, as if that meant anything in a death match.

He noted out of the corner of his eye she was standing there with her hands on her hips as if to say, *Get on with it, I'm hungry*.

He would have laughed if he hadn't noticed her original attacker slowly pulling himself to his feet, still armed.

"Julia, *down!*" Douglas barked.

His clever soon-to-be wife noticed the Russian too and disappeared behind the couch in an instant.

A flame of fire shot out of the fireplace at this point even though no fire had been blazing in its grate the moment before. The moan was still howling through the house, the windows flexing, the chandeliers veering crazily side-to-side.

Douglas whirled, gaining position on the gun, he used his attacker's weapon and aimed at the other Russian who had already fired, this time toward the spot where Julia had been.

Douglas's shot went wild as did his mind.

If he hit Julia, Douglas would rip him apart.

He let out a roar of rage and used his newfound fury to plant his feet and throw his attacker over his shoulder onto his back on the floor. Without hesitation, Douglas wrested the man's gun away, calmly aimed and fired two rounds into him, one in each kneecap.

The man's howls joined the unearthly thunder of the house and Douglas turned again to the other man who had decided against shooting him to give way to the crazed violence that blazed in his eyes. Charging toward him like a bull, Douglas braced for impact when two things happened at once.

First, the blast of a shotgun unloaded itself into the ceiling by the side doors that led toward the greenhouse.

This happened thanks to a wild-eyed Roddy Kilpatrick who followed the blast with an outcry of, "What the *bloody hell* is going on here?" and yet stood calmly as plaster rained down on him.

Second, another paperweight, this one bigger than the last, flew with alarming accuracy at Douglas's assailant, knocking him with a sickening thump on his head and succeeding in dropping him like a stone three feet away from Douglas.

Julia stood behind the couch heaving angry breaths and smartly yanking up the neckline of her strapless dress. Douglas stood amongst the carnage, one man unconscious at his feet, the other writhing in (now whimpering) agony.

The battle against the Russians won, Sommersgate still had a battle of its own.

"Are you all right?" Douglas asked Julia.

"*You* took your own damned time coming home!" she accused hotly.

He guessed, by that response, she was all right.

"Jesus, Doug. You made a mess. I'm always telling you, not the kneecaps. Christ, the man will never walk again."

Nick was in the room, staggering a bit, a huge lump had formed on his temple and the bruising had already begun.

"Oh Nick, your head." Julia started to rush forward in concern. "We need to get you some ice."

"*You're* bloody well not nursemaiding me. I know from experience you aren't very good at it."

"Well!" Julia halted with a skid halfway to her friend, clearly affronted.

"Girl," Nick returned, his voice low with anger, "next time I come tearing into this house and tell you to run, you... better... damned... well... *run!*"

"Will someone tell me what in *the hell* is going on?" Roddy Kilpatrick shouted from his position by the doors, a position from which he had not moved, his shotgun still pointed at the ceiling, his hair dusted white with plaster.

Coming up behind him on a wheeze was Margaret Kilpatrick.

"My goodness!" she panted. "Is there an earthquake?"

Roddy whirled. "Woman! I told you to stay with the children!" he yelled, his face going perilously red.

"Ronnie's with them, they're all fine!" she yelled right back, an angry flush forming on her own cheeks.

Douglas rolled his eyes to the ceiling in a brief prayer for patience at the utter bedlam in his house and saw the chandeliers lurch precariously.

"Julia, get over here," he demanded because if the house was going to fall on their heads, it was damned well going to do it when she was in his arms.

She didn't hesitate. Delicately stepping over bodies in her lovely shoes with her red toenails peeking out of a small, charming indentation in the toe, she muttered, "Should we do something about him?" She indicated the writhing Russian with a low wave of her hand.

"He'll survive," Douglas grunted.

She'd come within reach and he reached for her, yanked her forward, her body slamming against his.

"Are you all right?" he repeated his earlier question.

"Yes, fine," she answered distractedly, still looking down at the man. Then her eyes fluttered to his. "I knew you'd be home any minute so I just waited. You were late, though. That was a bit unfortunate. You've been hit."

Her eyes were now on his bleeding arm but he noted that she was completely calm, as if the house wasn't at that very moment shirking off a century old curse, as if bodies didn't litter the hall and drawing room of their home, as if she hurled deadly projectiles at villains every day.

He felt it tear through him. Feelings, emotions, love, desire, happiness, safety, beauty, laughter, everything that was Julia, it ripped through him with a stunning force and nearly brought him to his knees.

Or, more to the point, it mended him, taking the jagged, long-unused shards of his heart and rending them together, complete, functioning and healthy, the scars simply fading away.

He had not needed to put her back together.

He had needed her to do it for him.

His arms stole around her and he buried his face in her neck.

"God, I love you." His voice was hoarse with feeling, trembling with it and he felt a shudder go through her.

"I'm so glad," she whispered, her head turned so her lips were at his ear. "I didn't want to spend my life not telling you how I feel. I love you, Douglas." Then she tilted her head back, her throat arching and he lifted his head to watch in amazement as she shouted proudly, "Love you, love you, love you. *I love Douglas Ashton!*"

He would have kissed her but instead, the instant she finished her declaration, the night was pierced by a blood-chilling scream.

The house stilled completely and everyone in the room froze for a moment then scattered, running out to the grand stairwell.

Douglas halted at what he saw. He'd dragged Julia with him, grabbing her hand as he left the drawing room. She slammed into his back then wrapped her arms around his waist, peeking around him and they both, with Nick and the Kilpatricks, witnessed something hideous and momentous.

Douglas could not believe his eyes.

The ghostly vision of a woman was struggling at the foot of the stairs with an unseen attacker who was clearly choking the life out of her.

It was a death struggle.

And she was losing.

A raging howl came from behind them and they all shifted as one and if anyone had seen them, they would have noted it as almost comical.

But it was anything but funny.

Through the French doors they could see the ghost of a man, also fighting against an unseen attacker (or, to Douglas's way of thinking, more than one considering the bulk of his body, his obvious strength and the desperate nature of his struggle).

The howl he emitted had been fierce, shaking the windows.

And then a blaze of fire shot out of the grate by the leather couches but they all missed it as the ghost man tore away from his attackers and charged forward, up to and *through* the glass, finding himself for the first time in over a century in the glorious and grand home he built as a proud display of love for his adored wife.

He did not hesitate in triumph at his entry but rushed forward, throwing off her attacker and catching her body, swinging her around as she coughed, spluttered and weakly lifted her hands to hold onto his shoulders.

"Ruby." His mouth moved but the aching sound didn't come from

there, it came from everywhere, the walls, the floors, the furniture, the carpets.

It came from Sommersgate.

"Archie." Was her reply, the yearning in the sound was like a caress and it, too, filled the air like oxygen.

"Oh my God," Mrs. K breathed and Douglas felt a strange sensation behind him, realising that Julia was holding onto him tightly, her arms wrapped around his waist, her body pressed against his and hers was rent with silent sobs.

He pulled her around toward his front, his arms encircling her as she snuggled into his chest, pressing her cheek against him there all the while she watched the ghostly reunion.

Douglas looked again to the beings who had inhabited his home long before he'd come into the world. Beings Tamsin had sworn existed but he had never sensed.

They were embracing, kissing passionately and it was almost embarrassing to watch even though he could not, for the life of him, tear his eyes away.

With the spirits still kissing, the words came from Sommersgate, from the voices long since stilled in the past.

"Douglas, Julia, thank you. We wish you..."

Then they were fading, still embracing but slowly fading until they were completely out of sight.

"...love." It was a whisper and Douglas felt Julia's tremble communicate itself through his body.

Sommersgate was still, quiet, all that it was, all that it used to be, was gone, fading with the spectres.

Leaving behind only stones and mortar, wood and glass, iron and granite.

All of it built in love.

Douglas and Julia's home.

❧ 26 ❧

THE TOASTS

Julia stood at the back of the cathedral, her bridesmaids, Lizzie and Ruby, milling around her and Will yanking nervously at his collar but still looking quite dapper in his morning suit.

She'd peeked into the church to see Douglas and Oliver line up at the front and to watch Will escort Patricia to her seat. Patricia was wearing such an enormous, baby pink hat, replete with ruffles and rosettes, that Julia wondered how her mother managed to manoeuvre herself down the aisle without toppling over. Her nephew then turned and tried not to (but definitely did) scurry back to Julia.

It was Julia and Douglas's wedding day.

Monique was not in attendance, she sent word she was deathly ill with the flu.

Julia couldn't have been more pleased at the news but she tried to hide her reaction when she saw the dark look that crossed Douglas's face, though, he said not a word.

The very proud looking Kilpatricks sat in the front row on Douglas's side, next to Charlotte and Nick, with Sam and Ronnie (and their boyfriends) and Carter and his daughter sitting behind.

Julia thought happily that was a far better representation of Douglas's family than Monique would ever be.

Both sides of the church were filled to capacity. Julia had protested the guest list but Douglas demanded that every business and social acquaintance he had be present.

"If I could," he whispered into her neck one dark night, "I'd have the world watch me make you mine."

It was, of course, an atrociously possessive thing to say but who was she to argue?

For her part, a great number of her family and friends were there, mainly because Douglas had bought every seat on a commercial jet flying from O'Hare to Heathrow. That gesture made the trip a great deal more affordable for a lot of people.

Finishing this assemblage, there was enough paparazzi outside to make the BAFTAs look tame in comparison.

Julia was wearing what Gregory termed his "masterpiece" (in a short time, she had become known widely as Gregory's "muse").

Her wedding gown was a simple, long, backless, sleeveless, boat necked, ivory silk dress, the silk being the most extraordinary material Julia had ever touched. Cut on the bias, it fit superbly, flowing all the way down to her feet where the very pointed toes of her ivory pumps peaked out. The back hem fell in a graceful train three feet long. She wore ivory gloves up to her middle upper arms, a choker made of four rows of pearls separated by bars of diamonds imbedded in platinum, a matching bracelet and a set of earrings that had a teardrop pearl suspended from a beautiful diamond (this an "early" wedding gift from Douglas making her wonder what the "during" and "after" wedding gifts would be – for her part, she carried with her a secret that was Douglas's present that she prayed he would adore). She carried a bouquet made completely out of perfect white roses.

As usual in Julia's life, the day had not run smoothly (to say the least).

She had started it in her rooms surrounded by her girlfriends from Indiana *and* England, everyone wanting to help but doing nothing but getting in the way. Charlotte, Gregory and Patricia had a fight over how Julia was going to wear her hair even though Julia and Sylvie, the stylist, had long since decided on a style.

"She must wear it up, something soft, with curls at the back and tendrils around her neck with baby's breath," Patricia demanded (and Julia thought it sounded like something a girl would wear to a prom).

"Down! Straight! Edgy!" Gregory clipped out, speaking (as per usual) in as many exclamation-point-ending, one-word phrases as he could (Gregory, at last, a match for Patricia's dramatics).

"A sleek, elaborate up-do, with the front of her hair parted severely, smoothed over and tucked in..." Charlotte declared and then went on for several more words.

Julia let Charlotte win because that was the closest to what Sylvie and Julia had decided *and* because Charlie happened to be the editor of a glossy fashion magazine and likely knew what she was talking about.

Then Patricia decided she was not sure about the gloves.

Then Patricia launched into her (oft-heard) lecture about how high heels would ruin your back.

Then Patricia doubted the wisdom of having only *one* wedding colour, ivory, saying they should add a last-minute infusion of something else, like pink.

And so on.

Before preparations to her toilette began in earnest, Douglas had walked into Julia's rooms causing Patricia to shriek and Gregory to hyperventilate, waving his hand in front of his face like a wilting Southern belle.

"You can't see her before the wedding!" Patricia exclaimed, her voice shrill.

Douglas ignored his very-soon-to-be mother-in-law and just stared at Julia with an intense ferocity that she had learned from experience looked at lot worse than it was. Before he could say what he came to say, Julia spoke mainly because she'd had enough.

"You sure you want to do this? You've got a good fifteen, twenty years having to put up with this crazy old bat." She indicated her mother with a frustrated jerk of her head.

"Well, I never!" Patricia cried.

"I wish!" Julia retorted.

Charlie giggled.

Julia swung back to Douglas. "If you're going to pull out, pull out now. It's not too late. You're rich enough, you can buy us an island where we can live in sin and install ground-to-air missiles to shoot her down should she try to chopper in."

Apparently Douglas decided whatever he came to say that had caused that intense look was not nearly as important as exiting the room with all due haste.

Which he did but only after he quirked an arrogant brow at her while he awarded her with one of his diabolically sexy grins.

The Night of the Russians (as Julia now referred to it) or Archie and Ruby's Release (which was another way she liked to term it) or Villainous Valentine's Day (another of her favourites) ended with nearly more drama than it began.

Not five minutes after Lady Ruby and Archie had faded from sight, the police crashed through the house in a noisy rush, one of them actually breaking through the glass of the French doors. This caused everyone, already tense, to go wired.

Roddy Kilpatrick aimed his shotgun.

Nick pulled the knife out of the back of Douglas's belt and waved it about threateningly.

And Douglas thundered, "Is this what you call 'proceeding with caution'?"

Luckily they recognised Douglas and there was no further bloodshed.

Some high up official from some government organisation that outranked the police came not long after and took control of the situation. There was no press, only interviews with all involved (and signed gag orders masquerading as "confidentiality agreements") and dozens of people milling about taking pictures, gathering evidence, removing bodies or hauling others off to hospital.

It all seemed very curious to Julia but evidently this was somewhat of an international incident and the Russians wanted the criminals (or what was left of them) returned with as little muss and fuss as possible, issuing fervent apologies along the way.

Douglas was treated at the scene, a flesh wound to the upper arm that was stitched together by the same doctor who had come the last time.

Nick was taken to hospital for observation for a concussion. He'd been unconscious for quite some time and even though at first he refused, both Julia and Mrs. K nagged him until it became obvious that he could either go or expire due to extreme molly-coddling. Furthermore, what caused him to go down was a bullet that had ricocheted off something in the hall, grazing him in the back (also requiring nothing but a few stitches) but not entering his body. Remarkably, it glanced off a rib but with enough force to knock him off his feet and bang his head.

This caused him to slap his ribs and gloat, repeatedly, for weeks, "Bones of steel," anytime he saw Julia and Douglas.

Carter came home and promised to guard the house and Lord knew the children were safe with the shotgun-wielding Roddy. No one could really inhabit the house considering the number of bloodstains, broken doors, gunshot holes and shotgun blasts and it would likely take Mrs. K at least a day (maybe two), to sort out all the damage.

Once Douglas had cleaned himself up and changed clothes, he whisked Julia off to Bath anyway even though it was long past time to enjoy any kind of Valentine's Day celebrations. He seemed not to realise that evening's dramatics may have been an everyday occurrence for *him* but not for Julia.

On the way to Bath Douglas briefly, curtly and in no detail (because, he told her, in all seriousness, if he went into detail, there was a good possibility he would have to kill her, or, if not him doing the deed, someone else would) explained something about the MI6 (or MI5, she didn't hear him correctly and was too scared to ask), Russians, the mysterious two-year disappearance (training and undercover work) and white slavery.

There was a quick, impersonal account about Veronika, but Julia read between the lines and realised he'd saved her from a fate worse than death (thus Julia understood Ronnie's declaration of New Year's Night that Douglas was her hero, this caused a bit of the frightened-to-death, oh-my-God-we're-all-going-to-die feeling to melt away, but just a bit).

Nick was definitely involved and somehow, along the way, Carter was involved too (indeed, he'd *recruited* Douglas).

Douglas assured her, just as briefly and curtly, that he nor Nick and most definitely not Carter ("Retired," Douglas had grunted) were currently or would ever again be involved in what he called "the job".

Feeling (accurately) that he needed to leave it at that, she allowed him to do so but it was very, *very* hard.

She just had to trust him.

And she did.

Upon entering their room at the Royal Crescent Hotel, long past the time they should have been there, Douglas simply undressed Julia, undressed himself and pulled her into bed with him.

To sleep.

Facing her, he lifted one of her legs to drape over his hip and pulled her in his arms, tucking her head under his chin.

Regardless of this intimate position, with no apparent amorous intentions, he closed his eyes.

He muttered no seconding to his (somewhat wonderful) avowals of love. He didn't mention the fact that his childhood home had nearly erupted like a volcano. Or that he'd witnessed the ghosts of two dead lovers fade to heaven.

"Um," she muttered against his neck, "what are you doing?"

"Sleeping," was his weary reply.

He wasn't sleeping because he was speaking but she thought it best not to point that out.

Instead, she asked, "Now?"

"I'm tired."

Julia fidgeted. The adrenalin was still coursing through her body.

"Well, now I can say I've seen it all. Nothing seems to slow you down but I guess mortal combat, experiencing your ancestral home shake off an evil curse and witnessing the passionate reunion of two dead lovers finally has stalled the Great Douglas Ashton, Baron Blackbourne, ruthless business tycoon and secret agent –"

"Be quiet, Julia."

"I love you, Douglas."

His arms tensed fiercely, crushing her to him. He held her for long moments then his arms loosened but they didn't go away.

"Go to sleep," he ordered but this order was gentle.

"Okay," she obeyed on a whisper because even though it *was* an order, she liked the way it sounded.

And somehow his calm communicated itself to her, she felt the tenseness of the night drain away and she did as he commanded.

He'd loved the cufflinks and she'd adored the rubies.

They'd managed to keep it all from the children (and Ronnie) due to a quickly orchestrated dash to London which the children had to be pulled out of school for so they could be fitted for their dresses and morning suit for the nuptial festivities.

When they returned, the plaster and doors were fixed and there were no bloodstains to be found.

Several days later, while Julia was at her new consultancy, Douglas ordered Ronnie to move all of Julia's things to his rooms.

When Julia arrived home later than normal, she found no one waiting for her in the kitchen. Upon quick inspection of the house, she finally entered the last place she expected to find anyone, Douglas's sitting room.

He was on the couch, his briefcase open on the table in front of him, papers spilled everywhere and his mobile at his ear. His eyes came to her the minute she walked in and, even though they warmed, they were also wary.

Will was doing his homework sitting at the desk in the corner.

Mrs. K and Ronnie's disembodied voices came from the bedroom and Julia tore her gaze away from Douglas and wandered through the door dazedly.

"There's nothing for it, we'll have to build a bigger closet," Mrs. K's voice came from an opened door that Julia knew was Douglas's dressing room.

"She has many shoes," Ronnie noted.

Ruby was jumping on Douglas's bed and Lizzie was lying on it telling her to stop.

"May I ask what's going on?" Julia's voice was both bewildered and dangerous.

Will ran through and jumped on the bed, bowling over Ruby, making Ruby shriek and Lizzie groan.

Julia felt Douglas come up behind her and was about to whirl on him when Ruby informed her knowledgeably, "You're moving in with Unka Douglas, just like Mummy and Daddy. Mummy and Daddy *always* slept together."

Neither Lizzie nor Will had any reaction to this in any way, shape or form.

It was then she whirled on Douglas.

"You..." she started.

He caught her by the waist, pulled her to him and laughed, burying his face in her neck.

"I love you, darling," he said, clearly and distinctly, the first time he'd said it since The Night of a Thousand Russian Horrors (another one of her favourites) and the first time he said it in front of the children.

Her back was to them but she could feel their eyes on her and Douglas.

But she was too busy nearly dying in rapture at the sound of those words and she felt herself dissolve into happy laughter.

"I don't know why because you're such an arrogant, underhanded cad, but I love you too, sweetheart," Julia replied.

This scene was something with which the children were *very* familiar. They settled comfortably in the bed, annoying each other to the extreme while Douglas nuzzled Julia's neck, Ronnie and Mrs. K eventually gave up on the shoes and Mrs. K left the room to call the carpenter.

❧ ❧ ❧

The music had started in the Cathedral, the beautiful strains of the organ filling the air.

It was time to begin the wedding.

Ruby was first to have her turn up the aisle. She was wearing her pretty ivory dress with puffed sleeves, big tulle petticoats and a hem that dripped lace. It was completed with a wide, white-satin sash tied in a bow in the back.

She was supposed to be littering the aisle with white rose petals but halfway to her destination, she spotted her uncle and shouted, "Unka Douglas!" as if she didn't expect him to be anywhere near the Cathedral that day or even in the country (and hadn't been practising her role for a month). She threw aside her basket of petals and dashed forward, throwing herself against him as the congregation twittered.

"She'll ruin everything," Will hissed at Julia's side, his nerves in tangles.

Julia bent, not nearly as far as she had to ten months ago, to look him in the eye. "She's just being Ruby and it doesn't ruin the day, honey, it makes it perfect."

"If you say so," Will grumbled dubiously, clearly too overwhelmed by his looming responsibility to find rambunctious Ruby perfect at anything.

Lizzie, however, *was* perfect, serenely gliding up the aisle like she was a professional bridesmaid. She too was wearing ivory, a younger girl's version of Julia's dress (except not backless). It fell neatly in a column to just above her ankles. With it she wore gloves and a matching double-strand choker of pearls at her throat, wrist and tiny teardrop earrings (Douglas's "early" birthday present to Lizzie whose birthday just happened to be in July).

Julia saw that Douglas decided to calm Ruby by picking her up and positioning her at his hip to give her the best vantage point of the proceedings. Julia found this, too, endearing and her heart melted at the sight.

Then again, she found almost everything about Douglas endearing.

However, upon entering the aisle out of nowhere an unbidden wave of melancholia overwhelmed Julia.

She was afraid something like this would happen and as she walked hesitantly forward, she tried to focus on Douglas. No matter how hard she tried, she couldn't contain her trembling lips, her heart beating like a jackhammer, her legs feeling like jelly and her hand clutching Will's arm with vice-like pressure, all the while her throat burning like fire.

"You okay, Auntie Jewel?" Will asked out of the side of his mouth, wincing at her grip on his arm.

Halfway up the aisle Julia halted. Ignoring the gasps of the crowd, she turned to her nephew and put her hand on his cheek. Again, she bent toward him.

"I didn't say it before, when you told me you'd give me away, but I'm going to say it now. I miss your Dad with everything that is me, but

I'm *so proud* you're here with me now," she whispered to him, her eyes filling with tears.

Will stared at her a moment then gulped back his emotion, nodded slowly and finally shot a sidelong glance up the aisle.

"Um, Uncle Douglas looks kinda mad," he whispered, his face bright red.

Julia jerked upright and saw that Douglas didn't look mad, he looked *furious*. He'd put down Ruby (she was now standing by a bewildered-looking Lizzie) and was scowling at Julia.

Julia fairly raced up the aisle, pulling Will along with her.

"Sorry, sorry," she muttered when she reached him, avoiding his eyes, "we were having a moment."

"Perhaps, in future, you'll pick the timing for your 'moments' better," Douglas replied dryly and her eyes flew to his.

His were carefully blank.

Julia's heart sank.

"Er, shall I start the ceremony?" the Bishop asked in a low voice.

Douglas quirked a brow at the same time Julia cried, "Yes!"

After this incongruous start, Will's performance at giving her away was superb.

With Julia's hand held firmly in Douglas's (*very* firmly) the Bishop started the ceremony.

Julia muttered under her breath, "I'm sorry, Douglas-honey, I got a little overwhelmed with missing Gavin. It just came over me."

When the endearment came from her lips, the first time she'd ever used it when addressing him, Douglas's lithe body froze, statue-still and Julia misinterpreted it as anger.

She thought of his father, his mother, their hideous treatment of him and what he likely thought was her disrespect in the aisle.

She turned to him and vowed fervently (if a little hysterically), "If someone was choking you in Sommersgate, I'd spend all night trying to claw my way in, even if it killed me, I swear to God!"

At this dramatic pronouncement, Douglas turned only his head in her direction and she realised the Bishop had stopped talking again.

"Darling, would you care to be quiet long enough for us to get married?" Douglas asked politely.

Julia could have happily had the floor open up and engulf her at that moment.

"Yes, yes, *definitely,*" she turned to the Bishop and nodded at him encouragingly while giving him a shaky smile.

The Bishop looked at Douglas for a shade longer than was necessary, obviously giving him time to run from the Cathedral, but Douglas stood true.

When Julia looked out the corners of her eyes at her intended to gauge just how furious he was, she saw his lips twitching with humour and her breath left her in relief. She leaned into him, resting her body against his side and she let her head drop to his shoulder.

The Bishop started talking faster, his eyes widening at this new affront to tradition and decorum.

But Julia was finished making a fool of herself and the only thing that caused her to be anything but deliriously happy (and it was only to cause her to be even *more* deliriously happy) was when Douglas's deep voice rang out in the cathedral when he said his vows *and* when he said, "I do."

It might not have been the near-shout Gavin had used but it was damned close.

And although Gavin had given Tamsin a mighty kiss when they were pronounced man and wife, the entire congregation at Wells Cathedral shifted uncomfortably in their seats when Douglas kissed Julia.

It was not decorous and befitting a church.

It was long and hungry with possession, branding her as his in the eyes of God (literally) and everyone else and it left Julia swaying, dazed and utterly, thrillingly, rapturously, ecstatically happy.

❧ ❧ ❧

"I heard this house was frightful and actually haunted but it seems lovely to me." A woman Julia didn't know was speaking to her at the wedding reception which was being held at Sommersgate.

Julia nodded and stared in vague alarm out the French doors of the old entryway at a ten foot tall ice sculpture of swans sitting in the middle of the garden, their bills pressed together to form a heart.

She had heard no discussion about ice sculptures.

"If a little... *ornate*." The woman was still talking.

With a smile, Julia turned her attention to the woman and explained, "There are no ghosts here..." she smiled and winked before she finished, "anymore."

Before there was a chance for the woman to reply, there was a tinkling of glasses indicating that a toast was soon to be made.

Julia and Douglas had decided against a formal meal and traditional reception with the traditional toasts. Heavy hors d'ouevres and an even heavier open bar, good company and good conversation were all they were to provide. Julia simply wanted a party, a joyous celebration and nothing tired and staid.

Therefore she was a bit surprised that the glasses were being tapped for a toast and she looked to the stairs where Douglas stood on the sixth step.

Once the congregation quieted, Douglas said across the expanse, "Could I ask my wife to join me, please?"

A thrill ran down her spine at being referred to as his "wife" and she turned to the lady and murmured, "If you'll excuse me, my husband wants me."

"Of course," the woman replied, smiling brightly into Julia's glittering eyes.

Julia wended her way through the crowd all the while her eyes on Douglas and his on her. When she was close to the foot of the staircase, he came down to meet her (complete with a brush of his lips against hers) and then he helped her climb the steps to resume his position over the crowd.

Nick quickly approached holding three full glasses of champagne and Douglas took two, handing one to her.

"What are you doing?" she whispered. "I thought we agreed there would be no toasts."

"We agreed that no one *else* would make any toasts but I can say what I want in my own house," Douglas returned, the warmth in his eyes showing he was teasing.

There was a time when she would not have believed that Douglas Ashton could tease.

But he could, very well.

She beamed at him, too happy to be cross, and then turned to the crowd and linked her arm through his.

"Firstly," Douglas's strong voice carried throughout the cavernous space, "I'll tell you that my wife is rather fond of lists so I've decided to take my cue from her and recite a list of toasts. I ask you to charge your glasses because there will be several before I reach the end."

Julia felt a blush creep in her cheeks at the fondness in his tone and leaned into his side. Some of the hired staff (because all of the Sommersgate regulars were guests this day) were wandering around carrying two bottles of champagne each and filling glasses, others were carrying heavy trays on which filled glasses rested for those who had no drinks at all.

Finally, Douglas started, "I would like to thank you all for coming and celebrating this very special occasion."

"A long time coming," Patricia grumbled loudly and people laughed.

Douglas wisely decided to ignore her.

"I would also like to take this opportunity to thank Mr. and Mrs. Roderick Kilpatrick for their years of service to myself and my home. They have been faithful to me and my family in more ways than we often deserved. They have been exceedingly kind and welcoming to my wife and my new family and I," he turned to Julia, "*we* are lucky to have them. To Roddy and Margaret Kilpatrick."

He lifted his glass and Julia watched his gorgeous throat as he drank down a sip. She was already near tears, her hand clutching at her husband's arm. She swiftly took a drink and turned her eyes to the Kilpatricks who were both visibly moved by his toast (indeed, Mrs. K's eyes shone with tears).

Before she could respond further, Douglas began speaking again.

"I publicly acknowledge the interference of Charlotte Forsythe, interference which greatly hastened this day." Julia watched Douglas's chin dip to look at Charlie and he finished. "Thank you, Charlie."

The last three words were said more quietly as Charlie was standing at the foot of the stairs and they were directed warmly to her.

Julia noted, as the tears pricking the backs of her eyes began to spill, Charlie's own tears were falling over. The congregation twittered in curiosity but they took their cue from Douglas who lifted his glass in a salute to Charlie and took a sip.

"To Charlie!" Oliver shouted and everyone concurred.

Charlie's toast complete, Douglas carried on. "I must pay tribute to Patricia Fairfax, a good woman, a fine mother and a wonderful grandmother who has accepted me readily into her family, a position I hold with great honour. To Patricia," he toasted and Julia gave up the pretence of attempting to control herself and, letting the tears flow freely, she wrapped her arm around Douglas's waist and went up on tiptoe to put her mouth to his ear.

"I love you," she whispered, as he shifted his own arm around her waist to hold her tightly.

His only response was to kiss her temple then he looked back to the crowd and continued. "And now, to Elizabeth, William and Ruby Fairfax, who have, these last months, showed great courage and strength. Could you three please join your aunt and me?" Without further coaxing, the children melted out of the crowd and self-consciously (except Ruby who barrelled up to the steps with great vigour) joined them on the stairs. "I ask you all to lift your glasses to the courage of my nieces and nephew."

"Here, here!" Roddy Kilpatrick sang out.

"To Lizzie, Will and Ruby!" Nick shouted.

Mrs. Kilpatrick and Ronnie burst into loud tears.

Everyone toasted and took their sips and Douglas continued. "And lastly, I should toast my beautiful wife but I will salute her in an altogether different way later." He turned to give her a sexy smile and Julia's cheeks, already pink with emotion, flamed. He turned back to the crowd. "I will finish with a toast to two people who could not be here today. To Gavin and Tamsin Fairfax who bestowed on us the great honour of rearing their children in their absence and, in so doing, led me to Julia. I cannot find words to express my gratitude so I shall not try." When everyone began to lift their glasses to drink,

Douglas went on. "But especially to my sister, who always had faith in me, who was, in every way, a kind and loving soul, the light in an often dreary life. To Tamsin Fairfax!" His voice rang loud and Julia forced her face into his neck, too overcome to join in the shouts to Tammy.

"Thank you all," Douglas, finally, (and thankfully, Julia could take no more) was finished. "Please continue to enjoy –"

"Hold on a blasted minute."

Douglas quieted and Julia peaked out from her hiding place to see Patricia shouldering her way through the crowd. Luckily she'd divested herself of her hat or she might have caused injury.

"I have something to say," she announced upon arrival at the step.

The children were shifting uncomfortably and Julia stiffened at whatever dramatic pronouncement might come out of her mother's mouth. Douglas, however, was the soul of amiability and he smiled, actually smiled (and warmly too) at his new mother-in-law.

Patricia smiled back and turned to the crowd.

"I've been waiting fifteen years to do this, as long as it took him to figure out he was in love with my daughter. He may have a head for business and a reputation for quick decisions but I'm here to tell you, there are some ways he can be *very slow.*"

The crowd laughed but if Julia was stiff before, she was rock solid now. She would *not* allow her mother to badmouth her husband in front of hundreds of guests. She was about to interrupt when her mother continued.

"But, the longer we wait, the sweeter our victory, eh, Douglas?" Patty grinned, any sting in her earlier words taken out by the dancing light in her eyes.

Douglas merely inclined his head.

"I, for one," she told the crowd, "feel damned lucky to call Douglas Ashton my son. He's a good man, has taken care of my grandchildren during a very trying time and has, finally, after I fretted for years that it would ever happen, made my daughter unbelievably happy. I mean, look at the girl, she's *glowing!*" There was more laughter and Douglas's other arm wrapped around Julia.

"So please," Patricia continued, "join me in raising your glasses to

Douglas Ashton, my daughter's husband, my grandchildren's uncle, my new son and a very fine man. To Douglas!"

"Oh Mom!" Julia cried, reached across Douglas to embrace her mother and after she did so, Patricia gave Douglas a loud kiss on his cheek.

"You should know, my boy, I've put you in my will," she informed him grandly.

He nodded gravely, as if he needed to be put in her will and didn't have enough money to buy a small country. Patricia winked at Julia then hustled the children down the stairs.

Douglas kept hold of his wife, his arms loosely wrapped around her.

"That was well done of you," Julia praised him.

"Let's go," he answered, completely ignoring her compliment.

Julia laughed, light-hearted and carefree, the music of her laughter sounding through Sommersgate.

When she sobered enough to speak, she realised he was serious and therefore protested, "We can't leave our own wedding reception."

"We can," he insisted.

And Douglas was correct.

Because, without delay, they did.

EPILOGUE
SOMMERSGATE HOUSE

Julia Ashton, Baroness Blackbourne, finally bested Douglas in the present giving stakes.

That evening they arrived at The Ritz (several hours earlier than expected) for their wedding night.

Their honeymoon flight to Fiji would leave early the next morning.

Sometime deep into the night, when the room was dark and they lay naked and replete in each other's arms, in a low voice, Douglas explained his arrival during her wedding preparations. He expected her to have cold feet and was going to warn her that if she left him, he'd find her and drag her home. Upon her announcement that he should buy them a small island where they could live in sin, he realised she wasn't going to leave him.

Julia rewarded him for this admission by giving him his wedding present.

She shared her secret with him and informed him she was pregnant.

He was, for Douglas Ashton, beside himself with delight.

They named their daughter Margaret Tamsin Fairfax Ashton.

❦ ❦ ❦

A great number of happy years later, Douglas insisted to Roddy Kilpatrick that they lay his wife to rest in the family plot on the grounds of Sommersgate House.

No one, really, could think of anywhere more appropriate for Mrs. K to spend eternity.

Roddy joined his wife there shortly after.

Flowers were delivered to their graves, as well as the graves of Tamsin and Gavin Fairfax, on a weekly basis for as long as Douglas was alive.

Unfortunately, Margaret and Roddy's version of heaven meant that their ghosts, forever, benignly and often hilariously haunted Sommersgate and all of its inhabitants.

※ ※ ※

Many, many, *many* years later, Sommersgate was inherited by William Fairfax as Douglas's only male heir and because Douglas wanted his sister's beloved home to go to her only son.

Will kept his father's mellow, friendly ways but, after years spent with Douglas, acquired more than a hint of his uncle's arrogance and commanding authority.

Will eventually married a beautiful woman named Rebecca (under rather romantic circumstances) and sired three children of his own.

※ ※ ※

Elizabeth Fairfax married for love, the son of some friends of her Aunt Jewel's who had survived leukaemia many years before. Lizzie moved to Indiana and hosted the family Christmases there every third year and brought her ever-increasing family to Sommersgate for the other two.

Lizzie became a social worker, specialising in helping others to survive loss.

※ ※ ※

When she was in her teens, Ruby Fairfax helped Nick to investigate the murder of Lady Ruby Ashton (the children were eventually told of the lovers' release but that was the only thing they were informed about regarding that night) and the Sommersgate House Curse.

As the trail was cold, they found very little but both agreed that it had something to do with a woman whose cottage was burned down with her in it. The townspeople thought she was a witch and police suspected arson but the inquest was inconclusive. Her son, however, was discovered to be serial murderer who strangled his victims. Most of those victims were unveiled at the trial but in his dying moments he hinted at another, the first woman who didn't want him and, therefore, had to die.

❧ ❧ ❧

In adulthood, Ruby followed (unknowingly) in her uncle's footsteps, a noted clairvoyant and a very clever girl, she worked for MI6 (though never told her aunt and uncle, siblings, Ronnie or the Kilpatricks) and she did a variety of other things that would have caused distress or, indeed, heart failure.

After some rather significant troubles with a dashing agent, she married him and spent a great many years driving him delightfully mad.

❧ ❧ ❧

Ronnie married her (fourth) English boyfriend and they travelled widely during all their vacations but she always worked at Sommersgate.

Although Ronnie looked on it more as taking care of her family.

She took over the role of Housekeeper after Mrs. K left this world.

Many years later, William Fairfax, Baron Blackbourne, insisted to her husband that she be buried in the family plot and he made certain flowers were delivered to her grave every week.

❧ ❧ ❧

Nick never left the Gate House, never married (although he had a great deal of fun), spent most of his evenings at the dining room table at the main house and he watched over the Ashton family until he died in his sleep at the age of eighty-seven whilst having a particularly good dream.

* * *

Carter retired the year after the Baron and Baroness married and spent the rest of his days close to his daughter and grandchildren in sunny Devon.

* * *

Charlotte and Oliver Forsythe stayed the best of friends with the Baron and Baroness and Charlie and Jewel's antics, for decades, were the cause of great hilarity amongst their set and in the media.

Charlie cried loudly and dramatically when both "Gregory" and Julia gave her stunning salutes at the retrospective honouring her contribution to fashion that was held at the Victoria and Albert Museum.

* * *

Sam Thornton invested her life savings in some stock her boss had suggested, made an absolute fortune, quit her job and travelled the world.

She met an Australian who was the only being she'd ever known (besides her ex-employer) who couldn't be cowed by her energy, intelligence and wit.

So she married him and had five children which quickly depleted her energy but lovingly challenged her intelligence and wit.

* * *

Patricia Fairfax moved into the Ashton Dower House in Clevedon and meddled freely in the lives of her family, the Kilpatricks, Veronika, Nick, Samantha and the Forsythes and anyone else who wandered through their tight circle.

She also let slip a family secret during a public altercation with

Monique Ashton, calling her an unfit mother and a few (well maybe a number) of other choice words.

The stunned reaction easily read on the faces of the Baron and Baroness, both of whom witnessed this diatribe, laid testimony to the truth of Patricia's attack.

Monique was disgraced (most people never liked her anyway) and she spent most of the rest of her life alone. This was until her son and daughter-in-law (mostly her daughter-in-law) insisted she be cared for at Sommersgate when she eventually fell ill and infirm.

She was also buried in the family plot, as was her due, but her delivery of flowers was much smaller than the rest.

At the permission of the current residents, Patricia's ashes were sprinkled over the pond in the front yard of what used to be her family farm in Indiana.

The fish were very happy.

❧ ❧ ❧

The Baron and Baroness only had one child as their home was already full of three others, three cats, a dog (a mastiff, *not* named Babykins), six horses (those in the stables, of course) and a number of beloved servants.

They felt that was enough to watch after.

Julia learned to enjoy riding horses.

Douglas learned to tell his deepest secrets.

Douglas never lost interest in his wife, indeed, year after year, he fell deeper and deeper in love with her.

Julia lived her life always about ready to expire from the rapture of being loved so splendidly by her husband and enjoyed living a life of doing the same right back.

❧ ❧ ❧

Tamsin and Gavin's vision of heaven *did* indeed mean they were somewhere beautiful and they could see their family. They watched over their loved ones with humour and delight (and, in the beginning, not a little bit of frustration), thrilled when Archie and Ruby finally joined them.

One, the other or all four of them would come to open the window to their family's world at Sommersgate House, open it over and over, and watch their family grow in happiness and in love.

Precisely the purpose for which Sommersgate House was built in the first place.

The End

Next in the Ghosts and Reincarnation Series is
Lacybourne Manor

AUTHOR'S NOTE

Sommersgate House, Douglas and Julia's home in the book, is loosely based on Tyntesfield, a National Trust property. Tyntesfield, located in Wraxall, North Somerset, UK is an extraordinarily beautiful, gothic Victorian mansion that is, as far as I know, not haunted.

The National Trust is a UK charity dedicated to conserving and opening to visitors historic houses, gardens and large parts of the countryside and coastline.

I highly recommend, if you live in the UK or are just visiting, that you plan a trip to Tyntesfield or the many National Trust properties open to the public: www.nationaltrust.org.uk.

KristenAshley.net
NEW YORK TIMES BESTSELLING AUTHOR

In 1522, the very night they were wed, Royce Morgan and his new bride, Beatrice Godwin, were murdered on their way home to Lacybourne Manor. After the cruel deed was done, a local witch came across their bodies, witnessing firsthand the tragedy of star-crossed lovers. Vowing that Royce and Beatrice would someday uncross those stars, using magic mixed with murder as well as true love, she linked their spirits together with hers (because someone had to protect them) forever...or until their reincarnated souls find happily ever after.

Now arrogant forbidding Colin Morgan lives at Lacybourne. He knows from lore (as well as the portraits of Royce and Beatrice that hang in Lacybourne's hall and the small fact that he looks exactly like Royce Morgan) that he's the reincarnated soul of his ancestor.

One stormy night, flighty, free-spirited, scarily-kind-hearted Sibyl Godwin comes to Lacybourne and it doesn't escape Colin's notice that Sibyl is the spitting image of Beatrice.

However, murder, magic, a warrior's heart beating in a modern man's chest, a woman bent on doing good deeds even if they get her into loads of trouble, a good witch whose family has vowed throughout the centuries to protect true love, distrust and revenge make a volatile cocktail.

This means the path to happily ever after is paved with tranquilizer darts, pensioners on a rampage, Sibyl's bad morning moods, heart-breaking misunderstandings and all kinds of magic, good...and bad.

LACYBOURNE MANOR
PROLOGUE

People try to explain magic in a variety of different ways.

They use the excuse of science, miracle, divine intervention, luck, fate and coincidence.

It's all just magic in one form or another.

※ ※ ※

And the purest magic is love.

And the purest, *purest* magic is *true* love.

※ ※ ※

Everyone has magical powers.

Some know they do.

Some would never believe.

Some are greater than others.

Some are good and kind and true.

Some are evil and wicked and violent.

And sometimes they all get tangled together.

❧ ❧ ❧

This is the story of the purest, *purest* form of magic, *true love.*

It is a story about all kinds of magic, mixed up in a crazy, mystical mess.

❧ ❧ ❧

Esmeralda Crane was there when Royce Morgan first laid eyes on Beatrice Godwin.

It was the Year of our Lord, 1522, and even though Esmeralda had already lived a goodly number of years in two centuries, she had never been blessed to witness true love.

He was handsome, a rich, land-owning knight wearing shining spurs. He had thick hair the unusual color of sunshine mixed with honey and eyes the color of the richest, most fertile clay.

She was dark of hair and fair of skin, her hair so dark it was only a shade lighter than black, and her skin so fair it was without blemish except for the freckles that danced across her nose. She had extraordinary hazel eyes. Eyes that could be more green then brown on occasion (with ire, which was a good deal of the time, considering her fiery nature), more brown than green on other occasions (with love or happiness, which was also a good deal of the time, considering her kind heart).

Esmeralda watched their stormy courtship with fascination.

There were times that his personality (which was mostly autocratic, reserved and often cynical) would grate roughly against her personality (which was buoyant, free-spirited and often explosive).

Esmeralda feared both these stubborn souls would never see the magnificent stars in each other's eyes and understand what kind of precious gift they had been given.

As ever, the magic of true love was victorious. Esmeralda should never have doubted it.

Even though Esmeralda wasn't invited, she created a glamor for herself so she could attend Royce and Beatrice's wedding.

One rarely had the honor of witnessing true love in the giddy hours right before its consummation.

But she felt the black soul there that day, dark as midnight. The soul was sitting in the church, as bold as can be, even though lightning should have struck it dead the minute its foot crossed the sacred threshold.

As Royce and Beatrice stood in the front of the church, Esmeralda saw the stars in the lovers' eyes.

Alas, Esmeralda knew those stars were now crossed with darkness.

She hurried from the church before the ceremony was finished, jumped on her sweet-spirited, but not very swift, nag so she could quickly get to her larder. There, she pulled out herbs, incense and oils, all the while muttering to herself. She put all of her efforts, all of her energy, all of her (considerable) power and all of her (even more considerable) magic into a protection charm that would keep the lovers safe.

Once done, exhausted with her efforts, she shrugged off her fatigue and scurried to Lacybourne Manor, frightened that she would be too late.

Nearly to the doors of the grand house, Esmeralda found that she *was* too late.

She came upon the newly-wedded pair outside the house, lying entwined under a copse of trees, the blood from their slit throats now fertilizing the soil around them.

Esmeralda wanted to cry, to scream, to keen into the night all of her despair that their love had not been consummated. The glorious consummation of true love, the like of the love between Royce and Beatrice Morgan, would have protected them like a powerful shield.

The old witch, no matter how tired, was not yet done with magic that night.

She picked up the delicate hand of the fallen Beatrice and saw the flesh and blood beneath the girl's fingernails. The same could be found under the nails of the once mighty knight.

Taking her dagger, she gouged the human particles from beneath the lovers' nails and also collected a dagger blade full of the soil that had absorbed the couple's mingled life blood. Lastly, she pierced the point of the dagger into her finger and squeezed her own blood into her powerful brew.

Working swiftly, the witch mixed the protection charm with a fierce shake. More of her conjuring was muttered, she opened her charm and sprinkled her potion around them.

Forever linking them.

Forever, through eternity, binding them together.

Until one day, many, many years in the future, the stars in the lovers' eyes would uncross.

Esmeralda knew the black soul would hunt them but she prayed that her protection charm and the added power of violence, death and true love would protect them.

The witch knew one day, they would find each other again.

And that day, they would need her.

Lacybourne Manor is available for purchase in all formats

NEWSLETTER

Would you like advanced notification about Upcoming Releases? Access to exclusive content? Access to exclusive giveaways? The first to see a new cover reveal? Sign up for my newsletter to keep up-to-date with the latest from Kristen Ashley!

Sign up at <u>kristenashley.net</u>

ABOUT THE AUTHOR

Kristen Ashley is the *New York Times* bestselling author of over one hundred romance novels. She's a hybrid author, publishing titles independently and traditionally, with books translated into fourteen languages and millions of copies sold.

Kristen's novel, *Law Man*, won the *RT Book Reviews* Reviewer's Choice Award for best Romantic Suspense, her independently published title, *Hold On*, was nominated for *RT Book Reviews* best Independent Contemporary Romance, and her traditionally published title, *Breathe*, was nominated for best Contemporary Romance. Her titles *Motorcycle Man*, *The Will*, *The Hookup* and *Ride Steady* (which won the Reader's Choice award from *Romance Reviews*) all made the final rounds for Goodreads Choice Awards in the Romance category.

Although Kristen is super proud of all those accolades, she's just happy that—after years of writing with no publisher or agent interested in what she did—she now has a loyal readership who, on social media, she can share recipes with and regale with stories of her bent toward being a klutz.

Kristen was born in Gary and raised in Brownsburg, Indiana, but since leaving her home state (Hoosier by birth, Boilermaker by the grace of God!), she's lived in Denver and the West Country of England. All of these places were home, and she's put them in her books with all the love she still has for them.

Now, after years of cold, misty days in the UK (that she still misses, along with cream teas, custard and battered sausages), Kristen resides in almost constant sun. She writes at her desk in Phoenix or among the deer and javelina in her little cabin up in the Arizona mountains, regretting often that she forgets to put the sunshade over her windshield, thus her car often doubles as a human oven. Even so, she loves calling all the sun, saguaro and beautiful mountains home.

You can read more about Kristen and her books at KristenAshley.net.

facebook.com/kristenashleybooks

instagram.com/kristenashleybooks

pinterest.com/KristenAshleyBooks

goodreads.com/kristenashleybooks

bookbub.com/authors/kristen-ashley

tiktok.com/@kristenashleybooks

Manor and Mysteries Series:

Too Good to Be True

Mathilda, SuperWitch:

Mathilda's Book of Shadows

The Rise of the Dark Lord

Misted Pines Series

The Girl in the Mist

The Girl in the Woods

The Woman by the Lake

The Woman Left Behind

Moonlight and Motor Oil Series:

The Hookup

The Slow Burn

The Rising Series:

The Beginning of Everything

The Plan Commences

The Dawn of the End

The Rising

River Rain Series:

After the Climb

After the Climb Special Edition

Chasing Serenity

Taking the Leap

Making the Match

Fighting the Pull

Sharing the Miracle

Embracing the Change

Finding the One

The Three Series:

Until the Sun Falls from the Sky

With Everything I Am

Wild and Free

The Unfinished Hero Series:

Knight

Creed

Raid

Deacon

Sebring

Wild West MC Series:

Still Standing

Smoke and Steel

Smooth Sailing

Other Titles by Kristen Ashley:

Heaven and Hell

Play It Safe

Three Wishes

Complicated

Loose Ends

Fast Lane

Perfect Together

The Chaos Series:

Own the Wind

Fire Inside

Ride Steady

Walk Through Fire

A Christmas to Remember

Rough Ride

Wild Like the Wind

Free

Wild Fire

Wild Wind

The Colorado Mountain Series:

The Gamble

Sweet Dreams

Lady Luck

Breathe

Jagged

Kaleidoscope

Bounty

Dream Man Series:

Mystery Man

Wild Man

Law Man

Motorcycle Man

Quiet Man

Dream Team Series:

Dream Maker

Dream Chaser

Manor and Mysteries Series:

Too Good to Be True

Mathilda, SuperWitch:

Mathilda's Book of Shadows

The Rise of the Dark Lord

Misted Pines Series

The Girl in the Mist

The Girl in the Woods

The Woman by the Lake

The Woman Left Behind

Moonlight and Motor Oil Series:

The Hookup

The Slow Burn

The Rising Series:

The Beginning of Everything

The Plan Commences

The Dawn of the End

The Rising

River Rain Series:

After the Climb

After the Climb Special Edition

Chasing Serenity

Taking the Leap

Making the Match

Fighting the Pull

Sharing the Miracle

Embracing the Change